MIDWINTER
SACRIFICE

MONS
KALLENTOFT

MIDWINTER
SACRIFICE

Translated from the Swedish by Neil Smith

HODDER &
STOUGHTON

First published in Great Britain in 2011 by Hodder & Stoughton
An Hachette UK company

Originally published in Swedish in 2007 as *Midvinterblod* by Natur och Kultur

1

A CIP catalogue record for this title is available from the British Library

Hardback ISBN 978 1 444 72150 8
Trade Paperback ISBN 978 1 444 72151 5

Typeset in Plantin Light by Palimpsest Book Production Limited,
Falkirk, Stirlingshire
Printed and bound in Great Britain by Clays Ltd, St Ives plc

Hodder & Stoughton policy is to use papers that are natural, renewable and recyclable products and made from wood grown in sustainable forests. The logging and manufacturing processes are expected to conform to the environmental regulations of the country of origin.

Hodder & Stoughton Ltd
338 Euston Road
London NW1 3BH

www.hodder.co.uk

AUTHOR'S THANKS

I would like to thank the following people for their help with this book:

Bengt Nordin and Maria Enberg for their encouragement and unstinting commitment. Nina Wadensjö and Petra König for their open-mindedness and enthusiasm. Rolf Svensson for his ability to control reams of paper, among other things. My mother, Anna-Maria, and father, Björn, for detailed information about Linköping and the surrounding area.

I would also like to thank Bengt Elmström, without whose common sense and warm-heartedness there would probably never have been any books at all.

I owe my greatest debt of thanks to my wife Karolina, who has been absolutely invaluable to so many aspects of *Midwinter Sacrifice*. What would have become of Malin Fors, her family and colleagues without Karolina?

My main focus has always been on what is best for the story. For this reason I have taken certain liberties, albeit small ones, with police procedure, the city of Linköping, the geography of the surrounding area, and the people who live there.

Mons Kallentoft
21 March 2007

Prologue

Östergötland, Tuesday, 31 January

In the darkness

Don't hit me. Do you hear me? Leave me alone.

No, no, let me in. Apples, the scent of apples. I can almost taste them.

Don't leave me standing here, in the cold and wet. The wind feels like nails that tear at my hands, my face, until there is no frosted skin, no flesh, no fat left on my bones, my skull.

Haven't you noticed I'm gone? You couldn't care less, really, could you?

The worms crawl on the earthen floor. I hear them. The mice too, how they make love, going mad in the heat, tearing each other to pieces. We ought to be dead now, they whisper, but you have lit your stove and are keeping us alive, we are your only company in the cold. But what company? Was I ever alive, or did I die long ago, in a room so cramped that there was never any space for love?

I pull a damp blanket over my body, see the flames burn through the opening of the stove, feel the smoke spread through my black hovel and seep out to the sleeping pines, the fir-trees, the rocks, the ice on the lake.

Where is the heat? Only in the boiling water.

If I fall asleep, will I wake up?

Don't hit me. Don't leave me in the snow. Outside. There I'll turn blue, then white, like everything else.

Here I can be alone.

I am sleeping now, and in my dreams the words return: fucking runt, bastard brat, you're not real, you don't exist.

But what did I ever do to you? Just tell me: what have I done? What happened?

And where did the scent of apples first come from? The apples are round, but they explode, disappear in my hands, and there are biscuit crumbs on the floor beneath me.

I don't know who she is, but a naked woman is drifting above my body. She says, I'm going to look after you, you exist for me, we are human beings, we belong together. Then she is dragged away and the ceiling of my hovel is ripped open by a black wind. Out there I hear something slithering towards her legs. She screams and there is silence. Then she's back, but she is someone else now, the faceless person I have missed all my life. Who is she really?

I can wipe out the longing. I can give up breathing.

But if longing and breathing disappear, you are left with belonging. Aren't you?

I have woken up. I am many years older, but my hovel, the cold, the winter night and the forest are the same. I have to do something. But I've done it already; something has happened.

Where does the blood on my hands come from? And the noises.

The worms and mice are inaudible over all the commotion.

I hear your voice. I hear you banging on the nailed-together planks that make up the door of my hovel. You're here, you've finally come.

But is it really you? Or is it the dead?

Whoever is out there, tell me that you mean me no harm. Tell me that you have come in love.

Promise me that.

Promise me that much.

Promise.

PART ONE

This last sort of love

I

Love and death are neighbours.

Their faces are one and the same. A person need not stop breathing in order to die, and need not breathe in order to be alive.

There are never any guarantees where death or love are concerned.

Two people meet.

Love.

They make love.

And they love and they love and then, after a while, the love runs out, just as abruptly as it first appeared, its capricious source blocked by circumstances, internal or external.

Or else love continues until the end of time. Or else it is impossible from the start, yet still unavoidable.

And is this sort of love, this last sort, is it really nothing but a nuisance?

That's just what it is, thinks Malin Fors as she stands in her dressing gown by the kitchen sink, fresh from the shower, spreading butter on a slice of wholemeal bread with one hand, and lifting a cup of strong coffee to her lips with the other.

Six fifteen, according to the Ikea clock on the whitewashed wall. Outside the window, in the glow of the streetlamps, the air seems to have solidified into ice. The cold embraces the grey stone walls of St Lars Church, and the white branches of the maples seem to have given up long ago: not another night of temperatures below minus twenty; better to kill us outright and let us fall dead to the ground.

Who could love this sort of cold?

A day like this, Malin thinks, is not meant for the living.

Linköping is paralysed, the city's streets draped limply upon the crust of the earth, the condensation on the windows making the houses blind.

People didn't even make the effort to get to the Cloetta Centre last night for the ice hockey, just a couple of thousand instead of the usual full house.

I wonder how Martin's getting on? Malin thinks, her colleague Zeke's son, a local lad, a forward with a chance of a place in the national team and a career as a professional. She can't actually summon up much interest in ice hockey, but if you live in this town it's pretty much impossible to avoid hearing about events on the ice.

Hardly anyone about.

The travel agent's on the corner of St Larsgatan and Hamngatan mocks with its posters for one exotic destination after the other; the sun, beaches, the unnaturally blue skies belong to another planet, a habitable one. A lone mother is wrestling with a twin buggy outside the Östgöta Bank, the children nestled in black bags, almost invisible, sleepy, obstinate, yet still so unimaginably vulnerable. Their mother slips on patches of ice hidden under a powder of snow, she lurches but drives herself on as though there were no other option.

'Winters here are the devil's work.'

Malin can hear her father's words within her, his justification a few years ago for the purchase of a three-room bungalow in a retirement village on Tenerife: the Playa de la Arena, just north of Playa de las Américas.

What are you doing right now? Malin thinks.

The coffee warms from within.

You're probably still asleep, and when you wake up it'll be warm and sunny. But here, the frost reigns unchallenged.

Should I wake Tove? Thirteen-year-olds can sleep for ages, right round the clock if they're given the chance, and in a winter like this it would be lovely to hibernate for a few months, not having to go out, and waking up fully restored when the temperature creeps above zero.

Tove can sleep. Let her tall, gangly body rest.

Her first class doesn't start until nine. Malin can see it all in her mind's eye. How her daughter forces herself to get up at half past eight, stumbles to the bathroom, showers, gets dressed. She never wears make-up. And then Malin sees Tove skip breakfast, despite all her cajoling. Maybe I should try a new tactic, Malin thinks: Breakfast is bad for you, Tove. Whatever you do, don't eat breakfast.

Malin drinks the last of the coffee.

The only time Tove ever gets up early is when she wants to finish one of the mass of books she devours almost obsessively; she has unusually advanced taste for her age. Jane Austen. How many Swedish thirteen-year-olds apart from Tove would read something like that? But, on the other hand . . . She's not quite like other thirteen-year-olds, never has to try hard to be top of the class. Maybe it would be good if she did have to make more effort, encounter a bit of real resistance?

Time has run on, and Malin wants to get to work, doesn't want to miss the half hour between quarter to seven and quarter past when she is almost certain to be on her own in Police Headquarters and can plan the day ahead undisturbed.

In the bathroom she takes off the dressing gown. Tosses it on to the yellow synthetic floor.

The glass in the mirror on the wall is a little bowed, and even though it makes her height of 1.70 metres appear slightly squashed she still looks slim; athletic and powerful and ready to meet whatever crap comes her way. She's met it before, crap, she's dealt with it, learned from it and moved on.

Not bad for a thirty-three-year-old, Malin thinks, her self-confidence doing its job: *There's nothing I can't deal with*, and then the doubt, the old fixed belief: *I haven't amounted to much, and won't now, and it's my fault, all my own fault.*

Her body. She concentrates on that.

Pats her stomach, takes in a deep breath so that her small breasts stick out, but just as she sees the nipples pointing forward she stops herself.

Instead she quickly bends down and picks up the dressing gown. She dries her blonde pageboy with the dryer, letting her hair fall over her prominent but soft cheekbones, forming a pelmet above her straight eyebrows, because she knows that emphasises her cornflower-blue eyes. Malin pouts her lips, wishes they were bigger, but maybe that would look odd beneath her short, slightly snub nose?

In the bedroom she pulls on a pair of jeans, a white blouse and a loose-knit black polo-neck sweater.

Glancing at the hall mirror, she adjusts her hair, reassuring herself that the wrinkles around her eyes aren't too visible. She puts on her Caterpillar boots.

Because who knows what lies ahead?

Maybe she'll have to head out into the countryside. The thick, synthetic down jacket she bought from a branch of Stadium in Tornby shopping centre for eight hundred and seventy-five kronor makes her feel like a rheumatic spaceman, her movements sluggish and clumsy.

Have I got everything?

Mobile, purse in her pocket. Pistol. Her constant companion. The gun was hanging on the back of the chair next to the unmade bed.

By the mattress with space for two, plus enough room for a decent gap, a gap for sleep and loneliness during the very darkest hours of night. But how can you find someone you can put up with if you can't even put up with yourself?

She has a picture of Janne beside the bed. She usually tells herself that it's there to make Tove happy.

In the photograph Janne is suntanned and his mouth is smiling, but not his grey-green eyes. The sky behind him is clear, and beside him a palm tree is swaying gently in the wind, while in the background you can make out a jungle. Janne is wearing a light blue UN helmet and a camouflage cotton jacket bearing the logo of the Swedish Rescue Services; he looks like he wants to turn round, to make sure that nothing's about to jump out at him from the dense vegetation.

Rwanda.

Kigali.

He's told her about dogs eating people who weren't even dead yet.

Janne went, goes, has always gone as a volunteer. At least that's the official version.

To a jungle so dense that you can't hear the sound of the heart of darkness beating, to mined and blood-drenched mountain roads in the Balkans, trucks with sacks of flour rumbling past mass-graves, poorly concealed by sand and scrub.

And it was voluntary from the start, for us.

The short version: a seventeen-year-old and a twenty-year-old meet in a bog-standard disco in a bog-standard small town. Two people with no plans, similar but different, but with some shared essence, ideas that work for both of them. Then, after two years, the event to be avoided at all costs happens. A thin membrane of rubber breaks and a child starts to grow.

'We have to get rid of it.'

'No, this is what I've always wanted.'

Their words slip past each other. Time runs out and their daughter arrives, the sunbeam to end all sunbeams, and they play happy families. A few years pass and a silence falls. Things turn out differently from the way they were planned, if they were planned at all, and each of those involved moves off in his or her own direction, without rhyme or reason.

No explosions, just a damp squib leaving a long trail into history, and even further into the soul.

The serfdom of love, Malin thinks.

Bittersweet. As she thought back then, after they'd separated, when the removal van was heading for Stockholm and the Police Academy, when Janne moved to Bosnia: If I become really good at getting rid of evil, then goodness will come to me.

Surely it could be as simple as that?

Then love might be possible again. Mightn't it?

On her way out of the flat Malin feels the pistol pressing against her ribcage. She carefully opens the door to Tove's bedroom. She can make out the walls in the darkness, the rows of books on the shelves, can sense Tove's oddly proportioned teenage body under the turquoise duvet. Tove sleeps almost soundlessly, has done ever since she was two. Before that her sleep was disturbed, she used to wake several times a night, but then it was as if she realised that silence and calm were necessary, at least at night, as if the two-year-old instinctively knew that a person needs to keep the night free for dreams.

Malin leaves the flat.

Goes down the three flights of stairs to the door of the building. With every step she feels the cold come closer. It's practically below zero in the stairwell.

Please let the car start. It's almost cold enough to freeze the petrol to ice.

She pauses at the door. The chill mist is drifting in waves through the streetlamps' cones of light. She wants to run back upstairs, go into the apartment, tear off her clothes and creep back into bed. Then it comes again, her longing for Police Headquarters. So: pull the door open, run to the car, fumble with the key, open the door, throw yourself in, start the engine and drive off.

The cold takes a stranglehold when she walks out; she imagines she can hear the hairs in her nose crackle with every breath, and feels her tear-ducts grow treacly, but she can still read the inscription above one of the side doors of St Lars: 'Blessed are the pure in heart, for they shall see God'.

Where's the car? The silver Volvo, a 2004 model, is in its place, opposite the St Lars Gallery.

Padded, bulky arms.

With difficulty Malin gets her hand into the pocket where she thinks the car keys are. No keys. The next pocket, then the next.

Damn. She must have left them upstairs. Then she remembers: they're in the front pocket of her jeans.

Her stiff fingers ache as she thrusts them into the pocket. But the keys are there.

Open now, bloody door. The ice has somehow spared the keyhole and soon Malin is sitting in the driver's seat swearing: about the cold, about an engine that merely splutters and refuses to start.

She tries again and again.

But the car refuses.

Malin gets out. Thinks: I have to take the bus, which way does it go?

Damn, it's cold, fucking bloody car-fucker, then her mobile rings.

A clawed hand on the angry plastic gadget. She can't be bothered to see who it is.

'Hello, Malin Fors.'

'It's Zeke.'

'My fucking car won't start.'

'Calm down, Malin. Calm down. Just listen. Something big's happened. I'll tell you when I see you. Be with you in ten minutes.'

Zeke's words hang in the air. From his tone of voice Malin can hear that something serious has indeed happened, that the coldest winter in living memory just got a few degrees less forgiving, that the cold has just shown its true face.

2

German choral music blasts through the car as Zacharius 'Zeke' Martinsson keeps a firm grip on the wheel and drives past the detached houses on the outskirts of Hjulsterbro. Through the side window he glimpses the red and green gables of the rows of generously proportioned houses. The painted wood is covered with frost and the trees that have grown tall in the thirty years since the houses were built look emaciated and malnourished in the cold. But, even so, the whole area looks unusually cosy and well-cared-for; it looks prosperous.

The doctors' ghetto, Zeke thinks. That's how the area is known in town. And it is undeniably popular among the doctors at the hospital. Opposite, on the other side of the main Sturefors road, on the far side of a car park, are the squat white blocks of flats in Ekholmen, home to thousands of immigrants and Swedes at the bottom of the pecking order.

Malin sounded tired, but not newly woken. Perhaps she slept badly. Maybe I should ask if anything particular has happened? No, best let it be. She only gets cross if you ask how she is. Zeke tries to keep his mind off what they are on their way to. Doesn't even want to know what it's going to look like. They'll see soon enough, but the boys in the patrol car sounded seriously shaken, and no wonder, if it was as bad as they said. He's got good at this over the years, delaying, postponing the crap even if it sometimes hits him hard.

Johannelund.

The boys' league football pitches down by the Stångån River are covered with snow. Martin used to play there for the Saab team before he decided to concentrate full-time on ice hockey.

I've never been much of a football dad, Zeke thinks, and now, now things are starting to go really well for the boy, I hardly have the energy to get to his matches. Last night was terrible. Even though they beat Färjestad 4–3. No matter how I try, I just can't love that game, its overblown toughness.

Love, Zeke thinks, is either there or it isn't. Like my love of choral music.

They practise two evenings a week, Da Capo, the choir he's been a member of since he dared himself to go almost ten years ago. Concerts maybe once a month, a trip to some festival once a year.

Zeke likes the undemanding nature of his relationships within the choir; no one cares what anyone else does the rest of the time, they meet, they talk and then they sing. Sometimes, when he's standing with the others, surrounded by song in a bright church hall, he imagines that it might really be possible to belong to something, to be part of something bigger than his own insignificant self. As if there were a simplicity and self-evident joy to the singing that couldn't possibly contain anything evil.

Because it's a question of holding evil at bay, as best you can.

On their way towards evil now. That much is clear.

The Folkungavallen Stadium. The next rung in the ball-game ladder. The football stadium was run down, ripe for redevelopment. The Linköping women's team is one of the best in the country, a group of women bought for the purpose, including a lot of national players, but who have never succeeded in winning over the town's inhabitants. Then the swimming pool. The new buildings beside the multistorey. He turns into Hamngatan, past the big shops, Hemköp and Åhléns, and then he can see Malin standing there shivering outside her door. Why isn't she waiting inside?

She is huddled but still seems somehow indefatigable as she stands with her arms round her body, her whole being sort of anchored to the ground in spite of the cold, in the certainty that this is the start of another day where she can devote herself to what she's best suited to.

And she really is suited to it, to police work. If I'd done anything wrong, I wouldn't want her after me, Zeke thinks, and he whispers to himself, 'Right, Malin, fuck it, what's today got in store for us then?'

The choral music turned down to a minimum. One hundred whispering voices in the car.

What can a human voice tell us? Malin thinks.

Zeke's voice has a hoarseness like no other Malin has ever heard, a tempered, demanding tone that vanishes when he sings, but which became even more pronounced when he just told her what had happened:

'Apparently it's a bloody awful sight,' he says, the hoarseness making his words sharper, 'according to the boys in the car when they called in. But when is it ever anything else?'

Zeke is sitting beside her, behind the wheel of his Volvo, his eyes fixed on the slippery road ahead.

Eyes.

We depend on them. Ninety per cent of the impressions that make up our image of the world around us come from our eyes. What we can't see almost doesn't exist. Anything can be hidden away in a cupboard and it's gone. Problem solved, just like that.

'Never,' Malin says.

Zeke nods his clean-shaven head. Perched on an unusually long neck, his skull doesn't seem to belong to his short, sinewy body. His skin is stretched over his cheekbones.

Malin can't see his eyes from where she's sitting. But she trusts her memory of them.

She knows those eyes. Knows that they sit deep in his cranium, and are usually calm. In their dull grey-green colour there is always a polished, almost bottomless light that is harsh and gentle at the same time.

At forty-five, he's got a lot of the calmness that experience brings, although the years have somehow made him more restless, implacable, or, as he said to her after a few too many beers and shorts at the Christmas party: 'It's us against them, Malin.

Sometimes, no matter how sad it sounds, we have to use their methods. That's the only language a certain type of man understands.' He said it without bitterness or satisfaction, it was simply a statement.

Zeke's restlessness isn't visible, but she can feel it. What on earth must he go through at Martin's games?

'. . . a bloody awful sight.'

It had taken eleven minutes from when Zeke had phoned for him to pick her up outside her flat. His blunt assertion made her shiver even more, at the same time making her feel strangely elated, against her will.

Linköping through the windscreen.

The avaricious city, in spite of its size, the veneer over its history strangely thin.

What had once been a factory city and a marketplace for farmers soon became a university city, the factories largely shut down, the residents cajoled into education, into colleges, into the university, and soon the most self-aware city in the country was rising from the plains, with the most remarkable inhabitants in the country.

Linköping.

The city as though born in the 1940s, the city as an insecure academic with a past that must be swept under the carpet at all costs. With people who want to be better than they are, and put on dresses and suits to go and drink coffee in the city centre on Saturdays.

Linköping.

An excellent city to get ill in.

Or, even better, to get burned in.

The University Hospital is home to the pre-eminent burns unit in the country. Malin was there once, in connection with a case, dressed in white from head to toe. The conscious patients were screaming or moaning, the tranquillised dreaming of not having to wake up.

Linköping.

Domain of flyboys. The home of the aeronautics industry. Steel crows croaking in the air: the Flying Barrel, Draken, Viggen, Jas. It all bubbles up and spills over and suddenly the newly wealthy are strolling the streets, their technology companies sold to the Americans.

Then there are the surrounding plains and forests. Home to all those whose genes cannot accommodate rapid change, those whose coding protests, refuses. Those who feel that they never have their feet on firm ground.

Janne. Are you one of them?

Is it that our coding doesn't work at the same pace?

Indians of the primal forests. People in communities like Ukna, Nykil and Ledberg. You can see the natives in tracksuit bottoms and clogs alongside the doctors and engineers and test pilots out at Ikea on Saturdays. People forced to live side by side. But if their coding objects? If loving your neighbour is impossible? In the fracture between then and now, between here and there, inside and outside, sometimes violence is born as the only option.

They drive past Skäggetorp.

Happy white houses from the building boom of the sixties, around a deserted centre, their rented apartments now housing people from far away. People who know how it feels when your uniformed torturers knock on the door at night, who have heard machetes whine through the air just as dawn is waking the jungle, people who are not exactly the toast of the Immigration Office.

'Do we want to go through Vreta Kloster, or shall we take the Ledberg road?'

'This isn't really my territory,' Malin replies. 'But it should be straight on, I think. So, how was the match last night?'

'Don't . . . Those red seats there are torture on the backside.'

Zeke drives past the turning for the Ledberg road and carries on towards Vreta Kloster.

Off to the east Lake Roxen opens out. Covered in ice, like a misplaced glacier, and ahead of them, beyond the lake, the villas on Vreta Kloster's millionaires' row clinging to the slope rising from the reeds. The locks on the Göta Canal alongside, waiting for the summer's hobby sailors and canal boats full of rich American tourists.

The clock on the dashboard: 7.22.

A bloody awful sight.

She wants to tell Zeke to put his foot down, but stays quiet, closing her eyes instead.

By this time people have usually started to arrive at the station, and she would be saying good morning to the others in the Investigation Section of Linköping's Crime Unit from her place behind her desk in the open-plan office. She could work out their mood, identify precisely which tone would apply that day. She would think, Good morning, Börje Svärd. You've been up and walked your dogs; it's never too cold to show your Alsatians a bit of love, is it? There's dog hair on your sweater, on your jacket, in your own ever-thinning hair. Your dogs' barks are like voices to you. And how do you cope, really? What must it be like to see someone you love suffer the way your wife suffers every day?

Good morning, Johan Jakobsson. Trouble getting the kids to bed last night? Or are they ill? There's a winter vomiting bug going around. Have you been up cleaning sick all night, you and your wife? Or did you experience the simple joy of children falling asleep early and happy? Is your wife dropping them off today, and you picking them up? You're on time, you're always on time, Johan, even if there's never enough time. And the worry, Johan, I can see it in your eyes, hear it in your voice, it never goes. I know what it means because I've got it as well.

Good morning, boss. And how is Inspector Sven Sjöman today? Be careful. That stomach is far too big, in quite the wrong way. A heart-attack stomach, as the doctors at the University Hospital say. A widow-making stomach, as they joke in the staffroom of the intensive care unit before bypass operations. Don't look at me in that beseeching way, Sven; you know I always do my best. Be careful. I need everyone who believes in me to stay believing, because it's so easy to have doubts, even if our driving force is far greater than we might think. And then his words, advice:

You've got a talent for this, Malin, a real talent. Look after it. There are many talents in the world, but there aren't many realised ones. Look at what's in front of you, but don't rely on your eyes alone, rely on your gut feeling, Malin. Rely on your instincts. An investigation consists of a mass of voices, the sort you can hear, and the sort you can't. Our own, and others'. You have to listen to the soundless voices, Malin. That's where the truth is hidden.

Good morning, Karim Akbar. You know that even the youngest, most media-friendly police chief in the country needs to stay on the right side of us ground troops? You glide through the room in your well-pressed, shiny Italian suits and it's always impossible to guess which way you'll go. You never talk about *your* Skäggetorp, about the orange panel-fronted blocks in Nacksta up in Sundsvall, where you grew up alone with your mother and six brothers and sisters after you fled Turkish Kurdistan and your father had committed suicide in his despair at never finding a decent job in his new country.

'Malin, what are you thinking? You look like you're miles away.'

Now Zeke's words are the crack of a whip and Malin is yanked back from her game, back to the car, back to their progress towards the incident, towards the violence that exists in the cracks, back to the winter-bitten landscape.

'Nothing,' she replies. 'I was just thinking about how nice and warm it must be in the station right now.'

'You've got this cold weather on the brain, Malin.'

'How could I not get it on the brain?'

'If you harden yourself against it, it'll go away.'

'The cold?'

'No, thinking about it.'

They pass Sjövik's fruit farm. Malin points through the window, towards the frost-covered greenhouses. 'Now, over there,' she says, 'you can buy tulips in spring. Tulips in every colour you can think of.'

'Wow,' Zeke says. 'I can hardly contain myself.'

★

The lights of the patrol car were shining like flickering coloured stars against the white field and sky.

They approach slowly, and the car seems gradually to reel in metre after metre of cold, of snow-covered field, of the site's evident suitability for loneliness. Metre by metre, crystal by crystal, they get closer to their goal, a tussock, a swelling in the ground, an event that stems from an event that demands the attention of the present moment. The wind whips against the windscreen.

The Volvo's wheels slide over the cleared road, and some fifty metres from the play of the lights a solitary oak stands out hazily against the horizon, grey-white tentacles becoming a scrambling poisonous spider on the white sky, the fine tracery of branches a net of memories and suggestions. The oak's coarsest branches bend down towards the ground, and slowly the cold lets go of the veils that have thus far concealed what bends them from Zeke and Malin's eyes.

There's a figure outside the patrol car. Two heads in its rear window. A green Saab pulled up haphazardly a few metres away.

A protection barrier set up around the tree, almost reaching to the road.

And then in the tree. The not exactly great sight.

Something to make your eyes doubt what they see.

For voices to talk about.

3

In a way, it's nice hanging up here.

There's a good view and my frozen body is swaying pleasantly in the wind. I can let my thoughts meander wherever they like. There's a calm here that I've never experienced before, that I never imagined might exist. My voice is new, my gaze too. Maybe I'm now the person I never had a chance to be.

The horizon is growing lighter and the Östgöta plain is grey-white; it looks endless, the view only broken by clusters of trees encircling small farms. The snow is drifting in waves across the meadows and fields, pasture interchangeable with bare soil, and down there, far from my dangling feet, a young man in grey overalls stands beside a police car, looking anxiously and expectantly, almost relieved, towards the approaching vehicle. Then he turns his eyes towards me, somehow watchful, as if I might run off or something.

The blood has solidified in my body.

My blood has solidified in the heavens and the stars and far out in the most distant galaxies. Yet I am still here. But I need not breathe any more, and that would be tricky anyway, considering the noose around my neck. When the man got out of his car and approached in his red jacket – God knows what he was doing out here so early – he screamed, then he muttered, Oh fuck, oh fuck, oh fucking hell, oh God.

Then he rushed to his phone and now he's sitting in the car shaking his head.

God: yes. I tried with Him once but what could He offer me? I see it everywhere: this faithless invocation that people start up as soon as they get involved in anything they imagine is related to darkness.

I'm not alone now, there are infinite numbers of people like me all around, but it still isn't crowded, there's room for all of us, more than enough room; here, in my infinitely expanding universe, everything is simultaneously shrinking together. Becoming clear, yet still strangely murky.

Of course it hurt.

Of course I was scared.

Of course I tried to escape.

But deep within me I knew my life was done. I wasn't happy, but I was tired, tired of moving in circles around what I had been denied, what I, nevertheless, somewhere in my innermost being, still wanted to have, still wanted to participate in.

People's movements.

Never my movements.

That's why it's pleasant hanging here naked and dead in a lonely oak tree out on one of the most fertile acres in the country. I think the two lights on the car that's heading this way along the road are beautiful.

There was never any beautiful before.

Maybe it's just for us dead?

It's lovely, so lovely not to be troubled by all the worries of the living.

The cold has no smell. The naked, bloody body above Malin's head is slowly swinging back and forth, the oak a reluctant, creaking gallows whose sounds mingle with the rumble of an idling car engine. The skin has come loose in great flaps over the bulging stomach and across the back, and the bleeding flesh, frozen, is a confusion of dull shades of red. Here and there on the limbs, apparently at random, the wounds are deep, concave, as though carved by a knife in slices from the body. The genitals appear to have been left untouched. The face lacks contours, is a blue-black, swollen, frozen mass of beaten fat. Only the eyes, wide open and bloodshot, almost surprised or hungry, yet simultaneously full of hesitant fear, let on that this is a human face.

'He must weigh at least a hundred and fifty kilos,' Zeke says.

'At least,' Malin replies, thinking that she has seen that look on murder victims before, how everything becomes primal again when we are faced with death, how we revert to the new human being we once were. Scared, hungry, but right from the outset capable of surprise.

She usually reacts this way when confronted by scenes like this. Rationalises them away, with the help of memories and things she's read, tries to match up what her eyes are seeing with what she's gleaned from studies.

His eyes.

Most of all she sees fury in them. And despair.

The others are waiting over by the patrol car. Zeke told the uniformed officer to sit and wait in the car.

'No need for you to stand out here freezing. He'll keep on hanging where he's hanging.'

'Don't you want to talk to the man who found him?' The officer looked over his shoulder. 'That's who found him.'

'We'll take a look first.'

Then this swollen frozen body in this lonely oak; a gigantic overgrown baby that someone, or more than one, has tortured the life out of.

What do you want with me? Malin wonders. Why have you dragged me out here on this godforsaken morning? What do you want to tell me?

The feet, blue-black, the toes turning black, swing against all the whiteness.

The eyes, Malin thinks. Your isolation. It's like something moving across the plain, across the town, and into me.

First the obvious.

The branch is five metres above the ground, no clothes, no blood in the snow, no tracks in the thin covering around the tree, apart from the really fresh ones from a pair of boots.

From the man who found you, Malin thinks. One thing is certain: you didn't get up here by yourself; and the injuries on your body, someone else must have given you those. And you probably didn't get them here, otherwise the ground beneath you would be covered in blood. No, you froze for a good while somewhere else, so long that your blood turned solid.

'You see those marks on the branch?' Zeke says, looking up at the body.

'Yes,' Malin replies. 'Like someone's torn the bark off.'

'I swear, the man who did this must have used a crane to get him up into the tree, then tied the noose afterwards.'

'Or people,' Malin says. 'There may have been more than one.'

'No tracks between here and the road.'

'No, but it was a windy night. The ground changes by the minute. Loose snow, bits of ice. It's changing all the time. How long would any track last? Quarter of an hour. An hour. No longer.'

'We're still going to have to get the forensics team to check the ground.'

'They're going to need the biggest heater on the planet,' Malin says.

'Well, that's their business.'

'How long do you reckon he's been hanging there?'

'Impossible to say. But no longer than the first hours of darkness. Someone would have seen him during the day.'

'He could have been dead long before that,' Malin says.

'That's Johannison's job.'

'Anything sexual?'

'Isn't everything, Fors?'

Her surname. Zeke uses it when he's joking, when he answers a question he thinks is unnecessary or stupid, or just stupidly formulated.

'Come on, Zeke.'

'I don't think there's anything sexual involved here. No.'

'Good, we agree on that, then.'

They head back towards the cars.

'Whoever did this,' Zeke says, 'must have a bloody huge sense of purpose. Because no matter how you go about it, it's no easy thing to get that body up here and into the tree.

'You'd have to be absolutely livid,' he adds.

'Or really sad,' Malin replies.

'Sit in our car instead. It's still warm.'

The uniforms clamber out of the patrol car.

The middle-aged man in the back seat looks meaningfully at Malin and makes an effort to move.

'You can stay,' she says, and the man sinks down, still tense, his thin eyebrows twitching. His entire body seems to be saying one single thing: How the hell do I explain this? What was I doing out here at this time of day?

Malin sits next to him, Zeke gets into the front.

'That's better,' Zeke says. 'Much better in here than out there.'

'It wasn't me,' the man says, looking at Malin, his blue eyes wet with worry. 'I shouldn't have stopped, bloody stupid of me, I should just have kept going.'

Malin puts her hand on the man's arm. The padding under the red fabric sinks beneath her fingers.

'You did the right thing.'

'You see, I'd been—'

'It's okay,' Zeke says, turning towards the back seat. 'Just take it easy. You can start by telling us your name.'

'My name?'

'Yep.' Malin nods.

'I'm having an affair—'

'Your name.'

'Liedbergh. Peter Liedbergh.'

'Thank you, Peter.'

'Now you can go on.'

'I'm having an affair, and I'd been with her in Borensberg and was going home this way. I live in Maspelösa and it's the quickest route from there. I'll admit that much, but I didn't have anything to do with this. You can check with her. Her name is—'

'We'll check,' Zeke says. 'So, you were on your way home from a night of passion?'

'Yes, and I came this way. They keep the road clear, and then

I saw something odd in the tree, and stopped, and I got out, and, I mean, fuck. Fuck. Bloody hell.'

People's movements, Malin thinks. Headlights shining in the night, flickering points of light. Then she says, 'There wasn't anyone here when you arrived? Did you see anyone?'

'Quiet as the grave.'

'Did you pass any other cars?'

'Not on this road. But a kilometre or so before the turning I passed an estate car, I can't remember what make.'

'Number?' Zeke's hoarse voice.

Peter Liedbergh shakes his head. 'You can check with her. Her name's—'

'We'll check.'

'You know. First I just wanted to carry on. But then, well, I know what you're supposed to do in this sort of situation. I swear, I had nothing to do with it.'

'We don't imagine that you did,' Malin says. 'I, I mean we, think it's pretty unlikely that you would have phoned if you were involved.'

'And my wife, does my wife have to know?'

'About what?'

'I told her I was going to work. Karlsson's Bakery, I do nights there, but that's in the other direction.'

'We won't need to say anything to her,' Malin says. 'But she'll probably find out anyway.'

'What am I going to tell her?'

'Tell her you took the scenic route. Because you felt too awake.'

'She'll never believe that. I'm usually completely exhausted. And in this cold.'

Malin and Zeke exchange a glance.

'Anything else you think might be important to us?'

Peter Liedbergh shakes his head. 'Can I go now?'

'No,' Malin says. 'The forensics team will have to check your car, and take your footprints. We need to know they're your footprints out there and not anyone else's. And you can give your lover's name to our colleagues.'

'I shouldn't have stopped,' Liedbergh says. 'It would have been better to leave him hanging here. I mean, someone would have found him sooner or later.'

The wind is increasing in strength, forcing its way through the synthetic padding of Malin's jacket, through her skin, flesh, right into the smallest molecules of her marrow. The stress hormones kick in, helping the muscles to send pain signals to the brain, and her whole body aches. Malin imagines that this must be what it's like to freeze to death. You never die of cold, but as a result of the stress, the pain the body experiences when it can't maintain its temperature and goes into overdrive, trying to fool itself. When you're really cold, you feel a warmth spreading through your body. It's a terrible bliss: your lungs can no longer oxygenate the blood and you suffocate and fall asleep simultaneously, but you feel warm; people who've returned from this state say that it's as though they'd drowned, sinking down, down, only to float up again on clouds so soft and white and warm that all fear vanishes. It's a physiological trick, that softness, Malin thinks. It's just death caressing us so that we'll accept it.

A car approaches in the distance.

The technical team arriving already?

Hardly.

More likely the hyenas on the *Östgöta Correspondent* who've got wind of Picture of the Year. *Is it him?* Malin has time to wonder as the top of the oak creaks disconcertingly and she turns and sees the body quivering, and thinks, It can't be much fun hanging there.

Just hang on and we'll get you down.

4

'Malin, Malin, what have you got for me?'

The cold seems to eat up Daniel Högfeldt's words, muting the sound waves midway through the air. Even though he is wearing a padded jacket with a fur collar, there is something direct yet elegant about the way his body moves, his way of somehow owning and exercising power over the ground he's walking on.

She meets his gaze, and she sees a glimpse of a mocking smile in it, a story beyond this moment, a secret history that he knows she doesn't want anyone here to be aware of. And she sees the calculation: I know, you know, and I'm going to use that to get what I want, here and now. Extortion, Malin thinks. It won't work on me. When are you going to play your trump card, Daniel? Now? Why not? It's a good opportunity. But I won't back down. We may be the same age, but we're really not that similar.

'Was he murdered, Malin? How did he get up in the tree? You *have* to give me something.'

Suddenly Daniel Högfeldt is very close; his straight nose seems to be almost touching hers. 'Malin?'

'Not another step. And I'm saying nothing. I don't *have* to do anything.'

And the mocking smile in his eyes gets even clearer, but Daniel decides to retreat.

The photographer's camera clicks as she moves about just beyond the cordon round the tree and body.

'Not so close, you idiot,' Zeke shouts, and from the corner of her eye Malin sees the two uniformed officers rush off towards the photographer, who slowly lowers her camera and backs away nearer their car.

'Malin, he must have been murdered if you need to keep the site clean, so you have to say something. It doesn't look like a suicide, if you ask me.'

She shoves Daniel aside, feels her elbow touch his, wants to go back and repeat the gesture again, but instead she hears him calling after her, and thinks, How the hell could I? How could I be so stupid?

Then she turns back to face the journalist from the *Correspondent*: 'Not one step on to that field. Back to your car, and stay there, or, even better, get out of here. It's cold and there's nothing else going on; you've got pictures of the body, haven't you?'

Daniel smiles a practised boyish smile, which, unlike his words, cuts right through the cold.

'But Malin, I'm only doing my job.'

'All that's going to happen now is that the forensics team are going to turn up and start doing their job, that's all. We'll take it from there.'

'I'm done,' the photographer calls, and Malin thinks that she can't be more than eight or nine years older than Tove, and how her bare fingers must ache.

'She's freezing,' Malin says.

'I dare say she is,' Daniel says. Then he pushes past Malin towards the car without looking back.

When the thought first occurred to me, that she was actually going to help me down, I grew tired of hanging here. Because that is my state. I drift, and I am here. I am in one place, and everywhere. But this tree is no place of rest; perhaps rest will never come. I don't know yet.

So, all these people in their padded clothes.

Don't they see how vain they are?

Do they imagine they can keep out the cold?

Can't they get me down now?

I'm tired of hanging around like this, of this game you're playing with me down there in the snow below me. It's fun watching how

your steps in the snow become tracks, tracks I can amuse myself
by following, round, round, like restless memories hidden in inac-
cessible synapses.

'I can't stand that man,' Zeke says as the *Correspondent*'s car
disappears off in the cold. 'He's like a cocaine-fuelled leech with
ADHD.'

'And that's why he's so good at his job,' Malin says.

Zeke's American-inspired metaphors turn up when you least
expect them, and Malin has often wondered where they come
from. As far as she knows, Zeke has never shown any fondness for
American popular culture, and he probably hardly knows who
Philip Marlowe is.

'If he's so fucking clever, what's he doing on a local paper?'

'Maybe he's happy here?'

'Yeah, right.'

Then Malin looks over at the body. 'What do you think it's
like, hanging up there?'

The words hung in the cold air.

'It's just meat now,' Zeke says. 'Meat can't feel anything.
Whoever that person was, whatever sort of human being he was,
he isn't here any longer.'

'Even so, he still has things to tell us,' Malin says.

Karin Johannison, analyst, pathologist and researcher at the
National Laboratory of Forensic Science, with a part-time post
as a crime-scene investigator with the Linköping Police, is flapping her arms around her heavily padded body, elegant even
though conducting an inelegant gesture. Small fragments of
feathers fly up in the air like misshapen snowflakes and Malin
imagines that the jacket must have been incredibly expensive
considering how well-padded its red fabric is.

Even in her fur hat and with cheeks red from the February
chill, Karin is the spitting image of a slightly aged Riviera prin-
cess, like a middle-aged Françoise Sagan, without a cloud in
her sky, far too attractive for the job she does. The suntan from

her holiday in Thailand at Christmas is still lingering on her skin and sometimes, Malin thinks, I wish I could have been like Karin, married to money and the easy life.

They approach the body cautiously, stepping in footprints already there.

Karin is behaving like an engineer, pushing aside any thoughts of the naked human being in the tree in front of them, refusing to see the fat, the skin, what had once been the face, suppressing any empathy with the thoughts that might have passed through the swollen body's brain, and which are now slowly settling over the city, the plain and the forests like an ominous murmur; a whimper that could perhaps only be silenced in one way, through an answer to the question: Who did it?

'What do you see, Karin?'

I know, Malin thinks. You see an object, a screw or a nut, a narrative machine that needs to be analysed, that will be allowed to tell its innate story.

'He can hardly have got up there by himself,' Karin says, standing almost immediately below the body. She has just photographed the footprints around it, laying a ruler beside them, because even if they are in all likelihood merely their own and Peter Liedbergh's they need to be checked.

Malin doesn't answer. Instead she asks, 'How long do you think he's been dead?'

'Impossible to know just by looking at him. I'm going to have to work without any preconceptions on this one. We'll get answers to those questions in the post-mortem.'

The answer she was expecting. Malin thinks instead of Karin's suntan, her plump jacket and how the wind is cutting straight through her own Stadium coat.

'We need to take a look at the ground before we get him down,' Karin says. 'We'll have to bring in the heater the army have got up in Kvarn, and erect a tent so we can get rid of all this snow.'

'But won't you just end up with a quagmire?' Malin asks.

'Only if we carry on too long,' Karin replies. 'They can

probably have the heater here in a few hours. If they're not on duty somewhere else, that is.'

'He shouldn't be left hanging there much longer,' Malin says.

'It's minus thirty out here,' Karin says. 'Nothing's going to happen to the body in this sort of cold.'

Zeke has kept the engine running and there is probably a forty-degree difference in temperature between the inside of the car and the air outside. Warm breath is turning to ice crystals on the side windows.

Malin gets into the passenger seat.

'Quick, shut the door,' Zeke snaps. 'So, has Mrs Johannison taken charge of the situation?'

'Kvarn. She's getting the heater from there.'

Another two patrol cars have arrived, and through the tracery of the crystals Malin sees Karin direct the uniformed officers out in the field.

'We might as well go now,' Zeke says.

Malin nods.

As they drive back past Sjövik's fruit farm Malin turns on the radio, tuning it to P4. An old friend of hers, Helen Aneman, presents a programme on that channel every day between seven and ten o'clock.

Her friend's soft voice comes on as 'A Whiter Shade of Pale' fades out.

'During that last track I took a look at the *Correspondent*'s site. This is no normal day in Linköping, dear listeners. And I don't mean the cold. The police have found something in an oak tree in the middle of the plain, towards Vreta Kloster.'

'That was quick,' Zeke said over the noise of the radio.

'He's no slacker, Daniel,' Malin says.

'Daniel?'

'If you feel like starting the day with something stomach-churning,' the velvet voice on the radio says, 'have a look at the pictures on the *Correspondent*'s website. A very unusual bird in a tree.'

5

Daniel Högfeldt leans back against his office chair and the responsive backrest dips towards the floor.

He rocks back and forth like he used to in Grandfather's rocking-chair in the cottage out in Vikbolandet, the one that burned down soon after Grandma finally passed away at Vrinnevis Hospital in Norrköping. First Daniel looks out through the window at Hamngatan, then across the open-plan newsroom at his colleagues crouched over their computers, most of them completely indifferent to their work, happy with what they've got, and tired, so tired. If there's one poison worse than all the others for journalists, Daniel thinks, it's tiredness. It messes people up, ruins them.

I'm not tired. Not in the slightest.

He mentioned Malin in his article about the man in the tree: *Malin Fors of Linköping Police did not want to give any . . .*

Back and forth.

Just like most crime investigations he had covered.

The clatter of keyboards, the sound of people calling across the newsroom, and the smell of bitter coffee.

Several of his colleagues are so cynical it is affecting their productivity. But not him. It is a matter of maintaining respect for the people whose stories and mishaps are his daily bread.

A naked man in a tree. Hanged.

A blessing for anyone with newspaper pages to fill and sell.

But also something else.

The city will wake up. No question at all.

I'm good at what I do, because I know how to play the 'journalistic game', but also because I know how to keep my distance and how to play people.

Cynical?

Hamngatan was swept in winter outside.

Crumpled sheets in Malin Fors's apartment. Only two blocks away.

Sven Sjöman's wrinkled brow, his bulging gut, the denim shirt carelessly tucked into his brown wool trousers. His face as lifeless and grey as the jacket he is wearing, his thin hair the same colour as the whiteboard he is standing in front of. Sven prefers to keep meetings small, then to inform anyone else involved as and when. In his opinion, large meetings like they have in other police districts are never as productive.

He starts the way he usually does with a meeting of this sort, when they are about to start work on a big new case. The question *who?* needs to be answered, and it is his responsibility to set the question in motion, to give it a direction that will hopefully lead to the answer: *him, her, them.*

There is a deceptive emptiness, a trickling poison in the meeting room. Because all five of the officers assembled know that when that question is left hanging in the air, it can influence and change an entire community, a region, a country, a whole world.

The room is on the ground floor in one of the old military barracks in the A1-district that was rebuilt as the central police station about ten years ago when the regiment was disbanded: military out, law and order in.

Outside the barred windows is a ten-metre-wide, snow-covered lawn, then a playground, empty and desolate; the swings and climbing-frames are painted in primary colours but the white frost has turned them all into a collage of grey. Beyond the park, inside the nursery school's large windows, Malin can see children playing, running to and fro, doing all the things that make up their world.

Tove.

It's been a long time since you ran about like that.

Malin called her from the car, and Tove answered on her way out of the flat: 'Of course I got up.'

'Wrap up warm.'

'What, do you think I'm stupid or something?'

Zeke: 'Teenagers. They're like horses on a racecourse. They never do what you want.'

Sometimes when they've been working on particularly violent cases, with pictures pinned up on the walls of the meeting room, they close the blinds to shield the children in the nursery, so that they don't see the sort of thing they probably see on television every day, flickering past on an unguarded set, image added to image, as the child learns to trust its own eyes.

A slit throat. A burned corpse hanging from a lamppost, a swollen body in a flooded town.

And now Sjöman's words, the same words as always, his gruff voice: 'So, what do you think we've got here? Any ideas, anyone? There have been no new missing person reports, and if that was going to happen it would probably have happened by now. So what do we think?' A question tossed into the room by a standing man to people sitting round an oblong table, his finger pressing the play button, words like music, like notes, hard and brittle between the four walls.

Johan Jakobsson speaks up, and it is obvious he has been waiting to hear his own voice, that he has been wanting to say something, anything, if only to put an end to his own tiredness.

'It's got ritual written all over it.'

'We don't even know for sure that he was murdered,' Sven Sjöman says. 'We can't be sure until Karin Johannison is finished. But we can presume that he was murdered. That much is clear.'

You don't know anything for certain, Malin. Until you know. Until then: the virtue of ignorance.

'It looks like a ritual.'

'We have to keep an open mind.'

'We don't know who he is,' Zeke says. 'That would be a good start, finding out who he is.'

'Maybe someone will call in. The pictures are in the paper already,' Johan says, and Börje Svärd, who has been silent up to now, sighs.

'Those pictures? You can't see the face.'

'How many people that overweight can there be round here? And before too long someone will wonder where that fat man has disappeared to.'

'Don't be so sure,' Malin says. 'This city's full of people that no one would notice if they went missing.'

'But he looks different, his body—'

'If we're lucky,' Sven interrupts Johan, 'someone will call in. To begin with we'll have to wait for the results of the search of the scene and for the post-mortem. We can start knocking on doors in the area, find out if anyone saw or heard anything, if anyone knows anything we ought to know. We have, as you're well aware, one question that has to be answered.'

Sven Sjöman, Malin thinks. Four years left before he reaches sixty-five, four years left at risk of a heart attack, four years of overtime, four years of his wife's tasty and lovingly prepared but dangerously fatty food. Four years of too little exercise. *A widow-making stomach*. But Sven is still the voice of reason in the room, the voice of experience, pushing no particular angle, stressing sensible, disinterested, mature methodology.

'Malin, you and Zeke will be in charge of the preliminary investigation,' Sven says. 'I'll see that you get the resources you need for the foot-work. And you two can help them as much as you have time for.'

'I'd have been happy to take this on,' Johan says.

'Johan, we've got other things to do as well,' Börje says. 'We don't have the luxury of concentrating on just one case.'

'Is the meeting over?' Zeke asks, pushing back his chair and standing up.

The moment they have all got to their feet the door opens.

'You can all sit down again.'

Karim Akbar says these words with all the gravity his muscular, thirty-seven-year-old body can muster, then goes to stand beside Sven Sjöman and waits while the other four officers sink into their chairs again.

'You appreciate how important it is,' Karim says, and it strikes Malin that there isn't a trace of an accent in his speech, despite the fact that he was already ten years old when he arrived in Sweden. He speaks clear, empty, standard Swedish.

'How important it is,' he repeats, 'that we get this sorted out,' and it sounds just like he's talking about a dissertation that needs restructuring before a viva.

Hard work and application.

If you start on minus and want to get to double-plus, you can't afford to leave anything to chance. Karim has written controversial opinion pieces in *Svenska Dagbladet* and *Dagens Nyheter*, perfectly chiselled to match the needs of the age. His opinions have upset a lot of people: immigrants must meet certain requirements; benefits need to be linked to linguistic ability in Swedish after just one year in the country. Exclusion can only become inclusion with a lot of effort.

His face appears regularly on television discussion programmes. Make demands, liberate people's innate potential. Look at me, it can be done. I am living proof.

But what about the timid? Malin wonders. Those who were born diffident?

'We know this is what our job is about. Solving crimes like this,' Zeke says, and Malin sees Johan and Börje smiling furtively as Sven pulls a face that means: Calm down, Zeke, let him make his speech; just because you don't make a fuss doesn't mean that you're nothing but a manual labourer for him. *For God's sake, haven't you grown up, Martinsson?*

Karim gives Zeke a look that says: Show me respect, and don't use that tone, but Zeke doesn't look away. So Karim goes on instead: 'The press, the media, will make a big deal out of this, and I'm going to have to answer a lot of questions. We have to come up with the solution quickly; it's a matter of showing how efficient the Linköping Police are.'

Malin thinks that it sounds like Karim's words are being spoken by an automaton. No one talks like that in real life, and the competent individual in front of her is playing the role of a competent individual, when he would really prefer to relax and show . . . well, what? . . . his vulnerable side?

Then Karim turns to Sven. 'Have you allocated resources?'

'Fors and Martinsson are in overall charge. They have all necessary resources at their disposal. Jakobsson and Svärd will assist as much as they can. Andersson is off sick and Degerstad is still on her course in Stockholm. That's the situation right now.'

Karim takes a deep breath, holding the air in his lungs for a long time before breathing out.

'Okay, this is what we're going to do. Sven, as usual you will have overall responsibility as primary investigator, and you other four can form a team. Everything else will have to wait. This has the very highest priority.'

'But—'

'This is how it has to be, Martinsson. I don't doubt that you and Fors are very capable, but right now we need to focus our resources.'

Sven's stomach seems to have grown even larger, the furrows on his brow even deeper.

'Do you want me to contact the National Criminal Investigation Institute? We don't yet know formally that he was even murdered.'

Karim is heading towards the door.

'No National Crime. We're going to sort this out ourselves. You're to report to me every three hours, or whenever there are any new developments.'

The noise of the door slamming behind him echoes round the room.

'You heard what he said. You can divide the work up between you and report back to me.'

The children playing on the other side of the nursery windows are gone. A yellow, Calder-inspired mobile is swaying gently beneath the checked curtains.

Blue, fat-mottled skin.

Beaten and alone in the ice-cold wind.

Who were you? Malin wonders.

Come back and tell me who you were.

6

Now they have erected a tent beneath me, its green colour turned grey by the evening. I know they are warm in there, but none of that warmth reaches me.

Can I even feel warmth any more? Could I ever? I lived in the land beyond, free in one way from your world, but what a freedom it turned out to be.

But I no longer have any need of your warmth, not as you understand it; there is warmth around me. I am not alone, or rather I am exactly that, alone, I am loneliness, I am the core of loneliness. Perhaps I was the core of loneliness when I was alive? The most basic substance of loneliness, the mystery whose solution we are approaching, the chemical reaction, the seemingly simple yet all-encompassing process in our brains that gives rise to perceptions which in turn give us consciousness, the precondition for the reality we believe to be our own. The lamps burn late in researchers' laboratories. Once we have cracked that code, we will have cracked them all. Then we can rest. Laugh or scream. Stop. But until then?

Wandering, working, searching for the answers to all manner of questions.

It's hardly surprising, the way you carry on.

The snow melts, trickling away, but you won't find anything, so get rid of the tent, bring in a crane and get me down. I'm a strange fruit, I'm not supposed to hang here; it spoils the balance, and it's starting to make the branch creak. Even the tree is protesting, can't you hear it?

Well, exactly, you're all deaf. Just think, how quickly we actually forget. Think what the meanderings of our thoughts can do to us, where they can lead us.

★

'Mum, have you seen my eye-shadow?'

Tove's voice from the bathroom sounds desperate, annoyed and resigned all at the same time, yet simultaneously full of a resolved, focused and almost frightening determination.

Eye-shadow? That hasn't happened for a while. Malin can't remember the last time Tove wore any make-up, and wonders what's going on this evening.

'Do you *want* eye-shadow?' Malin calls from her place on the sofa. The news has just started, with the man in the tree as the third item, after a statement from the Prime Minister and some meteorological expert who says that the current spell of cold weather is conclusive proof of climate change, that we're heading for a new ice age which is going to cover the whole of Sweden under metres of granite-hard crystals.

'Why else would I be asking?'

'Are you seeing a boy?'

There is silence from the bathroom, then a single 'Damn' when the make-up bag balanced on the bathroom cabinet evidently tumbles to the floor. Then: 'It's here. I found it, Mum.'

'Good.'

A male reporter from the *Östgöta* newspaper is standing at the darkened crime-scene, floodlights illuminating the tree in the background, and you can just make out the body in the tree, but only if you know it's there.

'I'm standing in a frozen field several miles outside Linköping. The police have . . .'

Throughout the region people are watching the same pictures as me, Malin thinks. And they're wondering the same thing: Who was he? How did he get there? Who did it?

In the eyes of the television viewers, I am the provider of television truth, I make sure that evil people are locked up behind bars. I am the person who is expected to transform anxiety to security, but things are never so simple in reality, outside the screen. Out here everything is a test card, rich in nuances where it is impossible to take in everything, where meaning is everywhere and nowhere, with a clock ticking away and everyone waiting for something new, something clearer, better, to take over.

'Mum, can I borrow your perfume?'

Perfume?

She's got a date, Malin thinks. Which would be a first. Then: Who? Where? When? A thousand questions, thoughts, anxieties in myriad forms run through her in a fraction of a second.

'Who are you seeing?'

'No one. Can I borrow your perfume?'

'Of course.'

'. . . the body is still hanging here.'

The camera moves to one side, and in the abrupt darkness above the tent the body sways back and forth and Malin wants to change the channel, but at the same time she wants to watch. Cut to that afternoon's press conference. Karim Akbar in a well-pressed suit in the large meeting room in Police Headquarters, his black hair slicked back, his face serious, but his eyes can't conceal how much he loves the spotlight, how it seems to validate him.

'We don't yet know for certain that he was murdered.'

Microphones from TV4 in the foreground. A question from the mass of journalists; she recognises Daniel Högfeldt's voice.

'Why have you left the body hanging there?'

Daniel. What are you up to now?

Karim answers confidently. 'For technical reasons concerned with the investigation. As yet we don't know anything. We're keeping an entirely open mind.'

'Mum, have you seen my red polo-neck?' Tove's voice from her own room now.

'Have you looked in the drawer?'

A few short seconds, then a triumphant voice. 'Found it!'

Good, Malin thinks, then ponders what keeping an open mind means and is likely to mean: going round to every farm and cottage within a three-kilometre radius from the tree, knocking on the doors of farmers, commuters and workshy folk on sick leave.

'Really? No, I haven't noticed anything.'

'I'm always asleep at that time of day.'

'In this sort of cold I stay indoors.'

'I keep myself to myself, it's better that way.'

The same response for Johan and Börje as for her and Zeke: no one knows anything, no one has seen anything. It's as if the hundred-and-fifty-kilo body flew up into the noose in the tree, parking itself on the end of the rope in anticipation of attention.

Back to the studio.

'Naturally we'll be following developments in Linköping.' Pause. 'In London . . .'

Then Tove is standing in the door to the living room.

'I read about that on the net,' she says. 'Are you in charge of it?'

But Malin can't answer her daughter's question. Instead she just gawps when she sees her, the child who was lying in bed this morning; the little girl who went into the bathroom just quarter of an hour ago is transformed. She is wearing make-up and has tied up her hair, and something has happened, a hint of a woman has superimposed itself over her daughter's appearance.

'Mum? Mum, hello?'

'You look lovely.'

'Thanks, I'm going to the cinema.'

'I'm working on the case.'

'It's a good thing I'm going to Dad's tomorrow, so you can work late.'

'Tove. Please. Don't say that.'

'I'm off now. I'll be home by eleven. The last screening ends about then, but we're having coffee first.'

'Who are you going with?'

'Anna.'

'If I said I didn't believe you, what would you say?'

Tove shrugs. 'We're going to see the new Tom Cruise film,' then Tove gives the name of a film Malin has never heard of. Tove is as liberal in her choice of film as she is selective in her taste in books.

'I haven't heard of that one.'

'Oh Mum, you don't know anything about stuff like this.'

Tove turns and disappears from Malin's sight, but Malin can hear her rummaging in the hall. She calls, 'Do you need any money?'

'No.'

And Malin wants to follow her, doesn't believe any of this, but knows that she shouldn't, can't, won't. Unless she will?

'Bye!'

Anxiety.

Johan Jakobsson, Börje Svärd, Zeke: all parents are familiar with it, that anxiety.

It's cold out.

'Bye, Tove.'

And the flat closes around Malin.

She turns off the television with the remote.

Leans back on the sofa and takes a sip of her tequila, the one she poured herself after they'd eaten.

She and Zeke had been out to Borensberg and spoken to Liedbergh's lover. The woman was around forty, neither beautiful nor ugly, just one of the mass of normal women with passions to live out, to fulfil. She offered them coffee and home-baked buns. She told them she was single and unemployed, how she tried to fill her days while applying for any jobs she thought she might stand a chance of getting. 'It's hard,' Peter Liedbergh's lover had said. 'You're either too old or you haven't got the right qualifications. But something will turn up.'

The woman confirmed Liedbergh's story. Then she shook her head. 'It's a good job he went that way. Who knows how long that man might have been left hanging there otherwise in this cold.'

Malin looked at the porcelain figurines arranged on the kitchen windowsill. A dog, a cat, an elephant. A little porcelain menagerie for company.

'Do you love him?' Malin asked.

Zeke shook his head instinctively.

But the woman didn't take against the question.

'Who? Peter Liedbergh? No, not at all.' She laughed. 'You know, it's just something we women need, isn't it, a bit of company?'

Malin sinks further into the sofa. She thinks about Janne, about how difficult he finds it to talk, how he sometimes feels like a black outline superimposed over her own. In the window she can see the tower of St Lars, and waits for the bells to ring, tries to hear if there are any whispering voices in the darkness.

If you weren't deaf you would hear the sound of the branch breaking. You would hear the sound of fibres splitting, hear my body slicing through the cold and the air; you who are standing directly underneath would throw yourself to one side, but none of this happens. Instead all my many kilos land right on the tent, smashing the aluminium frame as if it were made of matchsticks, and the whole construction collapses and you who are standing there when I fall, you poor uniformed policeman, at first you notice something hitting you, then you feel my weight, and then you are flattened to the ground by my frozen hardness, and something inside you, you don't know what, breaks, but you're lucky, it's only a bone, nothing the doctors can't put right, your arm will be fine. I'm perfectly harmless in that respect, even now I'm dead.

Because you didn't get me down, in spite of my pleas, I had to persuade the tree, and to be honest it was tired of having me hanging on the oldest of its branches. It's ready to be cast off, the oak said, so go ahead and fall, fall on the tent, to the ground, and stir things up a bit down there.

And now I'm lying here on top of the screaming policeman, in a muddle of words, tent-pegs and canvas. The heater is roaring in my ear. I can't feel its heat but I know it's there. Beneath my hands I can feel the earth, made damp by your heat; pleasantly wet and nice, like the innards of something, anything.

Malin is woken by Tove's voice.

'Mum? Mum, I'm home. Don't you think you should go to bed instead?'

'Oh yes, of course.'

Malin wakes slowly, grows doubtful. Whenever she had done anything silly, she always woke Dad to say that everything was all right. But before Malin has time to doubt Tove, her daughter says, 'Have you been drinking, Mum?'

Malin rubs her eyes. 'No, just a bit of tequila.'

The bottle in front of her, the half-bottle of cask-aged tequila, bought on the way home from the station, a third empty.

'Okay, Mum,' Tove says. 'Shall I help you into bed?'

Malin shakes her head. 'That only happened once, Tove. You only had to do that once. ONCE.'

'Twice.'

Malin nods. 'Twice.'

'Well, goodnight, then,' Tove says.

'Sleep well,' Malin says.

The clock on the sideboard says quarter to twelve. From behind Malin can see that Tove's hair is now loose, and she looks like the little girl again.

A bit of tequila left in the glass. A lot more in the bottle. Another little one? No. No need. Malin gets up with an effort and stumbles towards the bedroom.

She can't be bothered to get undressed and falls on to her bed.

And dreams dreams that might have been best undreamed.

7

The jungle is at its most dense at night.

The damp, the insects, the damn wildlife, leaves, snakes, spiders, millipedes and mould growing in the sleeping-bag at night.

Then they land at the airport, endless masses of tiny lights, a starry sky on the ground and the Russian Tupolev plane plummeting straight down like a helicopter, the wings tear and he flaps with his soul in the cramped space, child and mother standing there, Tove, only little then, now: What are you doing here, Dad? You ought to be at home with me. I'm coming, I'm coming, and then they unload, break out of the plane's innards: food, plumbing pipes, and they come towards them in the darkness; you can only see their eyes, thousands of eyes in the darkness, eyes to trust in, and the hungry scared muttering and the salvos from the automatic rifles. Back off or we'll finish what the Hutus started. Back away and a millipede crawls over my leg, the mould grows, Kigali, Kigali, Kigali, the inescapable mantras of dream.

Get this fucking millipede away from me.

Janne, someone shouts. Tove? Malin? Melinda? Per?

Get this . . .

Someone cuts the leg off someone who's still alive, throws it in a pot of boiling water and then eats first, before someone else lets their children share the rest. No one cares, but if you stole milk from anyone still fully alive the punishment is death.

Don't shoot him, I say. Don't shoot.

He's hungry, he's ten, his eyes are large and yellowish white;

the pupils expand in time with the realisation that this ends here, now. *I can't even save you either.*

Then you shoot.

Dog, dog, dog, Hutu, Hutu, Hutu, your cries echo, and your greed, your fucking bastard humanity makes me want to drown you all in the latrines we came here to build for your sake, so that typhoid and cholera and other shit wouldn't kill you in numbers that even the Hutus couldn't match.

Janne. Dad. Come home.

Has the rain-sheet broken?

It's so fucking wet. How do the millipedes cope with all these drops?

Fuck, it stings, fucking savages, fucking things up for themselves.

Don't raise that machete against me, don't hit me, don't hit me, no no no and the scream is in the room outside the dream now, outside sleep, in the wakefulness of his room, in his loneliness and the dream-soaked sheets.

He sits up in bed.

The screams echo round the walls.

His hand on the fabric.

Soaking wet. No matter how cold it gets out there, it still seems to be warm enough in here for him to break into a full sweat.

Something crawls over his leg.

The last remnant of the dream, Jan-Erik Fors thinks, before he gets up to fetch a new sheet from the linen cupboard in the hall. The cupboard is an heirloom. He and Malin bought the house, in its isolated forest setting a couple of kilometres north of Linköping, not far from Malmslätt, just after Tove was born.

The floorboards creak as he moves, alone, from the bedroom and out into the rest of the house.

The dogs are barking round Börje Svärd's legs.

For the Alsatians there is no such thing as morning cold, not even at five o'clock in the morning; they're just happy to see him, excited about being able to run around in the garden, chasing the sticks he throws in different directions for them.

Entirely unconcerned.

Unaware of naked beaten dead men in trees. Every conversation with people in the area yesterday was fruitless. Silence and blindness. As if people were ungrateful at having senses that functioned.

Valla.

The district of detached houses built in the forties and fifties, wooden boxes with assorted extensions illustrating the way life just kept getting better and better and better; when this city still worked for ordinary people, before a factory worker was forced to get a university education to look after a robot.

But some things work.

Inside the house they're busy with her right now, the carers. They come once late at night to turn her, then they're there, in Börje and Anna's house, their home, all day and long into the evening, simultaneously more and less natural than the furniture, the wallpaper and the carpets.

MS. Multiple sclerosis. A few years after they got married Anna started to slur her speech. It progressed quickly after that. And now? The disease-modifying treatments came too late for her. Not a single muscle obeys her now, and Börje is the only person who can understand what she's trying to say.

Darling Anna.

This business of the dogs is crazy, really. But there has to be some sort of breathing hole, something that is his own, uncomplicated, full of happiness. Pure. The neighbours have complained about the kennels, the barking.

Let them complain.

And the children? Mikael moved to Australia about ten years ago. Karin moved to Germany. To escape? Almost certainly. Who could bear to see their mother like that? How do I bear it?

But you do bear it.

Love.

They may well have said that she can have a place in a home whenever you want it.

When *I* want it?

Dogs, pistols. Concentrating on the target. The firing range acts as purification.

But Anna, for me you are still you. And as long as you are still that for me, maybe you can bear to be the same for yourself.

'And then we open the garage.'

The spoon of cereal can't seem to find its way into the one-year-old's mouth, and for a moment Johan Jakobsson is brusque, holding the boy's head still with his hand and slipping the spoon into the reluctant mouth, and the boy swallows.

There.

Their terraced house is in Linghem. That was what they could afford, and as far as Linköping's dormitory villages are concerned, Linghem isn't the worst. Homogenous, rural, middle-class. Nothing remarkable, but nothing visibly dreadful either.

'Toot toot, here comes the lorry.'

From the bathroom he can hear his wife brushing their three-year-old daughter's teeth, hear her screaming and fighting, and how his wife's voice betrays the fact that she is on the brink of losing patience.

She asked him yesterday if he was working on the man in the tree and what was he supposed to answer? Lie and say no to keep her calm or tell it how it was: Yes, I'm working on that case.

'He looks so lonely up there in the tree,' his wife had said. 'Lonely,' and he hadn't been able to think of anything to say to that. Because you don't get much more alone than that.

'Brrm, brrm, here comes a Passat.'

After that she got annoyed because he didn't want to talk about it. The children were tired, out of control, until they collapsed for the night.

The children: they make him feel wiped out, their all-consuming will makes him exhausted, so tired. At the same time, they make him feel alive and adult. Life itself seems to go on somehow alongside the family. As if the crimes they investigate have nothing to do with the children. But they do. The children are part of the social body in which the crimes have taken place.

'Open wide . . .'

Breakfast television on in the background. The first news bulletin of the day. They mention the case briefly.

I'm going to miss these moments, Sven Sjöman thinks, taking a break from sanding down in the woodwork room in the cellar of their house in Hackefors. I'm going to miss the smell of wood in the mornings when I retire. Of course, I can carry on having that smell afterwards, but it won't be the same when I don't have police work ahead of me. I know that. I find meaning in shoring up the others. It's good to have young officers like Johan and Malin who aren't yet fully formed. I can feel I'm having some influence on them. Malin, in particular, seems to be able to take in what I say and make something of it.

He usually sneaks down to the workshop in the mornings before Elisabeth has woken up. Sand down the leg of a chair, apply some varnish. Something small and simple to get the day going before the first coffee.

Wood is simple and obvious. With his skills, he can make it do whatever he wants, in contrast to the rest of reality.

The man in the tree. The scarred corpse falling on top of one of his officers. It's as if everything is constantly getting worse. As if the boundary of violence is advancing relentlessly and as if people in their despair and fear and anger are capable of doing anything to each other. As if more and more people feel that they're somehow out of reach; beyond their own and that of everyone else as well.

It's easy to get bitter, Sven thinks. If you decide to mourn the fact that all decency and honour seem to have vanished into the darkness of history.

But you can't mourn something like that. It's better to be happy about each new day, about the fact that consideration and solidarity still seem able to hold the worst cynicism at bay.

*

Masks.

All these masks I have to put on.

Karim Akbar is standing in front of the mirror in his bath-room, freshly shaven. His wife has set off for school with their eight-year-old son, just as she usually does.

I can be many people, Karim thinks, depending what the situ-ation demands.

He pulls a face. He conjures forth anger, he smiles, looks surprised, attentive, reserved, inquisitive, watchful.

Which of all of these am I really?

How easy it is to lose your own view of yourself when you sometimes think you can be anyone at all.

I can be the tough police officer, the successful immigrant, the media manipulator, the gentle father, I can be the man who wants to cuddle up with my wife, feel the warmth of her body beneath the sheets.

Feel love.

Instead of cold.

I can be the man who pretends that the fat body in the tree never existed, but my task right now is a different one: the man who gives him justice. If only in death.

'What have you got planned?'

Malin's question to Janne and Tove echoes in her head.

It's just after eight. The day is fully awake now.

So far they haven't called from the station, but Malin is expecting the call any minute. The debacle yesterday evening at the crime-scene, when the body fell out of the tree, is on the front page of the *Correspondent*.

This whole thing is like a farce, Malin thought when she glanced through the paper fifteen minutes ago, far too tired to read it properly.

Janne is standing in the hall next to Tove. He looks tired, the skin stretched tight across his sharp cheekbones, and his tall, muscular body seems to be hanging from a swaying gallows. Has he lost weight? And aren't those a few mute grey hairs at his temples, scattered among the otherwise so glossy amber locks?

Tove off school, a study day, early Friday pick-up instead of late. Changes of shift. A jigsaw puzzle.

She sent Janne a letter in Bosnia when she had packed her and Tove's belongings and moved into a small flat in the city, a stop on the road to Stockholm.

'You can have the house. It suits you much better than me, you've got room for your cars. I've never liked the countryside that much, really. Hope you're well, and not having to witness anything awful. Or put up with anything awful. We can work out everything else later.'

His answer came on a postcard.

'Thanks. I'll get a mortgage when I get home and buy you out. Do as you like.'

Do as you like?

I would have liked to have things the way they were before. Back at the start. Before it all became routine.

Because there are events and days that can drive people apart, breaking points. We were young, so young. Time, what did we know of that then, other than that it was ours?

Malin thinks about his dreams, the ones he always wants to talk about when they meet, but which she can never quite bear to listen to and he can never quite articulate even when she is trying to listen.

Instead Janne's voice: 'You're looking tired, Malin. Don't you think, Tove?'

Tove nods.

'Working too much,' Malin says.

'The bloke in the tree?'

'Mmm.'

'You'll have your work cut out this weekend, then.'

'Did you come in the Saab?'

'No, I used the Volvo. It's got winter tyres. I haven't bothered to change the others.'

Men are car fanatics. Most of them. And Janne in particular.

He has four cars in the garage next to the house. Four cars in varying stages of decay, or restoration, as he would put it. She could never stand the cars, not even at the start; she couldn't bear what they represented. What? A lack of willpower? Or imagination? Listlessness? Crass systematic thinking. Love demands something else.

'What have you got planned?'

'Don't know,' Janne says. 'There's not too much you can do in this sort of cold. What do you think, Tove? Shall we rent some films and get a load of sweets and lock ourselves in? Or do you want to read?'

'Films sound good. But I've got some books as well.'

'Try to get a bit of fresh air anyway,' Malin says.

'Mum. That's not up to you.'

'We can go to the firestation,' Janne says. 'Play a bit of fireman's indoor hockey. Tove, what do you think, that would be fun, wouldn't it?'

Tove looks up at the ceiling, then adds, as if not quite daring to trust her father's sarcasm, 'Not in a million years.'

'Oh well. Films it is, then.'

Malin looks tiredly at Janne, and his grey-green eyes meet hers, he doesn't look away, he never has. When he disappears he takes his perfect physique and his soul and goes to places where someone might need the help he thinks he can't survive without giving.

Help.

The name he has given to flight.

When the flat, the house, everything got too cramped. And then over and over again.

She gave Janne a hug when he arrived today, held him tight and he responded, he always does and she wanted to keep hold of him, pull him to her for a long time, ask him to sit out the cold snap with them here, ask him to stay.

But instead she came to her senses, found a way of breaking free of him, as if he were the one who had initiated the embrace. A way of getting her muscles to ask quietly, 'What are you doing?

We're not married any more and you know as well as I do that it's impossible.'

'And what about you, have you been sleeping okay?'

Janne nodded, but Malin could see that the nod concealed a lie.

'I just sweat so much.'

'Even though it's so cold?'

'Even though.'

'Have you got everything, Tove?'

'Yep, everything.'

'Make sure you get some fresh air.'

'Mum.'

Then they're gone. Janne will bring her back tomorrow, Saturday evening, so we can have Sunday together.

What am I going to do now?

Wait for the phone to ring? Read the paper?

Think?

No. Thinking has a way of leading you into a very tangled forest.

8

'He died of his head injuries. The perpetrator used a blunt object, repeatedly, almost as if in a frenzy, to beat in the cranium and the face until it became the shapeless mass of flesh it is now. He was alive when he received the blows, but in all likelihood lost consciousness fairly quickly. The perpetrator or perpetrators also appear to have used a knife.'

Karin Johannison is standing beside the blue body, which is lying on the cold steel of the pathology laboratory. Arms and legs and head stick out from the trunk like lumpy, irregular stumps. The torso is cut open, with the skin and fat folded into four flaps, revealing a jumble of guts. The skull has been sawn open, dutifully, at the back of the head.

It looks methodical and haphazard at the same time, Malin thinks. As if someone had been planning it for a long time, and then lost their composure.

'I had to let him thaw out before I could start,' as Karin had put it over the phone. 'But once I got started it was pretty straightforward.'

Zeke is standing quietly beside Malin, apparently unconcerned; he's seen death many times before and realises that it's impossible to grasp.

Karin works with death, but she doesn't understand it. Perhaps none of us does, Malin thinks. But most of us appreciate what death can encompass. Karin, Malin thinks, doesn't understand a lot of what everything in this basement room is actually about; here she is useful, functional, as precise as the instruments she uses in her work. As precise as the room itself.

The most practical face of death.

White walls, small windows at ceiling height, stainless-steel cabinets and shelves along the wall holding textbooks and bandages, compresses, surgical gloves and so on. The linoleum floor is a bluish colour, easy to clean, hardwearing, cheap. Malin never gets used to this room, to its role and function, but she is nevertheless drawn to it.

'He didn't die from the rope,' Karin says. 'He was dead by the time he was hauled up into the tree. If he'd died of strangulation the blood wouldn't have run to his head the way it did. With a hanging the blood vessels are shut off directly, to put it in layman's terms, but here the physical blows made the heart pump faster, which accounts for the abnormal amount of blood.'

'How long has he been dead?' Malin asks.

'You mean now?'

'No, before he was strung up in the tree.'

'I'd say at least five hours, maybe a bit longer. Considering there was no great quantity of blood in his legs even though he was found hanging.'

'What about the blows to the body?' Zeke says.

'What about them?'

'What have you got to say about them?'

'Doubtless very painful, if he was conscious at the time, but they weren't fatal. There are marks on the legs that show he was dragged, that someone hauled the body over damp ground. The wounds have dirt in them, and fragments of fabric. Someone undressed him after the beating, and then moved the body. At least that's what I believe happened. He was finished off with a knife.'

'And his teeth?' Zeke asks.

'In too poor a state to be useful, most of his teeth were broken.'

Karin takes hold of one of the wrists. 'Do you see these marks here?'

Malin nods.

'They were made by chains. That's how they got him up into the tree.'

'They?'

'I don't know. But do you imagine a single man could have done this, considering the amount of physical strength required?'

'Not impossible,' Malin says.

Zeke shakes his head. 'We don't know yet.'

The snow had concealed nothing.

The only thing Karin and her colleagues found were a few cigarette butts, a biscuit wrapper and an ice-cream wrapper that didn't quite seem to belong in the field. Ice cream? Hardly at this time of year. And the wrappers and butts looked older, as if they'd been there several years. They, or he, or she, hadn't left any traces behind them on the ground.

'Did you find anything else?'

'Nothing under the nails. No signs of a struggle. Which suggests he must have been taken by surprise. Have you had any tip-offs? Anyone who's said anything?'

'It's been completely quiet,' Malin says. 'Nada, niente.'

'Not missed by anyone, then,' Karin says.

'We don't know that either yet,' Zeke says.

If I were still able to talk the way you do, if I could get up and tell you, cure your deafness, I would tell you to stop with all these questions.

What good are they?

It is the way it is, it's turned out the way it's turned out. I know who did it, I caught a glimpse out of the corner of my eye, had time to see death coming, slow, quick, black.

Then it went white, death.

White as freshly fallen snow. White is the colour when the brain fades, an optimistic firework burst, shorter than a breath. And then, when vision returned to me again I could see everything, I was free and unfree at the same time.

So do you really want to know?

Do you really want to hear this story? I don't think so. It is worse, nastier, darker, more merciless than you can imagine. If you carry on from here, you are choosing a path that leads right into the heart of the place where only the body, not the soul, can live and breathe, where we are chemistry, where we are code, the place outside, where the word feeling does not exist.

At the end of the path, in an apple-scented darkness clad in white, you will find waking dreams so black that they make this winter seem warm and welcoming. But I know that you will choose that path. Because you are human beings. And that is how you are.

'How long will it take you to fix him up?'

'Fix him up how?'

'Ideally we need to get his face sorted out,' Malin says. 'So we can give a picture to the press. So that maybe someone will realise he's missing, or at least recognise him.'

'I understand. I'll phone Skoglund at Fonus funeral services. He can probably help me with a quick reconstruction. We ought to be able to come up with something decent anyway.'

'Call Skoglund. The sooner we have a picture the better.'

'Okay, let's go,' Zeke says, and from the tone of his voice Malin knows he's had enough. Of the body, of the sterile room, but mainly of Karin Johannison.

Malin knows that Zeke thinks Karin gives herself airs and graces, and maybe he's also put out by the fact that she doesn't ask about Martin like everyone else does, no matter where or when. And, for Zeke, Karin's lack of interest in ice hockey and his son has become proof that she's arrogant. He's clearly tired of all the questions about Martin, but is still not happy if people don't ask.

'Do you use spray-tan?' Zeke asks Karin when they're on their way out of the lab.

Malin laughs, against her will.

'No, I use a solarium to keep up my suntan from Thailand over Christmas,' Karin says. 'There's a place on Drottninggatan that does spray-tans, but I don't know. It seems so vulgar. Maybe just my face, though.'

'Thailand? At Christmas?' Zeke says. 'Isn't that the most expensive time? I've heard that people who really know Thailand go at other times.'

9

'Malin, have you watered the plants? They won't make it through the winter otherwise.'

The question is so obvious, Malin thinks, that there was really no need to ask it. And the explanation just as unnecessary: his tendency to be overtly pedagogical to promote his own interests.

'I'm on my way to your flat to do it now.'

'Haven't you done it already?'

'Not since we last spoke, no.'

She got the call just as she was leaving Police Headquarters, waiting for a green light at the corner of the cemetery and the old fire station. The Volvo had deigned to start today, even though it was just as cold.

It was like she knew it was Dad by the way the phone rang. Annoyed, lovable, demanding, self-centred, kind: give me all your attention, I'm not giving up until you answer, I'm not interrupting anything, am I?

The meeting of the investigating team had been largely concerned with waiting.

Waiting for Börje Svärd who was late, something to do with his wife.

Waiting for someone to ask about Nysvärd's broken arm, injured when the body fell from the tree.

'On sick-leave for two and half weeks,' Sven Sjöman said. 'He seemed cheerful enough when I spoke to him, just a bit shaken up still.'

'It's a bit bloody macabre, having a hundred-and-fifty-kilo frozen-solid corpse land on you,' Johan Jakobsson said.

Then waiting for someone to say what they all knew. That they had nothing to go on. Waiting for Skoglund the funeral director to finish his work, get the picture taken and sent out.

Börje: 'What was it I said? That no one would recognise him from those first pictures.'

Waiting for waiting itself, all energy sucked out of tired police officers who know that the case is urgent but who can do little but throw up their hands and say, 'We'll see!' When every citizen, every journalist, wants to hear the police recount what happened, and who did it.

Waiting for Karim Akbar, who was late as well, if only late answering the phone out in his villa in Lambohov. Waiting for his son's stereo to be turned down in the background, then waiting for Karim's voice to stop resounding from the speakerphone.

'This isn't good enough, you know that perfectly well. Sven, you'll have to arrange another press conference tomorrow where you let them know what we've got so far. That'll calm them down.'

And you get another chance to show off, Malin thinks. Then: but you do stand there and soak up the questions, the aggression, and make sure we can work in peace and quiet. And you do stand for something, Karim. You understand the power of the group when everyone has a well-defined role.

Sven's tired words after Karim had hung up. 'If only we were like Stockholm. With our own press officer.'

'You're the one who's been on the media management course,' Zeke said. 'Couldn't you do it?'

Laughter. Release. Sven: 'I'm close to getting my pension and you want to throw me to the hyenas, Zeke? Thanks a lot.'

The red light turns green, the Volvo hesitates then rolls off along Drottninggatan into the city.

'How's Mum doing, Dad? The plants are fine, I promise.'

'She's having a nap. It's twenty-five degrees and glorious sunshine down here. How is it up there?'

'You don't want to know.'

'Yes I do.'

'Well I'm not going to tell you, Dad.'

'Well, it's sunny here in Tenerife, anyway. How's Tove?'

'She's with Jan-Erik.'

'Malin, I'm going to go now, otherwise it'll get expensive. Don't forget the plants.'

The plants, Malin thinks as she pulls up outside the ochre-coloured building on Elsa Brännströms gata where her parents have their four-room apartment. The plants must never be kept waiting.

Malin moves through her parents' apartment, a ghost in her own past. The furniture she grew up with.

Am I really so old?

The smells, the colours, the shapes can all get me going, make me remember things that make me remember other things.

Four rooms: one for best, a dining room, a living room and a bedroom. Nowhere for their grandchild to stay the night. They took out the contract on the apartment when they sold the villa in Sturefors thirteen years ago. In those days the housing market in Linköping was very different. If your affairs were in order and you could afford a decent rent, you had options. Today there's nothing, only shady deals can get you a contract. Or improbably good contacts.

Malin looks out of the sitting-room window.

From the third floor there is a good view of Infection Park, named after the clinic that was once housed in the barracks that have now been turned into housing.

The sofa she was never allowed to sit on.

The brown leather shines like new to this day. The table, lovely then, overblown now. The shelves full of books from Reader's Digest. Maya Angelou, Lars Järlestad, Lars Widding, Anne Tyler.

The dining table and chairs. Having friends over, children who had to sit and eat in the kitchen. Nothing odd about that. Everyone did the same, and children don't like sitting round the table anyway.

Dad, the welder, promoted to team-leader, then part-owner of a roofing company. Mum a secretary at the county administrative board.

The smell of people getting old. Even if Malin opened the window and aired the place the smell wouldn't go. Maybe, she thinks, the cold might make the apartment scentless at best.

The plants are drooping. But none of them is actually dead. She won't let it go that far. She looks at the framed pictures on the bureau, none of her or Tove, just her parents in different settings: a beach, a city, a mountain, a jungle. 'Can you water the plants?'

Of course I can water them.

'You can come down whenever you like.'

And how do we afford that?

She sits down on the armchair in the hall and the memory of the silent springs is in her body: she is five years old again, kicking her sandalled feet; there is water a little way away and behind her she can hear Mum and Dad's voices, not shouting at each other exactly, but in their tone of voice there is a chasm, and the gap between their voices conceals all that is painful, all that the five-year-old in the chair near the water feels but does not yet have a name for.

Impossible love. The coolness of some marriages.

Does it ever get a name? That feeling?

Then she is back.

The watering can in her hand.

Plant by plant. Methodically, in a way her father the team-leader would appreciate.

I'm not hoovering, Malin thinks. Dustballs on the floor. When she used to hoover, as part of her tasks in exchange for pocket money on Saturdays, Mum would follow her round the house, checking that she didn't knock against the furniture or door frames. When she was finished her mum would hoover again, hoovering the same places, right in front of her as if it were the most natural thing in the world.

What can a child do?

What does a child know?

A child is shaped.

And then it is finished.

All the plants watered. Now they will live a bit longer.

Malin sits down on her parents' bed.

It's a Dux. They've had it for years, but would they be able to sleep in it if they knew what had happened in this bed, that this was where she lost, or rather made sure she got rid of, her virginity?

Not Janne.

Someone else.

Earlier. She was fourteen and alone at home while her parents were at a party, staying the night with friends in Torshälla.

Whatever. No matter what had happened in this bed, it wasn't hers. She can't walk through this apartment, alone or with other people, without a sense of loss. She gets up from the bed, forcing herself through the thick veils of longing that seem to hang in the air. What's missing?

Her parents in pictures without frames.

In sun-loungers at the house on Tenerife. Three years since they bought it, but she and Tove have never been there.

'You're doing the watering?'

Of course I'm watering.

She has lived with these people, she comes from them, but even so the people in the pictures are strangers. Mum, mostly.

She empties the watering can in the kitchen sink.

There are secrets hidden in those drops, behind the green doors of the kitchen cupboards, in the freezer, rumbling away, full of last year's chanterelles.

Shall I take a bag?

No.

The last thing she sees before she closes the door of her parents' apartment behind her are the thick wool rugs on the floor of the sitting room. She sees them through the open double doors from the hall, average quality. They're not as good as Mum always pretends they are. The whole room, the whole home is full of things that aren't what they seem, veneers concealing a different veneer.

There's a feeling here, Malin thinks, of never being quite good enough, of nothing ever being quite right. That we aren't, that I'm not, good enough.

To this day she has difficulty with anything that's truly good enough, with people who are supposed to be genuinely good enough. Not just rich like Karin Johannison, but doctors, the upper classes, lawyers, that sort of good. Faced with people like that, she sometimes senses her prejudices and feelings of inferiority rise to the surface. She decides in advance that people like that always look down on people like her, and she adopts a defensive posture.

Why?

To avoid being disappointed?

It's better at work, but it can be stressful in her private life.

Thoughts are flying round Malin's head as she jogs downstairs and out into the early, wretched, Friday evening.

10

Just a little one, one little beer: I deserve that, I want to watch drops of condensation almost freezing to ice on a chilled glass. I can leave the car here. I can pick it up tomorrow.

Malin hates that voice. She usually tells herself, as if to drown it out: There's nothing worse than being hung over.

It's easiest that way.

But sometimes she has to give in.

Just a little one, a little . . .

I want to wring myself out like a rag. And that's when alcohol is useful.

The Hamlet restaurant is open. How far away is that? God, it's cold. Three minutes if I jog.

Malin opens the door to the bar. Noise and steam hit her. There is a smell of grilled meat. But most of all it smells of promise, of calm.

The telephone rings.

Or does it?

Is it something else? Is it the television? Is it the church bell? The wind? Help me. My head. There is something in the front of my head and now it's ringing again, and my mouth, I'm supposed to talk with it, but it's so dry, where am I?

Then it stops ringing.

Thank God.

But then it starts again.

Sufficiently awake now to recognise the mobile phone. The

hall floor. The rag rug. How did I get here? My jacket is lying next to me, unless it's my scarf? The letterbox from below. Jacket. Pocket. Mobile. Sandpaper mouth. My pulse, a pulsating cyst, an electronic globe spinning in the front of my head. Malin digs in the pocket. There, there it is. She holds her head with the other hand, fumbling blindly, puts the phone to her ear, scarcely audible: 'Fors, Malin Fors.'

'This is Sjöman. We know who he is.'

Who he is? Tove, Janne. The man in the tree. Missed by no one.

'Malin, are you there?'

Yes. Probably. But I don't know if I want to be.

'Are you okay?'

No, not okay. I gave in yesterday.

'I'm here, Sven, I'm here. I've only just woken up, that's all. Hang on a moment.' She hears some more words as she shifts from lying to sitting: '. . . have you got a hangover, ah . . .' Her head upright, black fog settles in front of her eyes, lifts, reappears as a vibrating pressure against her forehead.

'A hangover? A small one. The sort people have on Sunday mornings.'

'Saturday, Malin. And we know who he is.'

'What time is it?'

'Half seven.'

'Shit. Sven. Oh shit. Well?'

'They got the picture sorted yesterday. That funeral bloke, Skoglund, he did a good job. We sent it to the *Correspondent* and the news agencies, and the *Correspondent* put it up on their website at eleven and someone called straight away, and we've had more calls this morning. They all say the same name, so it should check out. His name's Bengt. Surname Andersson. But, and this is the funny thing, they all call him by his nickname; only one person knew his real name.'

Her head. Pulse. Don't put any lights on, no matter what. Focus on someone else's pain instead of your own; it's supposed to help. Group therapy. Or what was it someone said? The pain is always new, always different. *Personal?*

'Ball-Bengt. They called him Ball-Bengt. From what people have said so far, his life seems to have been as miserable as his death. Can you be here in half an hour?'

'Give me forty-five minutes,' Malin says.

Quarter of an hour later, just out of the shower, in fresh clothes, the rumble of painkillers in her stomach, Malin switches on her computer. She leaves the blinds closed even if it is still dark outside. The computer is on the desk in her bedroom, the keyboard hidden in a tangle of dirty underwear and vests, bills, paid and unpaid, mocking payslips. She waits, types in her password, waits, opens her browser, then the *Correspondent*'s website.

The light from the screen makes her head throb.

Daniel Högfeldt has done a good job.

The man in the tree. His face blown up in the most prominent part of the site. He looks like a human being, the swellings and bruises just shades of grey on the black and white photograph, like blemishes covered by make-up rather than traces of a fatal attack. Skoglund, whoever he is, is almost able to bring the dead back to life. The amount of fat makes this man, Bengt 'Ball-Bengt' Andersson's face shapeless. His chin, cheeks and brow hang together in a soft, round lump over his bones, making one big, plump mass. His eyes are closed, the mouth a small line, his upper lip full, but not the lower lip. Only the nose sticks out, hard, straight, noble, Ball-Bengt's only stroke of luck in the genetic lottery.

Can I manage to read?

Daniel Högfeldt's language.

Jaunty. Nothing for someone feeling sick and with a headache.

He probably knows more than we do. People call the papers first. To get the reward for a tip-off. So they can feel special. But who am I to blame them?

*

*The Östgöta Correspondent can today reveal the identity of the
man who . . .*

The letters form themselves into burning arrows firing into her
brain.

*Bengt Andersson, 46, was known as 'Ball-Bengt'. He lived in
Ljungsbro, where he was regarded as something of an eccentric, a
loner. He lived alone in a flat in the Härna district and had been
on social security benefits for several years, unable to work because
of mental health problems. Bengt Andersson got his nickname from
the fact that he would go to Ljungsbro IF's home games and stand
on Cloettavägen, behind the fence at the end of the Cloettavallen
pitch, and wait for the ball to be kicked over the fence.*

Balls, Malin thinks. Balls in my head now.
   *I can kick, Dad, I can kick all the way to the apple tree! Mum's
voice: No balls in the garden, Malin, you might hit the roses.*
   Tove wasn't interested in football.

A woman who wants to remain anonymous has told the Correspondent:
*'He was the sort of person everyone recognised, but no one really knew.
There's someone like him in every community.'*
   Bengt Andersson was found on Friday . . .

Direct quotes, not reported speech: Daniel's special trick for
added immediacy.
   Duplications. Repetitions.
   When will we leave the dead alone?

Malin walks out of the door of the building. It is just as cold
today. The wall of the church is a mirage, far, far away.
   But today the cold is welcome, throwing its weight over her
thoughts, wrapping her in a muffling fog.
   The car isn't where it is supposed to be.
   Stolen. Her first thought.
   Then she remembers. Her parents' apartment.
   'You'll water the plants, won't you?'

Hamlet.

Can I have another beer? Anonymous there, an older crowd, and me.

Taxi? No, too expensive. It'll take ten minutes to the police station if I hurry.

Malin starts walking. The walk will do me good, she thinks. The grit on the snowploughed pavement crunches under her feet. She can see bugs in front of her eyes. The gravel chips are bugs, an invasion that she has to crush with her Caterpillar boots.

She thinks about the fact that the man in the tree now has a name. That their work will be able to get started properly, and that they have to approach this with caution. What they came across out on the plain was no ordinary violence. It was something different, something worth being afraid of.

The cold was sharp against her eyes.

Sharp, cutting.

Have I got grasshoppers dancing in front of my eyes? she thinks. Unless the cold is forming crystals on the surface of my eyes. Just like yours, Ball-Bengt. Whoever you were.

11

What does this world do to a person, Tove?

I was twenty.

And we were happy, your dad and I. We were young and happy and we loved each other. The love of young people, pure and uncomplicated, clear and physical, and then there was you, our ray of sun to beat all rays of sun.

There was nothing beyond the three of us.

I didn't know what I was going to do with my life, apart from love the two of you. I could ignore his cars, how methodical he was, how different we were. It was like I had been given love, Tove; there was no doubt, no waiting, even though that was what everyone said, wait, take it slowly, don't tie yourselves down, live a little first, but I had got a scent of life, from my love for you, for Janne, for our life. I was vain enough to want more of it, and I thought it would last for ever. Because do you know what, Tove? I believed in love and I still do, which is something of a miracle. But back then I believed in love in its purest, simplest form, what we could maybe call family love, cave love, where we simply warm one another because we are human beings together. The first sort of love.

We argued, of course. I longed for other things, of course. And of course we had no idea what to do with all our time. And of course I understood when he said he felt as if he were trapped in a hole in the ground, even if it was in paradise.

Then he came home one day with a letter from the Rescue Services Agency, saying that he had to report to Arlanda Airport the next day for a flight to Sarajevo.

I was so angry with him, your dad. I told him that if he went, then we wouldn't be there when he got back. I said that you don't abandon your family for anything.

So, my question to you, Tove: Can you understand why your father and I couldn't manage back then?

We knew too much and too little at the same time.

12

No children in the nursery on a Saturday.

Empty swings. No sledges, no balls. The lights through the windows turned off. No games today.

'Are you okay with this, Malin? You look worn out.'

Stop going on, Sven. I'm at work, aren't I?

Zeke pulls a face from where he is sitting opposite her. Börje Svärd and Johan Jakobsson don't look exactly happy, but then you're not supposed to if you're at work just after eight on a Saturday morning.

'I'm okay. Just a bit of a party last night, that's all.'

'Well, I got to party with cheese puffs, crisps and a Pippi Longstocking DVD,' Johan says.

Börje doesn't say anything.

'I've got a list here,' Sven says, waving a sheet of paper in the air. He isn't standing at the end of the table today. He's sitting down. 'These are the people who phoned to identify Bengt Andersson, Ball-Bengt. We can start by questioning them. See what they have to say about him. There are nine names on the list, all in Ljungsbro or close by. Börje and Johan, you take the first five. Malin and Zeke can take the other four.'

'And the flat? His flat?'

'Forensics are already there. As far as we could make out, none of the violence happened there. They'll be done some time this afternoon. You can take a look after that if you like. Not before. When you're finished with the names on the list, try his neighbours. He was on benefits, so there must be a social worker somewhere who knows about his case. But we probably won't be able to get hold of them until Monday.'

'Can't we get it sorted any quicker?' Zeke's voice, impatient.

'Bengt Andersson hasn't been declared dead, or even officially identified yet,' Sven says. 'And until those two things happen, we have no authority to get access to any registers and databases containing the names of his doctor or social worker. But all the formalities ought to be sorted out on Monday.'

'Okay, let's get going,' Johan says, standing up.

I want to sleep, Malin thinks. Sleep as deep as is humanly possible.

My room is black, closed. But I can still see everything.

It's cold in here, but not as cold as in the tree out on the plain. But what do I care about the cold? And there is no wind here, no storm, no snow. I might miss the wind and snow, but I prefer the clarity that comes with a condition like mine. How much I know, how much I can do. Like finding words in a way that I never used to be able to.

And isn't it funny that everyone is suddenly concerned about me? How they all see my face and want to demonstrate that they knew me? Before they would turn away when I showed my face in public, they would cross the street to avoid my gaze, to avoid coming close to my body, my – as they thought – dirty clothes, which they thought stank of sweat, of urine.

Depressing and repulsive.

And the kids who would never leave me alone. Who would plague me, tease me, bully me. Their mums and dads truly had let a thousand evil flowers bloom in their children.

I was hardly even good enough to laugh at. Even when I was alive I was a tragedy.

The chimney of the Cloetta chocolate factory.

You can't see it from the roundabout beside the ancient abbey of Vreta Kloster, but you can see the smoke, whiter than white, as it climbs into a pretend-blue sky. The low morning clouds have drifted away and winter is getting bluer, the mercury sinks still further, the price you have to pay for the light.

'Do we turn off here?'

There are signs to Ljungsbro in both directions.

'Don't know,' Malin says.

'Okay, we're turning,' Zeke says, twisting the wheel. 'We'll have to check the GPS when we get closer.'

Malin and Zeke drive through Vreta Kloster. Past the dormant sluice-gates and empty locks. Bars closed for winter. Villas with people moving behind the windows, trees that have been left to grow in peace. An ICA supermarket. There's no music in the car. Zeke didn't insist and Malin appreciates the relative silence.

They pass a bus stop and the village spreads out to their left, the houses disappearing down a slope, and in the distance Lake Roxen opens out. The car heads down past a piece of woodland, then a field opens up on their right and a few hundred metres on more houses cling to the side of a steep incline.

'Millionaires' row,' Zeke says. 'Doctors' houses.'

'Jealous?'

'Not really.'

Kungsbro on another sign, Stjärnorp, Ljungsbro.

They turn off by a red-painted stable and a stone-built cowshed, no horses in sight. Only a few teenage girls in thermal clothes and moonboots carrying bales of hay between two outhouses.

They approach the houses along millionaires' row.

When they reach the top of another hill they catch a glimpse of the Cloetta chimney.

'You know,' Zeke says, 'I swear I can smell chocolate in the air today. From the factory.'

'I'd better put the GPS on, so we can find where we're going. The first name on the list.'

She didn't want to let them in.

Pamela Karlsson, thirty-six years old, blonde pageboy cut, single, sales assistant at H&M. She lived in a council block just behind the hideous white Hemköp supermarket. Only four flats in the grey-painted wooden building. She spoke to them with the safety chain on, freezing in white vest and pants, evidently woken by them knocking at the door.

'Do you have to come in? It's such a mess.'

'It's cold out here in the stairwell,' Malin said, thinking, A man has been found murdered, hanging in a tree, and she's worried about a bit of mess. Oh well. At least she phoned.

'I had a party yesterday.'

'Another one,' Zeke said.

'What?'

'Nothing,' Malin said. 'It really doesn't matter to us if it's a bit messy. It won't take long.'

'Well, okay.' The door closed, the chain rattled, then the door opened again.

'Come in.'

A one-room flat, sofa-bed, a small table, a tiny kitchenette. Furniture from Ikea, lace curtains and a stripped, rustic wooden bench, probably inherited. Pizza boxes, beer cans, a box of white wine. On the windowsill an ashtray, full to overflowing.

She saw Malin looking at the ashtray.

'I don't usually let them smoke in here. But I couldn't make them go outside yesterday.'

'Them?'

'My friends. We were doing some surfing last night as we drank, and that was when we saw him and the request for people to call in. I phoned straight away. Well, almost straight away.'

She sat down on the bed. She wasn't fat, but her vest bulged as she sat.

Zeke sat on a chair. 'What do you know about him?'

'Not much, except that he lives round here. And his name. Apart from that, nothing. Is it him?'

'Yes, we're almost certain.'

'God, it was all everyone was talking about last night.'

False memories, Malin thought. Recollections of other people are juicy conversation topics at parties. *Just wait till you hear what happened to a friend of a friend . . .*

'So you don't know anything about who he was really?'

'Not much. I think he was on the sick. And everyone called

him Ball-Bengt. I thought it was because he was so fat, but the *Correspondent* said different.'

They left Pamela Karlsson with her mess and her headache and went on to an address on Ugglebovägen, an architect-designed villa on four levels, where every room seemed to have a view of the fields and, in the distance, Lake Roxen. A hollow-eyed insurance broker named Stig Unning opened the door after they knocked on the gilded lion's head.

'It was my son who made the call. You'll have to talk to him, he's down in the basement.'

The son, Fredrik, was playing a computer game. Thirteen maybe, thin, acne, dressed in jeans and an orange T-shirt that were too big for him. Dwarfs and elves were dying in droves on the screen.

'You called us,' Zeke said.

'Yes,' Fredrik Unning said without looking away from the game.

'Why?'

'Because I recognised the picture. I thought maybe there was some sort of reward. Is there?'

'No, sorry,' Malin said. 'You don't get paid for recognising a murder victim.'

A gnu was blown to pieces, a troll had its limbs torn off.

'Should have called *Aftonbladet* instead.'

Bang. Dead, dead, dead.

Fredrik Unning looked up at them.

'Did you know him?' Malin asked.

'No. Not at all. I mean, I knew his nickname, and I knew he stank of piss. No more than that.'

'Nothing else we ought to know?'

Fredrik Unning hesitated and Malin saw a flash of fear cross his eyes before he once again fixed his gaze on the television screen and waved the joystick back and forth frenetically.

'No,' the boy said.

You know something, Malin thought.

'Are you quite sure you haven't got anything else to tell us?'

Fredrik Unning shook his head. 'Nah, nothing. Not a damn thing.'

A red lizard dropped a huge rock on the head of a hulking great monster.

The third person on the list was a Pentecostal pastor, Sven Garplöv, forty-seven, who lived in a fairly average newly built villa on the other side of the Motala River, on the outskirts of Ljungsbro. White brick, white wood, white gables, white on white as if to keep sin away. On the way there they drove past the Cloetta factory, its corrugated roof like an angry sugar snake, its chimney pumping out promises of a sweet life.

'That's where they make chocolate wafers,' Zeke said.

'I wouldn't say no to one right now,' Malin said.

Even though they were in a hurry, the pastor's wife, Ingrid, offered them coffee. The four of them sat on green leather sofas in the white-painted sitting room eating home-made biscuits, seven different sorts, as per tradition.

Butter in the biscuits. Just what she needed.

The pastor's wife sat in silence as he talked.

'I have a service today, but the congregation will have to wait. A sin of such a serious nature has to take precedence. He who waits to pray never waits for long. Wouldn't you say, Ingrid?'

His wife nodded. Then she nodded towards the plate of biscuits.

They both helped themselves for the second time.

'He was evidently a troubled soul. The sort of whom the Lord is fond, in His own way. We spoke about him briefly in the congregation once, and someone, I forget who, mentioned his name. We agreed that he was a very lonely man. He could have done with a friend like Jesus.'

'Did you ever speak to him yourself?'

'Sorry?'

'I mean, did you ever invite him to your church?'

'No, I don't think that ever occurred to any of us. Our doors are open to everyone, although perhaps slightly more open to some people than others. I have to admit that.'

And now they are standing outside the front door of a Conn Dyrenäs, thirty-nine, who lives in a flat on Cloettavägen, right behind the football ground, Cloettavallen. It doesn't take more than a few seconds for the door to open.

'I heard you come,' the man says.

The flat is full of toys, great drifts of them. Plastic in all manner of gaudy colours.

'The kids,' Conn Dyrenäs says. 'They're with their mother this weekend. We're divorced. Otherwise they live with me. You miss them terribly when they're not around. I tried to have a lie-in this morning, but still woke up at the same time as usual. I got up and surfed the net. Would you like coffee?'

'We've just had some, so no, but thanks anyway,' Malin says. 'Are you quite sure it's Bengt in the pictures?'

'Yes, no doubt at all.'

'Did you know him?' Zeke asks.

'No, but he was still part of my life.'

Conn Dyrenäs walks over to the balcony door, gesturing to them to follow.

'You see that fence over there? He used to stand there waiting for the ball whenever Ljungsbro IF played at home. It didn't matter if it was pouring with rain, or freezing, or boiling hot in the summer. He was always there. Sometimes he used to stand there in winter, looking out at the deserted pitch. I guess he missed it. It was like he'd sorted out a job for himself, something to do with his time here on earth. He ran after the ball when it went over the fence. Well, maybe not ran. Lolloped. And then he would throw it back. People in the stands used to laugh. Okay, it did look funny, but my laughter always stuck in my throat.'

Malin looks at the fence, white in the cold, the roofed stand with the clubhouse behind it.

'I kept thinking about asking him in for coffee one day,' Conn Dyrenäs says. 'So much for that idea.'

'He seems to have been a very lonely person. You should have asked him in,' Malin says.

Conn Dyrenäs nods, goes to say something, but remains silent.

'What else do you know about him?' Malin asks.

'I don't *know* much. There was a lot of gossip, though.'

'Gossip?'

'Yes, about his dad being mad. That he used to live in a house and one day smashed an axe into his father's head.'

'Really?'

'Yes, apparently.'

And Daniel Högfeldt hadn't managed to dig that out?

'But that could easily have been a load of rubbish. It must be a good twenty years since it happened. Maybe more. He was probably completely harmless. He had kind eyes. I could see that from here. You can't see that on the pictures in the *Correspondent*, can you?'

13

Malin is standing by the fence looking in at the football pitch, a grey-white field with some even greyer school buildings beyond. On the left is the clubhouse, a length of red wooden buildings with concrete steps leading to a green-painted door, and a hotdog kiosk bearing the Cloetta logo.

She sniffs the air. Maybe there is the slightest hint of cocoa?

Behind the kiosk is a tennis hall, a temple to the smarter sport.

She takes hold of the fence.

Through her black Thinsulate gloves she can't tell how cold the metal is, and it seems to be just clumsy, lifeless wire. She shakes the fence, closes her eyes and can see green, can smell new-cut grass, expectation in the air as the first team run on to the pitch, cheered on by eight-, nine-, ten-year-old boys and pensioners with their flasks, and you, Ball-Bengt, alone behind the fence, outside.

How does anyone get to be so alone?

An axe in the head?

They'll check your name in the records in the archive; it's bound to turn up. The ladies in the archive are diligent, good at their job, so we'll find you. We'll be able to see you. Don't doubt that.

Malin stretches her hands in the air. Catches the ball with her hands, before becoming heavy and motionless, before she stumbles backwards and to one side, thinking, They laughed at you, but not all of them, you and your hopeless attempts to catch the ball, your attempts to be part of these small occasions, the little things that make up life in a small community like this. Little did they understand that you were one of the ones who made this community what it is. You must have been a constant presence in many people's lives, visible yet invisible, known yet unknown, a walking tragic joke that brightened up completely normal lives simply by being told over and over again.

They'll miss you when spring comes. They'll remember you. When the ball sails over the fence they'll wish you were still there. Maybe then they'll appreciate that that's what having a nagging feeling at the bottom of your stomach feels like.

Is it possible to be any more alone than you? The butt of jokes when you were alive, unconsciously missed when you're dead.

Then her mobile rings in her pocket.

She can hear Zeke's voice behind her. 'It's probably Sjöman.'

And Sjöman it is. 'No one else has called, even though he was some sort of local celebrity. Have you found anything?'

'There are rumours of an axe to the head,' Malin says.

'A what?'

'Rumour has it that he smashed an axe into his father's head, sometime maybe twenty years ago.'

'We'll start looking,' Sjöman says. Then he adds, 'You can go to his flat if you want. Forensics have finished. They're certain he wasn't killed in the flat. Considering the level of violence used, there would have been at least some traces of blood left. But the Luminol test didn't come up with anything. Edholm and a few others are knocking on doors. Härnavägen 21b, ground floor.'

Four sliced Skogaholm loaves on a speckled grey, laminated kitchen worktop. The fluorescent lights in the ceiling make the plastic packaging look wet and unwholesome, their contents a danger to health.

Malin opens the fridge door, to find what must be twenty packets of sausages, full-fat milk and several packs of unsalted butter.

Zeke looks over her shoulder. 'A real gourmet.'

'Do you think he lived off this?'

'Yes,' Zeke says. 'It's not impossible. That bread is basically nothing but sugar. And the sausage is fat, so they go together nicely. Typical bachelor diet.'

Malin shuts the fridge door. Behind the lowered blinds she can make out the shapes of a few children braving the cold and trying to create something with the frozen snow. It had to be pretty hopeless, the harsh substance resisting every attempt to mould it. They are all immigrant children. These white, two-storey council blocks, plastered concrete and flaking brown wood, had to be the absolute pits of Ljungsbro.

Muted laughter from outside. But still joyful, as if the cold can be mastered.

Maybe not the pits after all.

People live their lives. Happiness breaks out, shining points of magma in everyday existence.

A sofa with garish 1970s fabric against a wall of yellow and brown mottled wallpaper. A card table with a green felt top, a couple of rib-backed chairs, a bowed bed in one corner, its orange bedspread neatly tucked in on all sides.

Spartan, but not terrible. No mess of pizza boxes, no cigarette ends, no piles of rubbish. Loneliness kept neat and tidy.

In one of the living-room windows there were three small holes, taped over, with tape carefully placed across the cracks radiating from the holes.

'Looks like someone's been throwing stones at the windows,' Zeke says.

'Yes, looks like it.'

'Do you think it means anything?'

'There are lots of kids in places like this, and they're always out playing. Maybe they just threw some gravel a bit too hard?'

'Unless he had a secret admirer?'

'Yeah, right, Zeke. We'll have to get forensics to take a good look at that window, if they haven't already done so,' Malin says. 'See if they can work out what made the holes.'

'I'm surprised they didn't take the pane with them,' Zeke says. 'But I dare say Johannison was here, and maybe she just didn't feel like it.'

'If Karin had been here, that glass would be in the lab by now,' Malin says, heading towards a wardrobe in the alcove containing the bed.

Enormous gabardine trousers in various muted colours in a row, neatly hung up on hangers, washed, ironed.

'This doesn't make sense,' Zeke says. 'Everything's neat, his clothes are washed, but he's supposed to have smelled of dirt and urine.'

'I know,' Malin says. 'But how do we know he actually did smell? Maybe he was just expected to? And then one person told another and so on, until it became accepted truth. Ball-Bengt, stinks of piss. Ball-Bengt, never washes.'

Zeke nods. 'Unless someone's been here since and cleaned.'

'Forensics would have noticed.'

'Are you sure?'

Malin rubs her forehead. 'Well, I suppose it could be difficult to tell.'

'And the neighbours? Didn't any of them notice anything unusual?'

'Not according to Edholm, who was in charge of the door-to-door.'

The last remnants of her headache are gone. Now there's just the feeling of being a bit swollen and unwashed left, the feeling when the alcohol is on its way out of her body.

'How long did Johannison say he'd been dead? Between sixteen and twenty hours? I suppose someone might have been here. Unless the dirt was just a myth.'

The hot chicken curry is on the stove, the smell of garlic, ginger and turmeric is spreading through the flat, and Malin is ravenously hungry.

Chopping, dicing, slicing. Frying and simmering.

The low-strength beer is poured. Nothing goes better with curry than beer.

Janne called a short while ago. Quarter past seven. They're on their way. And now the sound of the key in the door and Malin goes out to meet them in the hall. Tove is oddly animated, as if she's about to deliver a performance.

'Mum, Mum! We watched five films this weekend. Five, and all but one of them were good.'

Janne is behind the lively Tove in the hall. Looking sheepish but still confident. *When she's with me I decide, and you know that. We had that discussion a long time ago.*

'What were they?'

'They were all by Ingmar Bergman.'

So that was the plot, today's version of the little acts they usually put on for her.

Malin can't help laughing. 'I see.'

'And they were really good.'

Janne: 'Are you making curry? Perfect in this weather.'

'Okay, Tove. You think I'm going to fall for that! What films did you really see?'

'We watched *Wild Raspberries*.'

'Tove, it's called *Wild Strawberries*. And you didn't watch it.'

'Okay. We saw *Night of the Living Dead*.'

What? Janne? Are you mad? Then her brain goes into reverse. Thinks: *Living dead.*

'But we were down at the station as well,' Janne says. 'We did some weight-training.'

'Weight-training?'

'Yes, I wanted to try,' Tove says. 'I wanted to see why you think it's so good.'

'That curry smells delicious.'

The hours on the treadmill in the gym at Police Headquarters. Bench-presses, Johan Jakobsson standing above her: 'Come on, Malin. Come on, you can do better than that.'

Sweating. Straining. Everything becoming sharp and clear. There's nothing like physical exercise to give her new energy.

'What about you, Mum? How's work been? Are you working tonight?'

'Not as far as I know. Anyway, I've made dinner.'

'What is it?'

'Can't you tell from the smell?'

'Curry. Chicken?'

Tove can't hide her enthusiasm.

Janne with drooping shoulders.

'Okay, I'd better be off,' he says. 'Speak to you during the week.'

'Okay, speak to you then,' Malin says.

Janne opens the door.

Just as he is about to go, Malin says, 'I don't suppose you'd like to stay and have some curry, Janne? There's enough for you as well.'

14

Malin rubs the sleep from her eyes.

Wants to kick-start the day.

Muesli, fruit, soured milk. Coffee, coffee, coffee.

'Bye, Mum.'

Tove, all wrapped up in the hall, earlier than usual, Malin later. They stayed indoors all day yesterday, baking, reading. Malin had to suppress the impulse to go down to the station even though Tove said she could go to work if she wanted to.

'Bye. Will you be at home when I get back tonight?'

'Maybe.'

A door closing. The weather girl on TV4 last night: '. . . and it's going to get even colder. Yes, that's right, even colder air from the Barents Sea, settling over the whole country, right down to Skåne. Put on plenty of warm clothes if you absolutely have to go out.'

Have to go out?

Want to go out. Want to get on with this.

Ball-Bengt.

Who were you really?

Sjöman's voice on her mobile, Malin holding on to the cold steering-wheel with one hand.

Monday people on their way to work, shivering in the bus shelters by Trädgårdstorget, breath rising from their mouths and winding into the air towards the haphazard collection of buildings round the square: the 1930s buildings with their sought-after apartments, the 1950s blocks with shops on the ground floor, and the ornate house from the 1910s on the corner where for decades there was a record shop, now closed down.

'We had a call from an old people's home in Ljungsbro, Vretaliden, and they've got a ninety-six-year-old man there who evidently told one of the carers a whole load of things about Ball-Bengt and his family. She was reading the paper to him, because his eyes aren't good, and he suddenly started talking. The ward sister called, says she thinks we ought to talk to him ourselves. You may as well start off with that.'

'Does the old man want to see us?'

'Apparently.'

'What's his name?'

'Gottfrid Karlsson. The nurse's name is Hermansson.'

'First name?'

'She just said Sister Hermansson. It's probably best to go through her.'

'Did you say Vretaliden? I'm on my way.'

'Aren't you going to take Zeke with you?'

'No, I'll go on my own.'

Malin brakes, does a U-turn, just completing it ahead of the 211 bus on its way to the University Hospital. The driver honks his horn and shakes his fist.

Sorry, Malin thinks.

'Have they found anything in the archive?'

'They've only just started, Malin. You know he isn't on the computer. So now we're looking elsewhere. We'll see if anything turns up during the day. Call as soon as you can if you find out anything.'

Farewell pleasantries, then silence in the car, just the engine revving when Malin changes gear.

Vretaliden.

An old people's home and sheltered housing in one, extended and modified over the years, strict 1950s architecture jammed together with 1980s postmodernism. The whole complex is in a hollow a hundred metres away from a school, just a few culs-de-sac and some red-roofed council houses between the two institutions. To the south is a field of strawberries belonging to Wester Horticulture, ending abruptly in a couple of glasshouses.

But everything is white now.

Winter has no smell, Malin thinks as she jogs across the home's car park towards the main entrance, a glass box with a gently revolving door. Malin pauses. She worked at Åleryd nursing home one summer when she was sixteen, the year before she met Janne. She didn't like it, and afterwards she explained it by thinking that she was too young to appreciate the old people's weakness and helplessness, too inexperienced to look after them. And most of the practical work was off-putting. But she liked talking to the old folk. Playing at being a society lady when there was time, listening to them talk about their lives. A lot of them wanted to talk, to delve into their memories, those who could still speak. A question to get them started, and they were off, then just a few comments to keep the story going.

A white reception desk.

Some old men in wheelchairs that look like armchairs. Strokes? Late-stage Alzheimer's? 'You'll water the plants, won't you?'

'Hello, I'm from Linköping Police, I'm looking for a Sister Hermansson.'

Old age smells strongly of chemicals and unperfumed cleaning products.

The young carer, with greasy skin and newly washed, rat-coloured hair, glances up at Malin with a look of sympathy.

'Ward three. The lifts are over there. She should be at the nurses' station.'

'Thanks.'

While Malin is waiting for the lift she looks at the old men in the wheelchairs. One of them is drooling from the corner of his mouth. Are they supposed to be sitting there like that?

Malin goes across to the wheelchairs, takes out a tissue from the inside pocket of her jacket. She leans over towards the old man, wipes the saliva from his mouth and chin.

The nurse behind the desk stares, not in a hostile way, then smiles.

The lift pings.

'There,' Malin whispers in the old man's ear. 'That's better.'

He gurgles quietly, as if in response.

She puts her arm round his shoulder. Then she dashes over to the lift. The door is closing; damn, now I'll have to wait for it to come down again.

Sister Hermansson has short, permed hair which looks like crumpled wire-wool on her angular head. Her eyes are hard behind thick, black-rimmed glasses.

Maybe fifty-five, sixty years old?

She is standing in a white coat at the nurses' station, a small space situated between two corridors of hospital rooms. She is standing legs apart, arms crossed: my territory.

'Gottfrid Karlsson?'

'I'm really not in favour of this. He's old. In this sort of extreme cold, it doesn't take much to stir up anxiety on the ward. And that's not good for our old folk.'

'We're grateful for any help we receive. And he evidently has something to tell us?'

'I doubt it. But the carer who was reading today's *Correspondent* out loud to him insisted.'

Hermansson pushes past Malin and starts walking down the corridor. Malin follows, until Hermansson stops at a door, so abruptly that the soles of her Birkenstock sandals squeak.

'Here we are.'

Then Hermansson knocks on the door.

A faint but crystal-clear: 'Come in.'

Hermansson gestures towards the door. 'Welcome to Karlsson's territory.'

'Aren't you coming in?'

'No, Karlsson and I don't get on particularly well. And this is his business. Not mine.'

15

It's nice lying here waiting, not longing for anything in particular, watching time pass, being as heavy as I am yet still able to drift about.

So here I go, flying out of the cramped mortuary box, out into the room, out through the basement window (I prefer going that way, even if walls are no obstacle).

And the others?

We only see each other if we both want to, so I'm mostly alone, but I know all the others, like molecules in a great big body.

I want to see Mum. But maybe she doesn't know I'm here yet? I want to see Dad. I want to talk to them both, explain that I know that nothing is easy, talk to them about my trousers, about my flat, about how clean it was, about the lies, about the fact that I was someone, in spite of everything.

My sister?

She had enough problems of her own. I understood, understand that.

So I drift over the fields, over the Roxen, take the long way round to the beach and campsite in Sandvik, over Stjärnorp Castle, where the ruins seem somehow to glow white in the sunlight.

I drift like a song, like little German Nicole in the Eurovision Song Contest: 'Ein bisschen Frieden, ein bisschen Sonne, das wünsch' ich mir.'

Then over the forest, dark and thick and full of the very worst secrets. So you're still here?

I've warned you. There are snakes slithering along a woman's leg, their poisonous fangs biting her genitals bloody.

A glasshouse, a nursery, a vast field of strawberries where I sat as a lad.

Then I drift downwards, past the place of nasty kids. I don't want to linger there, and on instead to Gottfrid Karlsson's corner room on the third floor of Vretaliden's oldest building.

He's sitting there in his wheelchair, Gottfrid. Old and happy with the life he's lived, and which he will carry on living for a few years yet.

Malin Fors is sitting opposite him, on a rib-backed chair, on the other side of a table. She is rather subdued, unsure whether the old man opposite has good enough eyesight to meet her gaze.

Don't believe everything Gottfrid says. But most of it will do as 'truth' in your dimension.

The man opposite Malin.

Doses of creatine have made his nose broad and full and red; his cheeks are grey and sunken, but still full of life. His legs are bony under the thin beige fabric of the hospital trousers, his shirt white and well-ironed.

The eyes.

How much can he see? Is he blind?

The instinct of old people. Only life can teach us. When Malin sees him, memories of the summer in the nursing home come back to her. How some of the old people had come to terms with the fact that most of their life was behind them, and had found peace, while others seemed absolutely furious that it would all soon be over.

'Please don't worry, Miss Fors. It is Miss Fors, isn't it? I can only see the difference between light and dark these days, so there's no need for you to try to catch my gaze.'

One of the peaceful ones, Malin thinks, and leans forward, articulating clearly and speaking louder than usual.

'So you know why I'm here, Gottfrid?'

'Nothing wrong with my hearing, Miss Fors.'

'Sorry.'

'They read out the story in the paper to me, about the awful thing that's happened to Cornerhouse-Kalle's boy.'

'Cornerhouse-Kalle?'

'Yes, that's what everyone called Bengt Andersson's father. Bad blood in that family, bad blood; nothing wrong with the lad really, but what can you do with blood like that, with that bloody restlessness?'

'Please, tell me more about Cornerhouse-Kalle.'

'Kalle? By all means, Miss Fors. Stories are all I have these days.'

'Then please, tell me the story.'

'Cornerhouse-Kalle was a legend in this community. They say he was descended from the gypsies who used to stay on a patch of waste ground on the other side of the Motala River, over by Ljung, near the manor. But I don't know about that. Or maybe what they said was true, that he was the son of the brother and sister at Ljung Manor, the ones everyone knew were together like that. That the gypsies were paid to raise him, and that's why Cornerhouse-Kalle turned out the way he did.'

'When was this?'

'It was in the twenties, I think, that Kalle was born, or the early thirties. This area was different then. There was the factory. And the big farms and the estate. No more than that. Kalle was lost to the rest of us right from the start. You see, he was the blackest of black children. Not in his skin, but inside. As if the doubt had condemned him, as if uncertainty became a sorrow that drove him mad, a sorrow that sometimes made him lose his grip on time and place. They say it was him who set fire to the estate farm, but no one knows. When he was thirteen he could neither read nor write – the master had driven him out of the school in Ljung – and then the county sheriff got him for the first time, for stealing eggs from Farmer Tureman.'

'Thirteen?'

'Yes, Miss Fors, he must have been hungry. Perhaps the gypsies were fed up with him? Perhaps the smart folk at the manor had grown tired of paying? But what do I know? Things like that were impossible to find out, not as easy as nowadays.'

'Things like?'

'Paternity, maternity.'

'What happened after that?'

'Then Kalle disappeared, didn't come back for many years. There were rumours that he'd gone to sea, was in prison, terrible things. Murder, rape, child abuse. No one really knew. But he hadn't been to sea, or I would have known.'

'How?'

'I did my years in the merchant navy during the war. I know a sailor when I see one. And Cornerhouse-Kalle was no sailor.'

'What was he, then?'

'More than anything, he was a womaniser. And a drinker.'

'When did he come back here?'

'It must have been some time in the mid-fifties. For a while he worked as a mechanic in the factory garage, but that didn't last long, then he got some short-term farm work. As long as he was sober, he did the work of two men, so they put up with him.'

'Put up with what?'

'With the women and the drink. There can't have been many working women, maids or farmer's wives who didn't know Cornerhouse-Kalle. He was king of the dance floor at the People's Park. What he couldn't get into his head about numbers and letters, he made up for with his body. He had cloven hooves when he danced. He could turn on the charm like the devil. He took whatever he wanted.'

'What did he look like?'

'Ah, that was probably his secret, Miss Fors. The secret that made him irresistible to women. He looked like a beast of prey in human form, he was physical appetite made flesh. Broad, coarse, dark, close-set eyes and a jaw that seemed chiselled from marble.'

Gottfrid Karlsson falls silent, as if to allow the image of coarse masculinity to sink in to young Miss Fors.

'Men are no longer made like that, Miss Fors. Even if there are still a number of *unpolished* people around here.'

'Why "Cornerhouse"?'

Gottfrid puts his liver-spotted, withered hands on the chair's armrests.

'It must have been at the end of the fifties, or early sixties. I was working as a foreman at Cloetta then. Kalle had somehow come into a sum of money and bought a plot with an old red wooden cottage on it, down by Wester's, just a few hundred metres from here, by the bend, next to the tunnel under the main road, on what today is called Anders väg. The tunnel didn't exist then, and where the road is now used to be a meadow. I put in an offer on the house myself, so I know. It was a large amount of money in those days. There had been a robbery at a bank in Stockholm, and there were rumours that that was where Kalle's money came from.

'He had met a woman by then, Bengt's mother, Elisabeth Teodorsson, a woman so rooted in the soil that she seemed utterly unshakable, as if she would outlive the earth itself. But of course that didn't happen.'

Then the old man in front of her sighs and closes his eyes.

The flow of words seems to have stopped.

Perhaps the effort of digging through his memories has made him tired? Or has the story itself made him tired? Then his eyes open and the light in the foggy pupils is bright.

'From the moment he bought the house he was known as Cornerhouse-Kalle. Before that everyone knew who Kalle was, but now he got an extra name. I think that house was the start of the end for him; he wasn't made for what you might call ordered circumstances.'

'And then Bengt was born?'

'Yes, 1961, I remember, but by the time he was born Cornerhouse-Kalle was behind bars.'

Gottfrid Karlsson closes his eyes again.

'Are you tired?'

'No, not at all, Miss Fors. I haven't finished what I have to tell you yet.'

On her way out Malin stops at the nurses' office.

Sister Hermansson is sitting on the bench by the wall, writing up figures on some sort of diagram.

She looks up. 'Well?'

'Good,' Malin says. 'It was good.'

'Did you learn anything new?'

'In a way.'

'All those courses Gottfrid Karlsson took at the university after he retired have made him rather peculiar. So he may well have put ideas in your head. I presume he told you about the courses?'

'No,' Malin replies, 'actually he didn't.'

'Then I should keep quiet,' Hermansson says, and returns to her diagrams.

Down in the entrance the old men in the wheelchairs have gone.

When Malin emerges out of the revolving door and the cold hits her, Gottfrid Karlsson's final words come back to her, as she knows they will do, over and over again.

She was on her way out when he put his hand on her arm.

'Be careful now, Miss Fors.'

'Sorry?'

'Just remember one thing, Miss Fors. It is always desire that kills.'

16

The plot where the house, the cornerhouse, once stood.

The atmosphere now: middle-class pomp, a perfectly average, dull house. When could this pink-painted wooden villa with its factory-produced playful carvings have been built? 1984? 1990? Something like that. Whoever bought the house from Ball-Bengt knew what they were doing; presumably they bought cheap, sat out the recession, tore the house down, built a new bog-standard villa and sold up.

Did you build someone's life away?

No.

Because what is a house, other than property, and what does property do other than impose responsibility? Rent your house, own nothing. The mantra of the poor, the broad-minded.

Malin has got out of the car, letting air into its suffocating staleness. Behind the stiff crowns of the birch trees she can make out the pedestrian tunnel under the Linköping road. A black hole where the hill on the far side becomes an impenetrable wall.

The house opposite is a much extended 1950s villa, as is the neighbouring house to the left. Who lives here now? No Cornerhouse-Kalle. No drunks. Any womanisers? Any abandoned fatties whose souls were never allowed to grow?

Hardly.

Salesmen, doctors, architects, people like that.

Malin walks up and down beside the car.

Gottfrid Karlsson's voice: 'Cornerhouse-Kalle beat up a man at the People's Park. He did that a lot. Fighting was a way of life for him. But this time the other man lost an eye. He got six years for that.'

Malin walks over to the tunnel and the road and clambers up a slope via an unploughed cycle path. The aqueduct in the distance didn't exist back then. Cars disappear and reappear through the fog. Malin can see the greenery, the summer glory, the canal boats gliding on the water over the road in the summer. There comes the world! And it isn't yours, it isn't yours. Your world will still be this little community, your loneliness, the laughter of the others as you chase errant balls.

'Elisabeth made ends meet by sewing. She did adjustments for Slott's ladies' and gentlemen's outfitters on Vasagatan. She took the bus every morning with Bengt on her arm and went to fetch the garments, then took them back on the bus in the evening. The drivers let her travel without paying. Then the boy got fat, and people said she used to let him eat butter and sugar just to keep him quiet while she was sewing.'

Malin stands at the railing above the pedestrian tunnel, looking down at the house, at the red cottage that once stood there. So small, but, for a boy, a whole universe, the stars in the night sky reminders of how transitory our lives are.

'When Kalle got out Elisabeth was pregnant within a week or so. He was permanently intoxicated, old before his time. It was said that he was beaten by the other prisoners in the jail for something he had done in Stockholm. They said he had once grassed on someone to the police. But women were still just as crazy about him. He would spend Saturdays in the park. Skirts or fighting.'

Black tiles. Smoke from the chimney. Probably from an open fire.

'Then Bengt's sister Lotta was born. And it went on from there. Kalle drank and fought, he hit his wife and the boy, and the girl when she wouldn't stop crying, but somehow they managed. Somehow. Kalle used to stand outside the bakery roaring at people as they walked past. The police let him be. He had got old.'

Malin goes back to the house, hesitating before she steps on to the driveway. There's an ancient oak tree in the far corner of the plot. That oak must have been there in your time, Ball-Bengt, mustn't it?

It was there in my time.

I used to run round that oak with my sister. We played there to keep Dad away, to force him to stay away with our laughter, our yelling, our childish shrieks.

Oh, how I ate.

As long as I ate there was hope; as long as there was food there was faith; as long as I ate there was no other reality but food; as long as I ate, my grief at what never was stayed in its dark hole.

But what good did all the running and eating do?

Instead it was Mum who disappeared. First the cancer took her liver, she spilled away from us within a month or so, and then, yes, what happened then . . . that was when the never-ending night began.

'Social services should have taken the children away then, Miss Fors, when Elisabeth died. But they couldn't do anything. Kalle wanted to keep them and that was the law. Bengt was perhaps twelve years old, the little girl, Lotta, six. As far as Bengt was concerned, it was probably already over by then. Damaged goods, fit only for throwing away. He was the loneliest of the lonely, the corner kid, a monster to stay away from. How do you talk to people who look at you like you're a monster? I watched it happen from a distance, and if I have committed any sin, it was that I passed him by then, when he was somehow still there for real, if you understand my meaning, Miss Fors. When he needed me and the rest of us here.'

But the mother? Elisabeth. When is a raised hand to fend off a blow the only power you have left? When your hands are so badly beaten that you can no longer sew?

Malin walks round the house.

She feels eyes watching her from within. How they stare at her, wondering who she is. Fine, you carry on staring. Newly planted apple trees, an idyll of scented flowers: do you know how easy it is for that to fall apart and vanish, never to reappear?

Mum, even if you haven't got the strength, come back.
Was that your prayer, Bengt?

I can't say anything more now.
  Even we, I, have limits.
  I want to drift now.
  Drift and burn.
  *But I missed her, and I was worried about my sister; maybe that
was why I fought back, I don't know, to hold it together somehow. You
can see the houses that surrounded ours. I could see how it was
supposed to be, how it could be.*
  I loved him, my dad, that's why I raised the axe that evening.

Piss kids, dirt kids. Scared kids, teased kids. Never-go-to-school
kids. Alcoholic's kids.

A girl, a little Lotta who has stopped talking, who smells of
wee, who stinks of a misery that has no place in the newly polished
Social-Democrats' 'people's home'.

Two Caterpillar boots breaking the hard crust of the snow in
the back garden of a dream villa, a door opening, a suspicious
male voice: 'Excuse me, can I help you?'

The young police officer, expecting the question, holds up her
ID. 'Police. I'm just taking a look at the plot. Someone who lived
here a long time ago is under investigation.'

'When? We've lived here since 1999.'

'Don't worry. It was a long time ago, before this house was
even built.'

'Do you mind if I go in? I'm letting in so much cold air.'

The salesman variety. Highlights in his hair even though he's
almost forty.

'Go ahead. I'm almost done.'

A mother vaporised by cancer, a father who destroys anything
that comes within arm's length. A howl full of longing echoing
from the history of this place, these forests and fields.

Gottfrid's voice: 'He took the axe, Miss Fors. He wasn't even
fifteen at the time. He waited in the house for Cornerhouse-Kalle

to come home from one of his drunken fights. Then, when the old man opened the door, he hit him. The boy had sharpened the axe, but the blow wasn't clean. The blade hit him on the ear, almost severing it from the head in one clean cut. They say it was dangling like a flap from just a few sinews. And Kalle ran out of the cottage, blood pouring down his neck, down his body. His screams echoed right across town that night.'

The snow is white, but Malin can sense the smell of Cornerhouse-Kalle's alcohol-diluted blood. Can sense the smell of Ball-Bengt's fourteen-year-old despair, his little sister Lotta in the bed she has wet herself in, her mouth open, eyes full of a terror that will probably never fade.

'He never touched her. Even if there was talk of that as well.'

'Who never touched her?'

'Neither the old man, nor Bengt. I'm sure of that, even if neither of them escaped suspicion.'

Traces of blood running through history.

The girl was adopted. Bengt spent a year or so in a foster home, then was sent back to Kalle. His father was earless, with a bandage round his head and a white patch over the hole where his ear should have been.

Then the old man died early one spring. After a few furious years when they spent most of their time watching each other, him and Bengt. His heart gave out in the end. They found Ball-Bengt, who couldn't have been much more than eighteen at the time. 'He'd been living with the corpse for more than a month. Only going out to buy bread, apparently.'

'And then?'

'Social services organised the sale of the house. It was torn down, Miss Fors. And they put Bengt in a flat in Härna. Trying to draw a veil of forgetfulness over the whole affair.'

'How do you know all this, Gottfrid?'

'I don't know much, Miss Fors. Everyone round here knew what I have just told you. But most of us are dead now, or have forgotten. Who wants to remember such terrible people? Remember the madmen?'

'And after that, once they'd installed him in the flat?'

'I don't know. I've kept to myself these last ten years or so. He fetched balls. But he was clean and tidy the few times I saw him, so someone must have cared.'

Malin gets back in the car and turns the ignition.

In the rear-view mirror the tunnel quickly becomes a shrinking black hole. She breathes in, breathes out.

Someone may have cared, but who?

I close my eyes and feel Mum's warm hands on my three-year-old body, how she nips my bulges, how she burrows her nose into my round belly and how it tickles and feels warm and I never want her to stop.

Carry on looking, Malin, carry on looking.

17

Zeke's eyes are cold, annoyed when he meets her at the entrance of Police Headquarters. He has a go at her as they walk the few steps to her desk in the open-plan office. Johan Jakobsson nods from his own corner, Börje Svärd isn't there.

'Malin, you know what I think about you going off on your own. I tried to call but you had your mobile switched off the whole time.'

'It felt urgent.'

'Malin. It doesn't take much longer to pick me up here than it does to find a whore on the Reeperbahn. How long would it have taken to come by here? Five minutes? Ten?'

'A whore on the Reeperbahn? Zeke, what would the ladies in the choir say about that? Stop sulking. Sit down and listen instead. I think you're going to like this.'

Afterwards, when Malin has told him about Bengt Andersson's father, Cornerhouse-Kalle, and the world he created, Zeke shakes his head.

'Human beings. Wonderful creatures, aren't we?'

'Have they got anywhere with the archive?'

'No, not yet. But it'll be easier now. They can focus on specific years. He has no criminal record, but that's because he was only fourteen when it happened. We just need to get confirmation of what the old man said. It won't take long now. And the death certificate was issued this morning. So I managed to get a name in social services in Ljungsbro, a Rita Santesson.'

'Have you spoken to her?'

'Only briefly over the phone.'

'You didn't go out there? Or pick me up. Now I'll have to go back out there again.'

'For fuck's sake, Malin, you might go off on your own, but I don't. We're doing this together, aren't we? Anyway, going out to Ljungsbro is fun.'

'And the others?'

'They're following up the last of the door-to-doors, and they're helping the domestic burglary unit after a break-in at some Saab director's villa over the weekend. Apparently they stole a painting, some American, Harwool I think it was, worth millions.'

'Warhol. So a theft from a director's villa is more important than this?'

'You know how it is, Malin. He was only a fat, lonely man on benefits. Not exactly the foreign minister.'

'And Karim?'

'The media have calmed down, so he's calmed down. And a stolen Warhol might make it into *Dagens Nyheter*.'

'Okay, let's go and talk to Rita Santesson.'

Rita Santesson looks like she's falling apart before their eyes. Her light green crocheted top is hanging off her skinny shoulders, and her legs are little more than two sticks in a pair of beige corduroy trousers. Her cheeks are sunken, her eyes watery from the strip-lighting, and her hair has lost any colour it may have once had. Reproductions of Bruno Liljefors prints hang on the yellow-painted fabric wallpaper: a deer in snow, a fox attacking a crow. The blinds are pulled down, as if to keep out reality.

Rita Santesson coughs, and with unexpected force throws a black file bearing Bengt Andersson's name and ID number on to the worn pine top of the desk.

'That's all I have to give you.'

'Can we take a copy?'

'No, but you can take notes.'

'Can we use your office?'

'I need it to meet a client. You can sit in the staffroom.'

'We'll need to talk to you afterwards as well.'

'We can do that now. As I said, I really don't have much to tell you.'

Rita Santesson slumps down on to her padded chair. Gestures towards the orange plastic chairs, evidently for visitors.

She coughs, from deep in her lungs.

Malin and Zeke sit down.

'So, what do you want to know?'

'What was he like?' Malin asks.

'What he was like? I don't know. The few times he was here he seemed distant. He was on antidepressants. Didn't say much. Seemed withdrawn. We tried to get him to register for invalidity benefit, but he was strongly opposed to that. I suppose he still thought there was a place for him somewhere. You know, hope is the last thing that people let go of.'

'Nothing else? Any enemies? People who didn't like him?'

'No, nothing like that. He didn't seem to have any friends or enemies. As I said—'

'Are you sure? Please, try to remember.' Zeke's voice, forceful.

'Well, he did want to know about his sister. But that wasn't part of our job. I mean, helping him to keep tabs on his family. I don't think he dared contact her himself.'

'Where does his sister live now?'

Rita Santesson points to the file. 'It's all in there.'

Then she gets up and gestures towards the door.

'I'm seeing a client in a couple of minutes. The staffroom is at the end of the corridor. If you don't have any more questions?'

Malin looks at Zeke. He shakes his head.

'In that case . . .'

Malin gets up. 'Are you certain there's nothing else we ought to know?'

'Nothing that I want to go into.'

Rita Santesson seems suddenly energised, the sickly tiger master of its cage.

'Nothing you want to go into?' Zeke bursts out. 'He was

murdered. Hung up in a tree like a lynched nigger. And you "don't want to go into" something.'

'Please don't use that word.' Rita Santesson purses her lips tight and shrugs, the movement making her whole body shake.

You hate men, don't you? Malin thinks. Then she asks, 'Who did he used to see before you?'

'I don't know, it should be in the records. There are three of us in this office. None of us has been here longer than a year.'

'Can you give us the numbers of the people who used to work here?'

'Ask in reception. They should be able to help.'

A sour smell of burned coffee and microwaved food. A flowery waxed cloth on an oval table.

Sombre reading. They pass the pages between them, taking turns to read, make notes.

Bengt Andersson. In and out of mental hospitals, depression, a loner, different contact names, a transit station for social workers on the way up.

Then something happens in 1977.

The tone of the notes changes.

Words like 'lonely, isolated, in need of contact' start to appear.

The same social worker throughout this period: Maria Murvall.

Now the sister appears in the notes. Maria Murvall writes: *Bengt is asking after his sister. I checked the archive. His sister, Lotta, was first placed in a foster home, then adopted by a family in Jönköping. New name, Rebecka Stenlundh.*

So Lotta had to become a Rebecka, Malin thinks, Andersson became Stenlundh. Rebecka Stenlundh, her name changed like a cat with new owners after the old ones got tired of it.

Nothing else about the sister, except: *Bengt is worried about contacting his sister,* a phone number, an address in Jönköping, jotted down in the margin. Then an unthinkable reflection: *Why am I so concerned?*

Maria Murvall.

I recognise that name. I've heard that name before.

'Zeke. Maria Murvall. Don't you think it sounds familiar?'

'Yes, it does. Definitely.'

New words. *In a good mood. After all my visits and constant nagging, I've sorted out his hygiene and cleaning. Now exemplary.*

Then an abrupt end.

Maria Murvall replaced first by a Sofia Svensson, then an Inga Kylborn, then Rita Santesson.

They all form the same judgement: *Shut off, tired, difficult to get through to.*

The last meeting three months ago. Nothing odd about that.

They leave the folder with reception. A young girl with a nose-ring and jet-black hair smiles at them, and says, 'Of course,' when they ask for the phone numbers of Bengt Andersson's social workers.

Five names.

Ten minutes later the girl hands them a list. 'There you go. I hope it's useful.'

Before they leave Malin and Zeke do up their jackets and pull on their hats, gloves and scarves.

Malin looks at the clock on the wall. The institutional sort, black hands on a greyish-white background: 15.15.

Zeke's mobile rings.

'Yes . . . yes . . . yes . . . yes.'

With the phone still in his hand Zeke says, 'That was Sjöman. He wants us back for a group meeting at quarter to five.'

'Has anything happened?'

'Yes, some old boy from the history department at the university phoned. He evidently has some theory about what might have inspired the murder.'

18

Sven Sjöman takes a deep breath as he casts a quick glance at Karim Akbar, who is standing next to him in front of the whiteboard in the meeting room.

'Midwinter sacrifice,' he says, leaving a long pause before going on: 'According to Johannes Söderkvist, Professor of History at the university, that was evidently some sort of ritual where people long ago sacrificed animals to the gods. And the sacrifices were hung in trees, hence the clear connection to our case.'

'But this was a human being,' Johan Jakobsson says.

'I was coming to that. There were human sacrifices as well.'

'So we may be dealing with a ritual murder, carried out by some sort of latter-day heathen sect,' Karim says. 'We'll have to consider it as one of our theories.'

One of what theories? Malin thinks. She can see the headlines before her: SECT KILLING! HEATHEN GROUP REVEALED.

'What did I say?' Johan says. 'It's got ritual written all over it.' No triumph in his voice, just a blunt statement of fact.

'Do we know of any sects of that sort? Heathen sects?' Börje Svärd throws the question across the room.

Zeke leans back. Malin can see scepticism spreading through his body.

'We aren't aware of any sects of that nature right now,' Sven says. 'But that isn't to say that there aren't any.'

'If there are,' Johan says, 'they'll be on the net.'

'But going to such lengths,' Börje says. 'I mean, it's pretty far-fetched.'

'There are things in our society that we'd rather not think are possible,' Karim says. 'It feels like I've seen most of them.'

'Johan and Börje,' Sven says, 'you start looking into this business of sacrifices and sects on the net, while Malin and Zeke talk to Professor Söderkvist and see what he's got to say for himself. He'll be expecting you this evening in the faculty.'

'Okay,' Johan says. 'I can do this at home this evening. I think we can get a long way just by surfing around the net. If there's anything out there. But that means we'll have to drop the stolen painting.'

'Drop it,' Karim says. 'This is bigger.'

'It's best not to have any preconceptions at all as far as this is concerned,' Sven says.

'Okay, what else?' Karim, encouraging, almost parodically so.

'We've sent the window-pane from his flat to the Laboratory of Forensic Science for analysis,' Malin says. 'If possible, we want to know what made those holes. According to Karin Johannison, the edge of the holes might be able to give us an answer.'

Karim nods. 'Good. We can't leave any stone unturned. What else?'

Malin tells them what she and Zeke have found out during the day, concluding with the fact that she spent the drive back from social services in Ljungsbro calling three of the numbers on the list, without getting any answer.

'We ought to talk to his sister as well; she's now known as Rebecka Stenlundh.'

'Drive down to Jönköping tomorrow and try to get hold of her.'

'But don't expect too much,' Sven says. 'Considering the bloody awful start she got in life, anything could have happened to her.'

'You're not fucking trying.'

Johan Jakobsson is standing over her with his hands round the bar.

Seventy kilos.

The same as she weighs. Her back is pressed hard against the bench, the bar pushing down, down, down, as she fades away beneath the weight.

Sweat.

'Come on, you weakling, try!'

She's asked him to talk like that, call her a weakling, because otherwise he'd never say that sort of thing. He had trouble the first few times, Malin noticed, but now he sounds completely natural.

. . . three times, four, five, down, then six, seven, eight . . .

Her energy, so obvious just a few seconds before, is gone.

The curved armature in the ceiling above explodes, the room turns white, her muscles white, mute, Johan's voice: 'Try harder!'

And Malin pushes, but no matter how she pushes the bar is sinking towards her throat.

Then the pressure eases, the weight on her body disappears and the white walls and yellow ceiling come into view again, the apparatus in the windowless gym in the cellar, the smell of sweat.

She gets up. They are alone in the room. Most of their colleagues go to gyms in the centre of the city: 'They're better equipped.'

Johan is grinning. 'That eighth one seems to be the problem,' he says.

'You shouldn't have stepped in,' Malin says. 'I would have done it.'

'You'd have crushed your windpipe if I'd held back any longer.'

'Your turn,' Malin says.

'No more for me today,' Johan says, tugging his sweaty, washed-out blue Adidas top away from his chest. 'The kids.'

'Yeah, blame the kids.'

Johan laughs as he walks away. 'It's only exercise, Malin. No more, no less.'

Then she is alone in the room.

She gets on to the treadmill. Turns up the speed, almost to maximum. Then she runs until her vision starts to go white again, until the world disappears.

Jets of warm water on her skin.

Closed eyes, black around her.

A conversation with Tove some hours before.

'Can you heat up something from the freezer? Or there's some curry left from the weekend. Dad didn't quite manage to eat all of it.'

'Don't worry, Mum. I'll sort something out.'

'Will you be there when I get home?'

'I might go and study with Lisa. We've got a geography test on Thursday.'

Study, Malin thinks. Since when did you have to do that?

'I can test you if you like.'

'Thanks, that's okay.'

Shampoo in her hair, soap on her body, her breasts, unused.

Malin turns off the shower, dries herself, throws the towel in the wash-basket before taking her clothes out of her locker. She gets dressed, puts on the yellow and red Swatch Tove gave her for Christmas. Half past seven. Zeke would be waiting outside in the car. Best to hurry. The professor who is going to tell them about rituals probably doesn't want to have to wait all evening for them either.

19

They walk quickly between the panelled, brick-coloured buildings. The ground crunches beneath their feet, the grey paving carefully gritted, but with patches of ice every now and then. The path between the silent, oblong buildings becomes a wind-tunnel where the cold can gather its strength and get up speed to hit their bodies. The cones of light from the lamps hanging above them sway in the wind.

The university.

Like a rectangular city within the city, laid out between Valla and the golf course and Mjärdevi Science Park.

'I didn't know academic life could seem so bleak,' Zeke says.

'It isn't bleak,' Malin says. 'Just tough.'

She spent two years studying law part-time, with Tove crawling round her legs and Janne off in some jungle or on some mined road God knew where, and her patrol duties and nightshifts and night nursery, alone, alone with you, Tove.

'Did you say C-block?' The letter C shines above the nearest entrance. Zeke's voice sounds hopeful.

'Sorry, F-block.'

'Fuck, it's cold.'

'This cold stinks.'

'Maybe. But it still doesn't seem to have any smell, does it?'

A single light is shining on the second floor of F-block. Like an outsized star in a reluctant sky.

'He said to press B 3267 at the door, and he'd buzz us in.'

'You'll have to take your gloves off,' Zeke says.

And a minute later they are standing in a lift on the way up, Professor Söderkvist's voice vague and difficult to pin down over the speaker a few moments ago.

'Is that the police?'

'Yes, Inspectors Fors and Martinsson.'

A buzz, then warmth.

What was I expecting? Malin thinks as she settles on to an uncomfortable chair in the professor's office. A creaky old man in a cardigan? A history professor doesn't count as one of the really posh ones, the ones who make her so uncertain. But what about this one?

He's young, no more than forty, and he's attractive; maybe his chin's a bit weak, but there's nothing wrong with his cheekbones and his cool blue eyes. *Well hello, Professor.*

He is leaning back in an armchair on the other side of a pedantically tidy desk, apart from a messily opened packet of biscuits. The room is perhaps ten square metres in size, over-full bookshelves along the walls, and windows facing the golf course, silent and deserted on the far side of the road.

He smiles, but only with his mouth and cheeks, not with his eyes.

He is hiding one hand, the one he didn't shake hands with, Malin thinks. He's keeping it under the desk. Why are you doing that, Professor Söderkvist?

'You had something you wanted to explain to us?' Zeke says.

The room smells of disinfectant.

'Midwinter sacrifice,' the professor says, leaning even further back. 'Have you heard of that?'

'Vaguely,' Malin says.

Zeke shakes his head and nods to the professor, who goes on.

'A heathen ritual, something the people you would call Vikings used to do once a year round about this time of year. They made sacrifices to the gods for happiness and success. Or as a penance. To cleanse the blood. To be reconciled with the dead. We don't know for sure. There's very little reliable documentation about this ritual, but we can be sure that they made both animal and human sacrifices.'

'Human sacrifices?'

'Human sacrifices. And the sacrifices were hung in trees, often in open places so that the gods could get a good view of them. At least that's what we believe.'

'And you mean that the man in the tree on the Östgöta plain could be the victim of a modern midwinter sacrifice?' Malin asks.

'No, that's not what I mean.' The professor smiles. 'But I do mean that there are undoubted similarities in the scenario. Let me explain something: there are residential courses and hotels in this country that organise harmless midwinter sacrifices at this time of year. With no connection to the darker sides of the sacrifice, they arrange lectures about Old Norse culture and serve food that they suppose would have been served in those days. Commercial mumbo-jumbo. But there are others who have a less healthy interest in those days, so to speak.'

'A less healthy interest?'

'I come across them occasionally during my lecture tours. The sort of people who evidently have difficulty living in our age, and who prefer to identify themselves with history instead.'

'They live in the past?'

'Something like that.'

'Is this about the old Æsir beliefs?'

'I wouldn't put it quite like that. We're talking about the pre-Norse period here.'

'Do you know where they are, people like this?'

'I don't know that there are any specific societies. I've never been that interested in them. But they're probably out there somewhere. I'm sure I've had nutters like that come and listen to me. If I were you I'd start by looking on the Internet. They may prefer to live in the past, but they're extremely technologically literate.'

'But you don't actually know of any?'

'Not in particular. There are never any records kept of who attends my open lectures. It's like the cinema or a concert. You come, you watch and listen, then you go away again.'

'But you know that they're technologically literate?'

'Isn't everyone like that these days?'

'What about on your courses here at the university?'

'Oh, they never find their way here. And midwinter sacrifice gets little more than a mention in the greater scheme of things.'

Then the professor pulls out the hand he has been keeping hidden under the desk and strokes his cheek, and Malin can see angry scars criss-crossing the back of his hand.

The professor seems to lose his train of thought, and quickly lowers his hand.

'Have you hurt yourself?'

'We have cats at home. One of them had a bit of a turn when we were playing the other day. We took her to the vet. It turned out that she had a brain tumour.'

'I'm sorry to hear that,' Malin said.

'Thank you. The cats are like children for Magnus and me.'

'Do you think he's lying about his hand?'

Malin can hardly hear Zeke's voice in the wind-tunnel between the buildings.

'I don't know,' Malin shouts.

'Should we check him out?'

'We can get someone to take a quick look.'

As she is shouting the words her phone starts to ring in her pocket.

'Fuck.'

'Let it ring. You can call back once we're in the car.'

As they're driving past McDonald's on the Ryd roundabout, Malin calls Johan Jakobsson back, not caring that his wife might be trying to put the children to bed and that the sound of the phone ringing might keep them awake.

'Johan Jakobsson.'

The sound of children playing up in the background.

'Malin here. I'm in the car with Zeke.'

'Right,' Johan says. 'I haven't managed to find anything specific, but the idea of midwinter sacrifice pops up on a lot of sites. Mostly residential courses that—'

'We know all that. Anything else?'

'That's what I was coming to. Apart from the courses I found a site belonging to someone calling himself a soothsayer. Soothsaying is apparently some sort of Old Norse magic, and it says that according to these particular traditions, every February you have to make a midwinter sacrifice.'

'I'm listening.'

'Then I went on to a Yahoo group about soothsaying.'

'A what?'

'A discussion group on the Internet.'

'Okay.'

'It doesn't have many members, but the man running the group gives an address outside Maspelösa as his home location.'

'Maspelösa.'

'Exactly, Fors. Not much more than ten kilometres from the crime-scene.'

'Are you going to talk to him tonight?'

'Because he's got a website? It can wait till morning.'

'Is that wise?'

'Wise or not, unless the pair of you fancy driving out to Maspelösa now?'

'We can do that, Johan.'

'Malin, you're mad. Go home to Tove.'

'You're right, Johan. It can wait. You two take it tomorrow.'

The kitchen worktop is cold to her touch, but still feels somehow warm.

Soothsaying.

Old Norse magic.

Unexplained, thus far, holes in a pane of glass.

Does all this belong together?

The Æsir belief-system.

Zeke had laughed to begin with, then his face had taken on a rather uncertain look, as if it had struck him that if a naked man can be found hanging in a tree on a cripplingly cold winter's morning, then there could well be 'nutters' who live their lives according to Old Norse mythology.

But they had to follow several threads at once, looking under any stone where there might be something relevant. There were countless police investigations that had ground to a halt simply because the officers themselves had got hung up on one of their own theories, or, worse still, fallen in love with it.

Malin eats a couple of crispbread sandwiches with low-fat cheese before she sits down at her desk and starts phoning the people on the list she was given at Ljungsbro social services.

The clock on the computer says 21.12. Not too late to call. A note from Tove in the hall.

I've gone to Filippa's to study for a maths test tomorrow. Home by ten at the latest.

Maths? Didn't she say geography? Filippa?

No answer anywhere; she left messages, her name and number, why she was phoning: *Call me this evening or early tomorrow, as soon as you get this message.* How busy could people be on a Monday evening? But, on the other hand, why not?

Theatre, cinema, a concert, evening classes, the gym. All the things people do to stop themselves getting bored.

Maria Murvall's number was unobtainable. This number is no longer in use. Directory enquiries had no new number for her.

Half past nine.

Malin's body is tired after her exercise; she feels the fibres of her muscles protest as they grow. How her brain is tired after the encounter at the university.

Maybe this will be a peaceful night? Nothing holds the nightmares at bay like exercise and concentration, but she can still feel the anxiety and restlessness, how impossible it is to stay inside the flat even though it is so cold outside.

She gets up, pulls on her jacket, her holster out of habit, and leaves the flat again. She walks up Hamngatan towards Filbytertorg, then carries on up towards the castle and the cemetery, where the snow-covered graves keep their owners' secrets. Malin looks up at the memorial grove; she usually goes there to look at the flowers, trying to feel the presence of the dead and hear their voices, pretending that she can breach the dimensions, that she's a superhero with fantastic powers.

The rustle of the wind.

The panting of the cold.

Malin stands still in the memorial grove.

The oaks are drooping. Frozen branches hang in the air like stiff black rain. A few nightlights are burning around her feet, a floral wreath makes a grey ring on the snow.

Are you here?

But everything is silent and empty and still.

I'm here, Malin.

Ball-Bengt?

And the evening is destructively hard and cold and she leaves the grove, walking the length of the cemetery wall and then along Vallavägen and down towards the old water tower and the Infection Clinic.

She walks past her parents' apartment.

'You won't forget . . .'

There's something not right. There's a reddish light up in one of the apartment's windows. Why is there a light in the apartment?

I never forget to turn off the lights.

20

The stairwell: she leaves the light on.

She takes out her mobile, is about to dial her parents' number – whoever is up there will get a shock – but then she remembers that her parents had the phone disconnected.

She doesn't use the lift.

She climbs the three flights of stairs as silently as she can in her Caterpillar boots, feeling sweat break out on her back.

The door hasn't been broken open, there's no visible evidence.

Light behind the glass of the door.

Malin puts her ear to the door and listens. Nothing. She looks in through the letterbox; the light seems to be coming from the kitchen.

She tries the door-handle.

Should I draw my pistol?

No.

The hinges creak as she pulls the door open, voices, muffled, from her parents' room.

Then the voices fall silent, and instead the sound of bodies moving. Have they heard her?

Malin marches firmly across the hall, hurrying down the passageway to her parents' bedroom.

Pulls the door open.

Tove on the green bedspread. *Me, that's me.* Tove fumbling with her jeans, trying to find the buttons with fingers that won't obey.

'Mum.'

Beside the bed a long-haired, skinny boy trying to pull on a black T-shirt with some hard rock logo on it. His skin is unnaturally white. As if he's never been out in the sun his whole life.

'Mum, I—'

'Not a word, Tove. Not a single word.'

'I . . .' the boy says in a voice that has hardly broken. 'I . . .'

'And you can keep quiet too. Both of you, quiet. Get dressed.'

'We are dressed, Mum.'

'Tove. I'm warning you.'

Malin leaves the bedroom, shuts the door behind her, shouts, 'Come out when you're dressed.'

Feels like shouting a whole load of things, but what? Can't shout: Tove, you were a mistake, a condom that broke, and do you want to do the same as me? Do you think it's fun being a teenage mother, even if you do love your kid?

Whispers and giggling from the bedroom.

Two minutes later they come out. Malin is standing in the hall, and points to the sofas in the sitting room.

'Tove, sit down there. And you, who are you?'

Handsome, Malin thinks, but pale. But, good God, he can't be more than fourteen, and Tove, Tove, you're a little girl.

'I'm Markus,' the pale boy says, pushing his hair out of his face.

'My boyfriend,' Tove calls from the sofa.

'Yes, I worked that out,' Malin replies. 'I'm not that stupid.'

'I go to Ånestad school,' Markus says. 'We met at a party a few weekends ago.'

What party? Has Tove been to a party?

'Have you got a surname, Markus?'

'Stenvinkel.'

'You can go now, Markus. We'll have to see if we ever meet again.'

'Can I say goodbye to Tove?'

'Put on your coat and go.'

'Mum, I'm actually in love with him.'

The front door closes as Tove says the words.

'That's a bit serious.'

Malin sits on the sofa opposite Tove. The sitting room is dark around them. She closes her eyes and sighs.

Then starts to feel angry again.

'In love? You're thirteen, Tove. What could you possibly know about love?'

'As much as you, apparently.'

And the anger vanishes as quickly as it came.

'Studying with Filippa, Tove? Did you have to lie?'

'I thought you'd be angry.'

'What about? About you wanting a boyfriend?'

'No, because I haven't said anything. And because we were here. And, well, because I've got something you haven't.'

These last words cut straight to Malin's core, with no warning, and rather than think about what her daughter had just said, she chose to say, 'You have to be careful, Tove. This sort of thing can lead to no end of problems.'

'That's what I was afraid of, Mum, that you'd only see the problems. Do you think I'm stupid enough not to realise that you and Dad had me by mistake? I mean, who'd be mad enough to have a child at that age otherwise? I'm not that careless.'

'What are you saying, Tove? You weren't a mistake. Whatever makes you say that?'

'I know, Mum. I'm thirteen, and thirteen-year-olds have boyfriends.'

'The cinema with Sara, studying with Filippa . . . God, how stupid am I? How long have you been seeing each other?'

'Almost a month.'

'A month?'

'It's hardly surprising that you haven't noticed anything.'

'Why not?'

'What do you think, Mum?'

'I don't know, tell me, Tove.'

But Tove doesn't answer the question. Instead she says, 'His name's Stenvinkel. Markus Stenvinkel.'

Then they sit in silence in the darkness.

'Markus Stenvinkel.' Malin laughs, eventually. 'God, he's pale. Do you know what his parents do?'

'They're doctors.'

Better folk. The thought comes to Malin against her will.
'Nice.'

'Don't worry, Mum. Actually, I'm hungry,' Tove says.

'Pizza,' Malin says, slapping her hands down on her knees.
'I've only eaten a couple of crispbreads tonight.'

Shalom on Trädgårdsgatan have the biggest pizzas in the city,
the best tomato sauce, and the ugliest interior: plaster walls with
amateur frescoes of nymphs; cheap, plastic patio tables.

They share a calzone.

'Does Dad know about this?'

'No.'

'Okay.'

'What do you mean?'

Malin takes a sip of her Cuba Cola.

Her mobile rings again.

Daniel Högfeldt's name on the small display.

She hesitates, then clicks the call away.

'Dad?'

'It just feels important that you haven't told him either.'

Tove looks thoughtful. She takes a bite of the pizza before
saying, 'Weird.'

A fluorescent light flickers above their heads.

There's competition in love, Tove, Malin thinks. There's competition and loss in everything.

21

Tuesday, 7 February

It is just after midnight.

Daniel Högfeldt presses the door button on the wall and the main door to the *Correspondent*'s offices swings opens to the sound of manic squeaking. He's happy, job well done.

He looks down Hamngatan as he takes a breath of the icy air.

He called Malin. To ask about the case, and to ask about . . . yes, what was he going to ask her about?

Even though his thick jacket is done up to the neck, the cold wins in just a few seconds and forces its way through the fabric.

He heads home quickly along Linnégatan.

At St Lars Church he looks up at the darkened windows of Malin's flat, thinks of her face and eyes, and of how little he knows about her, and what he must look like to her: a fucking irritating journalist, a male chauvinist with some sort of irresistible sex appeal and charm. A body that does the job well enough when her own body needs fulfilment.

Fucking.

Hard or soft.

But people have to fuck.

He walks past H&M and thinks about the distance in that 'people'. Fucking isn't something you or I do, 'people' do it; an alien entity separate from our bodies.

The phone-call from Stockholm today.

Flattery and coaxing, promises.

Daniel wasn't surprised.

Am I done with this dump now?

The front page of the *Correspondent* confronts Malin from the hall floor as she stumbles towards the kitchen on tired, stiff legs, freshly showered and dressed.

In spite of the darkness she can read the headline, which, in its urgent, tabloid manner, bears Daniel Högfeldt's unmistakable signature: POLICE SUSPECT RITUAL KILLING.

You made the front page, Daniel. Congratulations.

An archive picture of a serious Karim Akbar, a statement given over the phone late yesterday evening: *I can neither confirm nor deny that we are investigating secret networks of people who follow the Æsir belief-system.*

Secret networks? The Æsir belief-system?

Daniel has interviewed Professor Söderkvist, who claims to have been questioned by the police for information, and that he had explained ritual killings to them during the day.

Then a screenshot of a website about the Æsir faith, and a passport photograph of a Rickard Skoglöf from Maspelösa, who is identified as a central character in such circles. *Rickard Skoglöf was unavailable for comment yesterday evening.*

A fact box about midwinter sacrifices.

Nothing else.

Malin folds the paper and puts it on the kitchen table, and makes a cup of coffee.

Her body. Muscles and sinews, bones and joints. Everything aches.

Then the sound of a car-horn down in the street.

Zeke. Are you here already?

Jönköping, we'll set off early. Zeke's final words as he dropped her off outside her flat.

The Ikea clock on the wall says quarter to seven.

I'm the one who's late.

What exactly is this winter doing to me?

★

Zeke at the wheel of the green Volvo. Tired shoulders, limp hands. German choral music in a minor key fills the car. The pair of them are equally tired. The E4 cuts through white-clad fields and the frozen landscape of the plain.

Mobilia outside Mantorp, a retail park, Tove's favourite outing, Malin's nightmare. Mjölby, Gränna, Lake Vättern as a strip of white hope in front of a horizon where nuances of grey meet other nuances of grey, forming a confusion of cold and darkness, an eternal lack of light.

Zeke's voice comes as a liberation, loud enough to drown out the music.

'What do you think about this Old Norse stuff?'

'Karim seemed fairly positive about it.'

'Mr Akbar. What do factory-farmed police chiefs like him know about anything?'

'Zeke. He's not that bad.'

'No, I suppose not. Mr Akbar presumably has to give the impression that we're making progress. And the holes in the window, have you had any more thoughts about them now you've had time to sleep on it?'

'No idea. Maybe they'll lead to something. But what, I don't know.' Malin thinks that this is just like every big investigation, that obvious connections are hidden somewhere close to them, just out of reach, mocking them.

'When was Karin going to have her analysis of the glass finished?'

'Today or tomorrow.'

'Just one thing,' Zeke goes on. 'The more I think about Ball-Bengt up there in the tree, the more it all feels like some sort of pagan invocation.'

'I've been feeling the same,' Malin says. 'Well, it remains to be seen if there are any links to Valhalla or anything else.'

Malin rings the doorbell of Rebecka Stenlundh's flat. She lives on the second floor of a yellow-brick block in the hills just south of Jönköping.

The view from the flat must be wonderful, and in the summer the area must be lush with the green of all the birch trees. Even the garages a little way down towards the road look attractive, with orange-painted doors, surrounded by well-maintained hedges.

The place where Rebecka Stenlundh lives is neither one thing nor the other. Not lovely, but nice enough, a *here* where children could grow up in decent surroundings.

Not a dumping-ground for social service cases and immigrants. The sort of place where people live out their lives unobserved, largely unnoticed and unwanted, but still well thought of. A life on the fault-line, close to the boundary of dysfunction. Malin is just as surprised every time she finds herself in a place like this, by the fact that they still exist. The quiet happiness of the old Social-Democratic 'people's home'. Two point three swings and slides per child.

No answer.

It is just after nine o'clock; perhaps they should have called and announced their arrival, but does she even know about what happened to her brother?

'No, we'll just head over there.' Zeke's words.

'We might be bringing bad news.'

'Wasn't she told before his name was made public?'

'No one knew he had a sister then, and it's a long time since the papers showed that level of consideration.'

Malin rings the bell again.

The rattle of locks on the neighbour's door.

An old woman's face, friendly, smiling. 'Are you looking for Rebecka?'

'Yes, we're from Linköping Police,' Malin says, and Zeke holds up his ID.

'From the police? Goodness.' The old woman screws up her eyes in alarm. 'I hope she isn't involved in any unpleasantness? I can't imagine that she is.'

'Don't worry,' Zeke says in his gentlest voice. 'We'd just like to talk to her.'

'She works down in the ICA supermarket. Try there. She's the manageress. You've never seen a nicer ICA shop. I can promise you that. And you should see her son. You won't meet a nicer boy. He's always helping me with one thing or another.'

Just as they are heading towards the automatic doors of the ICA shop, Zeke's phone rings.

Malin stops beside him, listens to him talk, sees him frown.

'Yes, okay, so it checks out, then?'

Zeke hangs up.

'They've found that business with the axe in the archive,' he says. 'What the old man told you seems about right. Lotta, Rebecka, saw it all. She was eight years old at the time.'

Vegetables and fruit in neat rows, and a smell of food that makes Malin hungry. Signs with beautiful lettering, every corner well-lit, everything announcing: *this is a clean shop.*

The old woman was right, Malin thinks. Nothing shabby or slapdash, just an apparent desire to give people something pleasant in their everyday lives. Someone wanting to make a bit of extra effort for other people. Showing a bit of consideration must surely be good for business. Anyone would want to return to this shop.

A middle-aged woman at the till, plump, with blonde, tightly permed hair.

Rebecka?

Zeke's voice: 'Excuse me, we're looking for Rebecka Stenlundh.'

'The boss. Try over at the butcher's counter. She's marking up the meat.'

Over at the butcher's counter a thin woman is crouched down, her dark hair in a net, her back bowed under a white coat with the red ICA logo.

It looks like she's hiding behind that coat, Malin thinks, as if someone's going to attack her from behind, as if the whole world wishes her ill and you can never be too careful.

'Rebecka Stenlundh?'

The woman spins round on her wooden sandals. A pleasant

face: gentle features, brown eyes with a thousand friendly nuances, cheeks with skin that radiates health and a light suntan.

Rebecka Stenlundh looks at them.

Then one of her eyebrows twitches, and her eyes shine bright and clear.

'I've been expecting you,' she says.

22

'Do you think he's expecting us?'

Johan Jakobsson leaves the words hanging limply in the air as they pull into the drive.

'Bound to be,' Börje Svärd says, flaring his nostrils in a way that makes the brown hairs of his moustache vibrate. 'He knows we're coming.'

Three grey stone buildings in the middle of the Östgöta plain, a few kilometres outside a sleepy Maspelösa. The buildings seem almost suffocated by the snow piled in drifts against the already inadequate windows. The thatched roofs are pressed down by the weight of all the white. There are lights in the building to the left. A newly built garage, with shrubs planted all round it, has been squeezed in between two large oaks.

Only one problem: Maspelösa never wakes up, Johan thinks.

A few farms, some detached houses built in the fifties, a few council houses scattered across the open landscape: one of those settlements on the plain that life seems to have left behind.

They stop, get out, knock.

From the building opposite comes the sound of mooing. Then the sound of something banging on metal. Börje turns round.

The low, crooked door opens.

A head almost entirely covered in hair peers out of the darkness inside.

'And who the hell are you?'

The beard shaggy, seeming to cover the whole of his face. But his blue eyes are as sharp as his nose.

'Johan Jakobsson and Börje Svärd, Linköping Police. Can we come in? I presume you're Rickard Skoglöf.'

The man nods. 'ID first.'

They hunt through their pockets, have to take off their gloves and undo their coats to find their ID.

'Happy now?' Börje asks.

Rickard Skoglöf gestures with one hand as he pushes the door open with the other.

'We're born with the gift. It arrives in our flesh the moment we arrive in this dimension.' Rickard Skoglöf's voice is as clear as ice.

Johan rubs his eyes and looks round the kitchen. Low ceiling. The draining-board full of dirty plates, pizza boxes. Pictures of Stonehenge on the walls, Old Norse symbols, rune-stones. And Skoglöf's clothes: obviously home-made trousers of black-dyed canvas and an even blacker kaftan-like affair hanging loosely over a fat stomach.

'Gift?'

Johan can hear how sceptical Börje sounds.

'Yes, the power to see, to influence.'

'Soothsaying?'

The house is cold. An old eighteenth-century farmhouse that Rickard Skoglöf has renovated himself: 'Got it cheap, but it's bloody draughty.'

'Soothsaying is the word for it. But you have to be careful about using the power. It takes as much life as it gives.'

'So why a website about your sooth?'

'My soothsaying. In our culture we've lost track of our roots. But I have comrades.'

Rickard Skoglöf crouches down and goes into the next room. They follow him.

A worn sofa against one wall, and a huge computer screen, switched off, set up on a shiny desk with a glass top, two whirring hard drives on the floor, a modern black leather office chair behind the desk.

'Comrades?'

'Some people who are interested in soothsaying and in our Old Norse forebears.'

'And you have meetings?'

'A few times a year. Most of the time we communicate on discussion forums and by email.'

'How many of you are there?'

Rickard Skoglöf sighs. He stops and looks at them. 'If you want to carry on talking you'll have to come out to the barn with me. I have to feed Sæhrimnir and the others.'

Cackling hens run to and fro in an even colder space with badly plastered walls. There is a pair of new cross-country skis leaning in one corner.

'You like skiing?' Johan asks.

'No, I don't.'

'But you've got a new pair of skis.'

Rickard Skoglöf doesn't reply, just carries on towards the animals.

'Bloody hell, it's below freezing in here,' Börje says. 'Your livestock could freeze to death.'

'No chance,' Rickard Skoglöf says as he scatters food for the hens from a bucket.

Two pens along one wall.

A fat black pig in one, a brown and white cow in the other. They are both eating, the pig grunting happily at the winter apples he has just been given.

'If you think I'm going to give you the names of the comrades who usually come to our meetings, you're mistaken. You'll have to find them yourselves. But it won't do you any good.'

'How do you know that?' Johan asks.

'Only harmless kids and old folk with no lives of their own are interested in this sort of thing.'

'What about you? Haven't you got a life of your own?'

Rickard Skoglöf gestures towards the animals. 'The farm and these beasts are probably more of a life than most people have.'

'That's not what I meant.'

'I've got the gift,' Rickard Skoglöf says.

'So what is this gift, Rickard? In purely concrete terms?' Börje is staring intently at the canvas-clad figure in front of them.

Rickard Skoglöf puts down the bucket of feed. When he looks up at them his face is contorted with derision. He waves the question away with his hand.

'So the power of soothsaying gives and takes life,' Johan says. 'Is that why you make sacrifices?'

The look in Rickard Skoglöf's eyes gets even more weary.

'Oh,' he says. 'You think I'm the one who strung up Bengt Andersson in a tree. Not even that journalist who was here before you thought that.'

'You didn't answer my question.'

'If I make sacrifices? Yes, I do. But not like you think.'

'And what do we think?'

'That I kill animals. And maybe people. But it's the gesture that matters. The willingness to give. Time, labour. The unity of bodies.'

'The unity of bodies?'

'Yes, the act can be a sacrifice. If one is open.'

Like my wife and I do every third week? Johan thinks. Is that what you mean? Instead he asks, 'And what were you doing on the night between Wednesday and Thursday last week?'

'You'll have to ask my girlfriend,' Rickard Skoglöf says. 'Right, the animals will be okay for a while now. They can stand a bit of cold. They're not as feeble as other creatures.'

When they come out into the yard a young woman is standing barefoot in the snow with her arms raised away from her body. The cold doesn't seem to bother her, she's wearing just pants and a vest, and she has her eyes closed, her head raised to the sky, her black hair a long shadow down the white skin of her back.

'This is Valkyria,' Rickard Skoglöf says. 'Valkyria Karlsson. Morning meditation.'

Johan can see Börje losing his temper.

'Valkyria,' he yells. 'Valkyria. Time to stop the mumbo-jumbo. We want to talk to you.'

'Börje, for God's sake.'

'Oh, shout away,' Rickard Skoglöf says. 'It won't help. She'll be done in ten minutes. There's no point trying to disturb her. We can wait in the kitchen.'

They walk past Valkyria.

Her brown eyes are open. But they see nothing. She's millions of miles away, Johan thinks. Then he thinks about the act, of opening yourself to someone else, something else.

Valkyria Karlsson's skin is pink with cold, her fingers somehow crystal clear. She is holding a cup of hot tea in front of her nose, inhaling the aroma.

Rickard Skoglöf is sitting at the table, grinning happily, evidently pleased that he is making things difficult for them.

'What were you doing yesterday evening?' Börje asks.

'We went to the cinema,' Rickard Skoglöf says.

Valkyria Karlsson puts down her cup.

'The new Harry Potter,' she says in a soft voice. 'Entertaining nonsense.'

'Did either of you know Bengt Andersson?'

Valkyria shakes her head, then looks at Rickard.

'I'd never heard of him until I read about him in the paper. I have a gift. That's all.'

'What about last Wednesday evening? What were you doing then?'

'We made a sacrifice.'

'We opened ourselves at home,' Valkyria whispers, and Johan looks at her breasts, heavy and light at the same time, breaking the law of gravity, floating under her vest.

'So you don't know of anyone in your circles who could have done this?' Börje asks. 'For heathen reasons, so to speak.'

Rickard Skoglöf laughs. 'I think it's time for you to leave now.'

23

The canteen of the ICA shop is pleasantly decorated, gently lit by an orange Bumling lamp. A smell of freshly brewed coffee permeates the room, while the almond tart is sticking to their teeth in a very pleasant way.

Rebecka Stenlundh is sitting opposite Malin and Zeke, on the other side of a grey laminate table.

In this light she looks older than she is, Malin thinks. Somehow the light and shadows emphasise her age, revealing almost invisible wrinkles. But everything she has been through has to show somewhere. No one escapes unblemished from that sort of experience.

'This isn't my shop,' Rebecka says. 'If that's what you're thinking. But the owner lets me do what I like. We're the most profitable shop of this size in the whole of Sweden.'

'Retail is detail,' Zeke says in English.

'Exactly,' Rebecka agrees, and Malin looks down at the table.

Then Rebecka pauses.

You're gathering your strength, Malin thinks. You're taking a deep breath, in it goes, helping to prepare you to talk.

Then she starts to speak again: 'I decided to leave everything to do with Mum and Dad and my brother Bengt behind. I decided I was bigger than that. Even if I hated my father in a lot of ways, I realised eventually, just after I turned twenty-two, that he couldn't own me, that he had no right to my life. In those days I was hanging out with the wrong guys, I smoked, drank, sniffed glue, ate too much, all the while exercising so hard that my body could hardly take it. I dare say I would have started shooting up heroin if I hadn't made that decision. I couldn't be angry and scared and sad any longer. It would have killed me.'

'You decided. Just like that?' Malin is taken aback at how the words come out, almost angry, jealous.

Rebecka starts.

'Sorry,' Malin says. 'I didn't mean to sound aggressive.'

Rebecka clenches her jaw before going on. 'I don't think there's any other way of doing it. I made up my mind, Officer. If you ask me, that's the only way.'

'And your adoptive parents?' Zeke wonders.

'I stopped seeing them. They were part of my old life.'

Wherever this case takes us, Malin thinks, it will be tied up with the warped logic of emotions; the sort of logic that makes someone torture another person and hang them up in a tree in the middle of a frozen plain.

Rebecka clenches her jaw again, then her face relaxes.

'Unfair, I know. Of course it was. There was nothing wrong with them, but this was a matter of life and death, and I had to move on.'

Just like that, Malin thinks. What was it T.S. Eliot wrote?
Not with a bang, but a whimper.

'Do you have family?' Right question, Malin thinks. But I'm asking it for the wrong reason.

'A son. A long time passed before I had a child. He's eight now, he's the reason I'm here. Have you got children?'

Malin nods. 'A daughter.'

'Then you know. Whatever happens, you want to be there for their sake.'

'And the father?'

'We're divorced. He hit me once, by mistake really, I think, a hand flying out one night after a crayfish party, but that was enough.'

'Did you have any contact with Bengt?'

'With my brother? No, none at all.'

'Did he ever try to contact you?'

'Yes, he phoned once. But I hung up when I realised who it

was. There was a before, and a now, and I was never, ever going
to let them meet. Ridiculous, isn't it?'

'Not really,' Malin says.

'A week or so after he rang I had a call from some social
worker. Maria, I think her name was. She asked me to talk to
Bengt, even if I wouldn't meet him. She told me how depressed
he was, how lonely; she genuinely seemed to care, you know?'

'So?'

'I asked her never to call me again.'

'One question, and it's a harsh one,' Malin says. 'Did your
father or Bengt ever abuse you sexually?'

Rebecka Stenlundh is remarkably calm.

'No, nothing like that, ever. Sometimes I wonder if I'm
suppressing something, but no, never.'

Then a long silence.

'But what do I know?'

Zeke bites his lip. 'Do you know if Bengt had any enemies,
anything we ought to know?'

Rebecka Stenlundh shakes her head. 'I saw the picture in the
paper. It felt like everything printed there was about me, whether
I liked it or not. You can't escape, can you? Whatever you do,
your past always catches up with you, don't you think? It's
like you're tethered to a post with a rope. You can move about,
but you can't get away.'

'You seem to be managing very well,' Malin says.

'He was my brother. You should have heard his voice when he
called. He sounded like the loneliest person on the planet. And
I shut the door.'

A voice over the Tannoy: 'Rebecka to the till, Rebecka to the till.'

'What were you doing on Wednesday evening last week?'

'I was with my son in Egypt. Hurghada.'

Hence the suntan, Malin thinks.

'We got a last-minute deal. This cold drives me crazy. We got
home on Friday.'

Malin finishes her coffee and stands up. 'I think that was
everything,' she says. 'Yes, I think so.'

24

Have I forgiven you, sister?

It didn't start with you, and it doesn't end with you. So what is there to forgive, really?

Arrange your apples in rows, raise your child the way we never were. Give him love. Mark your flesh with it.

I can't watch over you. But I can drift about and see you, wherever you choose to run.

I devoured Maria Murvall's friendliness like sandwiches made from ready-sliced loaves, like smoked sausage, like unsalted butter. I washed the way she told me to, I ironed my trousers, I listened to what she said, believed in her theories about dignity. But how dignified was what happened in the forest?

How clean?

How pure?

You ought to be drifting with me, Maria, instead of sitting where you sit.

Shouldn't you?

Shouldn't we all drift and glide about, like that green Volvo down there on the motorway?

Huskqvarna.

Lawnmowers and hunting rifles. Shotguns for all manner of prey and a matchstick troll looking out over Lake Vättern. The artist, John Bauer, drowned in those waters when his boat capsized. No trolls saved him. Is he resting in one of his dense forests now?

No music in the car. Malin refused. And the coughing of the engine reminds her to turn on her mobile.

It rings at once.

'You have one new message . . .'

'This is Ebba Nilsson. Social worker. You tried to get hold of me last night. I'm home all morning, so feel free to call me back.'

Add number. Call.

One, two, three rings.

No answer again? Ah.

'Yes, hello. Who is this?'

A shrill voice, like a larynx compressed by fat. Malin can see Ebba Nilsson before her: a short, round woman close to retirement.

'This is Malin Fors from Linköping Police. We keep missing each other.'

Silence.

'And what do you want?'

'Bengt Andersson. You were his social worker for a while.'

'That's right.'

'And you've heard about what's happened?'

'I haven't been able to avoid it.'

'Can you tell me anything about Bengt?'

'Not much, I'm afraid,' Ebba Nilsson says. 'I'm sorry. While I was working in Ljungsbro he only came to see me once. He was incredibly quiet, but that wasn't so strange. He hadn't had things easy . . . and of course looking the way he did.'

'There's nothing in particular that we should know?'

'No, I don't think so, but the girl who came after me got on well with him, or so I heard.'

'Maria Murvall?'

'Yes.'

'We've been trying to get hold of her. But the number we've got has been disconnected. Do you know where she is now?'

Silence on the line.

'Oh, dear Lord,' Ebba Nilsson eventually says.

'Sorry?'

Zeke takes his eyes off the road, looks at Malin.

'You were about to say something?'

'Maria Murvall was raped up in the woods by Lake Hultsjön a few years ago. Didn't you know?'

Rita Santesson: 'Nothing that I want to go into.'

Maria.

Murvall.

The name, it was familiar.

The Motala Police case. I remember now. I should have made the connection.

Maria Murvall.

Was she the only one who cared, Bengt?

Even your sister turned her back on you.

The logic of emotions.

A swirl of snow blows across the road.

Was she the only one who cared, Bengt?

And she was raped.

25

Hultsjön Forest, late autumn 2001

What are you doing in the forest all on your own?

This late, little girl?

No mushrooms at this time of year, and too late for berries. Dusk is falling.

Tree trunks, undergrowth, branches, treetops, leaves, moss and worms. They're all getting ready for the most intimate abuse.

Child-killers. Rapists. Is it one man? Or several? A woman, women?

They creep up on you as you walk through the forest, whistling. The eyes. They see you. But you don't see them.

Or are they waiting further on, the eyes?

Darkness is falling fast now, but you aren't scared, you could walk this track with your eyes blindfolded, getting your bearings by smell alone.

The snakes, spiders, everything that decays.

An elk?

A deer?

You turn round, still, silence falls over the forest.

Walk on. Your car is waiting by the road; soon you'll see Hultsjön lazing in the last of the evening light.

Then everything gets dark.

Footsteps on the track behind you.

Someone pulling your legs from under you, pressing you down on to the damp ground, hot and sweet breath on your neck. So many hands, so much force.

It doesn't matter what you do. Snake-fingers, spider-legs, they eat through your clothes, the black roots of the trees stifle your screams, tying you for ever to the silence of the earth.

The worms crawl up the inside of your thighs, sticking out their claws, tearing your skin, your insides.

How coarse, how hard is a tree trunk?

Flesh and skin and blood. How hard?

No.

Not like that.

No one hears your screams in the black vegetation. And if they heard your screams, would they come?

No one is listening.

There is no salvation.

Only the damp, the cold and the pain, the relentless harshness that burns in you, tearing apart everything that is you.

For ever silent.

Sleep, dream, wake.

The sweet breath in the air you are breathing in the forest night. Naked body, bleeding body, doomed to wander the edge of the forest around Hultsjön.

You must have walked a long way.

You were breathing. The night-chill fled in panic when you crept out on to the road. The car headlights.

You had walked so far.

The lights grow, blind, corrode.

Is it death that is coming? Evil?

Again?

It came yesterday, didn't it, with quick steps it ran up, from where it lay hidden behind scarred bushes.

26

'Maria Murvall.'

Zeke rubs his fingers against the steering-wheel.

'I knew I'd heard the name before. Shit. Me and names. She was the girl who was raped up by Hultsjön four years ago. A really nasty case.'

'Motala Police.'

'Right on the boundary, so they took it. They found her wandering about on a road almost ten kilometres from where it happened. Some truck-driver taking a load of shingle to a building site up in Tjällmo found her. She'd been torn to shreds, badly beaten as well.'

'And they never caught him.'

'No. I think it even got on to *Crimewatch*. They found her clothes and the place where it must have happened, but nothing else.'

Malin shuts her eyes. Listens to the sound of the engine.

A man hanging in a tree.

His concerned social worker raped four years ago. Wandering the forest.

Cornerhouse-Kalle. The debauched, mad father. *A real man's man.*

And it all keeps popping up in the investigation, all mixed up, yet it still fits together, somehow.

Coincidence?

Try the theory out on Zeke.

'Bengt Andersson. He must have come up during that investigation. If she really did care as much about him as everyone says.'

'Must have done,' Zeke says, pointing at a car they are over-taking. 'I've been thinking about getting one of those Seats. They're owned by Volkswagen these days.'

I know, Zeke, Malin thinks. Janne must have told me ten times or more when he got on to the subject of his cars.

'Isn't the car you've got now good enough?'

'Murvall,' Zeke says. 'Isn't that name familiar for some other reason as well?'

Malin shakes her head.

'Me and names, Malin,' Zeke says.

'I'll call Sjöman and ask him to order over the case files from Motala Police. Nordström there will get it sorted at once.'

Just as they are turning into Police Headquarters, the third social worker on the list calls, the one who took over after Maria Murvall.

'It's awful, what's happened. Dreadful. Bengt Andersson was depressed, withdrawn. At one meeting he just mumbled, "What does keeping clean matter? What does keeping clean matter?" If I'm honest, I never drew any connection to the rape. But perhaps there was a link? But the rapist? Bengt Andersson? He wasn't that sort of person. A woman can tell.'

Malin gets out of the car, her face forming an involuntary grimace as the cold hits her skin.

'At any rate, I never got as close to him as Maria Murvall. She evidently cared about him outside her work as well, she got him to pull himself together. Almost like a big sister, as I understand it.'

They walk into the station.

Sjöman is standing at Malin's desk, waving a bundle of fax paper in the air.

Their colleague in Motala evidently hadn't needed to be asked twice.

Sven Sjöman is talking in a strained voice. Malin and Zeke are standing beside him. Malin wants to tell him to calm down, to think of his heart.

'Bengt Andersson was one of the people the Motala force

interviewed in connection with the rape of Maria Murvall. He had no alibi for that night, but none of the evidence found at the scene, nor anything else, ever pointed to him. He was just one of twenty-five of Maria's clients who were questioned.

'It's pretty grim reading,' Sjöman says, handing the papers to Zeke.

'Reality is always worse than fiction,' Zeke says.

'She was, or rather is, the sister of the Murvall brothers,' Sjöman goes on. 'A gang of nutters out on the plain who were always causing trouble. Even if that was a long time ago now.'

'The Murvalls! I knew it,' Zeke says.

'Must have been before my time,' Malin says.

'Tough bastards,' Zeke says. 'Really nasty.'

'Evidently they found clothes in the forest with traces of DNA on them, but not enough to put together a profile.'

'And on her body?'

'It was raining that night,' Sjöman says. 'Everything got washed away, and evidently she was raped with a rough branch. She was scratched to hell, badly cut internally, it says here. They never worked out if she was penetrated any other way as well. There was no means of confirming it.'

Malin can almost feel the pain.

She raises her palms towards Sven. Thinks, That's enough.

Maria Murvall. The angel of the lonely. What a lovers' tryst you ended up having.

Malin can hear the words inside her. Wants to beat herself up, not be cynical now. Fors, don't be cynical, never be cynical . . . Maybe I am already? Cynical?

'She was never the same again,' Sjöman continues. 'According to the last notes, before the files were archived, she ended up in some sort of psychotic state. Apparently she's in the secure unit at Vadstena Hospital. That's the address given here, anyway.'

'Have we checked?' Malin asks.

'Not yet, but that's easily done,' Zeke says.

'Tell them it's urgent police business if some doctor starts making a fuss.'

'And we've had a message from Karin,' Sven says. 'She should have something for us later this afternoon about the holes in the glass.'

'Good. I'm sure she'll call when she's done. What about the Old Norse angle?' Malin asks.

'Börje and Johan are working on it. They spoke to a Rickard Skoglöf and his girlfriend Valkyria Karlsson while you were down in Jönköping. They're still following that angle.'

'Did they get anything from those two?'

'You never know,' Sjöman says. 'If you listen carefully, people may well say more than they think they are. We're taking a closer look at them now.'

A woman doctor's voice on the other end of the line.

'Yes, we've got a Maria Murvall here. Yes, you can see her, but preferably no men, and as few people as possible. Oh, you'll be coming in person, that sounds good.'

Then a long pause.

'Just don't expect Maria to say anything.'

27

The call from Karin Johannison came through when Malin had just got into her car and turned the ignition key.

'Malin? Karin here. I think I know what caused those holes in the glass now.'

Malin sinks into the icy car seat. In just a second she feels cold air spreading through the car, and longs desperately for it to warm up.

'Sorry, I was about to drive off. What have you found?'

'I can safely say that they weren't made by grit or stones, the edges are far too smooth for that. The holes have also caused some very large cracks, considering their size, so I think it's impossible that anyone threw anything through the window.'

'So what are you saying?'

'They're bullet-holes, Malin.'

Holes in glass.

A new door opening.

'Are you sure?'

'As sure as I can be. An extremely small-calibre weapon. There's no soot or powder on the holes, but that's often the case with glass. But it could also mean they were made by an air-rifle.'

Malin sits in silence, thoughts running through her head.

A small-calibre weapon. Was someone trying to shoot Bengt Andersson?

Air-rifle. Boys getting up to mischief?

Forensics didn't find anything odd in Bengt Andersson's flat. No bullet wounds in his body.

'In that case they must have been rubber bullets. Could that sort of ammunition have caused any of Bengt Andersson's injuries?'

'No, they cause a very particular type of bleeding. I've seen it before.'

Engine noise.

Malin, alone in her car, on her way to see a mute, raped woman.

'Malin, you've gone quiet,' Karin's voice comes over the phone. 'Have you gone off the road?'

'It's just me thinking,' Malin says. 'Could you go back to Bengt Andersson's flat and see if you can find anything new? Take Zeke with you.'

Karin sighs, then says, 'I know what you're looking for, Malin. You can rely on me.'

'Will you tell Sven Sjöman?'

'He's had an email already.'

What is it I, we, can't see? Malin thinks as she presses the accelerator.

This police officer, senior physician Charlotta Niima thinks, must be ten years younger than me, and the way she looks at you, through you, watchful and weary at the same time, as if she could do with a decent holiday away from all this cold. Same thing with her body: athletic, but still slow in its movements, hesitant in front of me somehow. Hiding behind matter-of-factness.

She's pretty, but she'd probably hate that word. And behind the penetrating eyes? What do I see there? Sorrow? But that must be to do with her work. What can't she have seen? Just like me. It's all a matter of compartmentalising, turning on and off like any other piece of machinery.

The black-framed glasses make Charlotta Niima look stern, but together with her big, red, permed hair, the glasses give her a slightly crazy look.

Maybe you have to be crazy to work with crazy people? Malin thinks. Unless you have to be entirely uncrazy?

There's something manic about Dr Niima, as if she maybe uses her patients' illnesses to keep her own problems under control.

Prejudices.

The hospital is housed in three whitewashed fifties buildings in a fenced-in area on the edge of Vadstena. Through the windows of Dr Niima's room Malin can see the ice-covered Vättern, frozen almost to the bottom: stiff fish panting below the ice, trying to force their way through a viscous, treacherous liquid. Soon we won't be able to breathe under here.

On the left, beyond the fence, she can make out the red-brick walls of the convent.

Birgitta. Prayer. Saints. Convent life.

She's here alone. Woman to woman. Zeke didn't protest.

The old madhouse, famous across the plain as a dumping ground for the lost, has been rebuilt as private apartments. Malin drove past the white art nouveau building on her way into the town. The white façades of the madhouse looked grey, and the drooping black branches of trees in the surrounding parkland must have heard a thousand madmen scream at night.

How could anyone choose to live in a place like that?

'Maria has been here almost five years now. She hasn't spoken once in that time.' Niima's voice, sympathetic, intimate, yet still distant. 'She doesn't express any wishes at all.'

'Does she look after herself?'

'Yes, she washes and eats. Goes to the toilet. But she doesn't talk, and refuses to leave her room. The first year we had her under watch, and she tried to hang herself from the radiator a few times. But now, as far as we can determine, she isn't suicidal.'

'Could she live in a flat outside the hospital? With proper support?'

'She fights if we try to get her out of her room. I've never seen anything like it. She's completely incapable, in our evaluation, of surviving out in wider society. She appears to view her whole body as a sort of prosthesis, a replacement for something she's lost. She's methodical in her daily hygiene, and puts on the clothes we lay out for her.'

Dr Niima pauses before going on.

'And she eats, three meals a day, but not enough to put on

any weight. Complete control. But we can't get through to her. Our words, even us as people, it's like we don't exist. Acutely autistic people can demonstrate similar symptoms.'

'Drugs?'

'We've tried. But none of our chemical keys has managed to break through Maria Murvall's complex locking mechanisms.'

'And why no men?'

'She starts to cramp. Not always, but sometimes. Her brothers visit her occasionally. That goes okay. Brothers aren't men.'

'Any other visitors?'

Dr Niima shakes her head. 'Her mother stays away. Her father died long ago.'

'And her physical injuries?'

'They've healed. But she had to have a hysterectomy. The things she had pushed inside her out in the forest did a great deal of damage.'

'Is she in pain?'

'Physical pain? I don't think so.'

'Therapy?'

'You have to understand, Inspector Fors, it's practically impossible to conduct therapy with someone who doesn't speak. Silence is the soul's most powerful weapon.'

'So you think she's somehow clinging on to herself through silence?'

'Yes. If she talked, she'd lose her grip.'

'This is where Maria lives.'

The female care assistant carefully opens the door, the third of seven in a corridor on the second floor of the building. The fluorescent lights in the ceiling make the linoleum floor of the corridor shine, and from inside one of the rooms comes a low groaning sound. Different detergent here to the old people's home. Perfumed. Lemongrass. Like in the spa at the Hotel Ekoxen.

'Let me go first and tell her who's come to see her.'

Through the crack in the door Malin can hear the care assistant's voice; it sounds like she's talking to a child.

'There's a girl from the police who'd like to talk to you. Is that okay?'

No answer.

Then the care assistant comes back. 'You can go in now.'

Malin opens the door wide, goes in through a little hall where the door to the shower and toilet is ajar.

A lunch tray with half-eaten food is on a table, there's a television, a blue-green rug on the floor, a few motorbike and dragster posters on the walls.

And on a bed in one corner of the room, Maria Murvall. Her body seems not to exist, her whole being is a vanishing face surrounded by well-brushed blonde tresses.

You're like me, Malin thinks. You're a lot like me.

The woman on the bed takes no notice when Maria comes in. She sits still, her legs hanging over the edge of the bed, down to the floor; her feet are wearing yellow socks, her head is hanging forward. Her eyes are open; an empty yet strangely bright gaze, fixed on some indefinable point in the air filling the room.

Cascades of snow against the window-pane. It's started to snow again. Maybe it will finally get a few degrees warmer.

'My name is Malin Fors. I work as a detective inspector with the Linköping Police.'

No reaction.

Just silence and stillness in Maria Murvall's body.

'It's very cold today. Windy, too,' Malin says.

Idiot. Babbling. Better to get straight to the point. Do or die.

'One of your clients at social services in Ljungsbro has been found murdered.'

Maria Murvall blinks, stays in the same position.

'Bengt Andersson. He was found hanging in a tree. Naked.'

She breathes. Blinks again.

'Was it Bengt that you ran into in the forest?'

A foot moving under yellow cotton.

'I understand that you helped Bengt. That you tried extra hard for him to have a better life. Is that right?'

New cascades of snow.

'Why did you care about him? Why was he different? Or were you like that with everyone?'

Words in the silence: *Go now, don't come here with your questions. Don't you understand that I die if I listen to them, or, rather, the opposite, that I have to live if I answer. I breathe, but that's all. And what does breathing mean anyway?*

'Do you know anything about Bengt Andersson that could help us?'

Why am I persisting with this? Because you know something?

Maria Murvall lifts her legs from the edge of the bed, shifts her spindly body to a lying position, her gaze following the same path as her body.

Just like an animal.

Tell me what you know, Maria. Use those words.

A black beast of prey in the forest. The same man as on a snow-clad, windswept plain?

Maybe?

No.

Unless?

Instead this: 'Why do you think someone would want to hang Bengt Andersson in a tree in the middle of the Östgöta plain in the coldest winter in living memory?

'Why, Maria? Didn't he have enough to put up with as it was?

'And who shot through his window?'

Maria shuts her eyes, opens them again. She breathes, resigned, as if breathing or not breathing had long ago lost their meaning. As if all that makes no difference at all.

Are you trying to comfort me?

What can you see that no one else sees, Maria? What can you hear?

'Nice posters,' Malin says before leaving the room.

In the corridor Malin stops the care assistant who is passing with a pile of orange handtowels in her arms.

'Those posters on her walls, they don't seem to belong here. Did her brothers put them up?'

'Yes. I suppose they think they'll remind her of home.'

'Are her brothers here often?'

'Just one of them. The youngest one, Adam. He comes every now and then, seems to feel guilty somehow that she's here.'

'Dr Niima said that more than one brother comes.'

'No, just one. I'm sure.'

'Did they get on particularly well?'

'I don't know. Maybe, seeing as he's the one who visits. There was another one here once, but he couldn't handle going into her room. He said it was too claustrophobic, that he couldn't do it. He said it was just like a wardrobe, those were his exact words. Then he left.'

28

'Are you there, Bengt?'

'I'm here, Maria. Can you see me?'

'No, I can't see you, but I can hear you drifting.'

'And there was me thinking that my drifting was silent.'

'It is. But you know, I hear things others can't hear.'

'Were you scared?'

'Were you?'

'I think so, but after a while you realise that fear is pointless, and then it fades away. That's what it's like, isn't it?'

'Yes.'

'It isn't too late for you, Maria. Not in the same way it is for me.'

'Don't say that.'

'It all fits together.'

'It smells of loneliness here. Is that you or me?'

'You mean the smell of apples? It's neither of us. That's someone else.'

'Who?'

'Them, him, her, all of us.'

'The one who shot at your window?'

'I remember getting home and seeing the holes, late, so late. I knew they were bullet-holes.'

'But who shot them?'

'I think they all shot at me.'

'Are there more of them?'

'If we all stick together then there are always more of us, aren't there, Maria?'

Zeke is standing three metres behind Karin Johannison in the doorway between the kitchen and the living room of Bengt

Andersson's flat. His jacket is done up; the heat has been turned down to the minimum by the landlord, just enough to stop the water freezing and the pipes bursting. That's happened in several places around the city this winter, peaking over Christmas when the smart folk disappeared to Thailand and wherever else they went, and their boilers slowed down, and bang! Water damage as a result.

I suppose my insurance premium will go up now, Zeke thinks.

Karin is kneeling on the floor, leaning over the sofa, picking at a hole in the stuffing with a pair of tweezers.

Zeke can't help it, but when she leans forward like that, seen from the back, she looks quite acceptable, not to say desirable. Well proportioned. No question.

They drove out in silence. With his whole body he left her in no doubt that he would prefer not to have any small talk. And Karin concentrated on the road, but still seemed to want to talk, as if she had been waiting for a chance to be alone with him.

The hole that Karin is digging in is in a direct line from the window. But the hole could have been made by anything.

Then Karin twists and pulls her hand, saying, 'That's it, that's it,' and then triumphantly pulls out the tweezers.

She turns round, holding the tweezers towards him, and says, 'If I look a bit longer, I promise I'm going to find a couple more of these little beauties.'

Malin is standing in the kitchen of her flat. She tries to shake off the image of Maria Murvall on her bed in that gloomy room.

'You and Zeke carry on looking into the Murvall angle. But if the Æsir line suddenly needs more work, we'll shift our focus on to that.'

Karim Akbar's voice earlier at the run-through, sounding like the whole chain leading to Maria Murvall had been his idea. Nice to be able to concentrate on one thing, though.

Sven Sjöman: 'We'll have to pull out the Murvall brothers' police records. And you and Börje, Johan, you carry on with the Æsir angle. Don't leave any rune-stone unturned. And we'll have to talk to Bengt Andersson's neighbours again, check if they saw or heard anything unusual, now that we know the window was fired at.'

Rubber bullets.

Karin and Zeke had found three green bullets in the sofa. Presumably one for each hole. The right size to fit a small-calibre weapon, most likely a small-bore rifle.

Rubber bullets.

Too serious to be lads messing around. But maybe not completely serious either. Probably meant to cause pain. Torment. Just as you were tormented, Bengt.

Rubber bullets.

Impossible to say what sort of weapon the bullets were fired from, according to Karin: 'You don't get enough of an imprint from the barrel. Rubber's more flexible than metal.'

Malin pours a splash of red wine into the stew bubbling in front of her.

Johan Jakobsson: 'We questioned a few Æsir fanatics in the Kinda area today. As far as we could make out, they were just harmless, shall we say *historically minded* individuals. That professor at the university, he must be one of the biggest media-tarts I've ever come across. And he looks pretty clean. His boyfriend, a Magnus Djupholm, confirms the story about the cat.'

Media-tart.

The words made Karim prick up his ears, as if he had suddenly become aware of an ailment.

And they made Malin laugh to herself.

Johan had brought copies of the national evening tabloids, *Aftonbladet* and *Expressen*, to the meeting. Nothing on the front. But whole pages devoted to the professor, big pictures, 'authority on Old Norse rituals', describing how a midwinter sacrifice would take place, and implying that he thought it could happen again.

Sven was silent for almost the whole meeting.

Malin stirs the stew on the stove, inhaling the smell of white pepper and bay leaves.

Their murder is disappearing from the public consciousness.

New murders, new scandals involving people on television, political manoeuvres.

What's a hanging body in a tree worth when it's no longer 'new'? Ball-Bengt, you're not news any more.

The front door opening into the hall.

Tove.

'Mum, are you home?'

'I'm in the kitchen.'

'You've made dinner? I'm starving.'

'Beef stew.'

Tove's cheeks rosy, beautiful, the most beautiful cheeks in the world.

'I saw Markus. We had coffee round his.'

A big white doctors' villa in Ramshäll. Dad a surgeon, one of the ones in white and green, his mum a doctor in the ENT clinic. Two doctors: a common combination in this city.

The phone rings.

'Can you get that?' Malin says.

'No, you get it.'

Malin picks up the phone from the wall where it's attached.

'Malin, Dad here. How are things?'

'Good. But cold. I've been watering the plants.'

'That's not why I'm calling. Is everything all right?'

'I just said it was. Everything's fine.'

'So it's cold up there, isn't it? We saw on TVSverige that there are radiators bursting in Stockholm.'

'That's been happening here too.'

He's got something on his mind, Malin thinks. I wonder if he'll manage to get it out. 'Did you want anything in particular?'

'Well, just that I . . . No, we can talk about it another time.'

Can't be bothered to wheedle it out of him, can't be bothered.

'Whatever you like, Dad.'

'Is Tove there?'

'She just went into the bathroom.'

'Well, it wasn't important. Talk to you soon, bye for now.'

Malin is left standing with the phone in her left hand. No one can end a conversation as abruptly as her father. He's there, then he's gone.

Tove comes back into the kitchen.

'Who was that?'

'Grandad. He sounded a bit odd.'

Tove sits down at the table, looks out of the window. 'All the clothes people have to wear at this time of year make them look ugly,' she says. 'They all look fat.'

'Do you know what,' Malin says. 'There's enough here for Janne as well. Shall we call and ask if he wants to come over?'

A sudden desire to see him. To touch something. Feel him. Just a whim.

Tove brightens up.

'You call him,' Malin says, and Tove's smile vanishes as quickly as it arrived.

'You'll have to do that for yourself, Mum.'

One, two, three, four, five rings. No answer.

Maybe he's on duty at the fire station.

At the station the operator says, 'He's off today.'

His mobile.

Janne's mobile, straight to the answering service: 'Hi, you've reached Janne. Leave a message after the tone and I'll get back to you.'

No message.

'Couldn't you get hold of him?'

'No.'

'Just the two of us, then, Mum.'

Tove is asleep in bed.

It is just after half past eleven. Malin is wide awake on the sofa.

She gets up, looks into Tove's room, at the perfect girl's body under the covers, the chest rising and falling.

Brothers aren't men.

An overflow of life.

Warm, warm blood circulating. Another body in another bed.

Janne, Janne, where are you? Come here. Come back. There's meat stew on the stove.

Can't. I'm driving sacks of flour over a mountain in Bosnia, the road's been mined. They need my help, here.

We need you.

Malin goes into her bedroom. Is sitting quietly on the edge of the bed when her mobile rings.

She rushes out into the hall and finds her mobile in her jacket pocket.

'Daniel Högfeldt here.'

First anger, then resignation, then hope.

'Have you got anything for me?'

'No, nothing new. What do you think?'

'I think you'd be welcome to come round, if you'd like to.'

'Are you home?'

'Yes. Are you coming?'

Malin looks at herself in the hall mirror, sees how the contours of her face seem to get weaker the more she looks at it.

Why resist?

She whispers down the phone, 'I'm coming, I'm coming, I'm coming.'

She drinks a large glass of tequila before leaving the flat. Leaves a note on the hall floor.

Tove

They called from work. I've got my mobile

Mum

PART TWO
Brothers

In the darkness

Are you coming? Are you coming with love?

Sketches, notes, and my little black book with little black words, pictures of now, of the future, of the past, of blood.

I'm not mad. It's only a part of me that's given in, that's come loose. What good did it do, talking to that psychologist?

It's in the wardrobe at home, the notebook; here there are only crumbs, apples and everything that needs doing, that's already done and needs doing again.

Let me in, do you hear? It's cold out here. Let me in.

Why are you laughing? You laughter is tearing me apart.

It's cold and damp. I want to go home. But this is probably my home now.

I want to join in and play.

Receive some love.

That's all.

29

Daniel Högfeldt's bedroom.

What am I doing here?

Are those his hands on my body? He's eager, firm, caresses, nips, slaps. Does he hit me? Oh, let him. Let him scratch a little, it might as well hurt a bit.

I give way. Let it happen. His body is hard and that's enough, I don't give a damn who he is.

Grey walls. My hands near the chrome headboard, he nibbles at my lips, his tongue in my mouth and he pumps and pumps.

Sweat. Minus thirty-four degrees.

Tove, Janne, Dad, Mum, Ball-Bengt, Maria Murvall.

Daniel Högfeldt on top of me, in charge. Do you think I'm yours, Daniel? We can pretend that if you like.

It hurts. And it's nice.

She takes control, rolls away from him, forces him down on the mattress. Clambers on, in.

Now, Daniel. Now.

I disappear into the lovely pain. And it's wonderful.

Can't that be enough?

Malin is lying next to Daniel, twists herself up into a sitting position. Looks at the sleeping muscular body beside hers. Gets up, puts on her clothes, leaves the flat.

It's five o'clock. Linköping deserted.

She walks towards Police Headquarters.

★

I heard you, Malin, I was awake, but you didn't notice.

I wanted to keep you here, I wanted that. It's so damn cold out there, I wanted to say that I wanted you to stay. Even the very toughest, people who seem hard, need warmth, everyone does.

There's nothing original in warmth.

But it still means everything.

I dig and root about in people's lives, try to uncover their secrets. There's no warmth in that, but I still like doing it.

How did I get like this?

The Murvall brothers.

Adam, Jakob, Elias.

Malin has their files in front of her on the desk, leafing through them at random, reading, drinking coffee.

Three people. Poured into almost the same mould.

The brothers' police records read like the report of a boxing match.

Round one: shoplifting, hash, souped-up mopeds, driving without a licence, obstruction of official duties, break-ins in kiosks, thefts from Cloetta trucks.

Round two: assault, fighting in bars.

Round three: poaching, extortion, stealing boats, possession of illegal weapons. Small-bore rifles, Husqvarna.

Then after that it's like the match is over.

The last notes in the brothers' files are some ten years old.

So what's happened to the Murvall brothers? Have they calmed down? Got families? Gone straight? Got smarter? Never the last of these. It doesn't happen. Once a gangster, always a gangster.

Which one is worst?

Notes, extracts from interviews.

The youngest brother, Adam. A hash-smoking petrol-head with violent tendencies, if the file is to be believed. He beat one of the drivers at Mantorp horse-trotting track until he was pouring with blood, after he failed to win a race that Adam had high hopes of.

Illegal betting? No question. Three months in Skänninge secure unit. Two elk poached in February. One month in Skänninge. Beating up his girlfriend. Suspicion of attempted rape. Six months.

The middle brother, Jakob. Illiterate, according to the files. Dyslexic. Prone to violent outbursts. And what does someone like that do? Hits a teacher in year seven, breaks the arm of a contemporary outside the kiosk in Ljungsbro. Juvenile institution. Dealing hash in the playground when he returned, broke a policeman's jaw when they came to pick him up. Six months in Norrköping, extortion of businesses in Borensberg, drink-driving. One year in Norrköping. Then nothing. As if whatever was wrong suddenly stopped.

The eldest brother, Elias. A perfect example. Some sort of talent for football, in the reserve team as a thirteen-year-old, until he broke into the kiosk at Ljungsbro IF and was expelled from the club. Causing death by dangerous driving when he hit a tree, drunk. Six months in Skänninge. Grievous bodily harm in the Hamlet restaurant. He smashed a beer-glass into another customer's head. The man lost the sight in one eye.

'Slow-witted, easily led, insecure.' The psychologist's words. Slow-witted? Insecure? Did people really write things like that?

Little sister Maria.

So these are your brothers, Maria? The ones who put up the posters in your room? Adam? In their language, his language, I suppose that's a sign of concern.

Bengt's blue body in the tree.

The revenge of three brothers?

Round four: murder?

Malin rubs her eyes. Sips her third cup of coffee.

She hears the door of the office open, feels a cold draught.

Zeke's voice, rasping and tired: 'Early today, Fors? Or just a very long night?'

Zeke puts on the radio.

Low volume.

'Interesting reading, isn't it?'

'They seem to have settled down,' Malin says.

'Or they just got a bit smarter.'

Zeke is about to say something else, but his voice is hidden by the sound of the radio. The song that is playing fades out, then an annoying jingle, then Malin's friend's voice: 'That was . . .'

Helen.

She grew up out there, Malin thinks. Almost the same age as the brothers. Maybe she knows them? I could call her. I'll call her.

'Hello, Malin.'

The voice as soft and sexy over the phone as on the radio.

'Can you talk?'

'We've got three minutes and twenty-two seconds until this track is over. But I can give us twice as long if I don't bother to talk before the next one.'

'I'll get straight to the point, then. Did you know three brothers by the name of Murvall, who grew up out in Vreta Kloster?'

'The Murvall brothers. Sure. Everyone knew them.'

'Infamous?'

'You could say that. They were always known as "the crazy Murvall brothers". They were pretty nasty. But all the same . . . there was something tragic about them. You know, they were the ones who everyone knew would never turn into anything, but who rage and rebel against the system. You know, the ones who are sort of on the periphery right from the start. Who are, I don't know, maybe doomed always to be outside normal society, knocking to get in. They were branded, somehow. They lived in Blåsvädret. The worst, most windswept hellhole on the whole plain. That was Murvall family territory. I wouldn't be surprised if they still live there.'

'Do you remember Maria Murvall?'

'Yes. She was the one who was going to make something of herself. She was in the parallel class to me.'

'Did you hang out with her?'

'No, she was sort of on the sidelines as well, somehow. As if she were branded the same way, like her good grades were almost, I don't know, it sounds awful, but a meaningless attempt to break free. Her brothers protected her. There was one boy who tried to bully her about something, I forget what, and they sandpapered his cheeks. Two horrible wounds, but he didn't dare tell anyone who did it.'

'And the father?'

'He did odd jobs. Blackie, that was his name. He was actually quite fair, but everyone called him Blackie. He had some sort of accident, broke his back and ended up in a wheelchair. Then he drank himself to death, although I think he'd already made a start on that. I'm pretty sure he broke his neck when he rolled down the stairs in their house.'

'Mother?'

'There were rumours that she was some sort of witch. But I dare say she was just an ordinary housewife.'

'A witch?'

'Gossip, Malin. A shitty little rural dump like Ljungsbro lives off rumour and gossip.'

The voice on the radio.

'And this next track is for my good friend Malin Fors, the brightest star of Linköping Police.'

Zeke chortles.

'Carry on the good work, Malin. Soon you'll be world-famous. Right now she's investigating the case of Bengt Andersson, which everyone in the city has such an interest in. If you know anything about the case, call Malin Fors at Linköping Police. Anything at all could help them.'

Zeke is chuckling louder now. 'You're going to get such a torrent of calls.'

The music starts.

'Country Boy' by Eldkvarn.

'This is my love song. This is my time on earth . . .'

Plura Jonsson's voice, tremulous with longing and sentimentality.

'. . . I am what I am . . . a country boy, call me a country boy . . .'

What am I? Malin thinks.

A country girl?

Not out of love. Maybe out of obligation.

30

As the song on the radio ends, the phone on Malin's desk rings.

'That's a bit quick,' Zeke says.

'Could be anything,' Malin says. 'Doesn't have to be about the case.'

The phone seems to vibrate on its next ring, demanding to be taken seriously.

'Malin Fors, Linköping Police.'

Silence on the line.

Breathing.

Malin makes a quick gesture to Zeke, holding up her hand.

Then a gruff voice that's only recently broken: 'I was the one with the computer game.'

Computer game? Malin ransacks her memory.

'Playing Gnu Warriors.'

'Sorry?'

'You came to ask me about—'

'Now I remember,' Malin says, and sees Fredrik Unning sitting in the basement of the smart house, joystick in hand, sees the father looking at his son, aloof.

'Yes, I asked you if there was anything else we ought to know.'

'Yes, that's right. I heard on the radio.'

The same fear in his voice now as there was in his eyes then. A quick, fleeting feeling, gone as soon as it appeared.

'And you know something?'

'Can you come out here, you and that other bloke?'

'We're heading out towards Ljungsbro later today. It may take a while, but we'll be there.'

'No one needs to know, do they? That you're coming?'

'No, we can keep this between us,' Malin says, thinking, It depends on what you've got to say, of course. And it strikes her how easily she is prepared to lie outright to a young person, as long as it helps the investigation. And she knows she would hate to be treated like that. But still she says, 'This is just between us.'

'Okay.'

Then a click, and Zeke's curious expression on the other side of the desk.

'Who was that?' he says.

'Do you remember Fredrik Unning? The teenager playing computer games in that posh house?'

'What, him?'

'Yes, he's got something to tell, but we'll do the Murvalls first. Don't you think?'

'Murvalls,' Zeke says, gesturing towards the door. 'Now what could be troubling young Unning?'

'When you cross this road property prices sink by thirty per cent,' Zeke says, as they turn off at a deserted Preem garage on to the road leading to the collection of houses that goes by the horribly appropriate name of Blåsvädret, 'windy weather'. The cold crackles through the melancholy outside the car. The chill seems to twist in the wind, picking up snow from the dead drifts, throwing it in transparent waves across the windscreen.

'God, it's windy,' Malin says.

'And the sky is white.'

'Shut up, Zeke. Just shut up.'

'I love it when you use platitudes, Malin, I just love it.'

An eerie place. That's the immediate feeling.

Good to have Zeke alongside. Because if anything happens, he can switch in a fraction of a second. Like when that junkie whipped out a syringe and held it to her neck. She didn't even have time to see what was happening, but Zeke lashed out and knocked the syringe from the junkie's hand. Then she saw Zeke kick the man to the ground and carry on kicking him in the stomach.

She had to drag Zeke off to stop him.

'Don't worry, Fors, it'll look like a couple of punches. But it'll hurt more. He was trying to kill you, and we can't have that, now, can we?'

Another, even more powerful, gust.

'God, this is weird, there was hardly any wind on the main road. What is this?'

'Blåsvädret is a Bermuda triangle,' Zeke says. 'Anything can happen here.'

One single street.

Blåsstigen, 'windy way'.

Five red-painted wooden houses on one side, garages and workshops on the other, one breezeblock building with drawn blinds. Another larger whitewashed house further on at the end of the road, almost invisible through the swirling snow.

The houses in Blåsvädret that aren't inhabited by the Murvall family are silent, their owners presumably at work. The clock on the dashboard says 11.30, almost lunchtime, and Malin feels her stomach rumble.

Food, please, not coffee.

The Murvall brothers live next to each other. The last two wooden houses and the breezeblock building are theirs, the white house their mother's. The windows of the wooden houses are dark, and car wrecks are randomly strewn about the plots, half covered by snow and ice. But there are lights on behind the blinds of the brick building. A broken, bowed, black iron-railing rocks in the wind. The workshop opposite has heavy, rusty metal doors, and in front of it stands an old green Range Rover.

Zeke stops the car.

'Adam's house,' Zeke says.

'Okay, let's see if he's at home.'

They do up their jackets, get out. More wrecked cars. But not like Janne's. These are wrecked beyond salvation; no loving hand will ever try to fix them up. In the drive is a green Skoda pick-up. Zeke peers at the back, running his glove through the snow, shakes his head.

The wind is howling beyond words, great angry gusts, with

hidden little bursts of Arctic chill that easily and nonchalantly push through the fabric of their jackets, the wool of their jumpers.

Sand on the concrete steps. The bell doesn't work and Zeke bangs on the door, but the house is silent.

Malin looks in through the green glass of the door. Vague shapes of a hallway, children's clothes, toys, a gun cabinet, mess.

'No one at home.'

'Probably at work at this time of day,' Malin says.

Zeke nods. 'Maybe they've gone straight.'

'It's odd,' Malin says, 'do you see how the houses seem to belong together somehow?'

'They're one and the same,' Zeke says. 'Not physically, but if houses have souls, then these share one.'

'Let's go to the mother's house.'

Even though the white wooden villa is just seventy-five metres down the road, it's impossible to make out anything but the outline, and the white wood that occasionally shimmers through the surrounding whiteness.

They walk towards the house.

As they get close the gusts of snow and chilly haze disperse and they see that the whole garden is full of mature apple trees. Their branches sway darkly in the wind, and Malin breathes in through her nose, closing her eyes briefly and trying to pick up the smell of apple blossom and fruit that must be here in spring and autumn.

But this world is scentless.

She opens her eyes.

The building's façade has settled and the crooked wood seems tired, yet somehow still defiant. Light is streaming through the windows.

'Looks like Mum's home,' Zeke says.

'Yes,' Malin says, but before she can say more she is interrupted.

A man, tall and with at least a week's worth of stubble around a well-defined mouth. He's dressed in green overalls, and has opened the door of the white house. The man is standing on the porch and staring askance at them.

'And who the fuck are you two? If you take another step on this property I'll get my shotgun and blow your brains out.'

'Welcome to Blåsvädret,' Zeke says with an expectant smile.

'We're from the police.'

Malin holds up her ID as they approach the man on the porch.

'Can we come in?'

And now she sees them.

All the people, the family watching them through the windows of the white house: tired women, children of various ages, a woman in a shawl with deep-set black eyes, a sharp nose and thin white hair draped over the shiny skin of her cheeks. Malin looks at the faces, the half bodies behind the windows, and thinks that it's as if the bits of these people that she can't see had grown together. That this family's thighs, knees, shins and feet were bundled together, inseparable, different, yet somehow superior.

'What do you want with us?' The man on the porch throws the words at them.

'And who do we have the honour of talking to?'

Zeke's bluntness seems to have an effect.

'Elias Murvall.'

'Okay, Elias, let us in. Don't leave us standing out here in the cold.'

'We don't let anyone in.'

From the house comes a sharp female voice, the mark of someone used to getting her own way.

'Let the police in, now, boy.'

Elias Murvall steps aside, follows them into the hall, where they are hit by the smell of burned cabbage.

'And you can take your shoes off.' The woman's voice again.

The hall is full of winter coats, garishly coloured children's jackets, cheap padded jackets, an army raincoat. Ahead of her Malin can see a living room: period furniture on Wilton rugs, reproductions of Johan Krouthén's sun-drenched Östgöta meadows. A misplaced computer screen of the latest, thinnest design.

Malin pulls off her Caterpillar boots, feeling exposed in her bare socks among these people.

The kitchen.

Around an enormous table laid for lunch in the middle of the room sits what must be the whole Murvall family, silent and expectant, more people than she saw in the windows, no longer grown together. Malin counts three women with small children, babies in their arms, children of various ages on other chairs; shouldn't some of them be at school? Home schooling? Or are they still too young?

Two more men in the room, one with a neatly trimmed beard, the other clean-shaven. They're dressed in the same sort of overalls as Elias who let them in, and they have the same powerful appearance. The clean-shaven one, who looks youngest, must be Adam. He is knocking a napkin on the table as if the tabletop were a door, his eyes such a dark blue that they are almost black like his mother's. The middle brother, Jakob, thinning hair, sitting in front of the stove, his gut showing through his overalls, looks at them with hazy eyes, as if he's encountered thousands of police officers who wanted something from him, all of whom he's told to go to hell.

The mother is standing by the stove. The short, thin old woman is dressed in a red skirt and grey cardigan. She turns towards Malin.

'On Wednesdays my family gets cabbage bake.'

'Nice,' Zeke says.

'What do you know about that?' the mother says. 'Have you ever tasted my cabbage bake?'

At the same time she points with one hand at Elias, gesturing as if to say, Sit down at the table. Now!

Several of the children lose patience, jump down from their chairs and run out of the kitchen into the living room, then up the stairs.

'Well?' The old woman stares at Malin, then at Zeke.

Zeke doesn't hesitate, in fact he even smiles slightly as he tosses the words into the room: 'We're here on account of the murder of a Bengt Andersson. He was one of the people questioned in connection with the rape of your daughter, Maria Murvall.'

And Malin, in spite of the incident the words refer to, feels a glow inside. This is what it should be like. Zeke is entirely unbowed, heads straight to the heart of the hornets' nest. Commands respect. I forget sometimes, but I know why I admire him.

No one round the table moves.

Jakob Murvall leans languidly across the tabletop, takes a cigarette from a packet of Blend and lights it. A baby in one of the women's laps whimpers.

'We don't know anything about that,' the woman says. 'Do we, lads?'

The brothers round the table shake their heads.

'Nothing.' Elias grins. 'Nothing at all.'

'Your sister was raped. And someone who was questioned during the investigation has been found dead,' Zeke says.

'What were you all doing on the night between Wednesday and Thursday last week?' Malin asks.

'We don't have to tell you a fucking thing,' Elias says, and Malin thinks that he says the words in an exaggeratedly tough voice, as if he doesn't want to look weak in front of the others.

'Well, yes you do, actually,' Zeke says. 'Your sister—'

Adam Murvall heaves himself up, throws out his arms and shouts across the table, 'That bastard could very well have raped Maria. And now he's dead, and that's a fucking good thing.'

The colour of his eyes shifts from blue to black as he spits out the words.

'Maybe she can get some peace now.'

'Boy, sit down.' The mother's voice from the stove.

Now several of the babies are crying, and the women try to comfort them, and Elias Murvall pulls his brother down on to his chair.

'That's better,' their mother says when silence has fallen once again. 'I think the bake is ready now. And the potatoes.'

'The old Æsir beliefs,' Malin says. 'Do you follow them?'

Scattered laughter from the adults round the table.

'We're proper men,' Jakob Murvall says. 'Not Vikings.'

'Do you have guns in the house?' Malin asks.

'We've all got hunting rifles,' Elias Murvall says.

'How did you get licences for them, with your records?'

'What, the sins of our youth? That's a long time ago.'

'Have you got a small-bore rifle?'

'What guns we've got is none of your business.'

'So you didn't use a short-bore rifle to fire through the window of Bengt Andersson's flat?' Malin asks.

'Has someone fired through his window?' Elias Murvall says. 'I don't suppose he'll be too bothered about that now, will he?'

'We'd like to see your gun cabinet,' Zeke says. 'You do keep your guns in one, I presume? And we've got a lot of questions. We'd like to talk to you one by one. Either here and now, or down at the station. Your decision.'

The women are all looking at me, Malin thinks. Their eyes are trying to work out what I want, as if I might try to take something away from them that deep down they don't really want anyway, but which they would defend to the death.

'You can call my boys in for questioning. And if you want to see the gun cabinet you'll have to come back with a warrant,' the old woman says. 'But right now, the Murvall boys are going to eat, so you can leave now.'

'We'll be wanting to talk to you as well, Mrs Murvall,' Zeke says.

Rakel Murvall lifts her nose towards the ceiling. 'Elias, show the police officers out.'

Malin and Zeke are standing in the cold outside the house, looking back at the façade, and the shapes behind the ever more fogged windows. Malin thinks how nice it is to have her shoes back on again.

'That there are still people living like that in Sweden today,' she says. 'Completely shut off from everything. It's anachronistic in an almost bizarre way.'

'I don't know about that,' Zeke says. Then he reaches for the first explanation that seems to come into his mind. 'It's benefits,' he says. 'It's all because of bloody benefits. I bet the whole lot of them are getting unemployment benefit, social support and everything else too. And the child support for a horde of kids like that must amount to a small fortune every month.'

'I'm not so sure about benefits,' Malin says. 'Maybe they don't get anything. But anyway. This is the twenty-first century. In Sweden. And here's a family that seems to live entirely according to its own rules.'

'They muck about with engines and hunt and fish while we work our backsides off. Do you expect me to feel any sympathy for them?'

'Maybe for the children. Who knows what their lives are like?'

Zeke stands still, evidently thinking.

'Living outside society isn't that unusual, Malin. In fact it isn't even anachronistic. Look at those people in Borlänge, Knutby, Sheike, and half of sodding Norrland. They're all around us, and as long as they don't upset the consensus too much, no one cares. Let them live their miserable lives in peace, and everyone else can live a normal life. The poor, the mad, the immigrants, the handicapped. No one cares, Malin. Except to get validation of the normality of their own lives. And who are we anyway to have opinions about how other people choose to live? It might be more fun than we think.'

'I don't want to think that,' Malin says. 'At any rate, as far as Bengt Andersson is concerned, they've got a motive.'

They head off towards the car.

'Nice sort of people, anyway, the Murvalls,' Zeke says as he turns the key in the ignition.

'You could see the fury in Adam Murvall's eyes,' Malin says.

'There are several of them, they could have done it together. And shooting at his window with rubber bullets? No problem for gentlemen like them. We'll have to get a warrant so we can check their guns. But they may have more without licences. I dare say they've got the contacts to get hold of weapons and ammunition.'

'Do you really think we've got enough evidence to get a warrant? There's not really anything concrete, in legal terms, to suggest that they might be involved.'

'Maybe not. We'll have to see what Sjöman says.'

'He was so incredibly angry. Adam Murvall.'

'Imagine it was your sister, Malin, wouldn't that make you angry?'

'I haven't got any brothers or sisters,' Malin says. Then she adds, 'I would have been livid.'

31

From a distance, and seen from above like this, Lake Roxen looks like a flattened greyish-white eiderdown. The trees and shrubs, almost tremulous, are pressed down along the edge of the lake, and the fields in front of it, cropped, wind-blasted, wait for a warmth that it is hard to believe will ever come.

White bricks and brown woodwork, stacked boxes in the best tradition of the 1970s, four privileged dwellings gathered together on a hillside above a steep slope.

They have knocked on the door with the lion's head, polished jaws gaping open.

The first time they spoke to Fredrik Unning, Malin was convinced he had something to say that he was frightened to come out with, and now she's certain, and with every step she takes towards the house expectation grows within her.

What is hidden in here?

They will have to be careful. Zeke beside her is restless, his breath misting from his mouth, his head bare, open for the cold to dig its stubby, infected claws into.

Rattling behind the door.

A crack that widens to an opening with Fredrik Unning's thirteen-year-old face behind it, his slightly pudgy, unexercised body in a light blue Carhartt T-shirt and grey army-style trainers.

'You've been ages,' he says. 'I thought you were coming straight away.'

If only you knew, Malin thinks, how well you've just summarised what a lot of people think about the police, Fredrik.

'Can we come in?' Zeke asks.

★

Fredrik Unning's room is on the third floor of the house. The walls are covered in skateboarding posters. Bam Margera from *Jackass* hangs in the air high above a concrete ramp, and on a reproduction of a vintage poster a young Tony Alva glides along a Los Angeles backstreet. Thin white curtains shield the view out of windows that stretch from floor to ceiling, and the pink carpet is stained in places. In one corner is a stereo that looks new, a floor-mounted flat-screen television with at least a forty-five-inch screen.

Fredrik Unning sits on the edge of the bed, focused on them this time, his previous nonchalance vanished, and gone too are his parents; his insurance broker father has taken his boutique manager wife on a little trip to Paris. 'They go there every now and then. Mum likes shopping and Dad likes the food. It's nice to be on my own.'

Empty pizza boxes in the kitchen, half-eaten Gorby pies, fizzy-drink bottles and an overflowing bag of rubbish in the middle of the floor.

Malin is next to Fredrik Unning on the bed, Zeke by the biggest window in the room, a dark silhouette against the light.

'Do you know anything about Bengt Andersson that we ought to know?'

'If I tell you anything, no one else will find out that I was the one who told you, will they?'

'No,' Malin says, and Zeke nods in agreement, adding, 'This will stay between us. No one will know where the information came from.'

'They never left him alone,' Fredrik Unning says, staring at the curtains. 'They were always getting at him. It was like an obsession.'

'Getting at Bengt Andersson?' Zeke over by the window. 'Who was getting at him?'

And Fredrik Unning gets scared again, his body slumps, moves away from Malin and she thinks how fear has become increasingly common around her over the years, how person after person seems to have understood that silence is always safest, that every word uttered carries the potential for danger. And maybe they're right.

'Bengt,' Fredrik Unning says.

'Who? It's okay,' Malin says. 'You can do it.'

And her words help Fredrik to relax.

'Jocke and Jimmy. They were always making fun of him, Ball-Bengt.'

'Jocke and Jimmy?'

'Yes.'

'What are their real names? Jocke and Jimmy?'

Fresh hesitation. Fresh fear.

'We need to know.'

'Joakim Svensson and Jimmy Kalmvik.' Fredrik Unning says their names in a firm voice.

'And who are they?'

'They're in year nine in my school, they're real bastards. Big and mean.'

Shouldn't you be at school now? Malin thinks, but she doesn't ask.

'What did they do to Ball-Bengt?'

'They used to follow him, tease him, shout things at him. And I think they messed up his bike, and threw things at him, stones and stuff. I think they might even have poured some sort of sludge through his letterbox.'

'Sludge?' Zeke asking.

'Flour, dirt, water, ketchup, anything, all mixed together.'

'And how do you know this?'

'They forced me to join in sometimes. Otherwise I'd get beaten up.'

'Did you get beaten up?'

Shame in Fredrik Unning's eyes, fear: 'They won't find out that I've told you, will they? The bastards torture cats as well.'

'In what way?'

'They catch them and stick mustard up their backsides.'

Brave lads, Malin thinks.

'Have you seen them do that?'

'No, but I've heard it from other people.'

Zeke from the window, his voice like the crack of a whip.

'Might they have shot through his window with a rifle? Did you join in with that as well?'

Fredrik Unning shakes his head. 'I've never done anything like that. Anyway, where would they get the gun from?'

Outside the clouds have thinned slightly, and through a few cracks some tentative rays of light are spreading across the greyish-white ground, making it clear and vibrant, and in her mind's eye Malin can see what the Roxen must look like in summer from up here, in warm light, when the rays have full access to a completely blank surface. But sadly a winter like this one doesn't make it easy to think of warmth.

'Bloody hell,' Zeke says. 'Those two sound pretty tough, Jocke and Jimmy. Serious hard cases.'

'I feel sorry for Fredrik Unning,' Malin says.

'Sorry for him?'

'You must have noticed how lonely he is? He must have been prepared to do anything to hang out with the tough kids.'

'So they didn't force him?'

'I don't doubt that they did. But it's not that simple.'

'It doesn't sound like they come from bad backgrounds.'

Fredrik Unning's words a short while before: 'Jimmy's dad works on oil platforms and his mum's a housewife. Jocke's dad's dead and his mum works as a secretary.'

Malin's phone rings. Sven Sjöman's name on the screen.

'Malin here.'

She tells him about their visit to the Murvalls, and about what they'd learned from Fredrik Unning.

'We're thinking of going to talk to Jimmy Kalmvik and Joakim Svensson right away.'

'We need to have a meeting,' Sven says. 'They'll have to wait an hour or two.'

'But—'

'We've got a team meeting in thirty minutes, Malin.'

★

The children are defying the cold.

The playground outside the windows of the meeting room is full of sluggish little moon-figures staggering about in their padded winter overalls. Blue children, red ones and one little orange warning child: be careful with me, I'm little, I might break. The assistants shiver in grey-blue fleece trousers, their breath like thick smoke. They jump on the spot when they're not helping some little one who's fallen over, flapping their arms round their bodies.

If this cold doesn't give up soon, everyone will have to learn how to live with it. Like a broken back.

Börje Svärd's report, people with links to Rickard Skoglöf. Interviews with kids who seem to live out their lives in front of a computer or as characters in role-playing games. 'Anything but real life.'

The hesitation in Börje's body. Malin can see it, smell it. As if all of life had given him just one single lesson: don't take anything for granted.

The results of the background checks.

Rickard Skoglöf seemed to have had a normal upbringing in an ordinary working-class home in Åtvidaberg; his father worked at Facit until it was shut down, then at Adelnäs fruit farm, where his son had also worked during summer holidays when he was at secondary school. Two years in sixth form. Then nothing. Valkyria Karlsson grew up on a farm in Dalsland. She got two-thirds of the way through an anthropology course at Lund University after sixth form in Dals Ed.

Karim Akbar. Also hesitant, but nonetheless: 'This Æsir angle. Keep digging, there's something there.'

His voice a little too confident, as if he were taking on the role of the convinced, encouraging boss.

Johan Jakobsson hollow-eyed. Winter vomiting bug, long nights awake, changed sheets. New wrinkles in his brow every morning, deeper and deeper. *Daddy, where are you? Don't want to, don't want to.*

Malin shuts her eyes. Has no energy for this meeting. Wants

to get out and work. To talk to Ljungsbro's own teenage bullies, see what they know. Maybe they can give them some leads, maybe they got hold of a gun and are responsible for firing into Ball-Bengt's flat, maybe their bad behaviour just got out of hand; who knows what two imaginative fifteen-year-olds are capable of?

Tove and Markus in her parents' apartment.

On the bed.

Malin can see them in front of her.

'And then we have the teenagers who made Bengt Andersson's life a misery,' Sven Sjöman says. 'You and Zeke will have to question them. Get them at school after this meeting. They ought to be there at this time of day.'

Sure, Sven, sure, Malin thinks, then says, 'If they aren't at school we'll find out where they live, and we've got their mobile numbers.'

After the two lads, she wants to bring the Murvall brothers in for questioning, bring the old woman in and put some pressure on her. Listen to the wives.

The brothers.

The looks on the women's faces.

No friendliness, just suspicion against *the stranger*. Alone, even if they stick together.

What is that sort of loneliness? Where does it come from? From the repeated unkindnesses of the world around them? From the fact that they keep getting no as an answer? From everybody. Or is that sort of loneliness granted to each of us? Is it within all of us, and, if it gets the chance to grow, does it simply over-whelm us?

The awareness of loneliness. The fear.

When did I first see that loneliness, that antipathy in Tove's face? When did I first see anything other than pure kindness and joy in her eyes?

She was maybe two and a half. Suddenly there among the innocence and charm was an element of calculation and anxiety. The child had become a human being.

Loneliness. Fear. Most people manage to hold on to some of

the child's joy, the naivety, when they encounter other people, when they feel a sense of belonging. Manage to overcome the possibly innate loneliness. Like Fredrik Unning tried to do today. Reach out a hand, as if he had realised he was worth more than being left to his own devices by his parents and forced to go along with boys who would really rather have nothing to do with him.

Happiness is possible.

Like with Tove. Like with Janne, in spite of everything. Like with myself.

But the women round the Murvall family table? Where did their unadulterated joy disappear to? Where did it go? Can it have run out for good? Could it be true, Malin thinks, as Sven summarises the state of the investigation, that there is only a finite amount of happiness free of guile, and that every time some of that sort of happiness is lost, it is gone for good and replaced instead by muteness, hardness?

And what happens if we are forced to give in to loneliness?

What sort of violence might be born then? In that point of fracture? In that final exclusion?

The child holding out its arms to its mother, to a nursery-school assistant.

Look after me, carry me.

Of course I'll carry you.

I won't just abandon you.

'Mum, I was thinking of staying at Dad's tonight, is that all right?'

Tove's message on her mobile. Malin listens to the message as she walks through the open-plan office.

Malin calls her.

'It's Mum.'

'Mum, you got my message.'

'I got it. It's okay. How are you getting out there?'

'I'll go down to the station. His shift ends at six, so we can head out then.'

'Okay, I'm probably going to be working late anyway.'

Sjöman's words at the meeting: 'I've already called them in for questioning. If the whole Murvall family doesn't turn up here tomorrow, we can go and get them. But we haven't got enough for a search warrant as far as the guns are concerned.'

When she ends the call to Tove, Malin calls Janne. Gets the answering service.

'Is it right that Tove's staying the night at yours? Just checking.'

Then she sits down behind her desk. Waits. Sees Börje Svärd hesitantly twisting the ends of his moustache on the far side of the room.

32

The façade of the main building of Ljungsbro school is matt grey, the low, dark-red-tiled roofs are covered by a thin layer of snow; small swirls of frozen moments, circular patterns etched on to several of the larger surfaces.

They park by the craft rooms, aquariums for handicrafts in a row of single-storey buildings along the road leading into town.

Malin looks into the rooms, empty, with dormant saws, lathes, firing and welding equipment. They walk past what must be a technology room; pulleys and chains hanging from the ceiling, one by one, as if ready for use. When she looks in the other direction she can just make out Vretaliden care home, and in her mind's eye she sees Gottfrid Karlsson sitting in his bed, under an orange health service blanket, quietly driving her on: 'What happened to Bengt Andersson? Who killed him?'

Malin and Zeke walk to the main building, past what must be the school dining room. Inside the frosted windows the staff are scrubbing pans and work surfaces. Zeke pulls open the door of the main entrance, eager to escape the cold, and in the large, airy space some fifty pupils are all talking at once, their breath fogging the windows on to the school grounds.

No one pays any attention to Malin and Zeke, their attention utterly absorbed by the conversations that belong to teenage life.

Tove's world.

This is what it looks like.

Malin notices a thin boy with long black hair and an anxious look, talking to a pretty blonde girl.

On the far side of the room a sign above a glass door announces: Head's Office.

'Vamos,' Zeke says as he catches sight of the sign.

Britta Svedlund, head of Ljungsbro school, has them shown in at once, perhaps the first time the police have been to the school in her time here.

But probably not.

The school is known to be problematic, and every year several of its pupils are sent to reform school, somewhere far out in the countryside, for further education in low-level criminality.

Britta Svedlund crosses her legs, her skirt riding up her thighs, revealing an unusual amount of black nylon, and Malin notes that Zeke has trouble controlling his eyes. He surely can't imagine that the woman in front of them is beautiful, cigarette-wrinkled, worn and grey-haired as she is.

The male curse, Malin thinks, trying to get comfortable on her chair.

The walls of the office are lined with bookcases and reproductions of Bruno Liljefors paintings. The desk is dominated by an antiquated computer.

After listening to Malin and Zeke's explanation of why they are there, Britta Svedlund says, 'They're leaving this spring, Jimmy Kalmvik and Joakim Svensson, Jimmy and Jocke; they've only got a couple of months left and it'll be a relief to be rid of them. Every year we have a few rotten eggs, and we get to send a few of them away. Joakim and Jimmy are craftier than that. But we do what we can with them.'

Malin and Zeke must have succeeded in looking curious, because Britta Svedlund goes on: 'They never do anything illegal, or if they have, they've never been caught. They come from stable backgrounds, which is more than you can say about a lot of pupils at this school. No, what they do is bully people, students and staff alike. And they're competitive. I swear that every lamp that gets broken in this school has been kicked in by them.'

'We'll need their parents' phone numbers,' Zeke says. 'Home addresses.'

Britta Svedlund taps on her keyboard, then writes down their names, addresses and numbers on a piece of paper.

'Here you are,' she says, handing the note to Malin.

'Thanks.'

'And Bengt Andersson?' Zeke asks. 'Do you know about anything they may have done to him?'

Britta Svedlund is suddenly defensive. 'How did you hear about this? I don't doubt that it's correct. But how do you know?'

'I'm afraid we can't tell you that,' Malin replies.

'To be honest, I don't care what they get up to outside these walls. If I cared about what the students get up to in their own time, I'd go mad.'

'So you don't know,' Zeke says.

'Precisely. But what I do know is that they don't play truant more than the exact amount that means they still get their grades, which are actually surprisingly good.'

'Are they at school at the moment?'

Britta Svedlund taps at her keyboard.

'You're in luck. They've just started their woodwork class. They don't usually miss that one.'

Inside the woodwork room there is a smell of fresh sawdust and scorched wood, with a background note of varnish and solvent.

When they walk into the room the teacher, a man in his sixties with a grey cardigan and matching grey beard, leaves one pupil at a lathe and comes over to meet them.

He holds out a hand covered in shavings and sawdust, then pulls it back with a smile, and Malin notices his warm blue eyes, which have evidently not lost their sparkle with age. Instead he raises his hand in a welcoming wave.

'Well,' he says, and Malin picks up a strong smell of coffee and nicotine on his breath, classic teacher's breath. 'We'll have to greet each other like Indians. Mats Bergman, woodwork teacher.

And behind me we have class 9B. I take it you're from the police? Britta called and said you were on your way.'

'That's right,' Malin says.

'So you know who we're looking for. Are they here?' Zeke says.

Mats Bergman nods. 'They're right at the back, in the paint room. They're working on a design for the petrol tank on a moped.'

Behind the teacher Malin can see the paint room. Squeezed into a corner, grey-green tins of paint on shelves behind shabby glass walls, two boys inside. They're sitting down, so Malin can only see their blond hair.

'Are they likely to be a problem?' she wonders.

'Not in here,' Mats Bergman says, smiling again. 'I know they can be rowdy outside, but they behave themselves in here.'

Malin pulls open the door to the glass-box paint room. The boys look up from their stools, their eyes dull at first, then watchful, tense and anxious, and she looks down at them with all the authority she can muster. A red skull painted on a black petrol tank.

Bullies?

Yes.

Shooters?

Possibly.

Murderers?

Who knows? She'll have to leave that question open.

Then the boys get up; they're both well-built, a head taller than her, both dressed in saggy hip-hop-style jeans and hooded jackets with designer logos.

Spotty teenage faces, they're oddly similar in their puppyish look, bony cheeks, noses a bit too big, suggesting nascent lust and an excess of testosterone.

'Who are you?' one of them asks as he gets up.

'Sit down,' Zeke snarls behind her. 'NOW!'

As if hit by a collapsing ceiling he is pressed back down on to the paint-spattered stool again. Zeke shuts the door and they leave a dramatic pause before Malin says, 'I'm Malin Fors, from the police, and this is my colleague Zacharias.'

Malin pulls her ID from the back pocket of her jeans.

She holds it out to the boys, who are now looking even more anxious, as if they're worried that a whole ocean of misdemeanours has caught up with them.

'Bengt Andersson: we know you tormented him, bullied him and made fun of him. We want to know all about that, and what you were doing on the night between last Wednesday and Thursday.'

Terror in the boys' eyes.

'So who's who? Jimmy?'

The one dressed in a blue hoodie nods.

'Okay,' Malin says. 'Start talking.'

The other boy, Joakim Svensson, starts to make excuses. 'What the fuck, we were just having a laugh. Cos he was so fat. Nothing wrong with that.'

Jimmy Kalmvik goes on: 'He was, like, completely fucked up, chasing after balls every match. And he stank. Of piss.'

'And that made it okay for you to torment him?' Malin can't hide the anger in her voice.

'Sure.' Jimmy Kalmvik grins.

'We've got witnesses who say you vandalised Bengt Andersson's home, and that you attacked him with stones and water-bombs. And now he's been found murdered. I can take you in to the station here and now if you don't talk,' Malin says.

She falls silent and lets Zeke continue: 'This is murder. Can you get that into your thick skulls?'

'Okay, okay.'

Jimmy Kalmvik throws out his arms and looks at Joakim Svensson, who nods.

'Attacked him? We threw stones at him, and we cut off the power to his flat, and sure, we put shit through his letterbox, but now he's dead anyway so what does it matter?'

'It might matter a very great deal,' Zeke says in a calm voice. 'What's to say you didn't go too far one day? That you got too close. That there was a fight. And you just happened to kill him? Try to see it from our side, boys. So what were you doing on Wednesday night?'

'How would we have got him out there?' Joakim Svensson says, then goes on: 'We were at Jimmy's, watching a DVD.'

'Yeah, my mum was at her bloke's. Dad's dead so she's got a new one. He's all right.'

'Can anyone confirm that?' Malin asks.

'Yes, we can,' Joakim Svensson says.

'No one else?'

'Do you need anyone else?'

Teenage boys, Malin thinks. They switch between arrogance and fear in a matter of seconds. A dangerous mixture of over-blown self-assurance and doubt. But still: Tove's Markus seemed very different. What would Tove make of these two? They're not exactly heroes in the Jane Austen mould.

'You silly little sod,' Malin says. 'Murder. Got it? Not torturing cats. Of course we need it confirmed, you can be fucking sure of that. What did you watch?'

'*Lords of Dogtown*,' the two boys answer at once. 'Fucking good film,' Jimmy Kalmvik says. 'It's about blokes who are as sound as we are.'

Joakim Svensson grins.

'And we've never tortured any cats, if that's what you think.'

Malin looks over her shoulder.

Outside the lathes and sanders and saws are in action as if nothing has happened. Someone is hammering frenetically at a box-like construction as she turns to face the boys again.

'Have you ever fired a gun at Bengt Andersson's flat?'

'Us? A gun? Where would we have got that from?'

Innocent as lambs.

'Are you interested in the Æsir belief-system?' Zeke asks.

And they both look nonplussed. Stupid, or guilty, impossible to tell which.

'Interested in what?'

'The Æsir belief-system.'

'What the fuck's that?' Jimmy Kalmvik says. 'Believing in *asses*? Yeah, I believe in them.'

Full-blown chauvinist pigs, when they're scarcely out of short trousers. Noisy, rowdy. But dangerous?

'Torturing cats? So he blabbed, Unning,' Jimmy Kalmvik says. 'The little shit. He's so fucking useless.'

Zeke leans over to him, his eyes looking like a snake's. Malin knows what that looks like. She hears his voice, its gruffness as cold as the night approaching outside the windows.

'If you touch Fredrik Unning I will personally see to it that you have to eat your own entrails. Shit and all. Just so you know.'

33

'Yes, she can stay over.'

Janne's text arrives at 20.15. Malin is tired, on her way home in the car from the gym at work, obliged to clear her head after a day full of too much human crap.

They went back to the station after talking to Ljungsbro's bullies, and in the passenger seat beside Zeke she summarised the situation to herself.

Bengt Andersson is teased and bullied and possibly more than that by testosterone-charged little bastards. We'll have to talk to their parents tomorrow. See where it comes from. Nothing to get them on so far. The offences against Bengt Andersson that they admitted to stopped being chargeable with his death, and may have been youthful mischief as much as anything else.

The shots through the living-room window.

Æsir nutters out on the plain. The murder apparently carried out as a heathen ritual.

And then the Murvall family casting its large shadow across the whole investigation. Weapons in a gun cabinet.

Maria Murvall silent and mute, raped. By whom? Bengt?

Malin wanted to answer no to that question. But knew that she couldn't yet close any doors in any direction, to any room. Instead she had to try to get an overview of something impossible to get an overview of. Listen to the voices of the investigation.

What else was still to emerge from the darkness of the plain, the forests?

'Yes . . .'

She sees the first word of the text.

Her concentration leaves the road for a few moments.

Yes.

We made that promise to each other once, Janne, but we didn't manage to find a way through what lay before us. How over-confident can you get?

Malin parks and hurries up to the flat. She fries a couple of eggs, sinks into the sofa and turns on the television. She gets stuck on a programme about some excitable Americans competing to build the most perfect motorbike.

The programme cheers her up in an uncomplicated way, and after a couple of advertising breaks she realises why.

Janne could easily be one of those Americans, happy beyond belief to let go of routine, of his memories, and just devote himself to his real passion.

She sees the bottle of tequila on the table.

How did that get there?

You put it there, Malin, when you cleared the plate and the remains of your eggs.

Amber liquid.

Shall I have a bit?

No.

The motorbike programme is over.

Then the doorbell rings and Malin thinks it must be Daniel Högfeldt, transgressing the final boundary and turning up unannounced, like they were officially in a relationship.

Hardly, Daniel. But maybe.

Malin goes out into the hall and pulls open the door without checking through the peephole. 'Daniel, you bastard . . .'

No.

Not Daniel.

Instead a man with blue-black eyes, a smell of engine oil, grease and sweat and aftershave. Burning eyes. They are screaming, almost in a fury, at her.

He stands outside the door. Malin looks into him: anger, despair, violence? He's so much bigger than he was in the kitchen. What the hell is he doing here? Zeke, you should be here now. Does he want to come in?

Her stomach clenches, she feels scared, in a fraction of a second she starts to tremble, invisibly. His eyes. The door, have to shut the door, nothing puppyish about this man's determination.

She slams the door, but no, a heavy black boot in the gap, a fucking boot. Hit it, kick it, stamp on it, but the steel toe-cap makes her stockinged feet useless, and the naked pain is hers instead.

He's strong. He puts his hands in the gap and starts to push the door open.

No idea to try and stop him.

Maria Murvall. Is the same thing happening to me?

Scared.

A thought more than a feeling now.

Adam Murvall.

Did you hurt your sister? Is that where the look in your eyes comes from? Is that why you got so angry today?

Nothing but fear. Force it aside.

Where's my jacket, with my pistol? But he's just staring at me, smiling, leering, and then he stares again, confused, pulls his foot back, doesn't force his way in, pulls his hands back, turns and leaves as quickly as he must have come.

Shit.

Her hands are shaking, her body twitchy with adrenalin, her heart racing.

Malin looks out into the stairwell. There's a note on the stone steps, shaky handwriting: *Let Murvall rest. You should leave us the fuck alone.*

As if all this were a steak, or dough, or a tired old man. Then a vague threat. You should . . .

Now Malin feels it again, the fear, it bubbles up as the adrenalin runs out of her body and fear becomes terror, and fast, shallow breathing takes over. *What if Tove had been at home?* Then the anger of terror.

How the hell could he be so fucking stupid?

The man outside the door.

He could have taken me, just like that. Broken me.

I was alone.

She goes back to the sofa. Sinks down. Resists the temptation to drink tequila. Five minutes pass, ten, maybe half an hour before she pulls herself together and calls Zeke.

'He's just been here.'

'Who?'

Suddenly Malin can't say his name.

'The one with blue-black eyes.'

'Adam Murvall? Do you want a patrol?'

'No, for heaven's sake. He's gone.'

'Fuck, Malin. Fuck. What did he do?'

'I think you could say that he threatened me.'

'We'll pick him up at once. Come in as soon as you're ready to. Or do you want me to come and pick you up?'

'I'll be fine on my own, thanks.'

Three cars with blue lights, two more than just a few hours ago. Adam Murvall sees them through the window, they stop outside his house; he makes himself ready, knows why they have come, why he did what he did.

'You have to say no.'

And a thousand other things. Little sister, big brother, events in the forest; if you persuade yourself of one truth, perhaps a different truth doesn't exist?

'Go and pay a visit to that female pig, Adam. Give her the note, then leave.'

'Mother, I . . .'

'Go.'

The doorbell rings. Upstairs Anna and the children are asleep, his brothers sleeping in their own houses. Four uniformed officers outside the door.

'Can I put my jacket on?'

'Are you arguing with us, you bastard?'

And the police are on him, he's fighting for breath on the floor, they force him down and Anna and the children are standing on the stairs, screaming and shouting, Daddy, Daddy, Daddy.

In the yard other policemen are holding his brothers back as they lead him like a chained wild dog to the waiting van.

Further off, in the illuminated window, stands Mother. He sees her, in spite of his bowed, stiff back.

34

The cold eats up the last of the anxiety and fear, and the effects of adrenalin have already worn off. The closer Malin gets to Police Headquarters, the more prepared she feels to face Adam Murvall now, and the other brothers tomorrow. Because however much they may want to live outside society, they have stepped into it now, and after that step there is no return, if there ever was.

When Malin walks past the old fire station, she comes to think of her mum and dad, without knowing quite why. How she gradually realised that her mother was always trying to make their home seem smarter than it was, but that the few trained eyes that set foot over their threshold must have realised that the rugs were of low quality, that the prints on the walls came from vast print-runs, that the whole décor was an attempt to appear significant. Unless it was something else?

Maybe I should ask you next time we meet, Mum? But you'd probably just push my question aside, even if you doubtless understood what I meant.

'What an idiot,' Zeke says.

Malin hangs her jacket on the back of the chair behind her desk, and the whole station is breathing expectation, and the smell of freshly brewed coffee is noticeable the way it usually is only in the mornings.

'Not too smart, was it?'

'Well, I'm not so sure,' Malin says.

'What do you mean?'

'They're the ones setting the pace here. Have you thought about that?'

Zeke shakes his head. 'Don't make things more complicated than they already are. Are you okay?'

'Oh, I'll be fine.'

Two uniformed male officers come in from the staffroom, their cheeks glowing with warm coffee.

'Martinsson,' one of them calls. 'Is your lad going to get a few goals against Modo?'

'He was bloody good against Färjestad,' the other one says.

Zeke ignores them, pretending that he's busy, hasn't heard.

Karim Akbar comes to Zeke's rescue. Stops alongside him and Malin.

'We're bringing him in,' Karim says. 'Sjöman has arranged for the van to pick him up. They ought to be here any minute.'

'What can we hold him on?' Malin wonders.

'Threatening a police officer in her own home.'

'He rang on my door, and left a note.'

'Have you got the note?'

'Of course.'

Malin digs in her jacket pocket, pulls out the folded sheet of paper, holds it out to Karim, who carefully unfolds it and reads.

'No problem,' he says. 'An obvious case of obstructing a criminal investigation, on the verge of threatening behaviour.'

'It is,' Zeke says.

'This is directed at you personally, Malin. Any idea why?'

Malin sighs. 'Because I'm a woman. I think it's as simple as that. Have a go at the easily scared woman. Tiresome.'

'Prejudice is always tiresome,' Karim says. 'It couldn't be anything else?'

'Not that I can think of.'

'Where's Sjöman?' Zeke asks.

'On his way in.'

A commotion over in reception.

Are they coming now? No, no flashing lights outside.

Then she sees him: Daniel Högfeldt, gesticulating, talking non-stop, but nothing can be heard through the bulletproof, sound-proofed pane of glass between the open-plan office and reception, just a familiar face, a figure in a leather jacket who wants something, knows something, looks serious but who somehow always seems to be playing a game.

Alongside Daniel is the young photographer. She is taking picture after picture of Ebba the receptionist, and Malin wonders if her nose-ring could ever get caught in the camera, if her rasta plaits ever get in the way of the lens. Börje Svärd is trying to calm Daniel down, then he just shakes his head in resignation and walks away.

Daniel glances in Malin's direction. Self-satisfaction washes across his face. Possibly also longing? Playfulness? Impossible to tell.

Fixed expression, Malin thinks.

'Meet the press,' Karim says, smiling at her as the skin on his face seems to change and become entirely new. Then he adds, 'By the way, Malin. You look like it's all getting to you. Is everything okay?'

'Getting to me? You'd never say that to a male colleague,' Malin says and turns towards her computer, trying to look busy.

Karim smiles again. 'But Fors, it was just an innocent remark, no harm intended.'

Börje comes over to them. A look of faint amusement on his face, like someone who knows something no one else does, but isn't telling.

'The pride of the press corps. He wanted to know if Adam Murvall is suspected of the murder, or if we're bringing him in for something else. He got angry when I said, "No comment."'

'Don't annoy the press for no reason,' Karim says. 'They're bad enough as it is.' Then: 'How does he know we've got something going on right now?'

'Eight police, eight mobile phones,' Zeke says.

'Plus ten others,' Malin says.

'Plus ridiculously low wages,' Karim adds, before leaving them and heading off towards Daniel.

'What was that about?' Börje says. 'An attempt to show solidarity with the foot soldiers?'

'Who knows?' Zeke says. 'Maybe he's had an epiphany that's gone beyond getting his own face noticed.'

'He's okay,' Malin says. 'Stop mucking about.'

Then blue lights do start to flash urgently outside the entrance and soon their gym-pumped colleagues are opening the doors of the white police van.

Muscles.

Iron fists on Adam Murvall's upper arms, bent back and up, the metal of the handcuffs cutting into his wrists, then a jerk, and his body leans forward instinctively to protect itself. His head is bent downwards, and their blue-clad legs, black boots and the magnetic blue light make the snow-covered tarmac look like a star-studded sky. Camera flashes. Automatic doors opening. One sort of cold exchanged for another.

A shrill voice, woman or man?

'Adam Murvall, do you know why you've been arrested?'

Do you think I'm stupid?

Then another door, a blue and beige pattern under his feet, voices, faces, the young girl, a couple of moustaches.

'Take him into the interview room right away.'

'Which one?'

'One.'

'We're waiting for Sjöman.'

A firm male voice. He probably thinks his accent can't be heard. But he's just a fucking coon.

Through the window of the interview room Malin sees Sven Sjöman turn on the tape recorder, she hears him give the date and time and his own name and the name of the person being questioned and the case number.

She sees Sjöman sit down on the black-lacquered metal chair.

The room.

Four metres by four.

Grey walls covered in perforated acoustic panels. A large mirror that doesn't fool anyone: behind that mirror I'm being watched.

The ceiling is painted black with recessed halogen spots. Confidences are built up, broken, guilt is allocated, admitted. The truth will out, and the truth needs silence and calm.

No one is calmer than Sven.

He has the gift.

The ability to get strangers to feel trust, to make a friend of someone who is an enemy. Briefed: 'What's it like where they live? Inside their homes? Details, give me details!'

On the other side of the table: Adam Murvall.

Calm.

Hands in handcuffs in front of him on the polished silver tabletop, the beginnings of bruises just above the metal rings. In the relative gloom the colour of his eyes fades and for the first time Malin notices his nose, how it sticks out tentatively at the root, then juts out in a sharp tip before easing into two flared nostrils.

Not really a peasant's nose.

Not a tap, as they say on the plain.

'So, Adam,' Sven says. 'You couldn't help yourself?'

Adam Murvall's face doesn't move an inch, he just shifts his hands, making a shrieking sound of metal on metal.

'We don't have to talk about that now. And not about your sister either. We can talk about cars, if you'd rather.'

'We don't have to talk at all,' Adam Murvall says.

Sven leans forward over the table. With a voice that is the very essence of friendliness and confidence he says, 'Come on, tell me a bit about all those cars you've got at home in your gardens. I dare say you get quite a bit of money from breaking them apart?'

35

Vanity, Malin. Find a way into their stories through vanity. Then they'll open up, and once they've opened up things usually turn out okay.

Sven Sjöman.

A master at coaxing, at getting people to talk.

Adam Murvall thinks that this policeman has been at it for a long time, but not long in this city, because then he should have remembered me. Because he couldn't have forgotten me. They usually never forget. Or is he pretending? Now they're standing behind the mirror, staring at me; fine, go on staring, what do I care? You think I'm going to talk, but how can you even think that? Don't bother with the cars, but, sure, if you're wondering about the cars I can always talk about them; what's so secret about the cars?

Adam reluctantly feels his antipathy slip a little.

'You weren't here ten years ago,' Adam Murvall says. 'Where were you then?'

'Believe me,' Sven says, 'my career is very dull. Ten years ago I was a detective inspector in Karlstad, but then the wife got a job here and I had to make the best of it.'

Adam Murvall nods and Malin can see he's happy with the answer. Why does he care about Sjöman's CV? Then it hits Malin: if Sjöman had been here for a while, he ought to have remembered the brothers.

Vanity, Malin, vanity.

'What about the cars, then?'

'Them? They're just something we do.'

Adam Murvall sounds confident, his voice a well-oiled engine.

'We take them apart and sell the good bits.'

'Is that all you live off?'

'We've got the petrol station as well. The one on the road down by the aqueduct. The Preem garage.'

'And you make a living from that?'

'More or less.'

'Did you know Bengt Andersson?'

'I knew who he was. Everybody knew that.'

'Do you think he had anything to do with the rape of your sister?'

'Shut up about that. Don't talk about it.'

'I have to ask, Adam, you know that.'

'Don't talk about Maria, her name shouldn't be grunted by your sort.'

Sven makes himself comfortable, nothing in his body language giving any indication that he's remotely upset by the insult.

'Are you and your sister close? I've heard that you're the one who visits her.'

'Don't talk about Maria. Leave her in peace.'

'So that was why you wrote the note?'

'This is nothing to do with you. We'll sort this out ourselves.'

'And what were you doing on the night between Wednesday and Thursday?'

'We ate dinner at Mother's. Then I went home with my family.'

'So that's what you did? You didn't hang Bengt up in that tree, then? Did you sort that out yourselves as well?'

Adam shakes his head. 'Pig.'

'Who? Me or Bengt? And was it you or one of your brothers who shot through the window into his living room? Did you creep down there one evening, just like you crept to Inspector Fors's flat tonight? To leave a message?'

'I don't know anything about any shots through any damn windows. I'm not saying anything else now. You can keep on all night. From now on I'm saying nothing.'

'Like your sister?'

'What do you know about my sister?'

'I know she was kind-hearted. Everyone says so.'

The muscles of Adam Murvall's face relax slightly.

'You know things don't look good for you, don't you? Threatening an officer, resisting arrest, obstructing an investigation. With your background, those are pretty serious charges.'

'I didn't threaten anyone. I was just handing over a letter.'

'I know how angry you can get, Adam. Were you angry with that repulsive fat Bengt? The man who raped your sister? The man who ruined her kind heart? Well? Adam? Did you hang—'

'I should have.'

'So you—'

'You think you know it all.'

'What is it I don't know?'

'Go to hell.' Adam Murvall whispers the words, before he slowly puts his finger in front of his mouth.

Sven turns off the tape recorder, gets up. He walks out of the room, leaving Adam Murvall alone behind him. He sits improbably straight-backed, as if his spine were one single beam made of steel, impossible to bend.

'What do you think?' Sven Sjöman looks round at them.

Karin Akbar watchful by the door.

'There's something that doesn't fit,' Malin says. 'Something.' But her brain can't work out what.

'He's not denying it,' Johan Jakobsson says.

'They're hard men,' Zeke says. 'Deny, admit? Never, either one would be giving in. It just isn't an option for people like them.'

'Sven's decided to hold him. We'll stick him in our coldest cell tonight, see if that softens him up,' Karim says, and the group falls silent; no one knows if he's serious or just joking.

'That was a joke,' he says. 'What did you think? That I was going to turn this station into some Kurdish hellhole?'

Karim laughs. The others smile.

The clock on the viewing-room wall. The black hands indicate twenty past eleven.

'I think,' Malin says, 'that it might be worth talking to the whole Murvall family. That's what I think. Tomorrow.'

'We can hold him for a week. The brothers and mother are due in tomorrow. We can bring the wives in as well.'

Behind the soundproofed glass Malin watches as two uniformed custody officers lead Adam Murvall out of the interview room, off to a cell in the detention unit.

The sky is crystal clear.

The Milky Way is smiling at humanity; the far-travelled light is dim yet simultaneously comforting and warm.

Malin is standing with Zeke in the car park, beside the black Mercedes belonging to Karim Akbar.

Almost midnight.

He is smoking one of his rare cigarettes. His fingers look like they're turning blue with the cold, but it doesn't seem to bother him.

'You should take it a bit easier, Fors.'

The light from the stars fades.

'A bit easier with what?'

'With everything.'

'Everything?'

'Just come down a gear or two, slow down.'

Malin stands still, waiting for the warmth of the moment to reappear, but it's taking its time, it's never going to come.

Zeke puts out his cigarette, hunts for his car keys.

'Do you want a lift?'

'No, I'll walk,' Malin says. 'I need a bit of fresh air.'

Adam Murvall lies on his bunk in the police station, the blanket pulled round his muscular frame, and thinks of the words Blackie always used to say, over and over again like a mantra, when he used to sit drunk in his wheelchair in the kitchen.

The day you give in it's over. Over, got it?

Blackie gave in. And he never even realised.

Then Adam Murvall thinks of Mother, of how she can rely on him like he has always been able to rely on her. She has somehow always stood like a wall between them and all the bastards.

Adam isn't the sort who'd talk, and the children, they must be asleep by now, even if it took Anna a long time to get them off.

Adam Murvall sees seven-year-old Anneli's thin ribcage rise and fall, he sees three-year-old Tobias's wavy blond hair against a sheet with its pattern of blue sailing-boats, and he sees the little eight-month-old lad on his back in his cot. Then Adam falls asleep, dreaming about a dog standing outside a door in the middle of winter. It's a crystal-clear night and the dog is barking so loudly that the rusty nails holding the door together shake. And Adam dreams that he is sitting at a nicely laid table in the kitchen of a big white house, and that a hand covered in the finest little veins pulls a leg off one of the roast chickens on the table, and how the same hand throws the leg out through the window to the dog.

He is still standing in the snow and barking.

The chicken leg makes him quiet.

Then the barking starts again.

A voice now: Let me in.

Don't leave me out here.

I'm freezing.

36

It is no bad dream.

It is just how it is.

Janne is walking up and down in the living room. The young boys from the refugee camp in Kigali came to him again tonight, just now. They were carrying their hacked-off feet on their upturned hands, approaching his bed with them like bloody trophies. The dark red blood dripped on to his sheets, steaming and smelling freshly of iron.

He woke up in a soaking wet bed.

Sweat.

As usual.

It's as if his body remembers the humid nights in the jungle and is adapting itself to the memory rather than the present.

He creeps upstairs and peers into Tove's room. She's asleep inside, safe in the warm.

Markus is asleep in the guest room. He seems an okay kid, from what Janne could tell during their short meal, before Tove and Markus disappeared into Tove's room.

He hadn't said anything to Malin about Markus staying over. She didn't seem to know, though he would always be able to say that he assumed she did. She would protest, but that's okay, Janne thinks, as he creeps back downstairs again. Better that we keep an eye on them than the alternative, so they don't have to sneak into his father-in-law's flat.

His father-in-law?

Did I just think that?

But I did phone Markus's dad to make sure it was okay with them.

He seemed friendly. Not full of himself like a lot of the doctors you run into at the hospital when you show up with an ambulance.

In the morning the Murvall family reports at Police Headquarters.

They arrive in the green Range Rover and a Peugeot minibus soon after eight.

The sun made the vehicles' paint shine, as they spewed out people, as Malin thought it looked.

The Murvall clan: men, women, child after child besieging the foyer of Police Headquarters.

Restless chatter.

People on the fault-line.

Waiting not to do what the authorities asked of them: talk. A conscious mix of obstinacy and resignation in every movement, every expression, every blink. Shabby clothes, faded jeans, jumpers and jackets in shrill, unfashionable colours, all thrown together, dirt, stains, children's snot as the glue holding it all together.

'Gypsies,' Börje Svärd whispered in Malin's ear as they looked out on the scene from the office. 'They're like a band of gypsies.'

In the middle of the group sat the mother.

Somehow alone among all the others.

'You have a fine family,' Sven Sjöman says, drumming his fingers on the table of the interview room.

'We stick together,' the mother states. 'Like in the old days.'

'That's unusual these days.'

'Yes, but we stick together.'

'And you have a lot of fine grandchildren, Mrs Murvall.'

'Nine in total.'

'It could have been more, perhaps. If Maria hadn't—'

'Maria? What do you want with her?'

'What were you doing on the night between Wednesday and Thursday last week?'

'Sleeping. That's what an old woman does at nights.'

'And your sons?'

'The boys? As far as I know, they were sleeping too.'

'Did you know Bengt Andersson, Mrs Murvall?'

'Bengt who, Inspector? I've read about him in the paper, if you mean the man they hung in the tree.'

'They?'

'Yes, I read that there was probably more than one of them.'

'Like your sons.'

Malin looks into Sofia Murvall's eyes. The bags beneath them hang way down on to her cheeks but her brown hair looks freshly washed, tied up in a neat ponytail at the back of her head. The meeting room is acting as an interview room.

Wife of Jakob, the middle brother. Four children, seven months to ten years. Exhausted from nursing, from sleepless nights, worn down to the bone.

'Four children,' Malin says. 'You should count yourself lucky. I only got one.'

'Can I smoke in here?'

'Sorry, no. They're very tough on that. But maybe I could make an exception, just this once,' Malin says, and pushes her empty coffee cup across the table. 'Use that as an ashtray.'

Sofia Murvall digs in the pockets of her grey hooded jacket, pulls out a packet of Blend Menthol and a free lighter from a haulage company. She lights a cigarette and the sweet, mint-like smell makes Malin feel sick, and she makes an effort to smile.

'It must be tough out there on the plain.'

'It isn't always fun,' Sofia Murvall says. 'But who says it has to be fun all the time?'

'How did you and Jakob meet?'

Sofia looks over her shoulder, takes a drag on the cigarette.

'That's nothing to do with you.'

'Are the two of you happy?'

'Really, really happy.'

'Even after what happened to Maria?'

'That didn't make any difference.'

'I can't really believe that,' Malin says. 'Jakob and his brothers must have been incredibly frustrated.'

'They looked after their sister, if that's what you mean, and now they're doing it again.'

'Did they take care of the person they thought did it as well? When they strung up Bengt Andersson in the tree?'

There's a knock on the door of the room.

'Come in!' Malin calls, and a newly recruited police constable called Sara looks through a gap in the door.

'There's a little boy crying out here. They're saying he needs feeding. Is that okay?'

The expression on Sofia Murvall's face doesn't change.

Malin nods.

The woman who must be Adam Murvall's wife carries in a fat, screaming baby and puts him in Sofia's arms. The boy opens his mouth wide and scrambles towards the nearest nipple, and Sofia Murvall puts out her cigarette and the hoodie goes up, revealing a bare breast, a pink nipple that the boy stretches out for and catches.

Do you appreciate your happiness? Do you feel it?

Sofia strokes the boy's head.

'Are you hungry, darling?' Then: 'Jakob couldn't have had anything to do with that. It's impossible. He's been asleep at home every single night, and he spends every day in the workshop. I can see him from the kitchen window whenever I look out.'

'And your mother-in-law. Do you get on well with her?'

'Yes,' Sofia Murvall says. 'You won't find a better person.'

Elias Murvall is shut off, his memories a clamped clam-shell.

'I'm not saying anything. I stopped talking to the police fifteen years ago.'

Sven Sjöman's voice: 'Oh, we're not that bad, are we, especially for a tough guy like you?'

'If I don't say anything, how will you find out what I have or haven't done? Do you really think I'm so weak that I'm going to give in to you?'

'That's just it,' Sven says. 'We don't think you're weak. But if you don't say anything, things get difficult for us. Do you want things to be difficult for us?'

'What do you think?'

'Was it you who shot . . .?'

Elias Murvall's mouth is sealed with invisible surgical thread, his tongue limp, slack in his mouth. The room is silent, apart from the sound of the air-conditioning.

From her place in the observation room Malin can't hear the noise, but she knows it's there, a gentle mechanical hum: fresh air for people trapped indoors.

Jakob Murvall laughs at the question: 'You think we had anything to do with that? You're crazy, we're law-abiding citizens now, we've kept quiet, within the bounds of the law. We're just ordinary car mechanics.'

Börje Svärd: 'Okay, what do you say about the rumours that you threatened anyone making an offer on houses for sale in Blåsvädret, that you threatened the estate agents?'

'Rumours. That's our stamping ground, and if we put in the highest bid, we get to buy, don't we?'

'The night between Wednesday and Thursday? I was in bed asleep next to my wife. Well, I wasn't asleep all night, but I was there in bed, with my wife.'

'Maria. You don't even have the right to say her name. Got that, you fucking pig? Bengt Andersson . . . Maria . . . Ball-Bengt, that fucking abortion, she should have stayed away from him . . .'

Jakob Murvall stands up forcefully.

Then a male body collapsing, muscles losing all their strength.

'She looked after him. She's the gentlest, warmest person God ever blessed this fucking planet with. She was only looking after him a bit, can't you understand that, you fucking pig? That's what she's like. No one can stop her. And if he thanked her by doing that in the forest, he deserved to die, and to go straight back down to hell.'

'But you didn't do it?'

'What do you think, pig? What do you think?'

37

An army on the retreat, Malin thinks.

The Murvall clan is evacuating the foyer of Police Headquarters, taking their places in their vehicles, shivering in the cold.

Elias and Jakob help their mother up into the front seat of the minibus, but surely the old woman could manage on her own?

A minute ago she was standing in the entrance, a shawl round her head, eyes open so wide they threatened to fly out of their sockets.

She was shouting at Karim Akbar.

'I'm taking my son Adam home with me.'

'The officer in charge of the preliminary investigation—'

Karim was nonplussed by the old woman's outburst, as sudden as it was taboo. He had been brought up to respect the elderly.

'He's coming home. Now.'

The rest of the family like a wall behind her, Adam's wife at the front, the children around her, snuffling.

'But—'

'Well, I want to see him, at least.'

'Mrs Murvall, your son can't have any visitors. The officer in charge of the preliminary investigation, Sven Sjöman—'

'The officer in charge of the preliminary investigation can go to hell. I'm seeing my boy. And that's that.'

Then a smile that quickly became a grimace, her false teeth unnaturally white.

Defiance as theatre, as a game.

'I'll see what I can—'

'You can't do a thing, can you?' And with that Rakel Murvall turned, raised one arm in the air and the retreat began.

The clock on the foyer wall says 14.50.

The meeting room. Too cold to open a window to remove the residual stink of menthol cigarettes.

'Lisbeth Murvall is providing an alibi for her husband, Elias,' Malin says.

'They're all giving alibis to each other,' Zeke says. 'One way or another.'

Johan Jakobsson: 'And they don't seem to have any connection to Bengt Andersson other than the fact that he was their sister's client and figured in the investigation into her rape.'

'We still ought to organise a search warrant for Blåsvädret,' Sven Sjöman says. 'I want to know what they've got in those houses.'

'Have we got enough for that?' Karim Akbar, hesitant. 'A motive, a few suspicions. That's all we've got.'

'I know what we have and haven't got. But it's enough.'

'We're only going to take a look,' Börje Svärd says. 'It won't be too bad. Will it?'

Only your world turned upside down, Malin thinks. Otherwise not too bad. Says, 'Sort out the warrants.'

'Okay,' Karim says.

'I want to talk to Joakim Svensson's and Jimmy Kalmvik's parents,' Malin says. 'Someone has to confirm what they were doing on Wednesday evening, and maybe we can find out more about how they used to torment Bengt Andersson.'

'The shots,' Zeke says. 'We still don't know who fired those shots.'

'Okay, this is what we do,' Sven says. 'First the search of Blåsvädret. Then you can talk to the boys' parents.'

Malin nods, thinking that they're going to need as much manpower as possible out in Blåsvädret. Who knows what those nutters might do.

Then she hears Fredrik Unning's frightened voice: 'This will

stay between us . . .' and she thinks back to her wretched responsibility to push that line of investigation as far as she can.

'Well, off to Blåsvädret,' Johan says, getting up.

'If you dredge the shit properly, something always comes up,'
Börje says.

Shit? You know quite a bit about that, don't you, Börje?

*You've been in the shit when you lie awake next to your wife,
listening to how hard it is for her to breathe, when her withering
diaphragm can hardly lift her lungs.*

*You've felt it cover you, the suction pipe between your fingers at
night in a dimly lit bedroom when she wants you to take care of her,
not one of the nameless carers.*

*Yes, you know a whole lot about shit, Börje, but you also know
that there are other things besides that.*

*In your own way you've been waiting for balls to fly over the fence
so you can throw them back. But no one has ever laughed at you.*

*You've never had to be really, really hungry, Börje. Really lonely.
Dangerously lonely. So lonely that you smash a freshly sharpened axe
into your father's head.*

*I drift across the plain, getting closer to Blåsvädret. From up here
the little cluster of houses looks like tiny black spots on an endless
white canvas, the tree where I hung a smudge of ash ten kilometres
or so to the west. I sink lower, see the cars, the freezing police officers,
how the Murvalls have gathered together in the kitchen in Rakel's
house, hear their curses, ill-contained anger. Do you understand the
principle of the pressure-cooker, the uncooled reactor that explodes?
Violence can only be contained for so long, and you are treading on
that fault-line. Do you imagine that four uniformed officers outside
their door can hold violence in?*

In the workshop, the largest, the big white-brick building.

*Malin and Zacharias, that's his name, open the door to one of the
inner rooms. It's cold in there, just ten degrees, but you can still smell
the smell.*

Vanity has driven you here.

Or curiosity?

Or perhaps absolution, Malin?

You will wonder why the Murvalls didn't clean up better, and your wondering will sow seeds of doubt within you. What is this? What animal doesn't buckle in the end?

You will see the chains hanging from the ceiling, the pulleys that help people lift heavier weights than they could otherwise lift to the roof, to the sky.

You will see clotted remnants.

Feel the smell.

And then you will start to realise.

'Do you see that, Zeke?'

'I see it. And I'm getting the smell as well.'

The stench of engine oil that dominated the first big room of the workshop seems to have been blown away in this inner room.

'Light, we need more light.'

The huge sliding iron doors separating the rooms have only just slid apart, easily and well-lubricated. You don't feel their weight, Malin thought, noting the wheel marks leading right up to the doors.

The realm of ease: a well-lubricated sliding door.

And then the windowless room. The concrete floor stained, the chains hanging motionless from the beams in the roof, but which still sound like rattlesnakes, the pulleys, neat little planets right up in the roof. Steel worktops along all the walls, shining faintly in the darkness, and then the stench, of death and blood.

'There.'

Zeke is pointing at the wall, at the circuit-breaker.

Seconds later the room is bathed in light. Zeke and Malin see the congealed blood on the floor, on the chains, the neat rows of knives placed on the polished steel worktops.

'Fucking hell.'

'Get forensics in here.'

'Okay, we're going to back out of here very carefully.'

★

Malin, Zeke and Johan Jakobsson are standing by the sink in the kitchen of Adam Murvall's house. Uniformed police officers are emptying out the contents of the drawers in the living room, the floor of which is covered with newspapers, photos, placemats and cutlery.

'So the whole inside room of the workshop looks like a slaughterhouse? They could have done it there?' Johan asks.

Zeke nods.

'And what have you found?' Malin asks.

'The entire cellar is full of meat. Big white freezers. Bags marked with the year and what cut it is: mince 2001, steak 2004, deer 2005. Same thing in all three houses. And presumably in the mother's as well.'

'Nothing else?'

'Only a lot of rubbish. Not much paperwork. They don't seem the sort to keep that kind of documentation.'

They are interrupted by a cry from the four-car garage belonging to Elias Murvall's house.

'We've got something here.'

The happy voices of the new recruits. Did my voice sound like that nine years ago? Malin wonders. When I had just graduated from Police Academy and was doing my first shifts on patrol, back in my home town? *Back for good?*

Malin, Zeke and Johan rush out of Adam Murvall's kitchen, sprint across the yard and out into the road, then over to the garage.

'Here,' one of the young uniformed officers calls, waving them over. His eyes are shining with excitement as he points to the flatbed of the Skoda pick-up.

'The back of this looks like it's been swimming with blood,' he says. 'Incredible.'

Hardly, Malin thinks, before she says, 'Don't touch anything.'

She doesn't notice how the young man's face goes from an expression of pride and happiness to the sort of itchy anger that only the arrogance of a superior officer can cause.

★

Börje Svärd walks with his stomach muscles clenched, feeling how their power spreads throughout his whole body.

The petrol pumps are well-maintained, he has to give these idiots that much. Nothing funny in the shop, nothing in the workshop. Well-managed and with an aura of competence. He would have been happy to leave his own car here.

Behind the shop is a small office, a few files on a shelf, a fax machine. And another door. Two strong padlocks, but not strong enough.

In the workshop Börje finds a heavy iron bar. Back to the office, where he pushes the bar behind the locks and presses down with all his weight. He hears the locks protest, and then, when he presses even harder with his chest, the metal gives way.

He looks inside the room. First he picks up the familiar smell of gun grease. Then he sees the rifles lined up against the walls.

Bloody hell, he thinks. Then it strikes him that petrol stations are always getting broken into. And if you keep weapons in your petrol station, you're not particularly worried about that happening. Otherwise you'd keep them somewhere else.

He grins.

He can imagine the talk among the petty crooks: 'Whatever you do, don't touch the garage in Blåsvädret. The Murvall brothers are crazy as fuck, so watch out.'

Darkness is starting to fall over on the horizon, as a whirl of activity surrounds Malin. Uniforms, plain-clothes officers, blood, weapons, frozen meat. The family is gathered in Adam Murvall's kitchen now that they are searching the old woman's house.

Malin is thinking that there is something missing. But what? Then she realises. Daniel Högfeldt. He *ought* to be here.

But instead there is some other reporter whose name she doesn't know. But the photographer is here, nose-ring and all.

Malin finds herself wanting to ask about Daniel, but that would be impossible. What reason would she have for asking?

Her mobile rings.

'Hi, Mum.'

'Tove, darling, I'll be home soon. Some serious stuff's happening at work today.'

'Aren't you going to ask if I had a good time at Dad's last night?'

'Of course, did you—'

'YES!'

'Are you at home now?'

'Yes. I thought I might catch the bus out to Markus's.'

Through the hubbub she hears Johan: 'Börje's found a load of guns down at the petrol station.'

Malin takes a deep, cold breath. 'To Markus's? Good . . . do you think you could get something to eat there?'

38

Karin Johannison's cheeks seem to absorb the glow from the floodlights and the brown nuances of her skin are emphasised by the wine-red fabric of her glamorous padded jacket. Not the same one she was wearing out at the tree, a different one.

Burgundy, Malin thinks, that's how Karin would describe the colour.

Karin shakes her head as she approaches Malin, who is standing waiting by the entrance to the workshop.

'As far as we can tell, it's just animal blood, but it'll take us several days to check every square centimetre. If you ask me, I think they slaughter animals in there.'

'Recently?'

'Most recently just a few days ago.'

'It isn't the season for hunting much right now.'

'I don't know about that sort of thing,' Karin says.

'But that's never stopped some people hunting everything throughout the year.'

'Poaching?' Karin frowns, as if the very thought of padding about in the forest in minus thirty degrees with a rifle on her shoulder is seriously off-putting.

'Not impossible,' Malin says. 'There's money in it. When I lived in Stockholm I always used to wonder how there was so much fresh elk meat in the markets all year round.'

Karin glides away, her eyes fixed on the garage. 'It looks like the same thing with the pick-up. But we don't know yet.'

'Animal blood?'

'Yes.'

'Thanks, Karin,' Malin says, and smiles without really knowing why.

Karin takes offence.

She adjusts her cap so that her earlobes peep out, little concave earrings with three inlaid diamonds shimmering in each one.

'Okay,' Karin says, 'when did we start thanking each other for just doing our jobs?'

The weapons are lined up in black bin-bags on the floor of the petrol-station shop.

Not the usual sort of shop, with hotdogs and groceries, but a hardcore garage, Malin thinks. A few dutiful chocolate bars and a rusty old cold-drinks cabinet rattling away in a corner are the only concessions made to a culture beyond engine oil, spare parts and motoring accessories.

Janne would like it.

Sporting rifles from Husqvarna.

Engravings of deer and elk, of men waiting in forest glades, flowers.

Shotguns from Smith & Wesson.

Pistols: Lugers, Colt and a SigSauer P225, standard issue for the police.

No Mausers. No air-rifles. No guns that could have been used to fire through Bengt Andersson's window, Malin can see that much. In the gun cabinets up in the houses there were just shotguns and sporting rifles. Could the brothers have a stash somewhere else? Unless, in spite of all these weapons, they don't actually have anything to do with the shots through the window? As they claim.

Most remarkable of all: two machine guns and a hand grenade.

It looks like an apple, Malin thinks, a misshapen apple in a mutated green colour.

'I bet you those machine guns and the hand grenade come from the break-in at the weapons store up at Kvarn five years ago,' Börje says. 'Ten machine guns were stolen, and a box of grenades. I bet you anything that's where they're from.'

He coughs, and walks up and down the room.

'They could start a war with all this lot,' Zeke says.

'Maybe they've already started one,' Börje says. 'When they strung Bengt Andersson up in that tree.'

Jakob and Elias Murvall are sitting on either side of their mother in the kitchen of her house, against a backdrop of drawers pulled open, crockery stacked up on the rag rugs.

The brothers are focused, as if they're waiting for orders that have to be carried out, come what may. As if they're at war, Malin thinks, just like Börje said, as if they're about to clamber out of their trench and rush at the enemy's lines. Rakel Murvall, their mother, like a matriarch between them, her jaw thrust forward slightly, her neck tilted back.

'Malin and Zeke, you take it,' Sven Sjöman had said. 'Put them under pressure, drop a few threats.'

Uniformed officers in the hall outside, in the living room: 'In case anything happens.'

Zeke beside Malin, opposite the trio. They agreed beforehand, the oldest trick in the book, good cop, bad cop. Zeke's eyes, the wolf on the plain with the scent of frozen winter blood.

'I'll be bad cop.'

'Okay. You're okay with that?'

'With you by my side, I'll be rock-solid.'

Malin leans over the table, looking first at Jakob, then Elias, and then at their mother. 'You're in a great deal of trouble.'

None of them reacts, they just breathe heavily and in time, as if their lungs and hearts had the same rhythm.

Zeke goes on: 'Five years each. Minimum. Breaking and entering, theft of weapons, possession of illegal firearms, poaching, and if we find traces of human blood then you'll be charged with murder as well. If we find his blood.'

'Breaking and entering? What breaking and entering?' Elias Murvall says.

His mother: 'Shh, not a word.'

'You don't think we can get you on the machine guns?'

'Never,' Elias whispers. 'Never.'

Malin can see how something in Elias Murvall's tone of voice pushes Zeke over the edge; she's seen it before, how his floodgates seem to open and his entire being turns to action, a mix of muscles, adrenalin and the here and now. He flies round the table in a single movement. Grabs Elias Murvall by the neck and forces his head down on to the wooden tabletop, pressing so hard that his cheek turns white.

'You fucking primitive,' Zeke whispers. 'I'm going to pluck the feathers from your arse and shove them right down your throat.'

'Keep calm, Jakob,' the mother says. 'Keep calm.'

'Did you kill him, you bastard, did you do it? Out there in the workshop? Like some fucking dog, then you strung him up in the tree for all to see, to show the whole of this fucking plain what happens if you mess with the Murvall family, is that how it was?'

'Let go of me,' Elias Murvall snarls, and Zeke presses harder. 'Let go of me,' he whimpers, and Zeke lets go, pulls his arms away.

That iron core, Malin thinks. You'd take the brothers on one by one or together if need be, wouldn't you?

'I understand,' Malin says calmly when Zeke has returned to their side of the table. 'If you couldn't let go of the thought that Bengt might have raped your sister, if you wanted to do something about it, just because. People will understand.'

'What do we care what people think?' Jakob Murvall says.

Their mother leans back in her chair, folds her arms over her chest.

'Not at all, Mother,' Elias Murvall says.

'Hasn't it gone far enough now?' Zeke says. 'We're bound to find Bengt's blood in the pick-up and then we'll have enough to charge you.'

'You won't find any of his blood there.'

'You must have been so angry. Did you give in to it last Thursday? Was it time for revenge?' Malin says in her gentlest voice, with her most sympathetic look in her eyes.

'Take the boys for poaching and possession of firearms,' the mother suddenly says. 'But they don't know anything about the rest of it.'

But you know, don't you? Malin thinks.

'But you know, don't you?'

'Me? I don't know anything. But tell her about the hunting, boys, about the cabin by the lake, tell her so we can put an end to this nonsense.'

39

The cabin, Malin.

The forest.

Things crawling between the tree trunks out there in the cold.

The brothers and the mother.

Were they the ones who hurt me, Malin? Who shot through my window, who strung me up in a tree? Who gave my body all its injuries?

They're resisting. Trying to keep what's theirs.

Or was it the young lads?

The believers?

The questions never stop.

Talk to the young boys' parents, Malin, I know that's what you're going to do now, you and Zacharias. Find clarity. Come closer to the truth that you think you seek.

Somewhere out there is the answer.

Somewhere, Malin.

Follow the plan.

Move according to the prearranged plan. Don't let go of anything until you know for sure.

Without preconceptions, Malin.

Sven Sjöman's favourite words.

Doors open wide, doors closed, like the one in front of her now.

Zeke's finger on the doorbell, the flat's little entrance hall painted red above them, light from the window next to the door, a kitchen, no one inside.

Pallasvägen.

Thirty or so similar blocks built some time in the late 1970s, to judge from the style, hidden out of the way on a patch of flat land beyond Ljungsbro's communal bathing area, icy but well-gritted paths lined with winter-dead bushes, little snow-covered patches of grass in front of each entrance.

Like villas, only not, Malin thinks. Like pretend houses for people who can't afford one. A form of living that is neither one thing nor the other. Do people become neither one thing nor the other if they live in places like this? Even the garages over by the shrub-edged car park make a confused, limp impression.

Joakim Svensson's mum. Margaretha.

She's at home, Malin thinks. So why isn't she opening the door?

Zeke rings the bell again, and his breath clouds from his mouth, white against the black of the approaching evening.

The clock in the car said 17.15 when they pulled up over in the car park. The evening, and possibly the night, would be long.

The brothers in custody.

The cabin in the forest.

Then Malin hears footsteps coming downstairs behind the door. She hears a lock clicking, sees a crack in the door open.

All these people, Malin thinks, who peep out at the world through cracks in their front doors. What are you so frightened of?

Then she sees Bengt Andersson's body in the tree.

The Murvall brothers.

Rakel.

Thinks that it's probably best to keep your door closed, Margaretha. Then she says, 'Margaretha Svensson? We're from Linköping Police and we'd like to ask you some questions about your son. Can we come in?'

The woman nods and the crack opens. Her body is wrapped in a white towel, her curly blonde hair is wet and dripping on the floor. Introductions and handshakes.

'I was in the bath,' Margaretha Svensson says. 'But come in, come in. You can wait in the kitchen while I put on some clothes.'

'Is Joakim at home?'

'No, Jocke's out somewhere.'

The kitchen could do with some serious work: the white paint is peeling from the cupboards and the hotplates on the stove look worn, but the room is still pleasant, the brown polished table and mixture of chairs lending a calm dignity to its simplicity, and when the cold has released its hold of her nose Malin detects a definite smell of allspice.

They take off their jackets, sit down at the kitchen table and wait. On the worktop are a bottle of olive oil and a fruit bowl containing various packets of biscuits.

Five minutes.

Ten.

Then Margaretha Svensson comes back. Dressed in a red tracksuit top and white jogging pants, made up; she can't be more than thirty-eight, forty at most, just a few years older than Malin, and she's attractive, a good figure, probably goes to the gym.

She sits down at the table, and looks inquisitively at Malin and Zeke.

'The head phoned and said you'd been to the school.'

'Well, as you may be aware, your son and Jimmy Kalmvik used to bully Bengt Andersson, the murder victim,' Malin says.

Margaretha Svensson lets the words sink in.

'That's what the head said. I had no idea. But it's not impossible. Who knows what they get up to together?'

'They spend a lot of time together?' Zeke asks.

'Yes, they're like brothers,' Margaretha Svensson says.

'And you don't know anything about what they might have done to Bengt Andersson?'

Margaretha Svensson shakes her head.

'Could they have had access to any weapons?'

'Knives and stuff, you mean? The kitchen drawers are full of them.'

'Guns,' Malin says.

Now Margaretha Svensson looks surprised. 'I don't think so. Absolutely not. Where would they have got a gun from?'

'The Æsir faith,' Zeke says. 'Has Joakim ever shown any interest in that sort of thing?'

'I can promise you he hasn't a clue what it is. Taekwondo and skateboarding, on the other hand, he knows all there is to know about those.'

'Can he drive?' Malin asks.

Margaretha Svensson takes a deep breath and runs a hand through her wet hair.

'He's fifteen. Those two could be up to anything.'

'They told us they were watching films here last Thursday, but that you weren't at home?'

'When I left at about seven they were here, and when I got home Jocke had fallen asleep. The film had finished, but the television was still on. That skateboarding film they always watch.'

'Where had—'

'I do aqua-aerobics in the local pool. Then I went back to my friend's. You can have his number if you like. I was back by eleven thirty or so.'

'Friend?'

'My lover. His name's Niklas Nyrén. I'll give you his number.'

'Good,' Zeke says. 'Does he have any contact with your son?'

'He tries. Probably thinks the lad could do with a male role-model.'

'Joakim's father is dead, isn't he?' Malin asks.

'He died in a road accident when Joakim was three.'

Then Margaretha Svensson straightens her back. 'I've done my best to bring him up on my own, working full-time as an accounts assistant at a god-awful construction company, trying to make a decent person out of him.'

But you haven't succeeded, Malin thinks. He seems largely to be a semi-criminalised, cruel bully.

And, as if she can read Malin's thoughts, Margaretha Svensson says, 'I know he isn't the best-behaved kid on the planet, and he can be pretty impossible sometimes. But he's tough, and I've encouraged that; he won't let anyone try to put him down, and he stands up for himself. And that means he's pretty well-prepared for all the battles he's got ahead of him, doesn't it?'

'Can we see his room?'

'Upstairs, straight ahead.'

Zeke stays at the table while Malin goes up.

The room smells musty. Lonely. Skateboarding posters. Hip-hop stars. Tupac, Outkast.

A bed, made, on a light blue fitted carpet, light blue walls. A desk. Malin checks the drawers, a few pens, some paper, an empty notebook.

She looks under the bed, but it's empty, just a few dustballs over in the corner where the walls meet.

Only for sleeping, Malin thinks.

Then she thinks how good it is that Tove hasn't met a boy like Joakim Svensson, that her doctor's son is a dream compared to these tough boys out on the plain.

The next house is another world.

Even though it's only five hundred metres from Margaretha Svensson's flat.

A large breezeblock house from the seventies with a double garage, located right on a slope leading up to the Göta Canal, one of maybe ten outsized houses in a square around a well-maintained playground, a black Subaru jeep parked out on the street by the bushes.

Malin's finger on the doorbell, the standard black and white model, their name written in shaky handwriting on a piece of paper behind the little plastic rectangle just beneath the button.

Kalmvik.

It's dark and cold now; evening has arrived in Ljungsbro, and, as time passes, night creeps in with its even fiercer cold.

Joakim Svensson and Jimmy Kalmvik were alone in the flat from seven to half past eleven. How can they be sure that the boys really were in the flat then? That they didn't sneak out and get up to anything? Could they have harmed Bengt Andersson in that time? Got him out to the tree? Or might Joakim Svensson have snuck out after his mum got home?

Nothing's impossible, Malin thinks. And who knows how many films they may have seen for inspiration? Could the whole thing have been a boyish prank that got out of control?

Henrietta Kalmvik opens the door wide.

No hesitant little crack.

'You're from the police? Aren't you?'

Big red hair, green eyes, sharp features. An elegant white blouse over stylish dark blue trousers: a woman in her mid-forties who knows what she looks good in.

'Is that your car?' Malin asks. 'Out on the street?'

'Yes. Nice, isn't it?'

Henrietta Kalmvik leads them into the house, gesturing to them to hang up their jackets in the second of two halls. As Malin shrugs off her padded jacket she sees her almost glide over the parquet floor into the living room, where two white leather sofas frame a table whose legs look like a fat lion's paws in red marble.

Henrietta Kalmvik sits down on the smaller of the sofas and waits for them.

There's a pink Chinese rug on the floor. On the wall above the larger sofa hangs a mostly orange painting of a naked couple on a beach at sunset. Outside the window is a snow-covered pool lit up by a floodlight, and Malin thinks how nice it must be to take a morning swim out there when the weather's warmer.

'Sit down.'

And Malin and Zeke sit down next to each other on the larger sofa, the leather sinking beneath them. It feels like she's disappearing into the soft padding. She notices a turned wooden bowl on the table, full of shiny green apples.

'I presume the head of the school called you,' Zeke says.

'Yes,' Henrietta Kalmvik says.

And then the same questions they asked Margaretha Svensson.

The same answers, yet somehow not the same.

Henrietta Kalmvik's green eyes fixed on the pool outside the window as she says, 'I gave up on Markus a long time ago. He's impossible, but as long as he stays within the law he can do what he likes. He has his own room in the basement, with his own entrance, so he can come and go as he pleases. If you tell me he was tormenting Bengt Andersson, I'd say he probably was. And guns? Not impossible. He stopped listening to me when he was nine. He used to call me a "stupid fucking bitch" when he didn't get what he wanted. And in the end I stopped trying. Now he comes home to eat. Nothing else. I do my own thing, I'm a member of the Lions, and the Jazz Club in town.'

Henrietta Kalmvik falls silent, as if she's said all she has to say.

'I suppose you want to see his room?'

She gets up and heads down some stairs leading to the basement.

They follow her once more.

In the basement they walk through a laundry room and another room containing a sauna and a large Jacuzzi, before Henrietta Kalmvik stops in front of a door.

'His room.'

She steps aside.

Lets Zeke open the door.

The room is a mess, the king-size bed unmade, oddly positioned in the middle of the room. There are clothes scattered all over the stone floor, along with comic books and sweet wrappers and empty drinks cans. The white walls are bare and Malin thinks that very little light must get in through the windows.

'Believe it or not,' Henrietta Kalmvik says, 'he likes being down here.'

They look in the chest of drawers, pick through the things on the floor.

'Nothing out of the ordinary here,' Zeke says. 'Do you know where Jimmy is now?'

'No idea. I dare say they're just hanging about somewhere, him and Jocke. They're like brothers, those two.'

'And Jimmy's father? Is there any chance we could talk to him?'

'He works on an oil rig out in the North Sea. Somewhere off Narvik. He's away three weeks, then home two.'

'It must get lonely,' Zeke says, closing the door to Jimmy Kalmvik's room.

'Not really,' Henrietta Kalmvik says. 'It suits us both not to be in each other's pockets. And he earns an awful lot of money.'

'Has he got a mobile out there?'

'No, but you can call the oil rig itself if it's urgent.'

'When will he be home?'

'Saturday morning. On the morning train from Oslo. But call the rig if it's urgent.'

40

A voice at the other end of the line, the crackling makes the Norwegian unclear, dreamlike, as Zeke reverses out of the Kalmviks' drive.

'Yes, hello? You wanted Göran Kalmvik? He hasn't been here for just over a week now. His shift ended last Thursday, and he's not expected back for two weeks. I can't hear you very well, not . . . Where he might be? At home . . . oh, I see . . . in that case I've no idea . . . yes, he works two weeks and is off for three.'

'Bloody hell,' Malin says when she has hung up. 'Kalmvik's dad isn't on the rig. Hasn't been there for over a week.'

'Henrietta didn't seem to have any idea about that,' Zeke says. 'What do you think it means?'

'It could mean anything. That he was at home last week when Bengt Andersson was murdered and that he could have helped the boys if they managed to go a bit too far with one of their pranks against him. Or he's been deceiving his wife and has a mistress or something even juicier somewhere else. Or maybe he's just having some time off on his own.'

'Is it Saturday he's due home?'

'Yes.'

'It'll be hard to get hold of him before that. Do you think Henrietta's lying? That she's only pretending not to know anything? Trying to protect him and their son?'

'It didn't look like it,' Malin says. 'I'd say not.'

'Okay, let's drop Kalmvik for now, Fors. Let's brave the cold and darkness and go and take a look at the Murvalls' cabin in the forest. It would be just as well to get a bit further with all this.'

Just as well, Malin thinks, closing her eyes and relaxing and letting the images in her head come and go as they like.

Tove on the sofa at home in the flat.

Daniel Högfeldt, bare-chested.

Janne's picture beside the bed.

And then the image that forces all the others aside, that expands and burns into her consciousness, an image impossible to shift: Maria Murvall on her bed in her room in the hospital, Maria Murvall among dark tree trunks one raw, damp night.

The car headlights illuminate the forest road, the trees like frozen figures from a horror film around them, deserted summer cottages turned to black outlines, stiff dreams of good days by the water; frozen now like a light grey smudge in the pale moonlight filtering through the gaps in the veils of cloud.

The directions Elias Murvall gave them earlier in his mother's house: 'Hultsjön, then after Ljungsbro head towards Olstorp, past the golf course and on to the Tjällmo road. After ten kilometres you'll get to the lake; the road to the other cottages is kept cleared, then you'll have to walk. The path is marked out. But you won't find anything there.'

Before that Jakob Murvall, suddenly talkative, as if his mother had pressed the play button. He went on about their organised hunting expeditions, about the sale of meat, about deer-traps, about how Russian millionaires were crazy about deer-traps.

'We'll head out there tonight. Now. Sjöman will have to sort out a warrant.'

Zeke hesitant. 'Can't it wait till tomorrow? The brothers are being taken into custody, they can't do anything.'

'No.'

'But I've got choir practice tonight, Fors.'

'What?'

'Okay, okay, Malin. But we'll deal with Joakim Svensson's and Jimmy Kalmvik's parents first,' and this time the hoarseness of his voice betrayed his awareness that she would tease him for months if he let choir practice with Da Capo take precedence over an entirely new lead.

The warrant went through, Sven Sjöman called to confirm.

And now Zeke has one hand on the wheel as some choir led by Kjell Lönnå is blasting through 'Swing it, Magistern!' Choral music: the non-negotiable condition for them driving out to the cabin. Zeke is dealing with the ice, pushing the car on by accelerating, braking, accelerating. The ditches alongside the road like a white-edged abyss beside them. Malin peers out in search of animals' glowing eyes: deer, elk, a stag that might decide to cross the road just as they approach. Few people can drive like Zeke, not with the uncompromising self-confidence of the professional driver, but with careful concentration on the goal: getting there.

They skirt round the lake, but get an idea of the frozen water continuing into the forest, narrowing to something like a river, leading right into the heart of darkness and night.

The clock on the dashboard reads 22.34. An ungodly hour for work like this.

Tove at home, never made it to Markus's: 'I heated up the rest of the stew. I'm fine, Mum.'

'As soon as things calm down at work we'll do something fun.'

Fun? Malin thinks as she sees the pile of snow ahead of them at the end of the road, how someone had forced a gap through the heap, and how reflecting patches fastened to the trees shine like stars in a line off into the distance.

What do you think is fun, Tove? It was easier when you were younger. We used to go to the swimming pool. And you'd rather go to the cinema with other people. You like shopping, but you're not as crazy about it as other girls your age. Maybe we could go to a concert in Stockholm, you'd like that. We've talked about doing that before but never managed it. Or maybe go to the book fair in Gothenburg? But that's in the autumn, isn't it?

'This must be the right place,' Zeke says, switching off the engine. 'I hope it's not too far to walk. Fuck, it feels even colder tonight.'

*

The geography of evil.

What does it look like? What sort of topography?

It wasn't far from here that traces of the attack on Maria Murvall were found, five kilometres to the west. None of her brothers knew what she was doing in the forest, no one mentioned the cabin then, the property they've got on loan free of charge from farmer Kvarnström for reasons no one wants to go into.

'We look after it, simple as that.'

Maria in the forest.

Cut up from inside.

A chill autumn night.

Damp-dripping world.

Ball-Bengt in the tree.

The cold of the plain.

Branches like snakes, leaves and rotting mushrooms like spiders, and then the worms under your feet, sharp thorns that cut into the soles of your feet. Who's that hanging there in the tree? Bats, owls, some fresh evil?

Is the geography of evil small outcrops of rock and shallow hollows? Half-grown forest, a woman with the tatters of black clothing hanging from her body, dragging herself along a deserted forest road at dawn.

Is the beast here in the forest?

Malin has time to think all this as she and Zeke pad through the snow towards the Murvall brothers' cabin. They light up the trees with their pocket torches, the reflecting patches shine, making the black trees tremble in the utterly silent night, making the snow crystals on the ground twinkle like countless watchful lemmings' eyes, little beacons for navigating through the unknown.

'How far, Fors? It's got to be at least minus fifteen and I'm still dripping with sweat.'

Zeke is walking ahead, heaving his way through the snow; no one has been this way since the last fall of snow, even if there are still earlier tracks to follow. Snowmobile tracks alongside.

The animals, Malin thinks. That must be how they get them out, by snowmobile.

'Pretty tough going,' Malin says, trying to instil a bit of courage in Zeke by showing that she shares his pain. 'We must have trudged a good kilometre by now.'

'How far was it supposed to be?'

'They wouldn't say.'

They stop next to each other, breathing out silently.

'Maybe we should have waited?' Malin says.

'Let's go on,' Zeke says.

After thirty minutes of struggling against the snow and the cold the forest opens out into a small clearing in front of them, and at its centre stands a small house, probably several hundred years old, with drifts of snow up to the eaves.

They train their torches on the cabin; long shadows fall from the beams of light and the trees in the forest become a curtain of dark nuances behind the snow-covered roof.

'Okay, let's go in,' Zeke says.

The key is hanging where the brothers said, on a hook under the soffit. The lock creaks in the cold.

'I don't suppose there's any electricity,' Zeke says as the door opens. 'No point looking for a light switch.'

Cones of light dance across a single, frozen room. Neat, Malin thinks. Rag rugs on the floor, a gas stove on a simple wooden worktop, a camping table in the middle of the room, four chairs, candles, no lamps, and three double beds along the windowless end walls.

Malin goes over to the table.

Its top is stained with light oil.

'Gun grease,' she says, and Zeke mutters in agreement.

On a dresser beside the kitchen worktop stand tins of pea soup and ravioli and meatballs, and in a box alongside are bottles of spirits.

'It reminds me somehow of a changing room,' Zeke says.

'Yes, it's very neutral. No feeling.'

'What were you expecting, Fors? They let us come out here precisely because we wouldn't find anything.'

'I don't know. Just a feeling.'

A room without feelings. What is there beyond that?

If you have wicked hearts, deep down inside, you Murvalls, then what sort of damage have you done?

Then Zeke hushes her and Malin turns round, sees him put a glove to his lips and then point out through the door as they simultaneously put their hands over the beams of their torches.

The resulting darkness is unshakable.

'Did you hear something?' Malin whispers.

Zeke says, 'Hmm,' and they stand there in silence and listen. A dragging sound coming towards them: a limping animal? Wounded by a misplaced shot? Dragging its way into the clearing? Then it is quiet once more. Has the animal stopped? The Murvall brothers are in custody. The old woman? Not here, not now. Maybe she can change her shape? The bullies? But what would they be doing here?

Malin and Zeke creep towards the open door, lean out carefully from either side, look at each other, then the noise starts up again, but further away now, and they leap out, training their torches in the direction the sound is coming from.

Something black drifts quickly towards the edge of the forest; a meditative movement. A person?

A woman?

A teenage boy? Two teenage boys?

'Stop!' Zeke shouts. 'Stop!'

Malin runs after it, following the black shape, but as she runs her boots cut through the crust of the snow and she stumbles, gets up again, runs, falls, gets up, hunting, calling, 'Stop! Stop! Come back here!'

Zeke's voice behind her, deadly serious: 'Stop or I'll shoot!'

Malin turns round. She sees Zeke standing on the porch in front of the cabin, holding his pistol out, taking aim at the empty darkness.

'Hopeless,' Malin says. 'Whatever it was, it's long gone now.'

Zeke lowers his weapon. Nods.

'And it came on skis,' he says, pointing with his torch at the narrow tracks through the snow.

41

Friday, 10 February

Tove in Malin's arms.

How much do you weigh now?

Forty-five kilos?

A good job Mum sometimes goes to the gym, isn't it?

Her legs ache, but at least the warmth has started to return to her feet.

They followed the tracks for two kilometres. In the meantime a storm blew up over the forests around Hultsjön and by the time they reached the end of the trail it was as good as hidden by white powder. The tracks ended at a forest road, and it was impossible to tell if there had been a vehicle parked there waiting. There was no oil on the ground. And any tyre tracks had been obliterated by the snow.

'Swallowed up by the forest,' Zeke said, then he made a note of their position from his mobile.

'It's only five kilometres. It'll be quicker to walk back to our car than wait for the station to send one.'

Tove was asleep on the sofa when Malin got home. The television was flickering and Malin's first thought was to wake Tove, get her to put herself to bed.

But then, as she saw the figure stretched out on the sofa, tall and slim for her age, her fine blonde hair over the cushion and her closed eyes, peaceful mouth, she wanted to feel her daughter's weight, the burden of living love.

She had to summon all her strength to move her, and was sure

Tove would wake up, but eventually she was standing there in the silent, dark living room with Tove in her arms, and now she is staggering through the hall, pushing the door to Tove's room open with her foot.

And then down on to the bed. But Malin loses her balance because of the uneven weight, she feels its warmth glide away from her and the body tumbles on to the mattress with a soft thud.

Tove opens her eyes. 'Mum?'

'Yes.'

'What are you doing?'

'I just carried you in here to bed.'

'Oh.' Then Tove closes her eyes and falls asleep again.

Malin goes out into the kitchen. She stops by the sink and looks at the fridge. It is rumbling in the dark, the cooler-unit dripping tiredly.

What was it you weighed, Tove?

Three thousand, two hundred and fifty-four grams.

Four kilos, five, and so on, and for every kilo of body, less dependent, less a child, more adult.

Maybe the last time I carry her like that, Malin thinks, closing her eyes and listening to the sounds of the night.

Is the phone ringing in a dream? Or in the room outside the dream?

Either way, it's ringing, and Malin reaches out a hand to the bedside table, to where the receiver ought to be, on the other side of the vacuum where she is now, the border between sleep and waking, where everything can happen, where for a few moments nothing can be taken for granted.

'Malin Fors.'

She manages to sound firm, but her voice is hoarse, so hoarse.

Their nocturnal walk must have found its way into her lungs, but she feels fine otherwise, her body is where it should be, her head as well.

'Did I wake you, Malin?'

She recognises the voice, but can't quite place it at first. Who? I hear this voice a lot, but not over the phone.

'Malin, are you there? I'm calling between two tracks and I haven't got long.'

The radio. Helen.

'I'm here. Still a bit sleepy, that's all.'

'Then I'll get straight to the point. Do you remember you called me about the Murvall brothers? There's something I forgot to tell you, something you might want to know. I read in this morning's paper that you're holding the three brothers, but it's not clear whether it's in connection with the murder or not, but then I remembered: there's a fourth brother, their half-brother. He was a bit older, a real loner; his dad was some sailor who drowned, I think. Whatever. I remember the others used to stick together, but not him.'

A fourth brother, a half-brother.

Silence like a wall.

'Do you know what his name was?'

'No idea. He was a little older. That's probably why I never really think of him as belonging with the others. You never used to see him much. It was a long time ago. Maybe none of this is right. I might be mixing things up.'

'That's a great help,' Malin says. 'What would I do without you? Time to meet up over a beer soon?'

'That would be great, but when? We both seem to work too much.'

They hang up. Malin can hear Tove out in the kitchen, and gets out of bed, feeling a sudden longing for her daughter.

Tove at the kitchen table, eating breakfast, reading the *Correspondent*.

'Those brothers, Mum, they seem really weird,' she says with a frown. 'Did they do it?'

Black or white, Malin thinks.

Done or not done.

In a way Tove's right, it's simple, yet still so incredibly more complicated, unclear and ambiguous.

'We don't know.'

'Oh well. I suppose they'll be locked up for the guns and poaching? And the blood, was it just animal blood, as that woman doctor says here?'

'We don't know yet. They're working on it in the lab.'

'And it says you've questioned two teenage boys. Who are they?'

'I can't say, Tove. Did you have a good time at Dad's the other night, by the way?'

'Yes, I said I did over the phone, don't you remember?'

'What did you do?'

'Markus and Dad and I had something to eat, then we watched television until we went to bed.'

Malin feels her stomach clench.

'Markus was there?'

'Yes, he stayed the night.'

'STAYED THE NIGHT?'

'Yes, but it wasn't like we slept in the same bed or anything. You didn't think that, did you?'

Both Tove and Janne spoke to her that afternoon. Neither of them mentioned Markus. Not that he would be staying over, not that he would be eating with them, not even that Janne was aware of his existence.

'I didn't even know your dad knew about Markus.'

'Why wouldn't he?'

'You said he didn't know anything.'

'But he does now.'

'Why hasn't anyone told me any of this? Why didn't you say?'

Malin can hear how ridiculous her words sound.

'You only had to ask,' Tove says.

Malin shakes her head.

'Mum,' Tove says. 'Sometimes you're incredibly childish.'

42

'There's another brother.'

From his desk, Johan Jakobsson waves a sheet of paper when he sees Malin walk into the open-plan office in Police Headquarters. Her mobile conversation with Janne is still running through her head.

'You could have said he was going to stay over.'

Janne had only just woken up, late getting to sleep after working the nightshift. But still clear and focused.

'What happens in my home, Malin, is my business, and if you if aren't keeping a close enough eye on Tove that she can keep things like this secret from you, maybe you need to have a bit of a think about your priorities in life.'

'Are you preaching morals to me?'

'I'm going to hang up now, okay.'

'So you mean it's Tove's responsibility and not yours?'

'No, Malin. YOUR responsibility, and you're trying to push it off on to Tove. Goodbye. Call when you've calmed down.'

'National registration records,' Johan calls. 'I got their file from the national registration office and it says there that Rakel Murvall has four sons; her eldest is called Karl Murvall. Must be a half-brother, because it says father unknown in the register. He's in the phone book, lives down on Tanneforsvägen.'

'I know about him,' Malin says. 'We need to talk to him as soon as possible.'

'Meeting in three minutes,' Johan says, pointing to the door to the meeting room.

Malin wonders if the children will be outside today. Let's hope so; isn't it a degree or so milder today?

*

There are no children playing outside the nursery, instead deserted swings, climbing-frames, sandpits and slides.

Karim Akbar has joined them for the meeting, dressed in a stern grey suit, sitting next to Sven Sjöman at the head of the table.

'So far they've only found blood from elk and deer,' Sven says. 'But they're hard at work in the lab. Until we're done we need to keep all our options open as far as the Murvall brothers are concerned. If nothing else, at least we've dug up a bit of shit.'

'Machine guns and hand grenades are more than a bit of shit,' Börje Svärd says.

'Speaking of weapons,' Sven says. 'According to the weapons experts at the National Laboratory of Forensic Science, none of the weapons we found at the Murvalls' could have been used to shoot rubber bullets into Bengt Andersson's flat.'

'Machine guns and hand grenades aren't shit. But they're not what we should be focusing on,' Karim says. 'Crime can deal with that.'

'The question is, who did you see out in the forest?' Sven says.

'We don't know,' Malin says.

'Whoever it was, they've got something to do with this,' Zeke says.

'Johan, tell us about the fourth brother,' Sven says.

When Johan has told them what they know, silence settles over the table.

Questions hang in the air, until Zeke says, 'None of the Murvalls has ever, not one single time, mentioned a half-brother. Did he grow up with them?'

'Looks like it,' Malin says. 'Helen seemed to think so.'

'Maybe he broke away,' Johan says.

'Some people might prefer a different sort of life to the one they offer,' Börje adds.

'Do we know anything else about this Karl Murvall?' Karim wonders. 'Do we know where he works, for instance?'

'Not yet,' Malin says. 'But we'll know by the end of the day.'

'And we can always ask the Murvall brothers, and their charming mother,' Zeke grins.

'I can try,' Sven says, and laughs.

'What about the Æsir angle?' Karim looks round the team expectantly. 'Considering the crime-scene, we can't just let that go.'

'In all honesty,' Johan says, 'we've been busy elsewhere. But we're definitely going to look more closely into that.'

'Carry on as much as you can now,' Sven says. 'Malin and Zeke, how did you get on talking to the parents of Joakim Svensson and Jimmy Kalmvik?'

'To their mothers,' Malin says. 'Joakim Svensson's father is dead, and Göran Kalmvik works on an oil rig. We didn't get anything new, really. It still isn't clear if the boys have an alibi for Wednesday evening. There's also some confusion about where Kalmvik's father actually is.'

'Confusion?' Sven asks. 'You know what I think about that.'

So Malin explains why the boys' alibi is doubtful, that they were alone in Joakim's flat, and that Göran Kalmvik is away, but that his wife thinks he's still on an oil rig out in the North Sea.

'But he'll be home tomorrow. Early. We thought we'd try to catch him then.'

'And Margaretha Svensson's lover? Might he have something to say about what her son gets up to? If he's been trying to build up a relationship?'

'We're going to talk to Niklas Nyrén today. We prioritised the Murvalls' cabin last night.'

'Good. But make the fourth Murvall brother the priority for now. I'll talk to the family.'

'What, Karl? He moved away to the city.' Rakel Murvall's voice over the phone.

Moved away to the city? It's only ten kilometres or so, but she makes it sound like the other side of the world, Sven Sjöman thinks.

'Nothing worth talking about,' Rakel Murvall says and hangs up.

★

'Here it is,' Zeke says, parking the car outside the white three-storey building on Tanneforsvägen, close to the Saab factory complex. The building was probably constructed in the forties, when Saab was expanding and they were building fighter planes in their hundreds in the city. A pizzeria on the ground floor promises a Capricciosa for thirty-nine kronor, and the ICA supermarket opposite has a special offer on Classic brand coffee. The pizzeria's yellow sign is peeling, and Malin can hardly read the name: Conya.

They dash through the chill across the broad pavement, tugging open the unlocked door into the stairwell. On the noticeboard: third floor, Andersson, Rydgren, Murvall.

No lift.

At the landing of the second floor Malin can hear her heart beat faster, and she is starting to pant, and by the time they reach the third floor she is almost having trouble catching her breath. Zeke is panting alongside her.

'It's always such a shock,' he says. 'How bloody awful stairs are.'

'Yes, the snow yesterday was nothing compared to this.'

Murvall.

They ring the bell, hear it ring behind the door. Silence from what seems to be an empty flat. They ring again, but there's no answer.

'Must be at work,' Zeke says.

'Shall we try the neighbours?'

Rydgren.

After two rings the door is opened by an elderly man with an outsized nose and deep-set eyes, and he looks at them suspiciously.

'I'm not interested,' he says.

Malin holds out her police ID.

'We're looking for Karl Murvall. He isn't at home. Do you happen to know where he works?'

'I don't know anything about that.'

The man is wary.

'Do you know—'

'No.'

The man slams the door shut.

The only other person who happens to be at home is an elderly lady who thinks they are from meals on wheels and have brought her lunch.

One by one the brothers are brought out of their cells, taken into the interview room, and answer Sven Sjöman's questions.

'I haven't got a brother called Karl,' Adam Murvall says, rubbing his forehead. 'You can say we're family if you like, and from your way of looking at it that's probably right, but not the way I see it. He chose his own path, and we chose ours.'

'Do you know where he works?'

'I don't have to answer that, do I?'

'What do you think, Malin? Shall we wait in the pizzeria over lunch, see if he comes home to eat?' They're standing by the car, and Zeke is fumbling with the keys as he talks. 'And it's been a bloody age since I had pizza.'

'Fine with me. Who knows, they may even know where he works.'

Inside the Conya pizzeria there is a smell of dried oregano and yeast. Not the usual woven wallpaper, but pink and green fabric and Bauhaus chairs around polished oak tables. A swarthy man with improbably clean hands takes their order.

I wonder if he's the owner? Malin thinks. It's no myth that immigrants have to start their own businesses if they want to make a living. What would Karim say about you? He'd probably call you a good example. Someone who hasn't given up your responsibility for earning a living to other people, but actively trying to look after yourself.

The virtuous circle we all have to hope in. Your sons, Malin thinks, if you have any, will doubtless be among the best on their courses out at the university. Hope so.

'What would you like to drink? It's included in the price of lunch.'

'Cola,' Malin says.

'Same here,' Zeke says, and when he gets out his wallet to pay he pulls out his police ID.

'Do you happen know a Karl Murvall who lives in one of the flats upstairs?'

'No,' the restaurant-owner says. 'No one I know. Has he done something stupid?'

'Not as far as we know,' Zeke says. 'We just want to talk to him.'

'Sorry.'

'Is this your place?' Malin asks.

'Yes, why do you ask?'

'I just wondered.'

They sit down at a table with a view of the entrance to the flats. Five minutes later the man places two pizzas in front of them, the cheese has melted and the fat is floating in pools over the tomato sauce, ham and mushrooms.

'Bon appétit,' he says.

'Great,' Zeke says.

They eat, looking out at Tanneforsvägen, at the cars driving past, at the angry grey-white exhaust fumes falling heavily to the ground.

What would cause such a breach between people who share the same blood? Sven Sjöman wonders.

He has just finished questioning Jakob Murvall. His words have stuck in his head.

'He lives his life. We live ours.'

'But you're still brothers.'

'Brothers aren't always brothers, are they?'

What makes people who ought to make each other happy, who ought to help each other, turn their backs on each other? Become something like enemies instead? People can fall out over any number of things: money, love, beliefs, pretty much anything. But family? Within a family? If we can't even hold things together on a small scale, how on earth are we going to manage on a larger one?

★

It is half past one.

The pizza is sitting like sluggish concrete in their stomachs and they lean back against the flexible wicker backrests.

'He's not coming,' Malin says. 'We'll have to come back tonight.'

Zeke nods. 'I thought I might go back to the station. Write up the report from yesterday,' he says. 'Do you mind going out to Ljungsbro on your own to talk to Niklas Nyrén?'

'Okay, I've got a few other things I want to check out,' Malin says.

'Do you need any help?'

'I'm happy to go alone.'

Zeke nods. 'Like you did with Gottfrid Karlsson in the home?'

'Hmm.'

They wave in thanks at the restaurant-owner as they leave.

'Pretty good pizza,' Zeke says.

Karl Murvall is a human being, but he is at best uninteresting in the eyes of his family, that much is clear.

'Karl?'

Elias Murvall looks at Sven Sjöman blankly.

'Don't talk about that jumped-up cry-baby.'

'What did he do?'

Elias Murvall seems to consider this, to soften slightly. Then he says, 'He's always been different, he's not like us.'

43

Malin's vision clears as she gets closer to the tree in the field.

Doesn't want to believe what her eyes are telling her.

The lonely tree in the field is no longer so alone. A green estate car with a roof-box is parked on the road, and on the snow, right where Bengt Andersson's body must have fallen, stands a woman wearing a white sheet, no, she isn't wearing anything, and she's holding her arms out from her body, her eyes closed.

She doesn't open her eyes even as Malin's car approaches.

Not a single muscle of the woman's face moves, and her skin is whiter than the snow, her pubic hair improbably black, and Malin stops the car and there is still no reaction from the woman.

Frozen to ice?

Dead?

Standing upright, but then Malin sees her ribcage moving gently in and out, and she seems to be swaying slightly in the wind.

Malin feels the midwinter open its door wide as she gets out of the car, how the season takes command of her senses, as if it were resetting her body and condensing the distance between impressions, thoughts and deeds. A naked woman in a field. This just gets madder and madder.

The car door slams shut, but it's as if the noise was nothing to do with any effort she herself made.

The woman must be freezing, and Malin approaches in silence.

Closer, closer, and soon she is only a few metres from the woman, who stands with her eyes closed, breathing, holding her arms out. Her face is quite calm, and her hair, raven-black, is hanging down her back in a plait.

The plain around her.

It's only just over a week since they found Ball-Bengt, but the police cordon has been pulled down and the snow that has fallen since then hasn't managed to hide the evidence left by curious visitors: cigarette ends, bottles, sweet wrappers, hamburger boxes.

'Hello!' Malin calls.

No reaction.

'Hello!'

Silence.

And Malin tires of the game, she knows who she has in front of her, remembers what Börje Svärd said after he and Johan Jakobsson went to see Rickard Skoglöf.

But what is she doing here?

Malin takes off her thick glove and taps the woman on the nose. Hard, twice, and the woman twitches, leaping back before yelling, 'What the hell are you doing?'

'Valkyria? Malin Fors from Linköping Police. What are you doing out here?'

'Meditating. And now you've disturbed me before I was finished. Do you have any idea how fucking irritating that is?'

It's as if Valkyria Karlsson is suddenly aware of the cold. She walks round Malin and heads towards her car. Malin follows her.

'Why here, of all places, Valkyria?'

'Because this is where he was found murdered. Because this place has its own special energy. You must be able to feel it too.'

'It's still a bit odd, don't you think, Valkyria, you have to admit that?'

'No, it's not odd at all,' Valkyria Karlsson says, getting into the green estate, a Peugeot, and wrapping a long sheepskin coat around her naked body.

'Did you and your partner have anything to do with this?' Stupid question, Malin thinks. But stupid questions can provoke good answers.

'If we did, I'd hardly tell you, would I?'

Valkyria Karlsson closes the car door, and soon Malin is

watching the smoke from the exhaust slowly rise into the sky as the car disappears towards the horizon.

Malin turns towards the tree.

Thirty-five metres away.

She forces the image of the naked Valkyria out of her mind, will deal with her later; now she is going to do what she came here for.

Are you here, Bengt?

And she sees the body, swollen and blue, beaten to a pulp, alone, swaying in the wind.

What did all the curious sightseers who have been out here expect to see?

A drifting spirit?

A corpse? To feel the stench of violence, of death, the way it looks in their worst nightmares?

Tourists in a chamber of horrors.

Malin carefully approaches the tree again, lets her heart-rate slow, shutting out all sound, letting the day disappear and be replaced by what happened here, trying to fix the scene in her mind: a faceless person struggling with a sleigh, chains round the body, feet, pulleys like black moons against the starry sky.

Malin is standing right where the branch broke, where Valkyria Karlsson has just been meditating.

Someone has laid a bunch of flowers on the ground, a card inside a plastic sleeve fastened to the bouquet.

Malin picks up the flowers, grey with frost, and reads: 'What are we going to do now, with no one to fetch our balls?' Ljungsbro IF football team.

Now you miss him.

In death comes thanks, and after thanks, fire.

Malin closes her eyes.

What happened, Bengt, where did you die? Why did you die? Who had so much hatred? If it was even hatred?

★

However much I shout you can't hear me, so I'm not even going to try, Malin Fors. But I am standing here beside you, listening to your words, and I'm grateful for all your efforts, all your trouble. But is it really that important?

Is this really the best thing that you could be spending your time doing?

Her naked white body.

She can make herself immune to the cold. I could never do that.

I know who had so much hatred.

But was it hatred?

Your question is justified.

Perhaps it was despair? Loneliness? Or anger? Or curiosity? A victim? A mistake?

Or perhaps something else, something much worse.

Can I make my words reach you? One single little word? In that case I would like it to be this word.

Darkness.

The darkness that arises when the soul never gets to see the light in another person, when it withers and eventually tries to save itself.

Malin sways with the wind, reaching for the broken branch, the part that is still attached to the tree, but she can't reach, and in the gap, the space between what she wants and what she is capable of, it becomes clear to her.

This isn't over for you, is it?

You want something, you want to have something, and this is how you show it.

What is it you want?

What can you get out of a naked body in a tree in a field tormented by winter?

What is it that is worth such longing?

Opposite the imposing yellow-brick façade of the Cloetta chocolate paradise, on the other side of a small park, is a row of houses built in the thirties, detached houses mixed with small blocks of flats, each flat with its own front door and staircase.

Niklas Nyrén lives in the block at the end of the street, in the middle flat of three.

Malin rings once, twice, three times, but no one answers.

In the car on the way back from the tree she called him on both his mobile and home numbers; no answer, but she still wanted to try.

But it's pointless. Not at home.

Margaretha Svensson said he worked as a travelling salesman, selling biscuits, for one of Cloetta's subsidiary companies, Kakmästaren.

He's probably out seeing customers, Malin thinks. And has his mobile switched off.

She left a message on the answering service.

'Hello, this is Malin Fors of Linköping Police. I'd like to ask you a couple of questions. Please call me on 070-3142022 as soon as you hear this.'

On her way back to the city Malin listens to P1 on the radio.

The television personality Agneta Sjödin has written another book, about a guru in India who meant a great deal to her.

'In his company,' Agneta Sjödin says, 'I became a whole person. Meeting him was like opening a door and finding myself.'

The reporter, an aggressive alpha male to judge by his voice, makes fun of Agneta without her realising.

'And who did you find in the incense-filled room, Agneta? A life coach, maybe, India's answer to Runar?'

Then music.

In front of her Linköping seems to be resisting the early fall of darkness, shimmering warm lights on the horizon promising security, a safe place to raise children.

And there are worse places, worse cities, Malin thinks. It's small enough to be as safe as you could ask for, while still being big enough, developed enough to give a scent of the outside world.

I felt that scent. Was going to stay in Stockholm. That would probably have been the right size for me in the long run. But a single mother in the police living in Stockholm? With no parents, with my daughter's father and his parents two hundred kilometres away, no real friends?

The retail outlets clustered beside Ikea. Babyland, Car-World, BR Toys. The sign to Skäggetorp. Lights taking hold of me, lights that are reluctantly forming themselves into a sense of home.

Malin and Zeke ring on Karl Murvall's door just after seven o'clock. Up at the station she told Johan Jakobsson and Börje Svärd about her visit to the crime-scene, and how Valkyria Karlsson had been there meditating in the cold.

Then she called Tove: 'I'm going to be late again tonight.'

'Can Markus come over?'

'Sure, if he'd like to.'

I don't want to be standing here at this door, Malin thinks. I want to go home and meet my daughter's boyfriend. Will he even dare to turn up? All he's seen of me was in Mum and Dad's apartment, and how friendly was I then? And maybe he's heard Janne's version of my personality. But what would that be like?

It's still quiet inside the flat. No mobile number on the net to call, not even an answer-phone on his home line.

Sven Sjöman on his questioning: 'It's like they're denying his existence. Whatever's at the bottom of it, it brings out the very worst in the Murvalls. I mean, it takes a lot for a mother to deny her son. It goes against nature, doesn't it?'

'He could be anywhere,' Zeke says, as they stand in the stairwell facing the door.

'On holiday?'

Zeke throws out his arms.

They turn and are just about to go down the stairs when they hear a car slow up and stop outside the front door.

Malin leans over and peers down at the car through one of the windows in the stairwell: a dark green Volvo estate, with a roof-box for skis that looks improbably pink in the light of the streetlamp. A thin-haired man in a black jacket opens the door, gets out and hurries into the building.

'Karl Murvall,' Zeke says, holding up his ID. 'We're from the police, and we'd like a word with you if that's all right.'

The man stops. Smiles.

'Yes, I'm Karl Murvall,' he repeats. 'Sure, come on in.'

Karl Murvall has the same strong nose as his half-brothers, only his is sharper.

He is short, with the beginnings of a pot-belly, and his whole appearance gives the impression that he'd like to sink through the floor, yet at the same time he exudes a peculiar, primitive power.

Karl Murvall puts his key in the lock, opens the door. 'I read in the paper about my brothers,' he says. 'I realised that you'd want to talk to me sooner or later.'

'You didn't think of contacting us yourself?' Zeke says, but Karl Murvall doesn't seem bothered by his words.

'Hang on, and I'll let you in,' he says instead, with a smile.

44

Karl Murvall's flat.

Two rooms.

Improbably tidy. Sparsely furnished.

It looks like Bengt Andersson's home, Malin thinks. Just as functional, with a bookcase, sofa, a desk by the window.

No ornaments, no plants, no decoration, nothing to disturb the simplicity, or rather the emptiness, apart from a bowl of fragrant yellow and red winter apples on the desk.

Books about computer programming, maths, Stephen King. An engineer's bookcase.

'Coffee?' Karl Murvall asks, and it strikes Malin that his voice is lighter than his brothers', and that he makes a milder, but nonetheless harder impression somehow. Like someone who has been through a lot, who has seen and heard a great deal. A bit like Janne, the way he looks when someone talks about the hardships they've endured on their walking holiday in the mountains, that mixture of derision and sympathy, and a hint of 'just be glad you don't know what you're talking about'.

'Too late in the day for me,' Zeke says. 'But Detective Inspector Fors here would probably like a cup.'

'Please.'

'Sit yourselves down in the meantime.'

Karl Murvall gestures towards the sofa and they sit down, hear him busying himself in the kitchen, and after five minutes or so he's back with a tray of steaming cups.

'I brought a third anyway, just in case,' Karl Murvall says, putting the tray on the coffee table before sitting down on the office chair by the desk.

'Nice flat,' Malin says.

'Well, how can I help you?'

'Have you been at work all day?'

Karl Murvall nods. 'Did you try to get me earlier?'

'Yes,' Malin says.

'I work a lot. I'm IT manager out at the Collins factory in Vikingstad. Three hundred and fifty employees, and increasing amounts of computerisation.'

'A good job.'

'Yes. I did computer engineering at university, and it's paid off.'

'You could afford something bigger,' Malin says.

'Material things don't really interest me. Property just means responsibilities. I don't need anything bigger than this.'

Karl Murvall takes a sip of coffee before going on: 'But that's not why you're here.'

'Bengt Andersson,' Zeke says.

'The man in the tree,' Karl Murvall says quietly. 'Awful.'

'Did you know him?'

'I've known who he was ever since my childhood in Ljungsbro. The whole family knew of him.'

'But no more than that?'

'No.'

'You didn't know he was questioned during the investigation into the rape of your sister?'

Without his tone changing, Karl Murvall replies, 'Well, that's only natural. He was one of her clients, and she cared about all of them. She got him to take care of his personal hygiene.'

'Are you and your sister close?'

'It's very hard to be close to her.'

'But before?'

Karl Murvall looks away.

'Do you visit her?'

Silence again.

'You and your brothers seem to have a strained relationship,' Zeke says.

'My half-brothers,' Karl Murvall says. 'We don't have any contact at all. That's correct.'

'Why is that?' Malin asks.

'I got an education. I've got a good job and I pay my taxes. That's the sort of thing that doesn't sit well with my half-brothers. I presume they're angry about it. They probably think I imagine I'm better than them.'

'And your mum as well?' Zeke goes on.

'Maybe my mother most of all.'

'You're half-brothers. On your birth certificate it says that your father's identity is unknown.'

'I'm Rakel Murvall's first child. My father was a sailor who disappeared in a shipwreck when she was pregnant. That's all I know. Then she met him, their father, Blackie.'

'What was he like?'

'To begin with, a drunk. Then a crippled drunk. Then a dead drunk.'

'But he took you on?'

'I don't understand what my childhood has to do with any of this, Detective Inspector Fors, I really don't.'

And Malin can see the change in Karl Murvall's eyes, how matter-of-factness turns to sadness, and then to anger.

'Maybe you two ought to be therapists instead. Those people out on the plain live their lives, I live mine, and that's just the way it is, all right?'

Zeke leans forward. 'Just for the sake of formality: what were you doing on the night between Wednesday and Thursday last week?'

'I was at work. I had a big update of the system to install and it had to be done at night. The security guard at Collins can confirm that. But is that really necessary?'

'We don't know yet, but no, probably not.'

'Were you working alone?'

'Yes, I always do when it's a difficult job. To be honest, no one else understands what needs doing, and they just get in the way. But the guard can confirm that I was there all night.'

'What do you know about your brothers' affairs?'

'Nothing. And if I knew anything I wouldn't tell you. They are my brothers, in spite of everything. And if you don't look after each other within your own family, when else would you?'

As they are pulling on their jackets and getting ready to leave the flat, Malin turns to face Karl Murvall.

'I noticed the roof-box on the car. Do you ski?'

'I have it for carrying things,' Karl Murvall says, before going on: 'I don't ski. Sport has never been my thing.'

'Well, thanks for the coffee,' Malin says.

'Thanks,' Zeke says.

'But you didn't touch yours,' Karl Murvall says.

'Maybe, but thanks anyway,' Zeke says.

Malin and Zeke are standing side by side next to Karl Murvall's estate. The back of the car is covered by blankets, and on top of the blankets is a large toolbox.

'He can't have had it easy, growing up out there,' Malin says.

'No, just thinking about it gives me nightmares.'

'Do you want to go out to see Niklas Nyrén?'

'Malin, we must have called him at least ten times. He'll have to wait till tomorrow. Go home and rest. Go home to Tove.'

45

The train moves forward slowly.

Göran Kalmvik is lying on the bunk in his compartment. Letting his thoughts come and go.

When won't there be anything to come home to? he thinks. You can be away so much that away becomes home. And I, at least, pick up things along the way.

It's still dark outside the windows of the train, but he can't sleep, in spite of the carriage's regular dunking against the joints of the rails, in spite of the fact that he is alone in a first-class compartment, and in spite of the fact that the sheets are crisp, yet warm and soft and smell soporific and freshly laundered.

Statoil is paying the fare.

He wonders how much longer he can do this.

It's time to pick a life. He's forty-eight and has been living a double life for almost ten years now, lying right in Henrietta's face every time he comes home.

But she never seems to suspect anything. She seems happy with the money, pleased at not having to work, just buying things.

It's worse with the lad. He gets more distant every time he goes away.

And the stories from school. Can it really be him acting up like that?

Little sod, Göran Kalmvik thinks, as he rolls over. Is it really so hard to behave properly? He's fifteen now, and has always had everything he wanted.

Maybe it would be better to pack up and leave? Move to Oslo. Give it a try.

Work is terrible at this time of year. So cold that something freezes deep inside you even if you're just moving back and forth in the icy wind on the drilling platform at the top of the rig, and your body never has time to warm up between shifts, and no one can be bothered to talk as they work.

But the pay is good.

It's worth having experienced people out on the rigs considering how much it costs every time production grinds to a halt. Pipes like cold snakes full of black dreams.

Soon Norrköping. Then Linköping.

Then home.

Quarter to six.

Henrietta won't meet him from the train. She stopped doing that a long time ago.

Home.

Unless it has now become away.

46

Sleeping-cars from Oslo sent on from Stockholm down towards Copenhagen, a slow, steady train full of people dreaming or about to wake up.

It is 6.15. The train is due at sixteen minutes past, and the morning has only just started to make itself felt. It is almost even colder than last night. But she managed to get up, wanted to check if Göran Kalmvik was actually on the train as they had been told, and, if he was, find out exactly what his secrets were.

She has called the security guards at Collins. They checked their logs and confirmed that Karl Murvall was in the factory from 19.15 on Wednesday evening until 7.30 the following morning. He had worked all night on a big update which had gone according to plan. She had asked if there was any other exit, or if there was any way he could have got out, and the guard had sounded certain: 'He was here all night. The main gate is the only way out. And the fence has sensors connected to our office. We would have noticed if anyone was messing about with it right away. And where. And he was up in the server room when we made our rounds.'

Dinner with Tove yesterday. They talked about Markus. Then they watched ten minutes of a Pink Panther film before Malin fell asleep on the sofa.

Now she can just make out the train coming over the Stångån bridge.

The Cloetta Centre like a UFO off to the left on the other side, and the chimney of Tekniska Verken obstinately struggling against the smoke, the lettering of the logo glowing red like eyes on an unsuccessful photograph.

The train appears to increase in size as it approaches, the engine now at the end of the platform, a grandiose projectile fashioned by engineers.

Malin is alone at the station. She wraps her arms round her padded jacket and adjusts her hat.

No Henrietta Kalmvik, Malin thinks. I'm the only one here to meet someone. And I'm hunting a murderer.

Only one train door opens, two carriages away, and Malin hurries over, feeling the frozen air tug at her lungs. Only one man gets out on to the platform, carrying two big red suitcases, one in each hand.

A weather-beaten face and a body that is heavy but still muscular, and his whole being radiates familiarity with cold and privation; his blue coat isn't even done up.

'Göran Kalmvik?'

The man looks surprised. 'Yes, and who are you?'

The door of the carriage closes again, and the sound of the conductor's whistle almost drowns out Malin's voice as she says her name and title. When the whistle has faded away and the train has left the platform, she quickly explains why she is there.

'So you've been trying to get hold of me?'

'Yes,' Malin says. 'For a few explanations.'

'Then you'll know that I wasn't out on the rig.'

Malin nods. 'We can talk in my car,' she says. 'It's warm. I left it running in neutral.'

Göran Kalmvik inclines his head. His expression is one of relief, tinged with guilt.

A minute later he is sitting beside her in the passenger seat, and his breath smells strongly of coffee and toothpaste, and he starts talking without her having to ask.

'I've had a woman in Oslo for about ten years now. I've been lying to Henrietta for ten years; she still thinks I work three weeks and have two off, but it's the other way round. I spend the missing week in Oslo, with Nora and her lad. I like him, he's more straight-forward than Jimmy. I've never really understood that boy.'

Because you're never at home, Malin thinks.

'And guns? Do you have any idea where Jimmy might have got hold of a gun?'

'No, I've never been interested in that sort of thing.'

'And you don't know what he used to do to Bengt Andersson?'

'Sorry.'

Because you're never at home, Malin thinks again.

'I'll need the number of your woman in Oslo.'

'Does Henrietta have to find out about any of this? I don't know what I want. I've tried telling her, but you know how it can be. So if she has to find out . . .'

Malin shakes her head. As an answer, as an attempt to get Göran Kalmvik to shut up, and as a reflection on the other gender's occasionally incurable weakness.

Malin is sitting in the car, watching Göran Kalmvik's taxi disappear off towards Ljungsbro, past the miserable brick box of the supermarket.

She is thinking.

Letting the possibilities wander freely through her head, then takes out her mobile and calls Niklas Nyrén's various numbers. But he doesn't answer, hasn't called back, and she wonders if he might be at Margaretha Svensson's, clicks up her number from the list, then stops when she sees what time it is: 6.59. Saturday morning.

It can wait.

There have to be some limits, even in a murder investigation. Let the worn-out single mother sleep.

Then Malin drives home. Gets into bed after checking on Tove. And before she falls asleep the image of Valkyria Karlsson comes back to her, naked in the field, like an angel, perhaps one of the devil's angels.

47

When does a case turn into a black waking dream?

When does the search for truth start to go in circles? When does the first doubt appear among the police officers working on the investigation, the feeling that we may not manage to solve this one, maybe this time the truth will elude us?

Malin knows.

It can happen early or late in a case, it can be there as a suspicion after a first phone-call. It can happen suddenly or build gradually, little by little. It can happen on a tired, early Saturday morning in a meeting room where five overworked officers who ought to be at home sleeping instead of drinking disgusting black coffee get to start the day with bad news.

'We've just received the final report from forensics about the raid at the Murvalls'. They've been working round the clock on this one and what good has it done?'

Sven Sjöman looks miserable, standing at the end of the table.

'Nothing,' he says. 'Nothing but animal blood, elk, deer, wild boar, hares. Animal hair in the workshop. Nothing else.'

Shit, Malin thinks, even if she has known deep down all along.

'So we're stuck,' Johan Jakobsson says.

Zeke nods. 'Stuck in solid concrete, I'd say.'

'We've got other lines of inquiry. The Æsir lead. Börje?' Sven asks. 'Anything new? Did you talk to Valkyria Karlsson after Malin found her out at the oak?'

'We've tried to get her on the phone, and we're aiming to catch up with her today,' Börje Svärd replies. 'We've also spoken to twenty other people with links to Rickard Skoglöf, but none of them seems to have the slightest connection to Bengt Andersson.

But we still have one big question to answer: what was she doing out at the crime-scene? Like that? And why?'

'Disorderly conduct,' Johan says. 'Isn't that what meditating naked comes under?'

'She wasn't harming anyone,' Malin says. 'I called Göran Kalmvik's woman in Oslo and she confirmed his story. And I'm hoping to talk to Niklas Nyrén today. It feels like he's the only unturned stone left in this line of inquiry.'

'Well, we'll simply have to keep going,' Börje says, and these words are no sooner out of his mouth than there's a knock at the door, and before anyone has time to shout 'come in', police constable Marika Gruvberg opens the doors and looks in.

'Sorry to interrupt. But a farmer's found some animal carcasses hanging in a tree in a field. We've only just taken the call.'

Circles, Malin thinks.

Seven circles.

Everything points downwards.

Shades of greyish white keep changing and blurring, impossible to detect with the naked eye, and it's hard to tell the difference between land and sky.

The animals are hanging in one of three pines in a small clump in the middle of a field between the Göta Canal and Ljung Church. Over by the canal the leafless trees are lined up in silent tribute, and some eight hundred metres to the east the white, coffin-like church building seems to be dispersing into the atmosphere, only held back by the dubious colours of the surrounding buildings, the ochre-coloured school, the buttercup-yellow head-teacher's house.

The bodies seem drained of blood, hanging by their necks from the lowest branches of the smallest pine. The snow is flecked red with frozen blood that must have poured from the wounds in the animals' bodies and throats. A Dobermann, a pig and a year-old lamb. The dog's mouth has been held closed with black and yellow hazard-warning tape.

Under the tree, in the blood and snow, there are cigarette butts and other rubbish, and in the snow Malin can see marks left by a ladder.

The farmer, a Mats Knutsson, is standing beside her in padded green overalls.

'I was taking a drive round my land in the car. I usually do at this time of year, just to keep an eye on things, and then I saw this in the tree; it looked odd from a distance.'

'You haven't touched anything, have you?'

'I haven't been anywhere near them.'

Zeke, increasingly suspicious of all life out on the plain.

'The whole lot of them seem inbred,' he snarled in the car on the way out to the crime-scene. 'What the fuck does this mean?'

'Well, it can't be the Murvall brothers.'

'No, they're in custody.'

'Could it be Jimmy Kalmvik and Joakim Svensson?'

'It's possible. According to Fredrik Unning, they've tortured cats before.'

'We'll have to talk to them again.'

'The same with Skoglöf and Valkyria Karlsson.'

A few metres beyond the branch where the animals are hanging, someone has written MIDWINTER SACRIFICE in the snow in uneven letters. Not using blood from the animals, but red spray-paint; Malin can see that much with her naked eye. Karin Johannison, who has just arrived, is crouched down, combing the ground with the help of a colleague Malin has never seen before, a young girl with freckles and tousled red hair under a turquoise hat.

Beyond the red lettering someone has urinated in the snow, spelling out the letters VAL, but then their bladder must have run dry.

Zeke, beside the tree, points up at the animals. 'Their throats have been cut. Drained of blood.'

'Do you think they were still alive?'

'Not the dog. They can kick up a real fuss when their instincts kick in.'

'The marks from the ladder,' Malin says. 'Between the bodies.

These cleared patches in the snow must be from a metal ladder, and these holes in the crust of the snow where the feet went in.'

Börje Svärd is walking up and down as he talks into his mobile. He ends the call.

'You see that dog up there in the tree. He must have been completely bloody helpless towards the end. The bastards couldn't even leave his mouth alone. As far as I can tell, he's an excellent example of the breed, which means he was bought from a kennel, probably tagged. So we'll be able to track down his owner from the tax register. So get him down. Now!'

'I just need to finish off here first,' Karin calls, looking up at them with a smile.

'Well, hurry up,' Börje says. 'He shouldn't be left hanging there.'

'Will we need the heater again this time?' Karin asks.

'No fucking heater,' Börje yells.

'Not for the animals,' Zeke says. 'What do you think, Malin?'

Malin shakes her head. 'It looks like we can get what we need here without it.'

They hear a vehicle approaching. They all recognise the sound of a police van and turn round. The van drives up as close as it can get on the road, and they see Karim Akbar get out and call in their direction.

'I knew it, I knew it. That there was something in the Æsir angle. In what that professor said. In those believers.'

Someone taps on Malin's shoulder and she turns round.

Farmer Knutsson is standing behind her, apparently unconcerned by the fuss. 'Do you need me here, or can I go? The cows . . .'

'Go on,' Malin says. 'We'll call you if there's anything else.'

'And the animals?' The farmer gestures towards the tree.

'We'll get them down.'

Just as she finishes the sentence she sees the car from the *Correspondent* in the distance.

Daniel, she thinks, where have you been?

But it isn't Daniel who gets out of the car. Instead it's the photographer with the nose-ring and a nicotine-wrinkled, grey-haired journalist whom Malin recognises: Bengtsson, an old hand, complete with a pipe and a genuine loathing of computers and word-processors.

Well, Malin thinks, Karim can take care of him, seeing as he's here.

Shall I ask about Daniel? Malin thinks. But once more she brushes the thought aside. How would that look? And how much do I care?

'Get the dog down at once,' Börje says.

Malin can see the frustration and anger in his body, all the emotion he's focusing on the dead dog in the tree.

She wants to say, Calm down, Börje, he can't feel anything hanging up there, but she keeps quiet, thinks, Anything he felt is long gone now.

'We're done here,' Karin says, and behind her Malin hears the click of the photographer's camera, and how Bengtsson is interviewing Karim in his hoarse voice.

'What conclusions do you . . .'

'Groups of . . . connection . . . teenage boys . . .'

Then Börje rushes towards the animals in the tree, leaps up and tries to grab the dog, but he can't reach his limp legs, flecked with small clumps of congealed blood.

'Börje, for fuck's sake,' Malin says, but he jumps again and again and again, trying to break the law of gravity in his attempts to save the dog from his helpless hanging.

'Börje,' Zeke shouts. 'Have you gone mad? They'll be here with a ladder soon, then we can get the dog down.'

'Shut up.'

And Börje catches hold of the dog's back legs, his hands seem to stick to them and reluctantly the dog follows the weight of Börje's body and the branch bends in an arching bow and the knot that held the dog in the tree gives way. Börje shouts, groans as he falls back into the red snow.

The dog lands beside him, his lifeless eyes wide open.

'This winter's sending everyone mad,' Zeke whispers. 'Completely fucking crazy.'

48

From the field Malin can see the forests where Maria Murvall was attacked and raped; the end of the trees is like a black band against the white sky. She can't see the water, but knows that the Motala River runs over there, bubbling like an overgrown stream under its thick covering of ice.

On a map the forest doesn't look anything much, a strip maybe thirty or forty kilometres across, stretching from Lake Roxen up towards Tjällmo and Finspång, and towards Motala in the other direction. But inside the forest it's possible to disappear, get lost, run across things that are incomprehensible to human beings. It is possible to be wiped out among the mud and decaying leaves, the unpicked mushrooms on their way to becoming part of the undercurrent of the forest. Long ago people in these areas believed in trolls, fairies, goblins and cloven-footed monsters, all wandering among the trees and trying to lure people to their doom.

What do people believe in today? Malin wonders, looking over at the church tower instead of the forest. Ice hockey and the Eurovision Song Contest?

Then she glances at the animal bodies in the snow.

Börje Svärd with his earpiece in. He's scribbling a number on a scrap of paper, then makes a call on his mobile.

Zeke on another phone.

Dennis Hamberg, a farmer outside Klockrike, has reported a break-in at his farm, very upset: 'Two organically reared animals stolen, a young pig and a year-old lamb. I moved here from Stockholm to get involved with sustainable farming, and now this happens.'

The forest.

Black and full of secrets, a girl from a John Bauer painting staring into a lake at her own reflection. Is there someone creeping up behind her?

Then they are all sitting in the police van, the muffled sound of an engine idling in the background, a treacherous heat that makes them undo their padded jackets, thaw out, open up again. A quickly convened meeting out in the field: Malin, Zeke, Börje and Karim; Sven Sjöman at the station, busy with paperwork.

'Well?' Karim says. 'Where do we go from here?'

'I'll take care of tracing the dog,' Börje says. 'It shouldn't take long.'

'The uniforms can go door-to-door,' Zeke says. 'And Malin and I will go and see the organic farmer and check out what Kalmvik and Svensson were up to last night. We can't let go of anything yet.'

'The connection looks pretty obvious, though,' Karim says from the driver's seat. 'The ritual, increased clarity of purpose and carelessness.'

'In cases like this the level of violence usually escalates,' Malin says. 'Experience suggests that. And to go from a human being to animals is hardly an escalation.'

'Maybe,' Börje says. 'Who knows what goes on inside some people's heads?'

'Check out Rickard Skoglöf and Valkyria Karlsson as well,' Karim says. 'The Æsir stamp on this is quite clear.'

When the meeting is over Malin looks over at the forest again. She closes her eyes, sees a naked, unprotected human body on scratchy moss.

She opens her eyes, trying to force the image away.

Karin Johannison walks past, carrying a large, yellow sports bag.

Malin stops her.

'Karin. The chances of analysing the DNA in traces of blood have got a lot better in recent years, haven't they?'

'You know they have, Malin. You don't have to flatter me by pretending you don't know. In the main British lab in Birmingham they've made huge progress. It's unbelievable what they can find out from practically nothing.'

'What about us?'

'We haven't got those resources yet. But we do sometimes send material over there for analysis.'

'If I had a sample, could you sort that out?'

'Of course. I've got a contact there. An Inspector John Stuart I met at a conference in Cologne.'

'I'll get back to you,' Malin says.

'Do,' Karin says, then heads off with her bag over the rough snow, and despite the weight she still manages to look as elegant as a model on a Paris catwalk.

Malin walks away from the others along the road, pulls out her mobile and calls the exchange in the station.

'Can you put me through to a Sven Nordström at Motala Police?'

'Of course,' the female receptionist says.

Three rings, then Nordström's voice: 'Nordström.'

'This is Fors from Linköping.'

'Hello, Malin. It's been a while.'

'Yes, but now I need your help. You know your rape case, Maria Murvall? The woman whose brothers have cropped up in our current case? Was she wearing any fragments of clothing when you found her?'

'Yes, but the blood on them was so filthy that forensics said they couldn't get anything out of it.'

'According to Johannison here, they've come up with a lot of new techniques. And she's got a contact in Birmingham who's a bit of a wizard at this sort of thing.'

'So you want to send the fragments of clothing to England?'

'Yes. Can you see that they get to Karin Johannison at the National Laboratory of Forensic Science?'

'It really ought to go through official channels.'

'Tell that to Maria Murvall.'

'We've got the samples in the archive. Karin will get them today.'

'Thanks, Sven.'

Just as Malin hangs up Karin passes her in her car. Malin stops her.

Karin winds down the window.

'You'll be getting some material today, from Nordström in Motala. Get it to Birmingham as soon as you can. It's urgent.'

'What is it?'

'Maria Murvall's clothes. Or the remains of them.'

Margaretha Svensson is tired when she opens the door of her flat. There is a smell of coffee from the kitchen and she doesn't seem surprised to see Malin and Zeke again, just gestures to them to come in and sit down at the kitchen table.

Is Niklas Nyrén here? Malin thinks, but if he was he would probably be sitting at the table or in the living room already. He would have been visible by now.

'Would you like coffee?'

Malin and Zeke stop in the hall once they've shut the door behind them.

'No thanks,' Malin says. 'We've just got a couple of quick questions.'

'Go ahead.'

'Do you know what your son was doing yesterday evening and last night?'

'Yes, he was at home. He and I had dinner with Niklas, then we all watched television together.'

'And he didn't go out at all?'

'No, I know that for certain. He's asleep upstairs at the moment. You can wake him and ask him.'

'That won't be necessary,' Zeke says. 'Is Niklas here now?'

'He's gone home. Went late last night.'

'I've asked him to call me, I left messages.'

'He told me. But he's been so busy with work.'

A murder investigation, Malin thinks. A fucking murder investigation and people can't even be bothered to call back. And they complain that the police are slow? Sometimes Malin wishes that people understood that the police are only the last link in a network covering the whole of society, where everyone, each and every one of us, has to do their bit to hold things together.

But everyone relies on everyone else doing their bit. And do nothing themselves.

SEP, as it's called in *Life, the Universe and Everything*: Somebody Else's Problem.

'What do you think?' Zeke asks as they head back to the car.

'She's telling the truth. He was at home last night. And Jimmy Kalmvik would hardly have done it on his own. Next stop the farmer.'

The group of buildings on a field a few kilometres outside Klockrike is covered in snow and cold, and the surrounding clusters of birches and a lovely dry-stone wall provide only slight protection for the garden in front of the newly built farmhouse.

The house is constructed of sandstone, with green shutters over the windows. In front of the porch, painted Mediterranean blue, stands a Range Rover.

It ought to smell of lavender, thyme and rosemary, but instead it smells of ice. At the end of the avenue leading to the house is a gate where someone has put up a sign saying: 'Finca de Hambergo'.

The green-painted door of the house opens and a man in his forties with bleached hair puts his head out.

'Thanks for coming so quickly. Come in.'

The ground floor of the house is a single open room, hall, kitchen and living room in one. When Malin sees the stone walls, the patterned tiles, the open kitchen cupboards, terracotta floor and earth colours, she feels transported to Tuscany or Majorca. Or Provence, maybe?

She's only been to Majorca, and the buildings didn't look like this. The flats where she and Tove were staying looked more like an overblown version of the council blocks in Skäggetorp. But nonetheless, she knows from interior design magazines that this is what the dream of the south looks like for a lot of people.

Dennis Hamberg notices them staring.

'We wanted it to look like a mixture of an Andalusian *finca* and an Umbrian villa. We moved here from Stockholm to start an organic farm. We really wanted to move further away, but the kids needed a Swedish school, so they're at secondary school in Ljungsbro. And my wife got a good job as head of PR for Nygårds Anna in Linköping. I went through a hell of a lot in the nineties and just wanted some peace and security.'

'Where are your family now?'

'In town, shopping.'

And you've got the urge to talk to someone, way out here on a desolate winter plain, Malin thinks.

'And the break-in to the barn?'

'Of course. Follow me.'

Dennis Hamberg pulls on a black Canadian Goose parka and leads them across the yard to a red-painted barn, and points to the marks left by a crowbar in the door frame.

'This is where they got in.'

'More than one?'

'Yes, there are loads of footprints inside.'

'Okay, we'll have to try not to stand on them,' Zeke says.

Prints from trainers and heavy boots. Military? Malin wonders.

In the barn there are several cages of rabbits. There's a single lamb in a pen, and in a square of concrete a black sow lies suckling something like ten piglets.

'Iberico. Pata Negra from Salamanca. I'm going to make ham.'

'This was where they took a pig?'

'Yes, they took one of the young ones. A lamb too.'

'And you didn't hear anything?'

'Not a sound.'

Malin and Zeke look round, then go back out into the yard, followed by Dennis Hamberg.

'Do you think there's any chance I'll get the animals back?' he says.

'No,' Zeke says. 'They were found hanged in a tree outside Ljung this morning.'

The muscles in Dennis Hamberg's face seem to wither away instantly, his whole body shudders, then he pulls himself together and tries to get a grip on something that seems completely incomprehensible.

'What did you say?'

Zeke repeats what he said.

'But things like that don't happen here.'

'It looks like they do,' Malin says.

'We'll be sending out a forensics team to conduct a search.'

Dennis Hamberg looks across the fields, pulling his hood over his head.

'Before we moved here,' he says, 'I never knew how windy it could get. Sure, it's windy in Egypt, on the Canary Islands, in Tarifa, but not like this.'

'Do you have a dog?' Malin asks.

'No, but we're going to get cats before summer.' And then Dennis Hamberg thinks for a moment before asking, 'The animals, will I have to identify them?'

Malin looks away, over the fields, and can hear from Zeke's voice that he's suppressing a laugh.

'Don't worry, Dennis,' he says. 'We can assume the animals are yours. But if you'd like to identify them, I'm sure that can be arranged.'

49

Börje Svärd clenches his fists in his pockets, feeling something approaching, something intangible. It's there in the air he breathes, and he recognises it. It's a feeling that something's about to happen, that an event has meaning for him in a way that goes far beyond his understanding.

The condensation on the windscreen increases with every breath.

The owner of the Dobermann, according to the tax register, is called Sivert Norling, and he lives at 39 Olstorpsvägen in Ljungsbro, on the side of the river where the roads lead up towards the forests near Hultsjön. It only took a few minutes to find out the owner's name, thanks to some helpful people in Stockholm.

Start with this.

The whole of his police instinct feels it. Closest, most possible. Skoglöf and Valkyria Karlsson will have to wait.

And now he and Johan Jakobsson are there. He wants to see what the bastard looks like, if it was the owner who did it. Either way, you have to keep a closer eye on your dog than to let a group of nutters get hold of it.

The whitewashed wooden house is squeezed in between other similar seventies constructions. The apple and pear trees are fully grown and in the summer the hedges are presumably tall enough to stop prying eyes.

'No point waiting,' Börje says. 'You never know. We might be getting close.'

'So how are we going to do it?' Johan wonders.

'We ring the bell.'

'Okay. That would be a start.'

They get out of the car, open the gate in the fence and go up the steps. Ring the bell.

They ring three, four times before they hear sluggish steps inside the house.

A lad in his late teens opens. He's wearing black leather trousers, has long black hair hanging over pierced nipples. His skin is as white as the snow in the garden and the cold doesn't seem to bother him.

'Yeah?' he says, and looks blearily at Börje and Johan.

'Yeah?' Börje says. 'Are you Sivert Norling?' he asks, holding up his police ID.

'No, that's the old man.'

'And you are?'

'Andreas.'

'Can we come in? It's cold out here.'

'No.'

'No?'

'What do you want?'

'Your dog. A Dobermann. Is it missing?'

'I haven't got a dog.'

'According to the tax office you do.'

'It's the old man's dog.'

Johan looks at the boy's hands. Small dots of red.

'I think you'd better come with us,' he says.

'Can I put a top on?'

'Yes—'

Without warning the boy takes a step back and slams the door with full force.

'Shit,' Börje shouts, rattling the door. 'You check the back and I'll take the front.'

They draw their weapons, split up, sticking close to the wall, their jackets catching on uneven planks.

Johan crouches, creeps under the windows along the terrace; the stained green planks creak beneath his feet. He reaches his arm up and tests the handle of the terrace door.

Locked.

Five minutes pass, then ten. Silence from inside the house, no one seems to be moving in there.

Börje sticks his head up, tries to see through the window into what must be a room. Darkness within.

Then Börje hears a noise from the door beside the garage, and it flies open and the boy races out with something black in his hand. Shall I take him? Börje has time to think, but he doesn't shoot him, instead starts chasing the boy as he sprints off down the road between the houses.

Börje chases the boy towards the centre of town and the Motala River, then into a street off to the left. There are children playing in a garden. His heart is racing fit to burst but with every step he gets a bit closer.

The boy is growing in his vision in front of him. The gardens seem to get bigger then smaller in turn to each side of him. His shoes drum on the gritted streets, left, right, left. The boy must know these streets like the back of his hand.

Tired now.

They're both running slower.

Then the boy stops.

Turns round.

Aims the black thing at Börje, who throws himself to the ground, towards a heap of snow.

What the fuck is he doing, the idiot, does he know what he's forcing me to do?

The heaped snow is sharp and cold.

Before him Börje Svärd sees his wife, motionless in bed, his dogs, excitable as he approaches their run; he sees the house and the children far away in distant countries.

He sees a boy before him, holding a gun aimed at him.

Torturing dogs. A child. The Dobermann's taped-up mouth.

Fingers closed around a trigger. The boy's, his own.

Aim for the leg. The shin. Then he'll go down, and there's no vein to tear open so he won't bleed to death.

Börje fires and the sound is short and powerful and before him on the road the boy collapses, as if someone had pulled his legs out from under him.

Johan heard the noise from the front of the house and rushed round.

Where did they go?

Two directions.

Johan runs upwards and then left. Are they round that corner?

Heavy breathing.

Cold in his lungs, then he hears the shot.

Shit.

And he runs towards the direction of the sound.

And he sees Börje creeping towards a body lying in the middle of the gritted street. Blood is running from a leg, a hand clawing at the snow, reaching for the wound. The boy's black hair like an array of shadow on the white snow.

Börje gets up, kicks something black away from the body.

Then the body starts to make a noise; a scream of pain, despair and fear, maybe also confusion, cuts through the walls of the residential area.

Johan runs up to Börje.

'He stopped and took aim at me,' Börje pants through the screaming. Then he points at the weapon in the snow. 'A fucking plastic replica. The sort of thing you can buy from a thousand websites. But how the hell was I supposed to see that?'

Börje crouches down next to the boy, says, 'Take it easy now. It'll get sorted.'

But the boy carries on screaming, holding his leg.

'We have to get an ambulance out here,' Johan says.

Malin looks out over the empty playground.

Thinks: What's going on round here? Why is all this happening now? She doesn't know why, but maybe it's because a breaking point has been reached, and something is collapsing right now, in a torrent of violence and confusion.

Young people.

Drifts of confused young people.

And it doesn't seem to fit.

'They've operated on him. We'll talk to him later.' Sven Sjöman's weary voice. 'His dad confirms that it was their dog, that he bought it for the boy.'

'What else did the father have to say?' Zeke asks.

'That the boy wasn't at home last night, that he's spent the last few years living in a world of computer games, Internet, death metal and, as his father put it, "a general interest in the occult".'

'Poor sod,' Zeke says, and Malin can see that he seems to be reflecting. Maybe he's getting a bit of sensible perspective and thinking that his anxieties before Martin's matches are ridiculous, that he knows his worries are silly and that he really ought to get over them, once and for all. There are ten thousand dads in Linköping who'd love to have a son like Martin. And when's the next home match?

Presumably Zeke has no idea.

He probably gets a sore backside at the very thought of the Cloetta Centre.

'The father's a sales executive for Saab,' Sven goes on. 'Spends three hundred days travelling each year. Places like Pakistan and South Africa.'

'Any friends?' Malin asks.

'None that the father could name.'

'Börje?' Johan Jakobsson, anxiety in his voice.

'You know how it is. Taken off active duties until the incident has been investigated.'

'It's open and shut,' Malin says. 'He fired in self-defence. Those replicas look exactly like the real thing.'

'I know,' Sven says. 'But when was anything that simple, Fors?'

Room ten of ward five in Linköping University Hospital is dark, apart from the light cast by the reading lamp above the bed.

Sivert Norling is sitting in a green armchair in the gloom by the window. He is a tall, gangly man, and even in the dim light

Malin can see that his blue eyes are hard. His hair is cropped and his legs stick out across the floor. Beside him sits his wife, Birgitta. She's blonde, dressed in jeans and a red blouse that makes her face, already red from crying, look even more swollen.

In the bed lies the boy, Andreas Norling.

He seems vaguely familiar to Malin, but she can't place him.

The boy's leg is in traction, and his eyes are cloudy with pain-killers and narcotics, but according to the doctors he can manage some questions.

Zeke and Malin are standing beside his bed, and a uniformed officer is sitting on guard outside the door.

The boy refused to say hello when they came in, and now he has defiantly turned his head away from them, his black hair looks like angry streaks of ink across the white pillow.

'You've got something to tell us,' Malin says.

The boy lies there silent.

'We're investigating a murder. We're not saying you did it, but we have to know what happened out at that tree last night.'

'I haven't been near any tree.'

The boy's father gets up, shouts, 'Now you just have the common damn decency to tell them what you know. This is serious. It's not some bloody game.'

'He's right,' Malin says calmly. 'You're in a whole lot of trouble, but if you talk to us perhaps things will get a bit easier for you.'

Then the boy looks at Malin. She tries to calm him with her eyes, persuade him that everything will all be all right, and maybe he believes her, maybe he decides that none of it matters.

He starts to talk.

About how they read in the paper about midwinter sacrifices, and how cool it sounded, and how he had been at home with his mum when the murder must have been committed, how they didn't have anything to do with that, that was murder, after all, and how he had been so tired of his flatulent dog and how his friend Sara Hamberg had said they could get some pigs from hers, and that their friend Henrik Andersson had an old EPA tractor with a flatbed trailer that they could use, and how he had found a site on the net all about sacrifices, and that Rickard Skoglöf, who they had read about in the paper, was the man behind the site. And that he was some sort of Æsir wizard and had encouraged them in several odd emails and one thing had led to another, it had become sort of unstoppable, as if some weird force was driving them to do it.

'We drank some cans, got hold of some knives. I didn't think there'd be so much sodding blood. It was like, wow, so much blood. It was pretty cool. But God it was cold.'

His mum begins to cry again.

His dad looks like he'd like to apply some corporal punishment.

The night is black behind the hospital window.

'Was Rickard Skoglöf with you?'

The boy shakes his head. 'No. Only those weird emails.'

'And Valkyria Karlsson?'

'Who?'

'Why did you run?' Malin asks. 'And why did you take aim at Detective Inspector Svärd?'

'I don't know,' the boy replies. 'I didn't want to get caught. Isn't that what you're supposed to do?'

'Someone ought to drop a bomb on Hollywood,' Zeke mutters.

'What did you say?' The boy suddenly interested.

'Nothing. Just thinking out loud.'

'One more question,' Malin says. 'Jimmy Kalmvik and Joakim Svensson, do you know them?'

'Know them? Jocke and Jimmy? No, but of course I know who they are. Bastards, both of them.'

'Did they have anything to do with this?'

'Not a thing. I'd never have anything to do with them if I could help it.'

On the way down in the lift Malin asks Zeke, 'Shall we bring in Skoglöf?'

'What for? Incitement to animal cruelty?'

'You're right. We'll leave him be for the moment. But we should probably have another talk with him and Valkyria Karlsson. Who knows what they might have got other people to do?'

'Yes, and Johan can talk to the other kids who were out in the field.'

'Okay. But we've only got one more thing to do today,' Malin says.

'What's that?'

'We're going to see Börje.'

The white-painted kitchen cupboards shine, newly polished, and the table is covered with an orange and black Marimekko table-cloth. Above it hangs a PH designer lamp.

The whole kitchen of Börje Svärd's house exudes calm, and the room has an aesthetic quality far beyond anything Malin imagines she might ever achieve. The entire house is the same: considered, restful, beautiful.

Börje is sitting at the end of the table. Beside him his wife, Anne, seems to be almost clinging to an armchair-like blue wheel-chair, the features of her face somehow rigid. Her laboured breathing fills the room, tormented, obstinate.

'What the hell was I supposed to do?' Börje says.

'You did the right thing,' Zeke says.

'Absolutely,' Malin agrees.

'So you say he'll be okay, no lasting damage?'

'Completely, Börje, the bullet hit him exactly where it should have.'

'Bloody awful, though,' Börje says. 'Attacking animals like that.'

Malin shakes her head. 'Madness.'

'I suppose I'll be off a couple of weeks,' Börje says. 'It usually takes a while.'

A gurgling sound, followed by some lighter noises from the wheelchair.

Language?

'She says,' Börje explains, 'that it's time we put a stop to these awful things.'

'Yes, it really is high time,' Malin says.

★

'What happened at work today, Mum?' Tove asks. 'You seem tired?'

Tove reaches for the pan of mashed potato on the kitchen table.

'Yes, what did happen? Some youngsters, not much older than you, who'd done a load of stupid things.'

'Like what?'

'Really, really stupid things, Tove.'

Then Malin eats a large forkful of potato before going on: 'Promise me you'll never do anything stupid, Tove.'

Tove nods. 'What's going to happen to them now?'

'They'll be called in for questioning, then social services will probably have to take care of them somehow.'

'How?'

'I don't know, Tove. Just take care of them, I suppose.'

50

Sunday, 12 February

Now the bell in the chapel is tolling eleven, eleven times, and then it starts ringing, and it is ringing for me, informing the district that Ball-Bengt Andersson is now being laid to rest, and in the ringing is the story of my life, the apparently wasted series of breaths that was mine. But oh, oh, how you deceive yourselves. I knew love, at least once, even if I was suspicious of it.

Although it is true: I was a lonely person, but not the loneliest.

And now they are going to talk about me. Then I shall burn. On a Sunday and everything! They made an exception for me, violent as my demise was.

But it doesn't matter, that part of me is past, only the mystery remains, and for its sake parts of me are preserved. I am a blood group, a complete code, I am the person lying in the white-painted pine coffin in the Chapel of the Resurrection's orange room, just the other side of Lambohov, on the way to Slaka.

A hundred metres away, along an underground tunnel, the oven awaits, but I'm not scared of the flames; they aren't eternal or hot, just a fashion to wear for today.

I'm no longer angry with anyone, but I wish Maria could have a little peace. She was friendly towards me, and that ought to mean something.

You look so serious, sitting there in your pews. There are only two of you: Malin Fors and a representative of Fonus funeral services, Skoglund, the man who made me look nice for my picture in the Correspondent. *Beside the coffin stands a woman, her priest's collar chafing her neck, and she wants to get this over and done with; death*

and loneliness of my variety scare her. That's how much faith she has
in her god, in his or her goodness.

So get on with it, get it over with.

I drift on.

The pain hasn't dissipated, and it's as capricious as ever, but I've
learned one thing: in death I own language.

I can whisper a hundred words, scream thousand upon thousand
of them. I can choose to be silent. I finally own my own story. Your
mumbling means nothing.

Just listen.

Malin greeted the representative of the funeral company, Conny
Skoglund, before she went into the chapel. They said hello under
the sand-coloured arches, and after the pleasantries they stood
beside each other in silent complicity before the bells started to
ring and they went into the large hall. Light was flooding into
the room in an almost indecent manner through the windows
which confidently, as if jealous of their view of the park, stretched
from floor to ceiling. It must be beautiful when it's green outside,
Malin thinks. Now it's just unnaturally light.

They sit on either side, as if trying somehow to fill the empty
room.

Alone in life.

Even more alone in death.

About a week since Bengt Andersson was found, and now his
funeral is to take place. A single wreath on the coffin, from
Ljungsbro Parish. The football club evidently thought it had done
enough with the wreath at the crime-scene. Malin has a white
narcissus in her hand, and the bells ring and ring and she thinks
that if they ring much longer both she and funeral director
Skoglund will go deaf. And the priest as well. She's around thirty-
five, red-haired and chubbily freckled, and now the bells stop
ringing and a hymn pipes up instead, and when it's over the
priest starts talking.

She says what she has to say, and when she gets to the part
where she has to add something personal she says, 'Bengt Andersson

was an unusual, normal person . . .' and Malin wants to get up, hold her mouth shut until the platitudes stop pouring out of it, but instead she shuts off and without knowing how it happens she is placing the white narcissus on Ball-Bengt's coffin as she thinks, We'll get them, we'll get him, you'll have peace, I promise.

Malin Fors, if you think that I need 'the truth' in order to have peace, you're mistaken, but you're looking for it for your own sake, aren't you?

You're the one who needs peace and quiet, not me.

But that's okay, we can be honest with each other, we don't have to hide our intentions and other such tiresome nonsense.

Now he's steering me down the path, the coffin is dark and warm and soon it will be even warmer.

His name is David Sandström, forty-seven years old, and everyone wonders how he can do a job like this. Corpse-burners aren't very well regarded, not much better than fatties who hit their own father over the head with an axe. But he's happy in his work, it's solitary, he doesn't have to worry about the living, and there are other advantages that don't need to be mentioned now.

We're inside the room containing the oven; it's big and spacious with sky-blue walls, located below ground with little windows up near the ceiling. The oven itself is entirely automated, the cremator just has to get the coffin on to a conveyor belt, then the doors open on a hearth that is lit by the press of a button.

Then I burn.

But not yet.

First David Sandström has to heave the coffin on to the conveyor belt, something that takes a great deal of effort.

God, it's heavy. You have to slide them the last bit of the way from the trolley to the conveyor belt and it's usually easy, but this one's bloody heavy.

Bengt Andersson.

David knows how he died, lets him lie in the coffin, under the lid, doesn't even want to look at him. Ideally they should be younger, he likes those ones, they grant him most peace.

There.

The coffin is on the conveyor belt.

He presses the button on the control panel, the door to the oven opens, he presses the next button and the flames lick hungrily for wood to bite into.

A bit more, just a bit.

Then the flames grab hold of the wood, and within ten seconds they have enveloped the coffin completely, and the door of the oven slowly returns to its starting point.

David Sandström pulls out his notebook from the inside pocket of his jacket. He takes out his special pen, then writes carefully on one of the last pages: *Bengt Andersson, 61 10 15-1923. No. 12,349.*

I feel the fire.

It is every feeling. I am transforming now. I am vaporised, becoming the smoke climbing from the chimney of the crematorium, the burned-smelling particles that drift in across Linköping, the air that Malin Fors hungrily inhales as she crosses the car park outside Police Headquarters.

What remains is ashes that will be emptied into the memorial grove beside the chapel in the old cemetery.

All our ashes there are beacons for memory, and my ashes will be there so that anyone who, against all expectation, wants to remember me will have a place to go.

We turn to our memories and thus revisit our lives.

Not much of a consolation for the dead, is it?

But such are the habits of the living these days.

PART THREE

The habits of the living

51

Plants that need watering, post that needs sorting, taps that need checking. Dust that needs sweeping up, a freezer that needs defrosting, a bedspread that needs straightening, and then the memories that need suppressing, events that need forgetting, suspicions that need denying, broken promises that need forgiving and love that needs to be remembered for ever.

Is that possible?

13.45, a few hours after Bengt Andersson's funeral.

Malin is moving through her parents' apartment. Remembers when she was last here. Tove, just like her, on her parents' bed, the same unsuspecting determination, the same naïve openness with her own body.

But still.

Malin laughs to herself. She has to give Tove full marks for her ingenuity in her hunt to find a love-nest for her and Markus in this cold. The two of them are at a matinée, a new action film based on the long-forgotten adventures of some comic-book hero from the fifties, updated for modern tastes: more violence, more – but just as chaste – sex, and a more obvious and happier ending. Ambiguity is the enemy of security, and security is necessary for success at the box-office.

Every age, Malin thinks, gets the stories it deserves.

The smell of her parents' apartment.

It smells of secrets.

In the same way as the hunting cabin in the forest, although it was clearer and cooler in the forest night, not as impenetrable and personal as here. You get twisted, Malin thinks, around your own axle if you spend too long in the past. At the same time, you're done for if you don't dare touch it. Psychotherapists know all about that.

Malin sinks into the sofa in the sitting room.

Feels exhausted and thirsty: Dad keeps his drink in the cupboard above the fridge in the kitchen.

Twist the soul.

Fine furniture that isn't really that fine.

'You'll water the plants, won't you?'

I've already watered them.

The plants. Smells. The smell of cabbage bake.

Of lies. Even here? Just like in Rakel Murvall's house in Blåsvädret. Just weaker, vaguer here. Have to go out there again, Malin thinks, have to go there and squeeze the secrets from the floorboards and walls.

Her mobile rings out in the hall.

It's in her jacket pocket, and she gets up from the sofa, runs out, fumbles.

International call.

'Hello, Malin.'

'Malin, Dad here.'

'Hello, I'm in the apartment, I've just watered the plants.'

'I don't doubt it. But that's not why I'm ringing.'

He wants something, but doesn't dare say, the same feeling as last time. Then her father takes a deep breath, and lets the air out before he starts to speak.

'You know,' he says, 'we've been talking about Tove coming out here, and it must be her half-term break soon? Perhaps that would be a good time?'

Malin takes the phone from her ear and holds it out in front of her, and shakes her head.

Then she pulls herself together. Puts the phone to her ear.

'In two weeks.'

'Two weeks?'

'Yes, it's half-term in two weeks. There's just one problem.'

'What's that?'

'We haven't got the money for a flight. I don't have any spare and Janne had to pay for a new boiler just before Christmas.'

'Yes, we talked about that, your mum and I. We can pay for her ticket. We went to a travel agent today, and there are cheap flights via London. Maybe you could get some time off as well?'

'Impossible,' Malin says. 'Not at such short notice. And we've got a difficult case right now.'

'So what do you think?'

'It sounds like a great idea. But of course you'll have to talk to Tove first.'

'She can go swimming here, go horse-riding.'

'She knows what she wants to do and what she doesn't. Don't worry about that.'

'Will you talk to her?'

'Call her yourself. She's at the cinema right now, but she should be home by ten.'

'Malin, can't you talk—'

'Okay, okay. I'll talk to her, then I'll call you back. Tomorrow.'

'Don't wait too long. Those tickets won't last.'

52

The voices.

Let them fly.

Listen to them all in the investigation.

Let them have their say. Then they'll lead you to your goal.

The hall of Niklas Nyrén's flat is full of transparent packs of biscuits, round, beige raspberry dreams, chocolate tops, chocolate balls that used to be called nigger-balls, and the green rug is covered in biscuit crumbs. There was a dark blue Volvo estate outside in the drive, parked far too close to a letterbox.

Be careful, Malin thought as she rang the doorbell. If the boys did it, he could have helped them with the body.

Niklas Nyrén leads her into the flat, into the tidy living room which is entirely dominated by a big red sofa in front of a wall-mounted flat-screen television.

There's nothing in the flat to suggest that Niklas Nyrén is anything but a completely ordinary middle-aged man.

He's wearing jeans and a green polo-neck sweater, his face is round and his stomach bulges out above his belt. Too much standing still. Too much driving, and too much of a taste for his own products.

'I was going to ring you,' Niklas Nyrén says, and his voice is oddly dark to belong to someone with a weight problem; his voice ought to be higher, hoarser.

Malin doesn't answer, and sits down on an imitation Myran chair at the little dining table by the window facing the Cloetta factory.

'You had some questions?' Niklas Nyrén says, sitting down on the sofa.

'As you know, Joakim Svensson's name has cropped up in

connection with the investigation into the murder of Bengt Andersson.'

Niklas Nyrén nods. 'I find it hard to imagine that the boy could be involved. He just needs to learn a few manners, get a few male role-models too.'

'You get on well with him?'

'I try,' Niklas Nyrén says. 'I try. I had a pretty crap childhood myself, and I wanted to help the lad. He's got keys to this flat. I want to show him I've got faith in him.'

'Crap in what way?'

'Nothing I want to talk about. But Dad was a hard drinker, if I can put it like that. And Mum wasn't exactly affectionate.'

Malin nods.

'And the night between Wednesday and Thursday last week, what were you doing then?'

'Margaretha was here, and I'm pretty sure Jocke was watching that film with Jimmy. Like they said.'

'Jimmy? You know Jimmy Kalmvik?'

Niklas Nyrén gets up, goes over to the window and looks out at the factory.

'They're joined at the hip, those two. If you want a decent relationship with one of them, you have to build bridges in various directions. I usually try to come up with things I think they'll like.'

'And what do they like?'

'What do boys like? I took them to a skateboarding show in Norrköping. We went to Mantorp Park. I let them drive my car on the gravel track out by the old I4. Hell, I even took them to the rifle range once last summer.'

You probably don't have to be too careful, Malin. Niklas Nyrén exudes thoughtlessness, unless he's just playing naïve?

'Do you hunt?'

'No, but I used to shoot as a sport. Small-bore rifle. Why?'

'I'm not going to get into trouble now, am I?' Niklas Nyrén is hunting through a wardrobe in his white-painted bedroom. 'You don't have to have a gun cabinet for a small-bore rifle, do you?'

'I think you probably should.'

'Here it is.' Niklas Nyrén holds a narrow, almost spindly, black rifle out to Malin, who loses her train of thought when she sees the weapon. No one is going to touch it until forensics have taken a look.

'Just put it on the bed,' she says, and Niklas Nyrén looks perplexed and lays the gun on his bed.

'Do you have any freezer-bags?' Malin says.

'Yes, in the kitchen. That's where I keep the ammunition as well.'

'Good,' Malin says. 'Go and get both of them. I'll wait here.'

Malin sits down on the bed beside the gun. Breathes in the sour, stale air and looks at the pictures on the walls: Ikea prints of different sorts of fish, in cheap frames.

Malin shuts her eyes and sighs.

Joakim Svensson has a key to the flat.

He and Jimmy Kalmvik must have taken the rifle some time when Niklas Nyrén was off on one of his sales trips, and gone up to Bengt Andersson's flat and fired a few shots just to scare him, to tease him. The little sods, Malin thinks, then stops herself. Testosterone and circumstances can cause a great deal of trouble for teenage boys, and someone who sees themselves as abandoned and downtrodden often ends up treading on others.

Malin opens her eyes to see Niklas Nyrén coming back from the kitchen.

In one hand he has a packet of freezer-bags, and in the other a box of ammunition.

'I usually use rubber bullets,' he says. 'Damn. I was sure this box hadn't been opened. But someone must have opened it. There are three bullets missing.'

Disappointment transforms Niklas Nyrén's face into a grimacing mask.

Put pressure on the Ljungsbro bullies and get them to confess that they fired shots at the window of Bengt Andersson's flat? Put a bit more pressure on them and get them to say even more?

If there is anything more to tell?

However much I want to go in one direction, it's too early yet, Malin thinks.

She presses harder on the accelerator pedal, on her way right across the snow-covered plain towards Maspelösa. She's already decided to wait, see what fingerprints Karin finds on the rifle, which is in the boot, wrapped up in a blanket. But Malin can't help playing with the idea. Shouldn't I turn round and go and put some pressure on Jimmy Kalmvik? I can do that on my own, child's play compared to the Murvalls. No, better to let Karin do her thing, work out if the rubber bullets in Bengt Andersson's flat come from Niklas Nyrén's rifle, and, if so, present the boys with hard facts. The uniforms can take their fingerprints, and Karin can match them against any she may have found.

Rickard Skoglöf's address is in her mobile, but it's not easy to find the house, and Malin spends a while driving among fields until she finds the little farm.

She stops.

The grey stone buildings are huddled against the cold, snow on the thatched roofs, and there is light coming from the windows of the main house.

Æsir nutters, Malin thinks, before she knocks. I can deal with them on my own as well.

It only takes a few seconds before the man who must be Rickard Skoglöf opens the door, wearing a kaftan and with his hair and long beard in one great tangle. Behind him a white-clad woman's form moves, presumably that of Valkyria Karlsson.

'Malin Fors, Linköping Police.'

'He must have been relieved of duty, that other one, after the shooting,' Rickard Skoglöf says with a smile as he lets her into the house. A damp warmth hits Malin, and she can hear the crackle of an open fire somewhere in the house.

'You can go in there.'

Rickard Skoglöf points to the left, into the living room, where a huge computer screen shimmers on a shiny desk.

Valkyria Karlsson is sitting on the sofa, her feet drawn up under a white nightgown.

'You,' she says as Malin walks into the room. 'The one who interrupted me.'

Rickard Skoglöf comes in, carrying three steaming cups on a plate.

'Herbal tea,' he says. 'Good for the nerves. If that's ever a problem.'

Malin doesn't reply, takes a cup and sinks on to the black office chair in front of the computer. Rickard Skoglöf stays on his feet after giving a cup to Valkyria.

'Does it feel good,' Malin says, 'encouraging young people to do idiotic things?'

'What do you mean?' Rickard Skoglöf laughs.

Malin gets an urge to throw the hot tea in his leering face, but controls herself.

'Don't play stupid. We know you sent emails to Andreas Norling, and who knows what else you might have got other people to do.'

'Oh, that. I read about that in the *Correspondent*. I never thought they'd go through with it.'

'Have you had any contact with Jimmy Kalmvik? Or a Joakim—'

'I don't know any Jimmy Kalmvik. I presume that's one of the teenagers the paper mentioned, the ones who had been tormenting Bengt Andersson. I want to say once and for all that I, the two of us, had nothing to do with that.'

'Nothing,' Valkyria says, stretching out her legs on the sofa, and Malin notices that her toenails are painted with luminous orange varnish.

'I'm going to confiscate your hard drive right now,' Malin says. 'If you protest I'll get a warrant to search the whole house within hours.'

Rickard Skoglöf is no longer grinning, looks afraid.

'Go. Go. You'll never get us, you police bitch.'

Tove comes home just after six o'clock. She slams the door shut, and it's impossible to tell if it's because she's happy or upset.

A reasonable Sunday, Malin thinks as she waits for Tove to come into the living room.

The rifle is at the National Laboratory of Forensic Science; Karin and her colleagues will check the weapon first thing tomorrow morning. Rickard Skoglöf's hard drive is safely secured at the station. Johan Jakobsson and the IT experts can get going on that, check if the bastard Æsir prophet had goaded anyone else to do anything really, really stupid, like murdering Bengt Andersson. If he has, there ought to be traces in his computer of emails and so on. Who knows how much more crap this winter, this landscape, can throw up?

Tove is standing in front of Malin, smiling, and her face and eyes are calm, free of anxiety and restlessness.

'Was the film good?' Malin asks from her place on the sofa.

'Hopeless,' Tove says.

'But you seem happy.'

'Yes, Markus says he can have dinner here with us tomorrow. Is that okay?'

Tove sits down on the sofa and takes a crisp from the bowl on the table.

'He's very welcome.'

'What are you watching?'

'Some documentary about Israel and Palestine and double agents.'

'Isn't there anything else on?'

'Bound to be. Have a look.'

Malin passes the remote to Tove, who zaps through the channels until she finds the local channel. Linköping have beaten Modo away, and Martin Martinsson scored three goals, and there are rumours that scouts from the NHL were at the match.

'I went round to Grandma and Grandad's earlier today.'

Tove nods.

'Grandad rang. He was wondering if you'd like to go and see them during half-term?'

Malin waits for a reaction, wants a smile to spread over Tove's lips, but instead she looks worried.

'But we can't afford the plane ticket?'

'They're paying.'

Tove looks even more worried.

'I don't know if I want to go, Mum. Will they be upset if I say no?'

'You can do what you want, Tove. Exactly what you want.'

'But I don't know.'

'Sleep on it, darling. You don't have to make a decision before tomorrow or Tuesday.'

'It's hot there, isn't it?'

'At least twenty degrees,' Malin says. 'Like summer.'

There are apples hanging in the trees and a boy, two boys, three, four boys are running around in a verdant garden. They fall and the grass colours their knees green, and then there's just one single boy left and he falls but gets up again and runs. He runs until he reaches the edge of the forest, then hesitates for a while before summoning his courage and heading into the darkness.

He runs between the tree trunks and the sharp branches on the ground cut his feet but he doesn't allow himself to feel any pain, he doesn't stop to fight the monsters roaring in the deep holes left by the roots of toppled trees.

Then the boy is standing by Malin's bed. He presses her ribcage up and down with even movements, helping her to breathe in the yellow air of the morning.

He whispers in her sleeping, dreaming ear, *What's my name, where am I from?*

53

A sullen morning mist over the city, the fields.

The investigation practically going in circles.

A weapon to examine.

Information on a hard drive to check this morning.

No wind over a desolate snow-covered field, nothing happening, just exhausted police officers sleeping or waking. Börje Svärd in his bed, alone under washed-out blue-flowered covers, his two Alsatians let in from their run on either side of the bed, and in the room at the end of the landing two of the nightshift's carers are turning his wife, and he makes an effort to fend off the sound of their activity.

Johan Jakobsson in his terraced house in Linghem, sitting, dozing on a sofa with his three-year-old daughter in his lap, a Lorenga & Masarin cartoon on the television, headphones over his daughter's ears. When are you going to learn that sleeping is nice? The previous day had been spent talking to the other youngsters who had been out in the field for the animal sacrifice. They had alibis for the night that Bengt Andersson was killed, they were just confused in the way that young people so often are. It turned into yet another day of hard slog, another day when he had to leave his family to its own devices.

Zacharias Martinsson is sleeping snuggled up to his freezing wife, the window in the bedroom open a crack, a draught that promises a cold. Sven Sjöman on his back in bed out in his villa, snoring loudly and audibly, his wife in the kitchen with a cup of coffee in front of her on the table, absorbed in *Svenska Dagbladet*;

she likes getting up before Sven sometimes, even if it doesn't happen often.

Even Karim Akbar is asleep in bed, lying on his side, breathing in and out, then he coughs and reaches out an arm for his wife, but she isn't there, she's sitting on the toilet with her face in her hands, wondering how she's going to sort everything out, what would happen if Karim knew.

Forensics expert Karin Johannison is awake, sitting astride her husband, her hair swinging back and forth, helping herself to her own body and consuming him beneath her, flesh that is more hers than his, because what else would she really want him for?

And Malin Fors is awake too. She is sitting behind the steering-wheel of her car. Focused.

The third line of inquiry in the investigation into Bengt Andersson's murder needs pushing, needs whipping, needs to have its back flayed.

Malin is freezing.

The car never seems to be able to warm up properly on mornings like this. Through the windscreen she sees the slender stone tower of Vreta Kloster, and beyond it lies Blåsvädret, and there, alone in her kitchen, sits Rakel Murvall with a cup of boiled coffee, looking out of the window and thinking that it would be good if the boys came home soon, workshops shouldn't stand idle.

Malin parks outside Rakel Murvall's house. The white wooden building seems more tired than last time she was here, as if it were starting to give way, both to the cold and to the person within. The path to the house has been cleared of snow, as if a red carpet were about to be unfurled.

She's bound to be up, Malin thinks. Surprise her. Come when she least expects it.

Just like Tove she slams the car door behind her, but she knows why: it's all about building up a feeling of determination, aggression, superiority that will make the mother obstinate, get her to open up, tell her stories, the ones Malin knows that she has to tell.

She knocks.

Pretends that Zeke is standing beside her.

Light yet oddly heavy steps behind the door, and the mother opens, her thin grey cheeks surrounding the sharpest eyes Malin has ever seen on a human being, eyes that somehow use her up, making her flat, apathetic and scared.

She's over seventy, what can she do to me? Malin thinks, but knows that she's wrong: she's capable of doing absolutely anything.

'Inspector Fors,' Rakel Murvall says in a welcoming tone of voice. 'What can I do for you?'

'You could let me in, it's cold out here. I have a few more questions.'

'But do you expect any more answers?'

Malin nods. 'I think you've got all the answers in the world.'

Rakel Murvall steps aside and Malin goes in.

The coffee is hot and just strong enough.

'Your boys aren't exactly little lambs,' Malin says, settling more comfortably on the rib-backed chair.

She sees first vanity, then anger flit across Rakel Murvall's eyes.

'What do you know about my boys?'

'I'm really here to talk about your fourth boy.'

Malin pushes her coffee cup aside, looks at Rakel Murvall, fixing her with her gaze.

'Karl,' Malin says.

'Who did you say?'

'Karl.'

'I don't hear much from the boy.'

'Who was his father? Not the same as the other boys. That much I do know.'

'You've spoken to him, I see.'

'I've spoken to him. He said his father was a sailor and that he drowned while you were pregnant.'

'You're right,' Rakel Murvall says. 'Off Cape Verde, the eighteenth of August, 1961. The M/S *Dorian*, she went down with all hands.'

'I think you're lying,' Malin says.

But Rakel Murvall merely smiles, before going on: 'Peder Palmkvist was his name, the sailor.'

Malin stands up.

'That was all I wanted to know for the moment,' Malin says, and the old woman stands up too and Malin sees her eyes take command of the whole room.

'If you come here again I'll have you for harassment.'

'I'm only trying to do my job, Mrs Murvall, that's all.'

'Boats sink,' Rakel Murvall says. 'They sink like stones.'

Malin drives past the Murvall family's petrol station. The Preem sign is switched off, the windows of the shop gape at her blackly, and the derelict foundry on the site is just begging to be torn down.

She passes Brunnby and Härna, doesn't want to see the building housing Ball-Bengt's flat. From the road only the roof can be seen, but she knows which building it is.

The landlord has probably cleared the flat by now; your things, the few that could be sold, have probably gone for auction and the money been sent on to the State Inheritance Fund. Rebecka Stenlundh, your sister by blood, if not legally, won't inherit the little you had.

Has someone else taken over your flat, Ball-Bengt? Or are the rooms lying empty, waiting for you to come home? Maybe you're home now, at last? Dust settling on the windowsills, taps rusting shut, slowly, slowly.

She drives under the aqueduct, past the school and picks up her mobile, thinking, I'll have to skip the morning meeting.

'Johan? It's Malin.'

'Malin?'

Johan Jakobsson's voice over the mobile, still sleepy, probably only just arrived for the meeting.

'Can you check something for me, before you get to work on Rickard Skoglöf's hard drive?'

Malin asks Johan to check the loss of the ship, the names of the sailors.

'It's too old to be in the database of the National Administration for Shipping and Navigation,' Johan says.

'That sort of thing must be on various websites. Someone must be interested enough in it?'

'Bound to be. The heroes of the merchant navy probably have admirers who make sure they aren't forgotten. If not, the information should be held by the Shipping Federation.'

'Thanks, Johan. I owe you one.'

'Don't make any promises until you know that I can come up with something. Then it's time for the hard drive.'

Malin hangs up as she turns into Vretaliden care home.

Malin doesn't make herself known at reception, but even though she walks quickly through the lobby she recognises the smell of unperfumed disinfectant, how its chemical unnaturalness makes the whole place seem depressed. In a home, Malin thinks, you use disinfectant that smells of lemons or flowers, but not here. And this is home for some people. People who really deserve a different smell than this.

She takes the lift up to ward three, and walks along the corridor towards Gottfrid Karlsson's room.

She knocks.

'Yes, come in.' The voice faint but still powerful.

Malin opens the door, walks in slowly, sees the thin body under a yellow blanket in bed. Before she has time to say anything the old man opens his mouth.

'Miss Fors. I was hoping that you would come back.'

Malin thinks that everyone waits for the truth to come and pay them a visit, that no one comes with the truth or helps it along of their own volition. But perhaps this is the nature of truth: is it not a sequence of elusive, shy occurrences rather than any one powerful supposition? That fundamentally there is only a *perhaps*?

Malin approaches the bed.

Gottfrid Karlsson pats the blanket next to him. 'Come and sit here, Miss Fors, beside an old man.'

'Thank you,' Malin says, and sits down.

'I've had the reports of your case read out to me,' Gottfrid Karlsson says, looking at Malin with almost blind eyes. 'Terrible things. And the Murvall brothers seem to be particularly delightful. I must have missed them just before I left. But of course I know about their mother and father.'

'What was their mother like?'

'She never made much fuss. But I remember her eyes, and I used to think, There goes Rakel Karlsson, and that woman is not to be messed with.'

'Karlsson?'

'The same surname as me. Karlsson is probably the most common name on the plain. Yes, that was her name before she married Blackie Murvall.'

'And Blackie?'

'A drinker and a braggart, but deep down he was probably just scared. Not like Cornerhouse-Kalle. Different mettle entirely.'

'And her son, she had a son before her marriage to Blackie, didn't she?'

'I seem to remember something of the sort, although his name escapes me. I think his name was . . . Ah well. Some names disappear from memory. As if time were erasing things inside my head. But one thing I do remember: the boy's father was shipwrecked while she was still pregnant.'

'How was she with the boy? It must have been difficult?'

'You never used to see the child.'

'Never saw him?'

'Everyone knew he existed, but you never saw him. You never saw him out and about with her.'

'And then?'

'He must have been two years old when she married Blackie Murvall. But, Miss Fors, there were rumours.'

'What sort of rumours?'

'I'm not the one to talk to about that. You should talk to Weine Andersson.'

Gottfrid Karlsson puts his old hand on Malin's.

'He lives in Stjärnorp care home. He was on the *Dorian* when she sank. He can give you a few facts straight from the horse's mouth.'

The door of the room opens and Malin turns round.

Sister Hermansson.

Her short curly hair seems to be sticking straight up, and today, now that she must have swapped her thick glasses for contact lenses, she looks a good ten years younger.

'Detective Inspector Fors,' she says. 'How dare you?'

54

'No one, not even the police, can come and see any of my residents unannounced.'

'But—'

'No one, Inspector Fors, no one. And that includes you.'

Sister Hermansson dragged Malin to the little nurses' station out in the corridor, then went on the attack.

'The residents here can appear stronger than they are, but most are weak, and at this time of year, when the cold is at its worst, we often lose several in quick succession, and then things get very anxious for my . . .'

To start with Malin got angry. Residents? Didn't that mean that this was their home? That they could do as they liked? But then she realised that Hermansson was right, and if she didn't make the effort to protect the old people, who else would?

Malin apologised before she left.

'Apology accepted,' Hermansson said, and looked visibly pleased.

'And you should change your disinfectant,' Malin added.

Hermansson looked at her quizzically.

'Well, you use unperfumed. There are hypoallergenic perfumed disinfectants that smell much nicer and probably don't cost much more.'

Hermansson thought for a moment.

'Good idea,' she said, and began to look through some papers as if to underline the fact that the conversation was over.

And now Malin is heading towards her car over in the car park, when her mobile rings.

She jogs back to the lobby, and, inside the chemical-scented warmth once more, pulls out her phone.

'We were right. The Shipping Federation had it on its database.'
Johan Jakobsson sounds very pleased with himself.

'So an M/S *Dorian* sank, and there was a Palmkvist on board
who drowned?'

'Exactly. He wasn't among the men rescued in lifeboats.'

'So some of them did survive?'

'Yes, it looks like it.'

'Thanks, Johan. Now I really do owe you one.'

Ruins.

And a lake where the ice seems to have settled for good. Malin
takes her eyes off the road for a few seconds to glance at Lake
Roxen. Cars driving along a ploughed path over the metre-thick
ice slip across in relative safety, and on the other side of the lake,
far off in the distance, smoke is streaming from the chimneys of
postage-stamp-sized cottages.

Stjärnorp Castle.

It burned down in the 1700s, was rebuilt, and to this day is
still the residence of the Douglas family, and it still reeks of
money.

The castle could hardly be more gloomy. It's a grey-stucco
two-storey stone building with shrunken windows, facing a practically featureless courtyard flanked by unadorned outhouses. The
ruins of the old castle slumber alongside, like a permanent
reminder of how badly things can turn out.

The old people's home is on the edge of the estate, just beyond
the bend where the road finally disentangles itself from the forest
and opens up to the view of the lake.

The three-storey building is whitewashed, and Malin estimates
that there can't be more than thirty old people living here, and
how quiet it must be, only a few random cars driving past.

She parks in front of the entrance.

What sort of Hermansson figure am I going to run into
here?

Then she thinks of that evening, how Tove has invited Markus
to dinner; she hopes she makes it back okay. She looks up at the

building, thinking, Weine Andersson, there's a chance there may be a problem with dinner.

Weine Andersson is sitting in a wheelchair by a window with a view straight out over Lake Roxen.

When Malin reported at reception the elderly nurse seemed pleased at her visit. The nurse didn't seem bothered, and certainly not annoyed, by the fact that Malin was a police officer on duty. Instead she said, 'That'll cheer Weine up. He doesn't get many visitors.' Then a pause: 'And he likes young people.'

Young people? Malin thought. Do I still qualify as that? Tove's a young person. Not me.

'His right side is paralysed. A stroke. It hasn't affected his speech, but he gets upset a lot.'

Malin nodded and went in.

The bald man in front of her has sailor's tattoos on both hands. On the lame hand, supported by a sling, someone has etched an anchor, and filled in the rough outline with ink.

His face is wrinkled and the skin covered with liver-spots, one eye is blind, but the good one seems to make up for it in brightness.

'Yes,' he says, his eye firmly fixed on Malin. 'I was on board that ship. I shared a cabin with Palmkvist. It would be going a bit far to say we were friends, but we came from the same parts so it was natural that we spent a lot of time together.'

'He drowned?'

'Off Cape Verde we got caught up in a storm. No worse than many others, but the ship was hit by a huge wave. We started to list and in just half an hour we had sunk. I swam for it and got into a lifeboat. We spent four days out in that storm before we were picked up by the M/S *Francisca*. We survived by drinking rainwater.'

'Weren't you frozen?'

'It was never cold. Just dark. Not even the water was cold.'

'And Palmkvist?'

'I never saw him. I think he was caught in the galley when the first wave hit. It probably filled up with water straight away. I was on watch up on the bridge.'

Malin can see it all in front of her.

The ship lurches.

A young man wakes up with a jolt, then everything is black and the water rises, comes closer in the darkness, like a mass of octopus tentacles; she sees how the cabin door is shut tight from the pressure on the other side, how his mouth, nose, head are covered, and how he finally gives up. Inhales the water and lets himself sink into a soft mist where there is nothing but peace and a warmer darkness than the one he has just left.

'Did Palmkvist know he was going to be a father?'

Weine Andersson can't suppress a chuckle. 'I heard those rumours when I got home. But I can tell you for a fact that Palmkvist wasn't the father of Rakel Karlsson's boy. He wasn't interested in women in that way.'

'He didn't want children?'

'Sailors, Inspector Fors. What sort of men used to become sailors in the old days?'

Malin nods, pauses for a moment before going on. 'So who was the boy's father if it wasn't Palmkvist?'

'I made it ashore afterwards. The third night in the storm, just when we thought it was easing, it started up again. I tried to hold on to Juan but he slid out of my grasp. It was night and it was dark and the wind was blowing like the worst night of winter. The sea was opening up for us, roaring out its hunger, it had us in its grip, it wanted to devour us, and even though . . .'

Weine Andersson's voice cracks. He raises his healthy arm to his face, bows his head and sobs.

'. . . even though I was holding on as hard as I could, he slid out of my arms. I could see the terror in his eyes, as he vanished down into the blackness . . . there was nothing I could do . . .'

Malin waits.

Lets Weine Andersson collect himself, but just when she thinks he's ready for the next question, the old man in front of her starts to cry again.

'I lived on,' he says, '. . . alone after that, there was no other choice for me . . . I don't think.'

Malin waits.

She watches the sadness draining out of Weine Andersson.

Then, without her having to ask, he says, 'Palmkvist was concerned about the rumour about Rakel Karlsson. It started before we even set off. But I knew, and a lot of other people knew who fathered the child she was expecting.'

'Who? Who was it?'

'Have you ever heard of a man called Cornerhouse-Kalle? He was the father of her boy, and they say he was the one who beat Blackie so he ended up in the wheelchair.'

Malin feels a warm glow course through her body. A warmth that is icy cold.

55

See the way he moves.

Tense muscles, dark eyes.

How the others shy away, how they steer their bodies aside instinctively when he comes with her, her and her or her.

How unending he is, Kalle.

How the sweet smells of the summer evening mingle with the sweat of the dancers' bodies, weekly toil being driven out, the expectations of the flesh, the blood coursing through the body, making it tender with longing.

He's seen me.

But he's waiting.

Warming up his dancing so that he's ready. Stand up straight, Rakel, stand up straight.

The band on the stage, the smell of sausages and vodka and lust. One, two, three . . . most of the others fat with the chocolate they eat from the conveyor belt, but not you, Rakel, not you. You're plump in all the right places, so stand up straight, stick out your breasts just for him as he dances past with her or her.

He's the beast.

Raw lust.

He's violence. The directionless, original blow, the one who doesn't know what flight is, the one who stands firm, obstinate, the one who has no voice or place in chocolate-land.

And tonight Kalle will dance with you, Rakel. Imagine, dancing with Kalle . . . Tonight it will be Rakel dancing the last dance with Kalle, the one who gets to smell the sweat on his shirt.

Then there is a break. The human mice stream into the evening; coloured lanterns and queues for sausages, quarter-bottles emptied, motorcycles over near the entrance, the almost tough guys and their broads, and Kalle walking past the queue, licking the mustard from the sausage and swallowing; the chocolate-fat girl by his side sways and now he sees me, breaks free from her and walks towards me but not yet, not yet. I turn round, head for the toilets, force my way into the Ladies and all the while I feel his steps, his eager, dark breathing behind me.

Not yet, Kalle.

I strut for no man.

'Democratic dance', says the sign. Men asking women to dance, women asking men.

And the women are at him, the man. The only one in the room who deserves the title.

But he denies them.

Looks over at me.

Shall I? I strut for no man. Then he is dancing again, it is someone else's body in his arms but it is me he is leading across the dance floor.

Now it is the gentlemen's turn to ask.

I turn down him, him, him and him.

Then Kalle comes.

I am pressed up against the wooden panelling.

He takes my hand. He doesn't ask, takes it, and I shake my head.

He pulls me out.

But no.

'Dancing, Kalle,' I say, 'is something you'll have to do with all those common chocolate girls.'

And he lets go of my hand, catches her beside me and then round, round, until the music falls silent and I am standing by the entrance to the park and see him walking, see him pass arm in arm with her, her or her.

Kalle, I whisper, quietly so no one hears.

I linger, the sound of disappearing motorcycle engines, of drink fading into dreams and headaches. Lanterns are extinguished, the band pack their things in the bus.

I know you're coming back, Kalle.

The canal is rippling quietly, it's black now, night, and not starlit; high above veils of cloud have swept in across the sky and are hiding the light of the stars, the moon.

How much time has passed?

An hour?

You'll come.

Are you finished with her, Kalle?

Because there you come, rounding the bend and you look so slight as you leave the yellow wooden façade of the bridge-keeper's cottage behind you.

But you're no boy.

That's not why I'm waiting here in the damp, gentle cool of a June night, that isn't why I feel so warm, so warm as you grow larger before my eyes.

Your shirt is unbuttoned.

The hair on your chest, your black eyes, all the power in your body directed at me.

'So you're still here.'

'I'm still here.'

And you take my hand, lead me along the road, past the newly built villas and lead me off to the left along the forest track.

What do I think will happen?

What am I expecting?

Your hand.

Suddenly it is unfamiliar. Your smell, your shadow are unfamiliar. I don't want to be here, in the forest. I want you to let go of my hand.

Let go.

But you squeeze even tighter and I follow you into the darkness, Kalle, even though I no longer know if I want to.

You're panting.

Talking about drink, muttering words and your smells mingle with the forest's; it's full of life but also of decay, of things that disappear.

Let go, let go.

I say the words now. But you pull me on, you tug and you drag and you are strong, you are just as raw as I expected.

Are you a lion? A leopard? A crocodile? A bear?

I want to get away.

I am Rakel.

Over-confident.

Panting.

Then you stop, black bands around us, and you turn round and I try to pull away but you catch my arm, pick me up, and there is no humanity in what you are. Gone is the light, gone is the dream.

Quiet, whore. Quiet.

And I am down on the ground now, no, no, no, not now, not like this and you hit me on the mouth and I scream but all I can feel is the taste of iron and something hard and powerful and long forcing its way upwards.

There, lie still now, here comes Kalle.

The ground cuts into me, burning.

Was this what I wanted so badly? Longed for?

I am still Rakel, and I strut for no man.

Kalle.

I can be like you, only sly.

You are breaking me, but I no longer protest, I lie nicely and it's odd how I can shrink this moment to nothing.

I break, I was broken and your weight means I can't breathe, but even so, you don't exist.

Then you're done.

You get up. I see you fasten your trousers, hear you mutter, Whore, whore, they're all whores.

Branches snap, you stumble, mumble, then the silence tells me you are gone.

But the night has just begun.

The darkness condenses around my midriff, two hands stretch up into the air, break through the clear, shimmering film and decide that here, here there will be life.

I feel it even then.

That in me is growing all the pain and torment of what it means to be human.

I crawl on the wet ground.

The branches writhe, the tree trunks mock, the twigs, leaves, moss eat me.

I huddle down. But then I get up.

Stand up.

And my back is straight.

56

'Let's shake hands.'

Markus holds out his hand and Malin takes it. His grip is firm and decisive, has direction but is still not painfully hard.

Well-drilled, Malin thinks, and sees a man in a doctor's white coat standing and practising handshakes with what is to be the perfect son.

'Welcome.'

'Thanks for inviting me.'

'I don't suppose we have as much space as your family,' Malin says, throwing out her arm in the little hallway and wondering why she feels the need almost instinctively to make excuses in the company of Tove's boyfriend.

'This is lovely,' he says. 'I'd love to live so close to the centre.'

'You'll have to excuse . . .'

Malin wants to bite her lip, and then falls silent, but realises that she has to finish the sentence.

'. . . the fact that I got a bit cross last time we met.'

'I would have done as well,' Markus says with a smile.

Tove comes out of the kitchen.

'Mum's made spaghetti with home-made pesto. Do you like garlic?'

'Last summer we rented a house in Provence. There was fresh garlic growing in the garden.'

'We mostly go on day trips in the summer,' Malin says, then quickly: 'Shall we sit down straight away? Or would you rather have something to drink first? A Coke, perhaps?'

'I'm quite hungry,' Markus says. 'I'd be happy to eat now.'

★

Malin watches him shovelling it in. He's trying to resist, to behave the way his parents must have tried to tell him, but Malin can see how he keeps losing the battle with teenage hunger.

'I think I might have overdone the parmesan . . .'

'This is great,' Markus says. 'Really good.'

Tove clears her throat. 'Mum. I've been thinking about what Grandad said. It sounds great. Really good. But couldn't Markus come too? We've spoken to his parents and they can get him a ticket.'

Hang on now. What's this?

Then she sees herself and Janne before her. She's fourteen, him sixteen. They're lying on a bed in an unidentified room, fingers on the buttons of each other's clothes. How shall we ever manage to be apart from each other for more than a couple of hours? The same feeling in Tove's eyes now.

Expectant, but with a first suspicion that time is finite.

'Good idea,' Malin says. 'They've got two extra bedrooms.'

Then she smiles. A teenage couple in love. With her mum and dad. On Tenerife.

'It's fine with me,' she says. 'But we'll have to ask Grandad.'

Then Markus says, 'Mum and Dad would like you to come to dinner some time soon.'

Help.

No. No.

Doctors' coats and a stuck-up woman around a table. Practised handshakes. Apologies.

'How lovely,' Malin says. 'Tell your parents that I'd love to come.'

When Markus has gone Malin and Tove are sitting at the kitchen table. Their bodies become black silhouettes reflected in the window facing the church.

'Isn't he sweet?'

'He's very well behaved.'

'But not too much.'

'No, Tove, not too much. But enough for you to watch out for him. The well-behaved ones are always the worst when it comes down to it.'

'What do you mean, Mum?'

'Nothing, I'm just rambling, Tove. He's fine.'

'I'll call Grandad tomorrow.'

An internal alarm clock rings and Malin is awake, wide awake, even though the clock on the bedside table says it's 2.34 and her whole body is screaming for rest.

Malin twists and turns in bed, trying to get back to sleep, and she manages to shut out all thoughts of the investigation, of Tove, Janne and everyone else, but sleep still won't come.

Have to sleep, have to sleep.

The mantra makes her more awake each time she thinks it, and in the end she gets up, goes out into the kitchen and drinks some milk directly from the carton, thinking how cross she used to get when Janne did that, how she thought it was disgusting and utterly uncivilised; and in another house, outside Linköping, Janne is lying awake and wondering if he's ever going to stop dreaming and then, to get rid of his memories of the jungle and the mountain roads, he conjures up Malin's and Tove's faces in his mind's eye and becomes calm and happy and sad, and thinks that only the people you really love can arouse such contradictory feelings inside you, and he pretends that his daughter is lying there, thinks about how she's growing away from them, that he never wants to let her go; and in the flat in the city Malin is standing beside Tove's bed and wondering if things could ever have been different or if everything was, is, already predetermined somehow.

She wants to stroke Tove's hair.

But maybe that would wake her up? Don't want to wake you, Tove, but I do want to hold you tight.

The early morning meeting was postponed yesterday, 'No point if you aren't here, Fors,' as Sven Sjöman said over the phone.

The others' breath is hanging heavy in the meeting room and they all seem more alert than her.

Maybe because they've had the results from the forensics lab?

The rubber bullets in Bengt Andersson's flat were fired from the small-bore rifle found in Niklas Nyrén's flat, and Joakim Svensson's and Jimmy Kalmvik's fingerprints were found on the weapon.

'So there we have it,' Sven says. 'We know who fired the shots through Bengt Andersson's window. Now Malin and Zeke can put some real pressure on our little tough guys and see if they're hiding anything else. Get hold of them as soon as you can. They ought to be at school at this time of day.'

Then Malin tells them what she's found out about the Murvall line of inquiry.

She can sense Karim Akbar's scepticism as she explains the connection between Cornerhouse-Kalle and the family. So what if he was Karl Murvall's father, what does that matter? What does it give us that we don't already have? That we don't already know?

'Murvall's a dead-end. We've got new paths to explore. We need more to go on with the Æsir angle; there must be something on the hard drive. Johan, how are you getting on with that? I see, you've got past the password, and found a load of protected files.'

But Malin persists: 'It makes Karl Murvall Bengt Andersson's brother. Something that presumably even he doesn't know.'

'If the old boy in Stjärnorp is telling the truth,' Karim says.

'We can easily check. We've got Bengt's DNA, and we can take a sample from Karl Murvall, and then we'll know.'

'Steady on,' Karim says. 'We can't just run round taking a load of integrity-compromising samples just because of what one man says. Especially if its significance for the investigation is, to put it mildly, questionable.'

After they had eaten last night she had called Sven and told him what Weine Andersson had revealed.

Sven had listened intently, and she didn't know if he was pleased or irritated that she was working on her own angle on a Sunday. But then he said, 'Good, Fors, we aren't done with that line of inquiry yet. And the Murvall brothers are still in custody, under arrest for the other offences.'

And perhaps that's why he now says, 'Malin, you and Zeke can go and talk to Karl Murvall again, see what else he knows. He has an alibi for the night of the murder, but try to find out if he knows anything about this. He may have been lying about how much he knew last time you spoke to him. Start with that, and then go and put some pressure on Kalmvik and Svensson.'

'And the DNA test?'

'One thing at a time, Malin. Pay him a call. See what you get. And the rest of you, look under every single stone, try to find angles and corners in this case that we haven't considered so far. Time is passing and you all know that the more time passes, the less chance there is of us catching the perpetrator.'

Zeke comes up to her desk.

He's angry, the pupils of his eyes are small and sharp.

Now he's annoyed that I went off without him yesterday. Isn't he ever going to get used to it?

'You could have called me, Malin. Do you think Karl Murvall knows about this? About Cornerhouse-Kalle?'

'I've been wondering about that. He might know, but not properly, if you get what I mean.'

'You're too deep for me, Fors. Okay, let's get out to Collins and have a chat with him. It's Tuesday, he ought to be there.'

57

Collins Mechanics AB, outside Vikingstad.

The tarmac car park stretches about a hundred metres from the edge of a dense forest to a security lodge and the heavy boom blocking the only opening in a ten-metre-high fence crowned with perfect coils of barbed wire.

The company supplies components to Saab General Motors. One of the few successful companies on the plain, three hundred people work on the automated construction of car parts. Just a few years ago there were seven hundred, but it is impossible to compete with China.

Ericsson, NAF, Saab, BT-Trucks, Printcom: they have all cut back or disappeared completely. Malin has noticed the changes that happen to areas when manufacturing industry is shut down: violent crime increases, as does domestic abuse. Despair is, contrary to what many politicians might say, a close neighbour of the fist.

But after a while everything reverts in a peculiar way to how it was before. Some people get new jobs. Others are put on training courses or forced or persuaded to take early retirement. They become either artificially necessary, or finished, and end up on a fault-line, on the edges of the society that the Murvall family wants no part in, at any cost. Other than on their own terms.

The realisation that one is used up, Malin thinks. I can't begin to imagine what it must be like to be faced with that conclusion. Being unwanted, unneeded.

Beyond the impenetrable fence lie windowless, hangar-like white factory buildings.

It looks like a prison, Malin thinks.

The guard in the lodge is dressed in a blue Falck uniform, and his face lacks any distinct boundary between cheeks, chin and neck. In the middle of all that skin, creation deigned to introduce a couple of grey, watery eyes that stare sceptically at Malin as she holds up her police ID.

'We're looking for a Karl Murvall. I gather he's IT manager here.'

'For what purpose?'

'It doesn't matter what purpose,' Zeke says.

'You have to state—'

'Police business,' Malin says, and the watery-eyed man looks away, makes a call, nods a couple of times before hanging up.

'You can go to main reception,' he says.

Malin and Zeke walk along the road leading to the entrance. They walk past enclosed production halls, a walk of several hundred metres, and halfway along there are a couple of open doors; worn pulleys hang in their hundreds from beams in the roof, as if they have long been idle and are just waiting to be used. A revolving etched-glass door beneath a ceiling held up by metal beams leads into the reception area. Two women are seated behind a mahogany counter; neither of them appears to notice their arrival. On their left is a broad marble staircase. The room smells of lemon-scented disinfectant and polished leather.

They walk up to the counter. One receptionist looks up.

'Karl Murvall is on his way down. You can wait on those chairs over by the window.'

Malin turns round. Three red Egg armchairs on a brown carpet.

'Will he be long?'

'Only a minute or so.'

Karl Murvall comes down the staircase twenty-five minutes later, dressed in a grey jacket, yellow shirt and a pair of too short dark blue jeans. Malin and Zeke get up when they catch sight of him and go to meet him.

Karl Murvall holds out his hand, his face expressionless. 'Detective Inspectors. To what do I owe this honour?'

'We need to talk in private,' Malin says.

Karl gestures towards the armchairs. 'Here, perhaps?'

'Maybe a conference room,' Malin says.

Karl Murvall turns round and starts to walk up the stairs, looking over his shoulder to make sure Malin and Zeke are following him.

He taps in a code on the lock of a glass door, and it slides open to reveal a long corridor.

Inside one of the rooms they pass can be heard the loud, whirring sound of fans behind a frosted-glass door. A dark shadow behind the door.

'The server room. The heart of the whole operation.'

'And you're responsible for that?'

'That's my room,' Karl Murvall says. 'I'm in control in there.'

'And that was where you were working the night Bengt Andersson was murdered?'

'That's right.'

Karl stops at another glass door, taps in another code. The door slides open, and round a ten-metre-long oak table are a dozen black Myran chairs, and in the middle of the table a dish of shiny red winter apples.

'The committee room,' Karl says. 'This should do.'

'Well?'

Karl Murvall is sitting opposite them, his back pressed against his chair.

Zeke squirms on his.

Malin leans forward. 'Your father wasn't a sailor.'

The expression on Karl Murvall's face doesn't change, not one single muscle tenses, no anxiety in his eyes.

'Your father,' Malin continues, 'was a Ljungsbro legend by the name of Karl Andersson, also known as Cornerhouse-Kalle. Did you know that?'

Karl Murvall leans back. Smiles at Malin, not scornfully, but an empty, lonely smile.

'Nonsense,' he says.

'And if that's true, then you and Bengt Andersson are, I mean, were, half-brothers.'

'Me and him?'

Zeke nods. 'You and him. Didn't your mother ever tell you?'

Karl Murvall clenches his jaw. 'Nonsense.'

'You don't know anything about this? That your mother had a relationship with Cornerhouse—'

'I don't care who was my father or not. I've left all that behind me. You have to accept that. You have to appreciate how hard I've had to fight to get where I am today.'

'Can we take a DNA sample from you so that we can compare it with Bengt Andersson's? Then we'd know for sure.'

Karl Murvall shakes his head. 'It's just not interesting.'

'Really.'

'Yes, because I know. You don't need to do any tests. Mum told me. But because I've tried to leave my other half-brothers and their life behind me, I really don't care about any of that.'

'So you are Bengt Andersson's half-brother?' Zeke asks.

'Not any more. Now he's dead. Isn't he? Was there anything else? I have another meeting I need to get to.'

On the way back to the car Malin looks over at the edge of the dark forest.

Karl Murvall didn't want to talk about his stepfather, didn't want to talk about what it was like growing up in Blåsvädret, didn't want to say anything about his relationship with his brothers, his sister. 'Not another word. You've got what you wanted. What do you know about what it's like being me? If there's nothing else you want to know, duty calls.'

'But Maria?'

'What about Maria?'

'Was she as kind to you as she was to Ball-Bengt? Kinder than Elias, Adam and Jakob? We understand that she was kind to Bengt. Did she know that you were his half-brother?'

Silence.

Karl Murvall's grey cheeks, little twitches at the corners of his mouth.

The boom across the entrance opens and they walk out.

Farewell, prison, Malin thinks.

Duty.

How miserable it can make a place.

Karl Murvall is also Rebecka Stenlundh's half-brother, she his half-sister.

But that isn't my duty, Malin thinks. They'll have to discover that for themselves, if they don't already know. Rebecka Stenlundh would probably rather be left in peace.

58

'Do you think Maria Murvall knew that Bengt Andersson and her half-brother had the same father? That that was why she took him on?' Zeke's voice is muffled by the food they are eating.

Malin takes a bite of her chorizo.

The fast-food joint at the Valla roundabout. Best sausage in the city.

The car is idling with the heater on, and behind them sit the yellow-brick council blocks and student accommodation of Ryd, quiet, as if aware of their position on the housing hierarchy; here live only people who don't have enough dosh, short-term, or for life, unless they win the lottery.

In the other direction is the motorway, and on the far side of some thin clumps of trees the buildings of the university. How scornful they must seem to a lot of the people living in Ryd, Malin thinks. There they sit every day like images of unattainable dreams, missed opportunities, bad choices, limitations. The architecture of bitterness, perhaps.

But not for everyone. Far from everyone.

'You didn't answer my question.'

'I don't know,' Malin replies. 'Maybe she felt there was a connection. Instinctively. Or else she knew.'

'Female intuition?' Zeke is chuckling.

'Well, we can't exactly ask her,' Malin says.

Play with a scorpion and it will sting you. Stick your hand in an earth and the badger will bite you. Tease a rattlesnake and it will bite. The same with darkness: force darkness into a corner and it will attack.

But the truth.

Which is it?

She whispers the word to herself as she and Zeke cross the yard to Rakel Murvall's house. Behind them the sun is sinking towards the horizon; the transition between light and dark is swift and cold.

They knock.

The mother has doubtless seen them coming, thinking, Not again.

But she opens.

'You two?'

'We'd like to come in,' Zeke says.

'Surely you've been here quite enough already.'

Rakel Murvall moves her thin body, backs up and stops in the hall with her arms by her sides, yet still oddly dismissive. Thus far, but no further.

'I'll get straight to the point,' Malin says. 'Cornerhouse-Kalle. He was the father of your son Karl.'

Her eyes turn black, keener. 'Where have you heard that?'

'There are tests,' Malin says. 'We know.'

'That makes Karl the half-brother of the murder victim,' Zeke says.

'What do you want to know? That I invented the entire story of that sodomite sailor when his ship sank? That I gave myself to Cornerhouse-Kalle in the park one night? I wasn't the only one who did that.'

Rakel Murvall looks at Zeke with calm derision in her eyes, then she turns round. Goes into the living room and they follow her and the words crack from her mouth like the end of a whip.

'He never knew, Kalle, that he was the boy's father. But Karl, I had him called that so that I'd never forget where he came from.'

You, Malin thinks, you never let him forget. In your own way.

Her eyes full of coldness now. 'What do you think it was like for me to have the boy here on my own? The sailor's boy, he's the sailor's boy, they swallowed that, the chocolate hags round here.'

'How did Karl find out?' Zeke asks. 'Did the boys and Blackie treat him badly?'

'He came and sat out here with some posh necklace for my seventieth birthday. He thought he was really something, so I told him how it was, that your father, he was Cornerhouse-Kalle, that's what I said to him. The computer expert! Pah! He was standing right where you are now.'

The old woman backs away. Raises a hand towards Malin and Zeke, waving, as if to say, Shoo, shoo, shoo.

'If you say anything about this to the boys I'll haunt you till you wish you'd never been born.'

She isn't afraid of threatening the police, Malin notes. Ghosts that have to be fended off at all costs. And you're still the one steering developments, Rakel. What does that mean?

Through her kitchen window Rakel Murvall watches the two police officers go back to their car. Sees them stepping in their own footprints. She feels her anger subside, her aggression become serious reflection. Then she goes out into the hall and picks up the phone on the little table.

59

Britta Svedlund has stood up, her eyes fixed on Joakim Svensson and Jimmy Kalmvik, who are just entering her office at Ljungsbro school. The room is vibrating with her anger and there is a thick smell of coffee and nicotine.

She must smoke in here sometimes, Malin thought when she came in a few minutes before.

When the boys first caught sight of Malin and Zeke they backed away, wanting to run, but the head's sharp stare held them where they were, is still holding them.

Earlier, when they were waiting for Joakim and Jimmy to come to her office from their English lesson, Britta Svedlund explained the philosophy behind her teaching.

'You have to understand that it's impossible to help everyone. I've always focused on the ones, not necessarily the most talented, but the ones who really want to learn. You can make pupils want more than they imagine, but some are hopeless and I've stopped wasting energy on them.'

You haven't given up on Joakim and Jimmy yet, Malin thinks as she watches Britta Svedlund take command of the boys with her look. Even though they're leaving this spring? Even though they're old enough to take responsibility for what they do?

'Sit down,' Britta says, and the two boys sink on to a couple of chairs, cowering under her voice. 'I've tried my best to protect you. And look what you've done.'

Malin moves so the boys can see her eyes. 'Look at me,' she says in an ice-cold voice. 'Enough lies. We know you fired those shots through the window of Bengt Andersson's flat.'

'We haven't—'

Britta Svedlund's voice from the other side of the table: 'HAVE SOME MANNERS,' and then Jimmy Kalmvik starts talking, his voice shrill, anxious, as if it has been dragged out of adolescence and shifted back to a more innocent age.

'Yes, we used that rifle to shoot at his flat. But he wasn't at home. We took the rifle and cycled there and then we fired the shots. It was dark and he wasn't at home. I swear. We scarpered at once. It was really creepy.'

'It's true,' Joakim Svensson says calmly. 'And we've got nothing to do with all that mad shit that happened to Ball-Bengt afterwards.'

'And when did you fire the shots?' Malin asks.

'Just before Christmas, a Thursday.'

'Will we go to prison now? We're only fifteen.'

Britta Svedlund shakes her head wearily.

'That depends on whether you co-operate or not,' Zeke says. 'Tell us anything you think could be of interest to us, and I mean everything.'

'But we don't know anything else.'

'We don't know shit.'

'So you didn't torment Bengt after that? Things didn't get out of hand one evening? Well?'

'Tell us what happened,' Malin says. 'We need to know.'

'But we didn't do anything else.'

'And the night between Wednesday and Thursday the week before last? Before Ball-Bengt was found?'

'We've already told you, we were watching *Lords of Dogtown*. It's true!' Desperation in Joakim Svensson's voice.

'You can go,' Zeke says, and Malin nods in agreement.

'Does that mean we're free?' Jimmy Kalmvik's voice, naïve.

'It means,' Zeke says, 'that you'll be hearing from us again in due course. You don't fire shots through someone's window without there being consequences.'

Britta Svedlund looks tired, seems to be longing for whisky and a cigarette, seems happy that the boys have left her office.

'God knows, I've really tried with those two.'

'Maybe they can learn from this,' Malin says.

'Let's hope so. Are you close to arresting anyone for the murder?'

Zeke shakes his head.

'We're following several lines of inquiry,' Malin says. 'We have to look into every possibility, every little chance, however improbable it might be.'

Britta Svedlund looks out through the window. 'What's going to happen to the boys now?'

'They'll receive letters calling them in for questioning, if the lead detective thinks it worth while.'

'Let's hope so,' Britta Svedlund says. 'They have to be made to realise that what they did was wrong.'

Back at Police Headquarters Karim Akbar meets them in reception.

Irritation like a cloud over his head.

'What have you two been up to?'

'We've—'

'I know. You've been out to see Rakel Murvall and bullied her with questions about who she had sex with forty-five years ago.'

'We didn't bully anyone,' Zeke says.

'According to her you did. She called and made a formal complaint. And she's going to ring "the paper", as she put it.'

'She's no—'

'Fors, how do you think this is going to look? She'll come across as a defenceless little old lady, and we'll be monsters.'

'But—'

'No buts. We've got nothing to go on there. We have to leave the Murvalls alone. If you, both of you, don't stop, Jakobsson will have to take over.'

'Shit,' Malin whispers.

Karim moves closer to her. 'One day of peace and quiet, Fors, that's all I ask.'

'Shit.'

'Suspicions, Fors, aren't good enough any more. Almost two weeks have passed now. We need something concrete. Not a load of crap about who is whose brother and the fact that we're bullying an old woman in the absence of anything better.'

The door to the open-plan office opens. Sven Sjöman. Resigned look.

'The evidence isn't strong enough to hold the Murvall brothers for the break-in at the weapons store in Kvarn. We have to let them go.'

'For God's sake, they had hand grenades from there. Hand grenades!'

'Yes, but who's to say they didn't buy them from someone in the underworld? Poaching and possession of illegal firearms isn't enough for the court to issue formal arrest warrants. And they've confessed.'

Then a voice from behind the reception desk. 'Call for you, Malin.'

She takes the call at her desk, the phone cold and heavy in her hand.

'Fors here.'

'This is Karin Johannison.'

'Hi, Karin.'

'I've just got an email from Birmingham. They haven't managed to get anything from that sample of Maria Murvall's clothes, it was evidently too messed up, but they're running another test. Something completely new.'

'Nothing? What can we hope to get from the new test?'

'You sound tired. Did what we came up with from the small-bore rifle help at all?'

'Yes, it pretty much means we can shut down that line of inquiry.'

'And?'

'Well, what can I say, Karin. Kids, or rather teenagers, left to their own devices. That's never a good idea.'

60

'Mum, Mum.'

Malin hears Tove calling her from the kitchen, presumes she's finished with her maths homework. Mathematics, yuk. Mathematics must be the language of things, seeing as it has never been mine.

'Mum, come here.'

The teenager.

The child.

The almost adult.

The adult.

All four in one person, with a desire to define her place in the world, a world that doesn't wait for you, and only reluctantly lets you have standing room. Even if you get a good education, Tove, it isn't certain you'll get a job. Become a doctor, a teacher, something secure. But is there anything secure? Follow your heart. Become whatever you like, as long as it's what you really want. Your response so far: I don't know. Maybe write books. So anachronistic. Write scripts for computer games instead, Tove. Do anything, just don't be in too much of a rush, see the world, wait a while before having children.

But somehow you already know all that. You're more sensible than I ever was.

'What is it, Tove?'

Malin settles on the sofa, turns down the television and the newsreader moves his lips without making a sound.

'Did you call Grandad?'

Shit. 'No, didn't we say you were going to call?'

'I thought you were going to call?'

'I don't know, but either way we have to do it now.'

'I'll call him,' echoes Tove's voice from the kitchen, and Malin hears her pick up the phone, dial the number and wait before saying, 'Grandad, it's Tove . . . yes, that sounds great . . . tickes . . . when? . . . the twenty-sixth? . . . well, there's something. You see, I've got a boyfriend . . . Markus . . . two years older . . . and I . . . thought maybe he could come too . . . yes, to stay with you . . . to Tenerife, his parents are okay about it . . . oh, I see . . . maybe you should talk to Mum . . . MUM, MUM, GRANDAD WANTS TO TALK TO YOU.'

Malin gets up and goes out to the kitchen. The smell of tonight's dinner is still in the air.

She takes the receiver from Tove's hand, puts it to her ear.

'Malin, is that you?'

He sounds upset, his voice almost falsetto.

'What do you mean by this? That some Markus should come too? Is this your idea? You always have to abuse the slightest little bit of faith anyone shows in you. Don't you realise that you've spoiled everything now, when all we wanted was to give Tove the chance to come to Tenerife . . .'

Malin holds the receiver away from her. Waits. Tove is standing beside her, expectant, but Malin shakes her head, has to prepare her for the inevitable. She sees disappointment settle over Tove's body, her shoulders drooping.

When she puts the phone to her ear again it has gone quiet.

'Dad, are you there? Have you finished?'

'Malin, whatever makes you put this sort of idea in Tove's head?'

'Dad. She's thirteen. Thirteen-year-old girls have boyfriends that they want to spend their free time with.'

Then Malin hears a click.

She hangs up.

Puts an arm round Tove's shoulders, whispers, 'Don't be sad, darling, but Grandad didn't think it was a very good idea about Markus.'

'Then I'll stay at home,' Tove says, and Malin recognises the defiance, as strong and defined as her own.

Some nights the bed is endlessly wide, some nights it contains all the loneliness in the world. Some nights it is soft and promising, when waiting for sleep is the best part of the day. Some nights, like this one, the bed is hard, the mattress an enemy that wants to force your thoughts into the wrong track, that seems to want to mock you for lying there alone, without another body to rest into and against.

Malin reaches out her hand and the empty space is as cold as the night outside the window, and it gets many times larger because she knows that the empty space is there even as she reaches out her hand to it.

Janne.

She thinks about Janne.

How he is starting to get older, how they are both getting older.

She feels like getting up, calling him, but he'll be asleep, or at the station, or else . . . Daniel Högfeldt. No, not that sort of loneliness tonight, a much worse sort. Real loneliness.

Malin kicks off the covers. Gets out of bed.

The bedroom is dark, a meaningless and empty darkness.

She fumbles with her portable CD player on the desk. Knows which disc to insert. Puts in the earplugs.

Then she lies down again and soon Margo Timmins's gentle voice is streaming through her head.

Cowboy Junkies. Before they got boring.

The abandoned woman alone, longing, but in the last verse triumphant: '. . . kinda like the few extra feet in my bed . . .'

Malin pulls out the earplugs, fumbles for the phone, dials Janne's number and he answers on the fourth ring.

Silence.

'I know it's you, Malin.'

Silence.

'Malin, I know it's you.'

His voice is the only voice she needs, gentle and calm and safe. His voice is an embrace.

'Did I wake you?'

'No worries. You know I don't sleep well.'

'Same here.'

'Cold night tonight, isn't it? Maybe the coldest so far.'

'Yes.'

'Luckily the new boiler seems to be working.'

'That's good. Tove's asleep. Nothing came of that plan with Markus and Tenerife.'

'He got angry?'

'Yes.'

'They never learn.'

'What about us, do we?'

But those aren't the words that pass her lips. Instead: 'You must be getting through a lot of oil this winter.'

Janne sighs down the line. Then he says, 'Time to sleep, Malin. Goodnight.'

61

Somehow the church seems to have grown accustomed to the cold. Got used to having its greying plaster covered by a thin layer of frost. But the trees are still protesting, and the pictures over in the travel agent's windows, the ones of beaches and clear blue skies, are just as mocking.

There's a smell of fresh baking. Malin was up early and had time to put some half-baked little baguettes in the oven. She's already eaten two, with apricot jam and Västerbotten cheese, and now she's sitting by the window in the flat.

Behind her on the kitchen table lies the *Correspondent*. She hasn't even bothered to open the paper. It's all there on the front page.

POLICE REPORTED FOR HARASSMENT IN MURDER CASE.

The headline is a joke, Malin thinks as she sips her coffee and looks down towards Åhléns, with its window displays of padded jackets and hats.

But if the headline is a joke, the article itself is a very bad one, an outright lie.

. . . even though the police have no evidence at all that the Murvall family is involved in the murder of Bengt Andersson, they have visited 72-year-old Rakel Murvall's home to interview her on no fewer than seven occasions. Only a year ago Rakel Murvall suffered a minor stroke . . . this looks very much like a clear case of harassment from the police . . .

Attributed to Daniel Högfeldt. So he's hitting back. In full form.
Hard. Where has he been?

A short article alongside, about the fact that the shots fired
into Bengt Andersson's flat have been cleared up, and that police
are not linking them to the murder itself. A quote from Karim
Akbar: *It is highly improbable that there is any connection.*

Malin sits down at the kitchen table.

Opens the paper.

Rakel Murvall identifies her and Zeke in one quote.

*They've been here seven times and forced their way in. The police
show no respect, even to an old woman . . . But at least my boys are
home again now . . .*

*The boys Mrs Murvall refers to are her sons, Elias, Adam and
Jakob, who were released from custody yesterday when the accusations
against them were found not to be sufficient to justify holding them
any longer . . .*

A picture of Karim.

His face captured in a slightly distorted pose. His eyes staring into
the camera: *Naturally, we are treating this complaint very seriously.*

He's not going to like that picture, Malin thinks.

*It looks as though the police have ground to a halt in their investiga-
tion of the murder. Chief of Police Karim Akbar did not want to
comment on the state of the investigation, claiming instead that he
could not talk about the case at the moment because of 'the sensitive
situation'. But according to the* Correspondent's *source in Police
Headquarters, the investigation has reached an impasse where the
police have run out of new leads to explore.*

Malin drinks the last of her coffee.

Source in Police Headquarters? Who? Maybe more than one.

She suppresses an urge to screw up the paper; she knows
Tove will want to read it. On the worktop sits the baking-tray
with the baguettes. Two for Tove. She'll be happy when she
finds them.

★

The area's morning paper.

Loved by almost everyone in the whole city; they know that from their opinion polls, from the tumult that ensues on the few occasions when the paper doesn't appear because of problems at the printers. Sometimes it feels like people are hugging the *Correspondent* to death, that they have no distance from what it prints, or just don't understand that the newspaper isn't their own personal mouthpiece.

Daniel Högfeldt is sitting at his computer in the newsroom.

The love, the response from the readers is still mostly a positive thing. If he writes something good, he'll get ten emails congratulating him instantly.

He's happy with the pieces in today's paper, and has rewarded himself with a fresh-baked cinnamon pastry from Schelin's down in Trädgårdstorget. Bengtsson, one of the old guard, doesn't have the energy to liven up his texts, and you need energy to cover a crime story like the murder of Bengt Andersson. Finely tuned energy to heighten the inherent drama. The city might be depressed, rendered mute by the cold. But from the emails he has received after those articles about the case, he can sense the disquiet, that fear is alive and well in Linköping, and there are the beginnings of anger that the police seem to be doing nothing.

'We pay fifty per cent tax and the police still aren't doing their job . . .'

Daniel has spent two days in Stockholm.

He stayed at the Hotel Anglais on Stureplan, with a view of all the swaggering fools around that ridiculous concrete mushroom.

Expressen.

He even got to meet the editor-in-chief, the fawning psychopath. But the whole thing felt wrong: sure, a bigger paper, higher salary, but so what?

Expressen.

Stockholm.

Not now. Not yet.

First follow the example of that woman from the *Motala Paper*

who dug up that scandal in the town hall and got the Great
Journalism Award.

If I'm going to go to Stockholm, I'm going to arrive as a king,
or at least a prince. Just like I am here.

I wonder what Malin Fors is up to now.

I wouldn't mind seeing her.

Bound to be worn out from work, angry and horny. Just
like I get when I'm working too much and sleeping too little.
Human.

Expressen.

I'll email the chief editor today and turn them down.

The three-year-old resists as Johan Jakobsson tries to open her
mouth. The blue tiles of the bathroom seem to be folding in on
them, but that mouth is going to open.

'We've got to brush our teeth,' he says. 'Otherwise the tooth
troll will come.' He tries to get his voice to sound both firm and
happy, but realises that he mostly sounds whiny and tired.

'Open wide,' but she wants to run off and instead he holds
her tight, and squeezes her jaw with his fingers, but not too
hard.

Then she pulls free. Runs out of the bathroom, leaving Johan
sitting on the toilet seat on his own. Fuck the tooth troll.

Work. When is this case going to open up? When is something
going to jump out at them? Soon they'll have been through the
whole of Rickard Skoglöf's hard drive and they haven't found a
thing. Sure, emails to the kids who hung the animals in the tree,
and some other weird emails to other Æsir types, but nothing
criminal. They've only got a couple more password-protected
files to check.

His whole life feels like a clenched mouth right now. And Malin
and Zeke just seem to get more and more frustrated. And Börje
suspended. But presumably he's with his wife, or the dogs, or at
the firing range. Although maybe that's the last thing he feels like
doing right now.

★

Karim Akbar passes the five-hundred-kronor note across the counter of the dry-cleaner's. He uses the one in the shopping centre in Ryd for two reasons: they open early, and they clean better.

Behind him the shopping centre: run-down and small. A Co-op shop, a newsagent's, a combined key-cutting and shoe-repair shop, and a gift shop that seems to have been left untouched since it went bankrupt.

Three suits on thin hangers covered in plastic. One Corneliani, two Hugo Boss, ten white shirts in a neat pile.

The man behind the counter takes the note, thanks him and makes to hand him his change.

'That's okay,' Karim says.

He knows that the man who runs the cleaner's is from Iraq, and fled here with his family during Saddam's time. Who knows what he went through? Once when Karim was leaving his suits the man wanted to talk about himself, about his engineering qualifications, about the man he could have been, but Karim pretended to be in a hurry. However much he admires the man for fighting for his family, he's part of the problem, part of what makes him and almost everyone else of foreign extraction a second-class citizen, makes them the sort of people who run the services that the Swedes won't touch. It ought to be forbidden for immigrants to run pizza restaurants and dry-cleaners, Karim thinks. That would get rid of the stereotype. The politically correct might object, but that's the reality. But of course it would be impossible. What about me? I'm not the slightest bit better than him, even if I'm made out to be.

Alienation breeds exclusion.

Exclusion breeds violence.

Violence breeds . . . Yes, what?

The infinite distance between people. The Murvall family that want nothing more than to be left outside, in peace, and then there is everyone who dreams of being inside, to feel that they belong. Dreams and reality match up in far too few cases.

My dad, Karim thinks as he leaves the dry-cleaner's. It was passive violence that drove him to his death.

But I never talk to anyone about him. Not even my wife.

The cold hits Karim when he opens the door.

His black Mercedes is glinting even in the gloomy winter light.

And then he thinks about the killers, or the killer, they're hunting. What is it that they want? What are they trying to achieve?

Zeke pulls open the door of Police Headquarters.

Walks into reception and it smells of sweat and overworked radiators, and one of the uniformed officers standing by the steps to the basement calls out, 'How's it going with Martin, is he going to play the next match? Wasn't there something to do with his knee?'

The ice-hockey player's dad.

Is that how they see me?

'He's playing, as far as I know.'

Martin has had offers from NHL clubs, but nothing has worked out so far. They don't quite seem to want to let him in yet. Zeke knows that ice hockey will make the lad rich sooner or later, rich in a way that's hard to imagine.

But not even a hoard of pirate treasure would make him have any respect for the game itself. The padding, the tackles, the sense that it's all make-believe.

Bengt Andersson isn't make-believe. Nor is the evil that's out there.

You can't have a load of padding on, Zeke thinks, when you're tackling the worst aspects of humanity. What we do is no game.

'Have you seen the way I look?'

Karim Akbar is standing by the counter in the coffee room and holding up the photo of himself in the paper.

'Couldn't they have chosen a different one?'

'It's not that bad,' Malin says. 'It could have been worse.'

'How? Have you seen what I look like? They're just choosing pictures that give the impression we're desperate.'

'Forget it, Karim. You'll probably be in the paper again tomorrow. Anyway, we aren't desperate. Are we?'

'Never desperate, Malin. Never.'

★

Malin opens up her email. Some of the usual administrative circulars, a bit of spam, and a message from Johan Jakobsson.

'Nothing on the hard drive so far. Only a few more folders to check.'

And then an email marked in red.

'CALL ME.'

From Karin Johannison.

Why couldn't she call herself?

But Malin knows how it is. Sometimes it just seems easier to send an email.

She types a reply: 'Have you heard anything?'

She presses send and it isn't more than a minute before her inbox pings.

She opens the new email from Karin. 'Can you come over?'

Answer: 'I'll be at the lab in ten minutes.'

Karin Johannison's office at the National Laboratory of Forensic Science has no windows, apart from a glass partition on to the corridor. The walls are covered from floor to ceiling with simple bookcases, and on the desk are stacks of files. The yellow linoleum floor is covered with a thick, red, high-quality carpet that Malin knows Karin has brought in herself. The carpet makes the whole room noble and pleasant, in spite of all the mess.

Karin is sitting behind the desk, as impossibly fresh as ever.

She invites Malin to sit down, and she settles on to the small stool by the door.

'I've had the results from Birmingham,' Karin says. 'And I've compared the results with Bengt Andersson's profile. They don't match. It wasn't him who raped his Maria Murvall in the forest.'

'Was it a man or a woman?'

'We can't tell. But we can tell that it wasn't him. Did you think it was?'

Malin shakes her head. 'No, but now we know.'

'Now we know,' Karin says. 'And the Murvall brothers can be told. Do you think one of them killed Bengt Andersson? And would maybe want to confess if they found out they got it wrong?'

Malin smiles.

'Why are you smiling?'

'You're good at chemistry, Karin,' Malin says. 'But you're not quite so good at people.'

The two women sit in silence.

'Why couldn't you have told me this over the phone?' Malin asks.

'I just wanted to tell you in person,' Karin replies. 'It seemed better somehow.'

'Why?'

'You're so shut off sometimes, Malin, tense. And we keep bumping into each other in the course of our work. It's no bad thing to meet like this, in a calmer setting occasionally. Don't you think?'

As she is walking out of the lab, Malin's mobile rings.

Malin talks as she crosses the car park, past a garage with its doors closed, towards the parking spaces over by the bushes where her Volvo is parked next to Karin's grey, shiny Lexus.

Tove.

'Hello, darling.'

'Hi, Mum.'

'Are you at school?'

'On a break between maths and English. Mum, you remember that Markus's parents want to have you over for dinner?'

'I remember.'

'Can you do tonight? They'd like to do it this evening.'

Smart doctors.

They'd like to.

The same evening.

Don't they know that other people have busy lives?

'Okay, Tove. I can manage that. But not before seven o'clock. Tell Markus I'm looking forward to it.'

They hang up.

As Malin opens the car door she thinks, What happens when you lie to your children? When you do your children harm? Does a star go out in the sky?

62

'Are there stones left unturned?' Zeke asks.

'I don't know,' Malin says. 'I can't see the whole thing properly right now. All the pieces, they don't seem to fit together.'

The clock on the brick wall is slowly ticking towards twelve.

The office at the station is almost deserted. Zeke is sitting behind his desk, Malin on a chair next to it.

Desperate? Us?

Not desperate, but fumbling.

When Malin got back from the forensics lab they had an endless meeting where they went through the state of the investigation.

First the bad news.

The disappointment in Johan Jakobsson's voice from his seat along one side of the table: 'The penultimate folder on Rickard Skoglöf's computer only contained a load of average porn, *Hustler*-style stuff. Fairly hardcore, but nothing remarkable. We've got one folder left with some sort of ingenious password mechanism, but we're working on it.'

'Let's hope there are some secrets in there,' Zeke said, and Malin could hear that his voice concealed the fervent wish that this whole thing would soon be over.

Then they stumbled about together. Tried to find the investigation's voice, the common, cohesive thread. But no matter how they tried, they kept coming back to the start: the man in the tree and the people around him, the Murvalls, Maria, Rakel, Rebecka; the ritual, the heathen faith, Valkyria Karlsson, Rickard Skoglöf; and the vanishingly small chance that Jimmy Kalmvik and Joakim Svensson might have done something really stupid during the few hours when only they could provide alibis for each other.

'We know all that,' Sven Sjöman said. 'The question is, can we do much more with any of it? Are there any other paths that might be more productive? Can we see any other paths?'

Silence in the room, a long, painful silence.

Then Malin said, 'Maybe we could tell the brothers that Bengt Andersson wasn't the person who raped their sister? Maybe they'd have something else to say if they knew that?'

'Doubtful, Malin. Do you think they would?' Sven said.

Malin shrugged.

'And they've been released,' Karim Akbar said. 'We can't bring them in again just for that, and if we go out and talk to them now without anything more concrete, they'd doubtless make allegations that we're harassing the whole family. The last thing we need is more bad publicity.'

'No new tip-offs from the public?' Johan tried.

'Nothing,' Sven said. 'Total silence.'

'We could make a new request,' Johan said. 'Someone must know something.'

'The media are chewing us up already,' Karim said. 'We'll have to manage without another request for information at the moment. It would only lead to more bad press.'

'The National Criminal Investigation Department?' Sven suggested. 'Maybe it's time to call them in. We have to admit that we're not making any progress.'

'Not yet, not yet.' Karim sounding self-confident, in spite of everything.

They had left the meeting room with a general feeling that they were all waiting for something to happen, that they could really only follow developments, wait for whoever had hung Bengt Andersson in the tree somehow to make themselves visible again.

But what if he, she or they remained invisible? If the whole thing was a one-off?

Then they were stuck.

All the voices of the investigation had fallen silent.

But Malin remembered how she had felt out by the tree: that there was something left unfinished, that something was in motion out in the forests and the snow-swept plain.

And now the clock on the brick wall is almost at twelve. As it hits, Malin says, 'Lunch?'

'No,' Zeke says. 'I've got choir practice.'

'You have? At lunchtime?'

'Yes, we've got a concert in the cathedral in a few weeks' time, so we're squeezing in some extra practice.'

'A concert? You haven't mentioned it. Extra practice? You sound like a hockey player.'

'God forbid,' Zeke says.

'Can I tag along?'

'To choir practice?'

'Yes.'

'Sure,' Zeke says, nonplussed. 'Sure, Malin.'

The assembly hall of the city museum smells musty, but the members of the choir seem happy enough in the large space. There are twenty-two of them today. Malin has counted them, thirteen women, nine men. Most of them are over fifty and they're all well dressed and well ironed in typical provincial style. Coloured shirts and blouses, jackets and skirts.

The members have crowded together, standing in three rows on the stage. Behind them hangs a large tapestry with embroidered birds that seem to want to take off and drift around the room, up to the vaulted ceiling.

Malin is sitting in the back row, by the oak panelling, listening to the members tune up, giggle, chatter and laugh. Zeke is talking animatedly to a woman the same age as him, tall, with blonde hair and wearing a blue dress.

Nice, Malin thinks. Both her and the dress.

Then one woman raises her voice and says, 'Okay, then, let's get to work. We'll start with "People Get Ready".'

As if on command the members line up neatly, clear their

throats one last time, and adopt the same look of concentration.

'One, two, three.'

And then the singing, a harmonious sound, fills the hall and Malin is surprised at its gentle strength, and how beautiful it sounds when the twenty-two voices sing together as one single voice: '. . . you don't need no ticket, you just get on board . . .'

Malin leans back in her chair. Closes her eyes, letting herself be embraced by the music, and when she looks up the next song has started and she can see that Zeke and the others really enjoy being up on stage, that they're somehow united in their singing, in its simplicity.

And suddenly Malin feels an oppressive loneliness. She isn't part of this, and she feels that this loneliness means something, that the sense of being an outsider somehow has a meaning beyond this room.

Over there is a door.

An opening into a closed room.

Intuition, Malin. Voices. What are they trying to tell me?

63

Bad deeds.

When do they start, Malin? When do they end? Do they go in circles? Are there more of them over time, or is the practice of evil constant? Is it diluted or enriched whenever a new person is born?

I can think about all this as I move over the landscape.

I look at the oak where I hung.

A lonely place. Perhaps the tree liked my company? The balls. I fetched the balls and threw them back, and they came back again and again and again.

Maria?

Did you know?

Was that the reason for your friendliness? The connection between us? Does it matter? I don't think so.

Air beneath and above me, I reside in my own vacuum. All the dead around me whisper, Carry on, Malin, carry on.

It isn't over yet.

I'm scared again.

Is there a way out?

There has to be.

Just ask the woman down there. The woman that black-clad person is approaching from behind, hidden behind a row of bushes.

The early evening is silent and cold and dark. The garage door refuses to open, creaking and squealing, and the sound seems to catch on the frozen air. She presses the button on the wall again; the key is where it should be and the power is on, that much is sure.

Behind her the buildings, the deep-frozen vegetation, lights in most of the windows. Almost everyone is home from work. The garage door won't move. She'll have to open it by hand. She's done it once before. It's heavy but not impossible, and she's in a hurry.

Rustling in the bushes behind her. Maybe a bird. At this time of year? Maybe a cat? But don't they stay indoors in this sort of cold?

She turns round and that's when she sees it, the black shadow racing towards her, taking one two three four steps before it is on her and she flails with her arms, screaming but nothing comes out; something that tastes chemical pressed into her mouth and she tears and hits but the gloves on her hands turn her blows into caresses.

Look out of your windows.

Look at what's happening.

He – because it must be a he? – is wearing a black balaclava and she sees the dark brown eyes, the rage and pain in his gaze, and the chemical smell is in her brain now, it's soft and clear yet it still makes her disappear, her muscles relax and she can no longer feel her body.

She can see. But she is seeing double.

She sees the person, people standing over her. Are there several of you?

No, stop it, not like this.

But there's no point fighting. As if everything has already happened. As if she is defeated.

The eyes.

His, hers, theirs?

They aren't here, she thinks. The eyes are somewhere else, far away.

Sweet breath, warm, and it ought to be unfamiliar, but it isn't.

Soon the chemical feeling reaches her eyes, then her ears. And pictures and sound are gone, the world is gone and she doesn't know if she's falling asleep or dying.

Not yet, she thinks. I've been drugged, haven't I? His face there at home, my face.

Not yet, yet, yet, yet . . .

★

She is awake.

She knows that. Because her eyelids are open and her head is aching, even if it is completely dark. Or is she sleeping? Confused thoughts.

Am I dead?

Is this my grave?

I don't want to be here. I want to go home, to my loved ones. But I'm not scared. Why aren't I scared?

That sound must be an engine. A well-maintained engine that does its job with joy in spite of the cold. Her wrists and feet ache. It's impossible to move them, but she can kick, tense her body in a bow and kick against the four walls of the space.

Shall I scream?

Of course. But someone, him, her, them, has taped her mouth shut, a rag between her teeth. What does it taste of? Biscuits? Apples? Oil? Dry, drier, driest.

I can fight.

Like I've always done.

I'm not dead. I'm in the boot of a car and I'm freezing and kicking, protesting.

Thump, thump, thump.

Can anyone hear me? Do I exist?

I hear you.

I am your friend. But I can't do anything. At least not much.

Perhaps we can meet afterwards, when all this is over. We can drift side by side. We can like each other. Run round, round the scented apple trees in a season that is perhaps one eternal long summer.

But first: a car feeling its way forward, your body in the boot; the car stops in a deserted lay-by and you are drugged again, your kicks were too much; the car drives across the field and up into the very closest darkness.

64

Ramshäll.

The very brightest side of Linköping.

Perhaps the very finest part of the city, to which the door is closed to most people, where the most remarkable people live.

Maybe it's the case, Malin thinks, that everyone, consciously or unconsciously, assumes the guise of importance if the opportunity arises, whether large- or small-scale.

Look, we live here!

We can afford it, we're the kings of the 013 area-code.

Markus's parents' house is in Ramshäll, among houses owned by Saab directors, successful entrepreneurs, well-heeled doctors and successful small businessmen.

The villas are almost in the middle of the city, clambering up a slope with a view of the Folkungavallen Stadium and Tinnis, a large communal outdoor swimming pool whose site every property developer in the country covets greedily. At the end of the slope the settlement disappears into the forest or rolls away in narrow streets down towards Tinnerbäcken pond where the dirty-yellow boxlike hospital buildings take over. Best of all is living on the slope, with a view, closest to the city, and that's where Markus's parents live.

Malin and Tove are walking side by side in the glow of the street-lamps, and their bodies cast long shadows along the well-gritted pavements. The residents would probably like to put up a fence around the whole area, or an electric fence with barbed wire and a security guard on the gate. Ideas of gated communities aren't entirely alien to certain right-wing politicians on the city council. So a fence around Ramshäll isn't perhaps as unthinkable as it might seem.

Stop. Thus far but no further. Us and them. Us against them. Us.

It doesn't take more than fifteen minutes to walk from the flat to Ramshäll, so Malin decided to brave the cold, in spite of Tove's protests: 'Look, I'm coming with you. So you can walk with me.'

'I thought you said it was going to be fun?'

'It will be fun, Tove.'

On the way they walk past Karin Johannison's villa. A yellow-painted house from the thirties with a wooden façade and a veranda.

'It's cold, Mum,' Tove says.

'It's healthy,' Malin says, and with every step she feels her restlessness subsiding, how she is preparing herself to get through the dinner.

'You're nervous, Mum,' Tove suddenly says.

'Nervous?'

'Yes, about this.'

'No, why would I be nervous?'

'This sort of thing always makes you nervous. Going to some-one's house. And they *are* doctors.'

'As if that makes any difference.'

'Over there,' Tove says, pointing along the street. 'Third house on the left.'

Malin sees the villa, a two-storey building of white brick, surrounded by a low fence and with clipped shrubs in the garden.

Inside her the house expands. It becomes a fortified Tuscan hill-town, impossible for a lone foot-soldier to capture.

Inside the house there is a smell of warmth and bay leaves and the cleanliness that only a hard-working Polish cleaner can conjure forth.

The Stenvinkels are standing in the hall, they have shaken Malin by the hand and she is swaying, unprepared for the unrelenting friendliness.

Mum, Birgitta, is a senior physician at the Ear Clinic, and wants to be called Biggan, and it's sooo lovely to meet Malin at laaast, when they've read so much about her in the *Correspondent*. Dad, Hans, a surgeon, wants to be called Hasse, hopes they like pheasant, because he got hold of a couple of lovely ones down at Lucullus. Stockholmers, upper middle class, brought to the back of beyond by their careers, Malin thinks.

'Am I wrong,' she asks, 'but can I hear that you're both from Stockholm?'

'Stockholm? Does it really sound like it? No, I'm from Borås,' Biggan says. 'And Hasse's from Enköping. We met when we were studying in Lund.'

I know their life history, Malin thinks, and we haven't got further than the hall.

Markus and Tove have disappeared into the house, and now Hasse is leading Malin into the kitchen. On a sparkling stainless-steel worktop sits a misted cocktail shaker and Malin capitulates, doesn't even contemplate trying to resist.

'A martini?' Hasse asks.

Biggan adds, 'Watch out, though. He makes them *very* dry.'

'Tanqueray?' Hasse says.

'Please,' Malin replies, and minutes later she is standing with a drink in her hand and they say a toast, and the alcohol is clean and pure and she thinks that at least he knows his drink, Hasse.

'We usually have an aperitif in the kitchen,' Biggan says. 'It livens up the atmosphere so.'

Hasse is standing by the cooker. With one hand he waves Malin over to him as his other hand opens the lid of a blackened, well-used cast-iron casserole.

The smell hits Malin as she approaches.

'Take a look,' Hasse says. 'Have you ever seen such lovelies?'

Two pheasants swimming in a puttering yellow sauce and Malin feels hunger grip her stomach.

'Well?'

'That looks wonderful.'

'Oops, that disappeared quickly,' Biggan says, and at first Malin doesn't understand what she means, then she sees the empty glass in her hand.

'I'll mix you another,' Hasse says.

And as he is shaking the cocktail in the air Malin asks, 'Does Markus have any brothers and sisters?'

Hasse stops shaking abruptly.

Biggan smiles before saying, 'No. We tried for a long time. But then we had to give up.'

Then the ice rattles in the cocktail shaker again.

65

Her head.

It's heavy, and the pain is like a fruit-knife thrust between the lobes of her brain. If you feel pain like that you don't sleep. In dreams there is no physical pain. That's why we love them, dreams.

No, no, no.

She remembers now.

But where's the engine? The car? She isn't in the car any more.

Stop it. Let me go. I've got someone who needs me.

Take this blindfold off my eyes. Take it off. Maybe we could talk about this? Why me?

Is there a smell of apples here? Is that earth under my fingers, cold but still warm earth, biscuit crumbs?

There's a stove crackling.

She kicks in the direction the warmth is coming from, but strikes no metal; she tenses her back but doesn't get anywhere. Only a dull thud, a vibration through her body.

I am . . . Where am I?

I'm lying on cold earth. Is this a grave? And I am dead, after all? Help me. Help me.

But it's warm around me and if I was in a coffin there'd be wood.

Take this rope off, for God's sake.

The rag in her mouth.

Strain hard enough and it might break, the rope. Twist back and forth.

Eventually the cloth is pulled away from her eyes.

A flickering light. A vaulted cellar? Earth walls? Where am I? Are those spiders and snakes moving around me?

A face. Faces?

Wearing a ski mask.

The eyes. Looking, yet not looking.

Now they've gone again, the faces.

Her body aches. But now is where the pain starts, isn't it?

I wish I could do something.

But I am powerless.

I can only watch, and I will do, because the look in my eyes may give you some comfort.

I shall stay even if I would rather avert my gaze and disappear to all the places I can disappear to.

But I stay in the fear and the love and all the other feelings. It isn't over yet, but do you have to do that? Do you imagine they'll be impressed?

It hurts, I know, I had to feel the same. Stop it, stop it, I say, but I know, you can't hear my voice. Do you think her pain will eradicate another pain? Will her pain open the doors? Mine didn't, after all.

So I beg you: stop, stop, stop.

Did I say stop?

How can a single noise come out of my mouth when it is taped up, the rag pressed deep between my teeth?

She is naked. Someone tore off her clothes, splitting the seams with a knife and now someone brings a candle close to her shoulders and she is frightened, the voice mumbling, 'This must, must, must happen.'

She screams.

Someone brings the candle close, close, and the heat is sharp and she screams as if she doesn't know how to scream, as if the sound of her burning skin and the pain are one. She twists back and forth but gets nowhere.

'Shall I burn your face off?'

Is that what the mumbling voice is saying?

'Perhaps that would be enough. Perhaps I wouldn't have to

kill you then, because you won't exist properly without a face, will you?'

She screams, screams. Soundlessly.

The other cheek. Her cheekbone burns. Circular movements, red, black, red, the colour of pain, and there is a smell of burned skin, her skin.

'Shall I get the knife instead?

'Hang on now.

'Don't faint, stay awake,' the voice mumbles, but she wants to be gone.

The blade shines in the light, the pain has disappeared, adrenalin is pumping through her body and the only thing is her fear that she might never get away from here.

I want to get home to my loved ones.

He must be wondering where I am. How long have I been here? They must be missing me by now.

The knife is cold and warm and what is that warmth running down my thighs? A woodpecker with a steel beak is pecking at my breasts, eating its way down to my ribs. Let me vanish; my face burns when someone hits me in vain attempts to keep me awake.

But it doesn't work.

I'm going now.

Whether you like it or not.

How much time has passed? I don't know.

Are those chains rattling?

I'm tied to a post now with forest around me.

I'm alone.

Have you gone? Don't leave me here alone.

I'm whimpering. I can hear it.

But I'm not freezing and I wonder when the cold stopped being cold.

When does pain stop hurting?

How long have I been hanging out here now? The forest is thick around me; dark but white with snow. There's a little clearing, and a door leading down to a hole.

My feet don't exist. Nor my arms, hands, fingers or cheeks. My cheeks are burning holes, and everything around me lacks any smell.

Away.

Away from here.

That's all that's left.

Away, away, away, at any cost.

But how can I run if I don't have any feet?

Something is approaching again.

Is it an angel?

Not in this darkness.

No, it's something black approaching.

'What have I done?'

Is that what the black thing says?

'I have to do this.' That's what the black thing says.

She tries to lift her head but nothing happens. She makes a real effort and there, there, she slowly lifts her head and the black thing is close now and is swinging a cauldron of boiling water backwards and she thinks herself away, and then the sound, someone roaring as the water is thrown at her.

But it doesn't reach. No heat arrives, just a few drops of warmth.

Now the black thing itself again.

With a branch in its hand?

What's that for?

Shall I scream?

I scream.

But not because anyone will hear me.

66

Candles are burning in the dining room and on the wall behind Hasse and Tove hangs a large oil painting by an artist called Jockum Nordström, who according to Biggan is supposed to have become some sort of big noise in New York. The painting is of a coloured man dressed in boy's clothes against a blue background, and Malin thinks the painting looks naïve and mature at the same time; the man is alone but still anchored in a sort of context on the blue background, and in the sky drift guitars and billiard-cues.

The pheasant tastes good, but the wine is even better, a red from a region of Spain that Malin doesn't know, and she has to exert all her willpower not to slug it down, it's so good.

'More pheasant, Malin?' Hasse gestures towards the pot.

'Have some more,' Markus says. 'It'll make Dad happy.'

The conversation during the evening has covered everything from Malin's work to weight-training, the reorganisation of the hospital and local politics and the 'reaaally dull' programme at the city's concert house.

Hasse and Biggan. Equally politely and genuinely interested in everything, and no matter how Malin has tried, she hasn't been able to find a single false note. *They seem to like us being here, we aren't intruding.* Malin takes a sip of the wine. *And they know how to get me to relax.*

'Great about Tenerife,' Hasse says, and Malin looks at Tove across the table. Tove looks down.

'Are the tickets all booked?' Hasse asks. 'We need an account number before you go so we can pay in some money. Remind me, will you?'

'I . . .' Tove begins.

Malin clears her throat.

Biggan and Hasse look at her anxiously and Markus turns towards Tove.

'My dad changed his mind,' Malin says. 'I'm afraid they've got other guests that week.'

'Their own grandchild!' Biggan exclaims.

'Why haven't you said anything?' Markus says to Tove.

Malin shakes her head. 'They're a bit odd, my parents.'

Tove breathes out, and Malin realises that the lie has made her feel relief, at the same time as she feels ashamed at not having the bravery, the honesty to come out with the simple truth: that it was Markus who wasn't welcome.

Why am I lying? Malin thinks.

So as not to disappoint anyone?

Because I'm ashamed at my own parents' social incompetence?

Because the truth hurts?

'How strange,' Hasse says. 'Who could possibly be more welcome than their own granddaughter and her friend?'

'It was an old business acquaintance.'

'Well, never mind,' Biggan says. 'Now the two of you can come with us to Åre instead. As we suggested in the first place. I don't mean to criticise Tenerife, but winter is for skiing!'

Malin and Tove are walking home along the well-lit villa-lined streets.

A cognac after the meal makes Malin's mouth run away with her. Biggan had one, but Hasse didn't, had to work the next morning. 'A small martini and a glass of wine. No more than that if I'm going to be wielding a scalpel!'

'You should have explained how things were to Markus beforehand.'

'Maybe, but I—'

'And now you've made me lie. You know what I think about that. And Åre, have they asked you to go to Åre? You could have mentioned that. Who am I really, you—'

'Mum. Can't you just be quiet?'

'Why? I've got things I want to say.'

'But you're saying such stupid things.'

'Why haven't you mentioned Åre?'

'Oh Mum, you know why. When was I supposed to tell you? You're hardly ever at home. You're always working.'

No, Malin feels like shouting at Tove. No, you're wrong, but she stops and thinks. Is it really as bad as that?

They walk on in silence, past Tinnis and the Hotel Ekoxen.

'Aren't you going to say anything, Mum?' Tove asks as they pass the City Mission's charity shop.

'They were nice,' Malin says. 'Not at all what I imagined.'

'You imagine so much about people all the time, Mum.'

67

I'm bleeding.

Something is lifting me up, away from the post and down on to a soft, hairy bed.

I'm alive.

My heart is beating.

And the black thing is everywhere, laying cloth, wool on my body and it's warm and the black thing's voice, voices, say, 'He died too soon. But you, you're going to hang the way it's supposed to be.'

Then the trees above me, I'm moving through the forest. Am I lying on a sledge? Can I hear the sound of runners over the crust of snow? I'm tired, so tired, and it's warm.

It's a real warmth.

It's in my dream and in wakefulness.

But away from the warmth.

It kills.

And I don't want to die.

The engine sound again. I'm in a car now.

In the sound of the engine, in its persistent running is a suspicion. That my body has one more chance, that it isn't yet too late.

I breathe.

Welcome the pain from every battered and smashed body part, the tearing of my bleeding innards.

It is in pain that I exist now. And it will help me survive.

I am drifting here.

The field lies open. Between Maspelösa, Fornåsa and Bankeberg,

at the end of an unploughed road covered by just a thin layer of snow,
stands a lone tree, like the one I was hanging in.
   The car with the woman in the boot stops there.
   I wish I could help her now.
   But she must do that herself.

The black thing has to open up. It has to help me out. Then
I shall be an engine. I shall explode, I shall get away, I shall
live.

The black thing opens the boot, heaves my body over the edge
and down on to the snow by the exhaust.

It leaves me lying there.

A tree trunk, thick, ten metres away.

The stone is covered by snow, but I still see it. Is it my hands
that are free, is it my hand, that swollen red lump I see to my
left?

The black thing at my side now. Whispering about blood.
About sacrifice.

If I twist to the left and then grab the stone and strike at what
must be its head, it might work. That could get me away.

I am an engine and I am turning the key.

Now I ignite.

I exist again and I grip the stone, and the whispering stops;
now I strike, I am going to get away and I strike myself away
from here. Don't try to fend me off, I strike, I want more, my
will is what sits deep, deep down, it's brighter than the darkness
can manage to blacken.

Don't try.

I strike at the blackness, and we roll around in the snow, and
cold does not exist and it gets a tight grip on me, but I explode
once more and then I strike. The stone against its skull and the
blackness goes limp, glides off me, on to the snow.

I crawl up on to my knees.

Open field in all directions.

I get up.

In the darkness. I have been there.

I stagger towards the horizon.
I am on my way, away.

I drift beside you as you stumble on across the plain. You will arrive somewhere, and wherever you go, I will be there to meet you.

68

Johnny Axelsson puts both hands on the steering-wheel, feels the vibrations of the vehicle, how the cold is making the engine run unevenly.

Early morning.

Clouds of snow are drifting in across the road from the fields and farms, in shifting, almost blinding veils.

It takes nearly fifty minutes to get from Motala to Linköping, and at this time of year it can be dangerous as well, with the uncertain state of the roads, ice that comes and goes, no matter how much they salt them.

No, best to take it cautiously. He always goes via Fornåsa, much prefers that road to the main road through Borensberg.

And you never know what's going to come out of the forest. He's come close to hitting deer and elk before now.

But at least the roads are straight, built as they were to be able to function as runways in case of war.

But how likely is it that war will ever come?

Unless it's already here.

Motala. Junkie capital of Sweden.

Few if any jobs, unless you want to work in the public sector.

But Johnny Axelsson grew up in Motala, and that's where he wants to live. So what if he has to spend a couple of hours commuting? That's a price he's willing to pay to live somewhere he feels at home. When the job advert from Ikea appeared in the paper he didn't hesitate. And he didn't when he was offered the job either. Don't be a burden. Contribute. Do the right thing. How many of his old friends are living off benefits? Still claiming unemployment even though their jobs disappeared ten years ago. God, we're thirty-five, how can they even bear to think about it?

Go fishing. Out hunting. Play the pools. Watch trotting races. Do a bit of carpentry on the sly.

Johnny Axelsson drives past a red farmhouse. It's close to the road and inside he can see an elderly couple. They're eating break-fast, and in the light of the kitchen their skin looks golden, like two fish in an aquarium, safe and sound in the middle of the plain.

Keep looking ahead, Johnny thinks, the road, that's what you should be concentrating on.

Malin goes straight to the coffee room when she gets to the station. The coffee in the pump-action flask is fresh.

She sits on a chair at the table by the window facing the inner courtyard. Only a white mass of snow at this time of year, a little paved area with a few dubious flower-beds in the spring, summer and autumn.

There's a magazine on the table next to her. She reaches for it. *Amelia*. An old issue.

Headline: YOU'RE GREAT THE WAY YOU ARE! Headline on the next page: AMELIA'S LIPOSUCTION SPECIAL!

Malin closes the magazine, gets up and walks off to her desk.

There's a yellow Post-it note on top of it, like an exclamation mark among the mess of paper.

From Ebba in reception:

Malin.
Call this number. She said it was important. 013-173928.

Nothing else.

Malin takes the note and walks out to reception, but Ebba isn't there. Sofia is sitting on her own behind the counter.

'Have you seen Ebba?'

'She's in the kitchen. She went to get coffee.'

Malin finds Ebba in the kitchen, sitting at one of the round tables, leafing through a magazine.

Malin holds up the note. 'What's this?'

'There was a woman who rang.'

'I can see that from the note.'

Ebba wrinkles her nose. 'Well, she didn't want to say why she was calling. But it was important, I understood that much.'

'When did she call?'

'Just before you got in.'

'Nothing else?'

'Yes,' Ebba says. 'She sounded scared. And hesitant. She was sort of whispering.'

Malin tries to identify the number through Yellow Pages.

Nothing.

It must be ex-directory, and not even they could get round that without a load of time-consuming paperwork.

She calls.

No answer, not even an answer-machine.

But a minute later her phone rings.

She picks up the receiver. Says, 'Yes, this is Malin Fors.'

'Daniel here. Have you got anything new for me about the Andersson investigation?'

She gets cross, then strangely calm, as if she had been wanting to hear his voice, but pushes the thought aside.

'No.'

'The harassment accusation, any comment?'

'Have you suddenly turned stupid, Daniel?'

'I've been away a few days. Aren't you going to ask where?'

'No.' Wants to ask, doesn't want to ask.

'I was in Stockholm. At *Expressen*, they were after me. But I turned them down.'

'Why?' The question pops out of her mouth.

'So you do care after all? Never do what they expect you to, Malin. Never.'

'Goodbye, Daniel.'

She hangs up, then the phone rings again. Daniel? No. Unknown number on the display, silence at the other end of the line.

'Fors here. Who is this?'

Breathing, hesitation. Maybe fear. Then a soft but anxious female voice, as if it knows it's speaking words that are forbidden.

'Well,' the woman says, and Malin waits.

'My name is Viveka Crafoord.'

'Viveka, I—'

'I work as a psychoanalyst here in Linköping. It's about one of my patients.'

Malin instinctively wants to tell the woman to stop, not to say anything else; she isn't allowed to hear confidential information about a patient, just as this woman who calls herself Viveka Crafoord isn't allowed to reveal it.

'I've been reading,' the woman says. 'About the case you seem to be working on, the murder of Bengt Andersson.'

'You mentioned—'

'I think one of my patients . . . well, there's something you need to know.'

'Which patient?'

'You'll appreciate that I can't say.'

'But perhaps we can talk anyway?'

'Not like this. But come to my practice at eleven o'clock today. It's on Drottninggatan, number 3, opposite McDonald's. The door-code is 9490.'

Viveka Crafoord hangs up.

Malin looks at the time on her computer screen: 7.44. Three and a quarter hours.

Martini and wine and cognac. She feels bloated.

Gets up and heads towards the stairs leading down to the gym.

How long have I been walking now?

Dawn has broken but it still isn't day. I'm moving across the fields, but I've got no idea where I am.

I am an open wound, but the cold means that I can't feel my body. I put one foot in front of the other, can't get far enough away. Am I being hunted? Has the blackness woken up? Is it close to me?

Is that a colour, the blackness coming with its car? Is that the engine of darkness?

Turn off the light.

It's blinding me. Be careful of my eyes.

They might be the only thing that's left of me intact.

Eyes on the road, Johnny Axelsson thinks.

Eyes. Use them carefully and you'll arrive safely.

Out in the patches of forest now.

The open fields are nice, but the cold and wind are making the visibility worse than usual, as if the earth were breathing and its air is turning to mist when it meets the chill atmosphere.

Eyes.

A deer?

No.

But.

But what the hell is that?

Johnny Axelsson changes down the gears and slows down, flashing his lights to scare the deer away from the verge, but hell, it isn't a deer, it's, it's a . . .

What is it?

The car seems stuck to the road.

A what?

A person? A naked person? Oh fuck, fuck, what does she look like?

And what's she doing here?

Out on the plain? Like this? In the morning?

Johnny Axelsson rolls past, stops, and in his rear-view mirror he sees the woman stagger past, how she doesn't take any notice of the car, just carries on.

Wait, he thinks.

He's in a hurry to get to work in the Ikea warehouse, but she can't just carry on walking like that. It's completely wrong.

He opens the car door, his body remembers how cold it is, and he hesitates, then runs after the woman.

He puts his arm on her shoulder and she stops, turns round

and her cheeks, has she burned them or is it the cold, the skin on her stomach, where is it, and how can she walk on feet like that, they're black, as black as the currants in his garden at home?

She looks past him.

Then into his eyes.

She smiles.

Light in her eyes.

And she falls into his arms.

The twelve-kilo dumbbell doesn't want to leave the floor no matter how hard Malin tries to lift it.

Damn, that's heavy, and I ought to manage at least ten reps.

Johan Jakobsson beside her, came down just after her and now he is driving her on, as if he wants them to drive out the bad news together.

Johan had managed to get into the last folder in Rickard Skoglöf's hard drive last night at home, once the children had gone to bed. The only thing in the folder had been more pictures, of Rickard Skoglöf himself and Valkyria Karlsson in various sexual positions on a large animal skin, their bodies painted with patterns resembling tribal tattoos.

'Come on, Malin!'

She raises the dumbbell, pushes it upwards.

'Come on, damn it!'

But it won't work. She lets the weight fall to the floor.

A dull rattle.

'I'm going to do a bit of running,' she tells Johan.

The sweat is pouring from her brow. The alcohol from dinner last night is being forced out, step by step, on the treadmill.

Malin looks at herself in the mirror as she runs, the sweat dripping down her brow; how pale she is even if the exercise is making her cheeks red. Her face. The face of a thirty-three-year-old. Lips that look plumper than usual because of the workout.

In recent years her face seems to have found itself, as if the skin has settled into its proper place over her cheekbones at last. The girlish quality she used to have has gone for good, no trace of it left after the exertion of the past few weeks. She looks at the clock on the wall: 9.24.

Johan has just gone.

Time for her to shower and then head off to Viveka Crafoord.

The internal phone rings.

Malin sprints across the room and picks up the receiver.

Zeke on the line. Agitated.

'We've just had a call from A&E. A Johnny Axelsson has brought in a woman he found naked and badly beaten up out on the plain.'

'I'm coming.'

'She's in a bad way, but according to the doctor I spoke to she evidently whispered your name, Malin.'

'What did you say?'

'The woman whispered your name, Malin.'

69

Viveka Crafoord will have to wait.

Everyone else will have to wait.

Apart from three.

Bengt Andersson.

Maria Murvall.

And now this other woman, found in exactly the same state.

The victims run out of the black forests, out across the white fields. Where's the source of the violence?

Zeke is driving at seventy kilometres an hour; forty too fast. The stereo is silent. Nothing but the abrupt, stressed sounds of the engine. They've had to take a detour, there are roadworks; a frozen pipe must have burst.

Djurgårdsgatan, the trees of the Horticultural Society, grey and straggly, but still somehow sparkling. Lasarettsgatan and the pink-brick blocks of flats put up in the eighties.

Postmodernism.

Malin read the article about the architect in the *Correspondent*, in the paper's series about the architecture of the city. The word struck her then as absurd, but she knew what the writer meant.

They swing up towards the hospital, the yellow façade of the main building faded by the sun, but the council's money is needed for other things than replacing the cladding. They take a short cut over a traffic island, knowing that they really shouldn't, that they're supposed to drive round, a long way round, but today there just isn't time.

And they're in front of the entrance to the A&E department, braking as they swing round the turning circle. They park and run towards the entrance.

A nurse meets them, a short, stocky woman with close-set eyes that make her thin nose stick out from her head.

'The doctor wants to talk to you,' she says as she leads them down a corridor, past several empty treatment rooms.

'Dr who?' Zeke asks.

'Dr Stenvinkel, he's the surgeon who's going to be operating on her.'

Hasse, Malin thinks, and at first she feels a resistance to meeting Markus's dad on duty, then realises that it makes absolutely no difference whatsoever.

'I know him,' Malin whispers to Zeke as they follow in the nurse's wake.

'Who?'

'The doctor. Just so you know. He's Tove's boyfriend's dad.'

'It'll be fine, Malin.'

The nurse stops in front of a closed door. 'You can go in. No need to knock.'

Hans Stenvinkel is a different man now compared to last night. Gone is the easy-going social individual, and instead there is a strict, sombre and focused person sitting before them. The whole of his green-clad body exudes competence, and the way he greeted her was personal but formal; subtext: we know each other, but we've both got important work to do.

Zeke is squirming on his chair, evidently wound up by the authority of the room. How the person in the green jacket bestows a sort of worthiness to the whitewashed textured walls, the oak-veneer bookcase and the worn wooden top of the simple desk.

This is what it used to be like, Malin thinks, when people had respect for doctors, before the Internet made it possible for everyone to be an expert in their own ailments.

'You can see her in a moment,' Hans says. 'She's conscious, but she'll have to be anaesthetised soon so that we can take care of her injuries. She needs a skin transplant. But at least we can do that here. We're the best place in the country for dealing with burns.'

'Frostbite?' Zeke asks.

'That too. But from a medicinal point of view, they're more like actual burns. So I dare say that she couldn't be in better hands.'

'Who is she?'

'We don't know. She just keeps saying that she wants to see you, Malin, so I expect you know who she is.'

Malin nods in agreement. 'Then it's probably best that she gets to see me. If she's up to it. We really need to find out who she is.'

'I think she could handle a short conversation.'

'Is her condition very serious?'

'Yes,' Hans says. 'She couldn't possibly have caused those injuries herself. She's lost a lot of blood. But we're giving her transfusions at the moment. We've relieved the shock with adrenalin. Burns and frost damage, like I said, knife wounds, cuts, compression injuries, and her vagina has been seriously wounded. It's astonishing that she didn't lose consciousness. You can't help but wonder what sort of monster is running loose on the plain.'

'How long could she have been out there?'

'I'd say all night. The frost damage is severe. But we should be able to save most of her toes and fingers.'

'Have you documented the injuries?'

'Yes, exactly as you want them.'

It's obvious from Hans's voice that he's done this before. With Maria Murvall?

'Good,' Zeke says.

'And the man who came in with her?'

'He left his number. He works at Ikea. We tried to get him to wait but he said, "The spirit of Ingvar, old IK himself, isn't happy if you get to work late." We couldn't persuade him to stay.'

Then Hans looks her in the eye. 'I'm warning you, Malin. She looks like she's been through the fires of hell. It's terrifying. You have to have incredible willpower to get through what she must have suffered.'

'People tend to have a ridiculous amount of willpower when their survival is at stake,' Zeke says.

'Not always, not always,' Hans replies, in a voice that sounds heavy and sad.

Malin nods to him, to indicate that she knows that he means. But do I? she wonders.

Who is she? Malin thinks, opening the door to the hospital room. Zeke is waiting outside.

A single bed against a wall, thin strips of light filtering through Venetian blinds and spreading across the grey-brown floor. A monitor is bleeping quietly, and two little red points of light on its screen shine like a pair of badger's eyes in the gloom. Drip-stands with blood-bags and fluids, a catheter-bag, and then the figure on the bed under thin yellow blankets, her head reclining on a pillow.

Who is it?

The cheek facing Malin is covered with a bandage.

But who is it?

Malin approaches cautiously and the figure on the bed groans, turns her head towards her, and isn't that something like a smile between the gaps in the bandages?

Hands wrapped in gauze.

The eyes.

I recognise them.

But who is it?

The smile is gone and the nose and eyes and hair become a memory.

Rebecka Stenlundh.

Bengt Andersson's sister.

She raises her bandaged hand towards Malin, beckoning her to the bed.

Then a huge effort, all the words to get out at once, a whole sentence to finish, as if it were her last.

'You have to take care of my boy if I don't make it. See that he ends up somewhere good.'

'You're going to make it.'

'I'm trying, believe me.'

'What happened? Can you bear to tell me what happened?'

'The car.'

'The car?'

'That's where I was taken.'

Rebecka Stenlundh turns her head, laying her bandaged cheek on the pillow.

'Then a hole. In the forest, and a post.'

'A hole, where?'

'In the dark.'

'Where in the dark?'

Rebecka shuts her eyes in a negative, in a: 'I have no idea.'

'And then?'

'Sledge, and car again.'

'Who?'

Rebecka Stenlundh shakes her head slowly.

'You didn't see?'

She shakes her head again. 'I was going to be hanged, like Bengt.'

'Was there more than one?'

Rebecka shakes her head once more. 'Don't know, couldn't see properly.'

'And the man who brought you in?'

'He helped me.'

'So you didn't see . . .'

'I struck the blackness, I struck the blackness, I . . .'

Rebecka drifts off, shuts her eyes, mumbles, 'Mum, Mum. Can we go and play under the apple trees?'

Malin puts her ear close to Rebecka's mouth. 'What did you say?'

'Stay, Mum, stay, you're not ill . . .'

'Can you hear me?'

'My boy, take . . .'

Rebecka falls silent, but she's breathing, her chest is moving; she's sleeping, or is unconscious, and Malin wonders if she's dreaming, hopes that Rebecka can escape dreaming for many nights to come, but knows that she's going to dream.

The machine beside her bleeps.

Glowing eyes.

Malin stands up.

Stands beside the bed for a while before leaving the room.

70

Zeke on his way to Ikea, Malin on her way up the stairs of number 3, Drottninggatan, million-year-old fossils embedded in the stone of the steps. Viveka Crafoord's clinic is on the third floor of four.

No lift in the building.

Crafoord Psychotherapy: a brass sign with curling letters, in the middle of a brown-lacquered door. Malin tries the handle. The door is locked.

She rings the bell.

Once, then twice, then a third time.

The door opens and a woman in her forties looks out. Frizzy black hair and a face that is round and sharp at the same time. Her brown eyes sparkle with intelligence even though they are half covered by a pair of horn-rimmed glasses.

'Viveka Crafoord?'

'You're an hour late.'

She opens the door a little more and Malin can see how she is dressed. A suede waistcoat over a puffy lilac-blue blouse, which in turn hangs over an ankle-length, green-checked, velvet skirt.

'Can I come in?'

'No.'

'You said—'

'I'm seeing a client at the moment. Go down to McDonald's and I'll call you in half an hour.'

'Can't I wait here?'

'I don't want anyone to see you.'

'Have you got . . .'

The door to the clinic closes.

'. . . my mobile number?'

Malin lets the question hang in the air, thinks that it's about time for lunch, and she now has the perfect excuse to partake of the American fast-food Satan.

She really doesn't like McDonald's. Has stuck absolutely to her decision never to take Tove there.

Baby carrots and juice.

We're taking our responsibility seriously and helping to combat childhood obesity.

So stop selling fries, then. Fizzy drinks. Half a responsibility: how much is that worth?

Sugar and fat.

Malin opens the door reluctantly.

Behind her a bus drives into Trädgårdstorget.

One Big Mac and one cheeseburger later she feels ready to throw up. The restaurant's garish colours and almost tangible smell of frying make her feel even worse.

Call now.

Twenty minutes. Thirty. Forty.

Her mobile rings.

Answer quickly.

'Malin?'

Dad? Not now, not now.

'Dad, I'm busy.'

'We've been thinking about the matter.'

'Dad—'

'Of course Tove is welcome to come down with her boyfriend.'

'What? I told you, I'm—'

'. . . so can you see if they still want to . . .'

Call waiting.

Malin clicks away from the call from Tenerife, takes the new one. 'Yes?'

'You can come up now.'

Viveka Crafoord's consulting room is furnished like the library of an upper-class home at the turn of the last century. Books,

Freud, metre after metre of shiny new leather book-spines. A black and white portrait of Jung in a heavy gold frame, thick rugs, a mahogany desk and a paisley-patterned armchair beside a chaise longue covered in leather the colour of oxblood.

Malin sits down on the chaise longue, turning down the invitation to stretch out and thinking how much Tove would like this room, its updated Jane Austen feeling.

Viveka is sitting in the armchair with her legs crossed.

'What I'm about to tell you stays between us,' she says. 'You can never mention it to anyone. It must never find its way into a police report or any other form of documentation. This meeting never took place. Is that okay?'

Malin nods.

'We're both risking our professional reputations if this ever gets out. Or if anyone knows it came from me.'

'If I act upon anything you tell me, I'll just have to say it was my intuition.'

Viveka Crafoord smiles. But only reluctantly.

Then she is serious again and starts to talk.

'Eight years ago I was contacted by a man, he was thirty-seven then, who said he wanted to get to grips with his childhood. Nothing unusual in that, but what was unusual about this case was that he made no progress at all for the first five years. He came once a week, he had a comfortable life, a good job. He wanted to talk, he said, about how things had been when he was little, but instead I got to hear about pretty much anything else. Computer programs, skiing, apple trees, various forms of faith. Everything apart from what he originally said he wanted to talk about.'

'What was his name?'

'I'm coming to that. Or I will, if it proves necessary.'

'I think it might.'

'Then something happened, three years ago. He refused to say what, but I think someone in his family was the victim of a violent crime, she was raped, and in some way it was as if this event had made him let go.'

'Let go?'

'Yes, and start talking. To begin with I didn't believe him, but afterwards . . . It could have been something else as well.'

'Afterwards?'

'When he persisted.'

Viveka Crafoord shakes her head. 'Sometimes,' she says, 'you wonder why some people have children.'

'I've thought the same thing.'

'His father had been a sailor who died when he was still in his mother's womb.'

That's wrong, Malin thinks. His father was someone else . . .

But she lets Viveka Crafoord go on.

'His earliest memory, the first thing we could reach together, was how his mother locked him in a wardrobe when he must have been about two. She didn't want to be seen out with a child. Then his mother remarried, a violent man, and they had children. Three brothers and a sister. The new husband and the sons saw it as their duty to torment him, and the mother seems to have cheered them on. In the winter they locked him outside in the snow, naked, so he had to stand in the cold while they were all sitting eating in the kitchen. If he protested he was beaten, even more than usual. They beat him, cut him with knives, poured hot water over him, threw crumbs at him. The brothers seem to have crossed the boundary, encouraged by their father; children can be incredibly cruel if cruelty is encouraged. They don't know it's wrong. A selective sort of violence. Almost like a sect in the end. He was the eldest brother, but what use was that? Adults and children against a lone child. The brothers must have been damaged by the situation as well, become confused, hard, insecure, yet simultaneously determined, bound together in something that we all know deep down is wrong.'

You believe in goodness, Malin thinks, and asks, 'How did he survive?'

'Fantasy worlds. His own universe. Some hole in a forest, he never said where. Computer programs. Different faiths. Everything that we human beings clutch at to get a grip on life.

Education. And by getting away from them. He managed it. He must have had immense internal strength. And a sister who seems to have cared about him. Even if she couldn't do anything on her own. He talked about her, albeit fairly incoherently, about something that had happened in the forest. It was like he lived in parallel worlds, and had learned to distinguish between them. But then it was as if every time we met the horrors of his childhood took over more and more. He was quick to lose his temper.'

'Violent?'

'Never in here. But possibly elsewhere. They burned him with candles. He described a cabin in the forest where they tied him to a tree and burned him, then threw hot water over him.'

'How could they?'

'People can do anything to another human being when they somehow stop seeing them as a human being. History is full of examples. It's nothing particularly unusual.'

'And how does it start?'

'I don't know.' Viveka Crafoord sighs. 'In this case with the mother. Or even further back. I think it was her refusal to love him, combined with the fact that she needed him. I don't know why she never had him adopted. Maybe his mother needed something to hate? Something to channel her fury at? Her hatred must also have been what fuelled the contempt of her husband and sons.'

'Why didn't she want to love him?'

'I don't know. Something must have happened.'

Viveka pauses.

'During that last year he would lie on that chaise longue where you're sitting now, crying and raging in turn. He would often whisper, "Let me in, let me in, I'm freezing."'

'And what did you do?'

'I tried to comfort him.'

'And now?'

'He stopped seeing me about a year ago. The last time we met he stormed out. Lost his temper again. Yelled that no words could ever help, that only action could put everything right, and now he knew, he'd found out something, he yelled, said he knew what needed to be done.'

'And you didn't contact him again?'

Viveka Crafoord looks surprised. 'All my treatments are voluntary,' she says. 'My patients have to come to me. But I thought you might be interested in this.'

'What do you think happened?'

'His cup has overflowed. All his worlds have merged together. Anything could happen.'

'Thank you,' Malin says.

'Do you want to know his name?'

'I don't need to.'

'I thought as much,' Viveka Crafoord says, and turns towards the window.

Malin gets up to leave.

Without looking at Malin, Viveka Crafoord asks, 'What about you, how are you?'

'What do you mean?'

'It's written all over you. You don't often see it so clearly, but it's like you're carrying a sorrow, a loss, that you haven't come to terms with.'

'I really have no idea what you're talking about.'

'I'm here if you want to talk.'

Outside great snowflakes are sailing to the ground; Malin thinks that they look like the remnants of beautiful stars that were pulverised far out in space, billions of years ago.

7 I

The disgusting little shit.

I'm putting a terry nappy on him.

I've padded the inside walls of the wardrobe. I might toss him an apple, a bit of dry bread, but he doesn't scream any more. If you hit a kid on the nose enough times he learns that screaming means pain, and that it doesn't help.

So I shut him in.

He cries silently as I put his two and a half years in the wardrobe.

Post-natal depression.

Thanks a lot.

Child benefit.

Thanks a lot.

Drowned father. One thousand, six hundred and eighty-five kronor every month. They bought it, the authorities, seeing as it was so tragic. Fatherless. But I didn't want to give him up and not get the money.

My lies aren't lies because they're mine alone. I am creating my own world. And the interloper in the wardrobe makes it real.

So I lock up.

And go off.

They sacked me from the factory when they saw my stomach; we can't have that at the chocolate conveyor-belt, they said.

And now I lock the wardrobe and he cries and I want to open up and tell him that he only exists here because he doesn't exist;

choke on the apple, stop breathing, then perhaps you'll get away. Fucking little brat. And yet not.

One thousand, six hundred and eighty-five old riksdaler a month.

I saunter through town to the grocer's, and I hold my head high but I know how they whisper – Where's she put the boy? Where's the boy? – because they know you exist, and I feel like stopping and curtseying to the ladies, telling them that the boy, the sailor's boy, I've got him in a dark, damp, padded wardrobe. I've even put in an air-vent, just like the one they put in the box when they kidnapped Lindbergh's son; you probably saw the report in the *Weekly News*.

I am quiet around him, but still, somehow, words find their way into his head.

Mummy, Mummy

Mummy

Mummy

and those noises disgust me, they're like damp snakes on a wet forest floor.

Sometimes I see Kalle. I named him after Kalle.

He looks at me.

He looks all wrong on his bicycle, and he's given in to the bottle now, and the woman, the fair one, has borne him a son. What does he want that for? Does he imagine he can get any order to that bloodline? I've seen the boy. Blown up like a balloon, he is.

The secret is my revenge, a kiss blown through the air.

Don't think you can get at me, Kalle. That you did get at me. No one gets at Rakel.

No one, no one, no one.

Then I open the wardrobe.

And he smiles.

The fucking little brat.

And I hit him to wipe the smile from his face.

72

I glide through the cold, the day as chalky-white as the fields below me. The tower of Vreta Kloster is a sharpened point on my way out to Blåsvädret and the Hultsjön forest.

The voices are everywhere. All the words they have spoken over the years twisted around each other to form a terrifying and beautiful web.

I have learned to distinguish the voices I want to hear, and I understand them all, even far beyond the apparent meaning of the words.

So who do I hear?

I hear the brothers' voices: Elias, Jakob and Adam. How they resist, but still want to talk. I start with Elias, listen to what you have to say.

You must never show you're weak.

Never, ever.

Like he did, the illegitimate one. He was older than me, Jakob and Adam, but he still blubbed in the snow, like a woman, like a weakling. If you show you're weak, they'll take you.

Which they?

The bastards. Everyone out there.

Sometimes, but I never say this to Mother or my brothers, I wonder what harm he really did. Why Mother hated him, why we had to hit him. I look at my own children and wonder what harm they could do, what harm Karl could really have done? What did Mother turn us into? Maybe you make children commit whatever cruelties you like.

But no, mustn't think like that.

I know that I am not weak. I am nine, and I am standing at the entrance to the newly built, white-plastered building of Ljungsbro school, it's early September and the sun is shining and the woodwork teacher, Broman, is standing outside smoking. The bell has gone and all the children rush to the entrance, me first, but just as I'm about to open the door Broman holds up first one arm, then the other, in the air and he shouts, STOP, NO FILTHY LITTLE BRATS IN HERE. And he shouts louder and louder and his words make the whole crowd of children stop, their little muscles frozen. He grins, grins, and everyone thinks they're the little brats, and then he shouts, IT SMELLS FILTHY HERE, ELIAS MURVALL, IT SMELLS FILTHY, and that's when the giggling starts, then laughter, and Broman's cigarette-hoarse shouting, LITTLE BRAT. He shoves me to one side, holds me hard against the glass of one door with his hairy arm as he opens the other door and lets in the rest of the children and they laugh and go past and whisper, Little brat, shit, it smells of shit here, and I won't put up with it. I make sure I explode, I open my mouth, and I bite, I dig my eye-teeth deep into Broman's arm. I feel the flesh give way and just as he starts to scream I feel the taste of iron in my mouth and who's crying now, you bastard, who's crying now?

I let go.

They wanted Mother to come to the school and talk about what had happened.

That's shit, she said, as she held me tight in the kitchen, we don't do that sort of shit, Elias.

I am still drifting and listening. I'm high up now, where the air is too thin for human beings, and the cold is quick to destroy, but your voice is clear here, Jakob, so pure and radiantly clear, transparent like a window frame without glass.

Hit the bastard, Jakob, Dad yelled.

Hit him.

He's not one of us, no matter what he might like to think.

He was skinny and thin and although he was twice my height I kicked him right in the stomach while Adam held him. Adam four years younger, but still stronger, run wild.

Dad in his wheelchair on the porch.

How it happened?

I don't know.

They found him in the park one night. His back broken, his jaw too. Mother said he must have run into a real man there in the park and that it's all over for Blackie now, and then she passed him another drink, let him drink himself to death, it's high time, and oh how he drank. We would push him round the houses and he would rave in his drunkenness and try to stand up.

I was the one who found him when he fell downstairs. I was thirteen then. I came in from the garden where I'd been pulling unripe apples off the trees to throw at cars driving past on the road.

The eyes.

They were staring at me, white and dead, and his skin was grey instead of the usual red.

I was scared. Wanted to scream.

But instead I closed his eyes.

Mother came down the stairs, just out of the bath.

She stepped over the body, reached out to me and her hair was wet but still warm, and it smelled of flowers and leaves and she murmured in my ear, Jakob. My Jakob.

Then she whispered, If you have to do something, you don't hesitate, do you? You know what has to be done, don't you? And she hugged me tight, tight, and then I remember the church bells and the black-clad people on the patch of gravel in front of the church in Vreta Kloster.

The patch of gravel.

Edged with walls and remains from the twelfth century.

I've landed there now and I can see what you must have seen, Jakob. What did the sight do to you? But everything had already happened long, long before then, hadn't it? And I think you're doing what has to be done, just as I'm doing now.

But it isn't your voice that's strongest here. That's Adam's, and what he says sounds sensible and mad at the same time, as despairing and obvious as the winter cold.

What's ours is ours, and no one can take it from us, Adam.

Mother's voice with no space for me.

I was probably two the first time I realised that Dad hit him, that there was someone who was always there, but who was only there to be hit.

There is an obvious quality to violence that doesn't exist in anything else. Drink your skull to pieces, smash a skull to pieces, smash to pieces, smash apart.

That's how it is.

I smash things apart.

Mother.

She also likes things to be obvious.

Doubt, she says, isn't for us.

It was different with the new kid.

He didn't know.

Turkish. Came to our class in year five. From Stockholm. His mum and dad had got jobs in chocolate heaven. He must have thought he could mess me about. I was the little one, after all, the one on the edge, with all the stains on his clothes, the one you could, well, do what you liked with, just to prove you were someone in the new place.

So he hit me.

Or tried to.

He used some fucking judo technique and got me down, then he punched me until my nose started to bleed, and then, just when I was about to fly at him again, the teacher and the caretaker and the PE teacher, Björklund, showed up.

My brothers got to hear about it.

The Turk lived in Härna. We waited for him by the canal, under the birches by the water, hidden down the slope behind the tree trunks. The fool used to go home that way.

And he came, just as my brothers had planned.

They leapt up and knocked him off his bike and he was lying there in the gravel by the side of the canal, screaming and pointing at the tears in his jeans.

Jakob stared at him, Elias stared, and I stood by a birch tree and I remember wondering what was going to happen now, but I knew.

Elias started kicking the Turk's bike, and when he tried to get up Jakob kicked him, first in the stomach and then in the mouth, and the Turk started whimpering and blood was coming out of the corners of his mouth.

And then I bent the bike frame and heaved the bike right out into the canal. And I ran up and kicked the Turk.

And I kicked.

Kicked.

Kicked.

His parents didn't even report it to the cops.

They moved just a few weeks after that. At school they said they'd gone back to Turkey, but I don't believe that. They were that other sort, Kurds. Like fuck would they have gone back.

On the way home from the canal I was sitting behind Elias on his Puch Dakota. I was holding on to his waist and the whole of his big body was vibrating, and Jakob was riding his moped next to us.

He smiled at me. I could feel warmth from Elias.

We were, we are, brothers.

One and the same.

Nothing odd about that.

73

It's warm here. No one will find me.

The earth roof above me is a heavenly vault of its own. There are biscuit crumbs on the ground.

Is she hanging?

If not, I shall have to try again and again and again. Because if I get rid of the blood you'll have to let me in. If I sacrifice it to you, you'll let me in.

It was easier with him, Bengt. He was heavy, but not too heavy, and I drugged him by the car park up in Härna when he was walking past. I had my other car, the one I bought with a normal boot. Then the same as with her, brought out here by sledge.

But he died too soon.

The pulleys came from the factory. I'd disconnected the sensors in the server room before I cut a hole in the fence. Not easy. A coat on a hanger was me through the frosted glass when the guards walked past.

That night, in the forest, I took him. I drove out the blood, took away the blood, so you would let me in. I made it clean.

The chains, the noose. The sacrifice.

I had made a sacrifice for you.

But what happened with her?

I remember waking up in the field and she was gone. I snaked back to the car, crept in and managed to start it. I made my way back here.

But was she hanging in the tree?

Or was she somewhere else?

She must have been hanging. I drove out what was wrong, I made the sacrifice.

So you'll soon be here to open the door.
You'll be coming with love, won't you?
What's happened? What's been done?
It smells of apples in my hole. Apples, biscuits and smoke.

The Philadelphia Church sign is illuminated in the middle of the day, as if to advertise: God is here! You just have to step inside and meet Him. The church building is right next to McDonald's on the other side of Drottninggatan, and it has a faithful and well-heeled congregation. She remembers Free Church people from her sixth-form days. They were polite, wore fairly trendy clothes, but they were still geeks, or at least that was how she saw them. As if there were something missing. As if there were a remarkable hardness in all that fluff and softness. Like candy-floss with sharp tacks in.

Malin peers up the street.

Where's Zeke?

She's just called him, told him to pick her up outside the church, that they were going out to Collins to bring in Karl Murvall.

There's the Volvo.

He pulls in, and before he has completely stopped the car Malin has opened the door and jumped into the passenger seat.

Zeke eager: 'What did the psychologist say?'

'I promised not to say.'

'Malin,' Zeke sighed.

'But it was Karl Murvall who murdered Bengt Andersson and tried to murder Rebecka Stenlundh. There's absolutely no doubt at all.'

'How do you know that? Didn't he have an alibi?'

Zeke is heading along Drottninggatan.

'Female intuition. And what's to say he couldn't have disconnected the sensors with the help of the computer system, cut a hole in the fence surrounding Collins, and just crept out that night? That he didn't sort out the business of the update beforehand?'

Zeke accelerates. 'Okay, why not, maybe the sensors were controlled from inside that server room,' he says. 'But they saw him in the room.'

'Maybe they only looked through the frosted glass,' Malin says.

Zeke nods, says, 'Family's always worst, isn't it?'

The gate at the entrance to the Collins site seems to have grown since they were last there, and the forest by the car park gives the impression that it's got thicker, become more enclosed. The factory buildings slouch like the depressed barracks of an internment camp behind the fence, ready to be shipped off to China any day now, and filled with workers earning a hundredth of what those working inside currently earn.

You again, the guard at the gate seems to think. Won't you ever stop asking me to open this hatch and let in the cold?

'We're looking for Karl Murvall,' Malin says.

The guard smiles and shakes his head. 'Then you've come to the wrong place,' he says. 'He was fired the day before yesterday.'

'So he got fired. You don't happen to know why? I don't suppose you get to hear things like that?' Zeke says.

The guard looks insulted. 'Why does anyone get fired?' he asks.

'What do I know? You tell us,' Zeke says.

'In his case it was for strange and threatening behaviour against his work colleagues. Anything else you want to know?'

'That'll do,' Malin says. She doesn't feel up to asking about the night of the murder and the fence. Somehow Karl Murvall managed to get out that night.

'Can't we put out an alert for him?' Malin asks Zeke as they are heading away from Collins' car park towards the main road. They pass a lorry whose trailer is weaving alarmingly on the road.

'No. You have to have something concrete to go on.'

'I have.'

'Which you can't reveal.'

'It's him.'

'You've got to come up with something else, Fors. You can always take him in for questioning.'

They pull out on to the main road, swerving to avoid a black BMW patrol car driving at least forty kilometres an hour too fast.

'But we have to find him.'

'Do you think he'll be at home?'

'We can always give it a try.'

'Is it okay if I put on some music?'

'Whatever you want, Zeke.'

Seconds later the car is filled with a hundred German voices.

'Ein bisschen Frieden, ein bisschen Sonne . . .'

'Eurovision classic as a choral work,' Zeke shouts. 'Always cheers you up, doesn't it?'

It's half past three by the time they ring on the door of Karl Murvall's flat on Tanneforsvägen. The varnish on the door is peeling and for the first time Malin notices that the whole stairwell could do with some work; no one seems to look after the communal areas.

No one opens.

Malin looks in through the letterbox. Newspapers and post untouched on the floor.

'We can't ask for a sodding search warrant either,' Malin says. 'I can't refer to what Viveka Crafoord told me, and just because Rebecka Stenlundh has been attacked doesn't mean we can march in here.'

'Where can he be?' Zeke wonders in a loud voice.

'Rebecka Stenlundh mentioned a forest and a hole.'

'You don't mean we have to go out in the forest again?'

'Who else could we have seen that night? It must have been him.'

'Do you think he's staying in the hunting cabin?'

'Hardly. But there's something in the forest. I just know there is.'

'No point waiting, then,' Zeke says.

★

The world shrinks in the snow. Collapses into a dark space that contains everything under the atmosphere. Packed together into a sluggish black hole.

You're hiding secrets, Malin thinks. You dark old Östgöta forest. The snow is harder than last time, the crust is bearing my weight. Maybe the cold has slowly turned the snow into ice? An ice age created in just a few months, forever changing the vegetation, the landscape, the tone of the forest. The trees around them are rough, abandoned ancient pillars.

One foot in front of the other.

Of all the children whom no one sees, who are abandoned, whose fathers and mothers don't care about them, who are forsaken by the world, some will always fall out, go mad, and the world that deserted them will have to take the consequences.

In Karin's Thailand.

In Janne's Bosnia and Rwanda.

In Stockholm.

In Linköping.

In Ljungsbro, Blåsvädret.

It's no more complicated than that, Malin thinks. Look after those who are small, those who are weak. Show them love. There is no innate evil. Evil is created. But I still believe that there is such a thing as innate goodness. But not now, not in this forest; goodness fled from here long ago. Here there is only survival.

Aching fingers in gloves that can't be made thick enough.

'Fuck, it's cold,' Zeke says, and it feels as if Malin's heard him say that a thousand times in the past month.

Her legs are becoming less and less willing the more darkness descends, the more the cold seeps into her body. Her toes have vanished, as well as her fingers. Not even pain is left.

The Murvall cabin lies cold and deserted. The snowfall has erased any trace of ski tracks.

Malin and Zeke stand still in front of the cabin.

Listening, but there is nothing to hear, only an odourless, silent winter forest around them.

But I feel it, I feel it, you're close now.

I must have nodded off, the stove is cold, no burning lumps of wood. I'm freezing, have to get the fire going again, so it's warm when they come to let me in.

My hole is my home.

Has always been my only home. The flat on Tanneforsvägen was never home. It was just rooms where I slept and thought and tried to understand.

I get the wood ready, light a match, but my fingers slip.

I'm freezing.

But it has to be warm when they come to let me in, when I'm to receive her love.

'There's nothing here, Fors. Listen to me.'

The clearing in front of the cabin: a completely soundless place, encircled by trees, by the forest, and an impenetrable darkness.

'You're wrong, Zeke.'

There's something here. Something moving. Is it evil? The devil? I can smell something.

'It's going to be completely dark in five minutes. I'm going back now.'

'Just a bit further,' Malin says, and starts walking.

They walk perhaps four hundred metres into the dense forest before Zeke says, 'Okay, we're going back.'

'Just a bit further.'

'No.'

And Malin turns round, walks back, never sees the clump of trees fifty metres further on, where grey smoke is starting to seep out of a narrow chimney in the roof of an earthen cellar.

The engine roars as the car gets going properly, just as they are passing the golf course at Vreta Kloster.

Peculiar, Malin thinks. They leave the flags out over the winter. I've never noticed them before. It's like they've hung them out in someone's honour.

Then she says, 'Let's go and see Rakel Murvall. She knows where he is.'

'You're mad, Malin. You're not going within five hundred metres of the old woman. I'll make sure of that.'

'She knows where he is.'

'That doesn't matter.'

'Yes, it does.'

'No. She's reported you for harassment. Turning up there now would be career suicide.'

'Shit.' Malin bangs the dashboard. 'Take me back to my car. It's in the multistorey near McDonald's.'

'You look energetic, Mum,' Tove says from her place on the sofa, looking up from the paperback she's reading.

'What are you reading?'

'*The Wild Duck*. Ibsen. A play.'

'Isn't it a bit odd, reading a play? Aren't you supposed to watch them?'

'It works if you've got a bit of imagination, Mum.'

The television is on: *Jeopardy!* Adam Alsing fat and over-familiar in a yellow suit.

How can Tove read proper literature with that on in the background?

'Have you been out, Mum?'

'Yep, in the forest, actually.'

'Why?'

'Zeke and I were looking for something.'

Tove nods, not worried about whether they found what they were looking for, and returns to her book.

He murdered Bengt Andersson. Tried to murder Rebecka Stenlundh.

Who is Karl Murvall? Where is he?

Damn Rakel Murvall.

Her sons.

A social science book is open on the table in front of Tove. The section heading is 'The Constitution', and it is illustrated with pictures of Göran Persson and an imam Malin has never seen before. People can be turned into anything at all. That's it.

'Tove. Grandad called today. You'd both be welcome to go. You and Markus, to Tenerife.'

Tove looks away from the television.

'I don't really want to go any more,' she says. 'And it would be hard to explain to Grandad that he has to play along with our lie that they were supposed to have other guests.'

'Good grief,' Malin says. 'How can something so simple get so complicated?'

'I don't want to go, Mum. Do I really have to tell Markus that Grandad's changed his mind?'

'No.'

'But what if we go some other time, and Grandad suddenly starts talking about how we didn't want to go last time even though we'd been asked?'

Malin sighs. 'Why not tell Markus how it really is?'

'But how is it, though?'

'That Grandad's changed his mind but you don't want to go.'

'What about the lie? Doesn't that matter?'

'I don't know, Tove. A little lie like that can't cause too much trouble, can it?'

'Well, in that case we could go then.'

'I thought you didn't want to go.'

'No, but I could if I wanted to. It's better for Grandad to be disappointed. Then maybe he'll learn his lesson.'

'So you're going to Åre?'

'Mmm.'

Tove turns away from Malin and reaches for the remote.

When Tove has gone to bed Malin sits alone on the sofa for a while before getting up and going into the hall, pulling on her holster and pistol, and then her jacket. Before leaving the flat she hunts through the top drawer of the chest in the hall. She finds what she's looking for and puts it in the front pocket of her jeans.

74

Linköping at midnight, on the night between Thursday and Friday, in the depths of February. The illuminated signs on the buildings in the centre struggle to match the streetlamps and lend a bit of apparent warmth to the streets where the thirsty and the lonely and the pleasure-seekers hurry between different restaurants and bars, clumsy polar explorers hunting for company.

No queues anywhere.

Too cold for that.

Malin's hands on the wheel.

The city beyond the car windows.

The red and orange buses are idling in Trädgårdstorget; inside them sit teenagers on their way home, tired, but with expectation still in their eyes.

She turns the wheel and swings into Drottninggatan, towards the river, past the windows of the Swedish Real-Estate Agency.

The dream of a home.

Of views to wake up to.

There are dreams in this city, no matter how cold it gets. No matter what happens.

What do I dream of? Malin thinks.

Of Tove. Of Janne. Daniel.

My body can dream of him.

But what do I expect of myself? What longings do I share with those teenage girls on the bus?

*

The door to the block of flats opens; it isn't even locked at
night.

Malin goes cautiously up the stairs, silently, not wanting to
announce her presence to anyone.

She stops outside Karl Murvall's door.

Listens.

But the night is silent, and behind the door the floor is still
covered by untouched newspapers.

She knocks.

Waits.

Then she sticks the skeleton key in the lock. Twists and turns
and the lock opens with a soft click.

A stale smell, musty, but warm, the radiators turned up to stop
them freezing. The conscientiousness of the engineer, the defiance of a certainty that must exist somewhere inside Karl Murvall:
I'll never live here again, so what does it matter if the radiators
freeze?

But he could be here. There's a very slight chance.

Malin stands still.

Listens.

Should I draw my pistol?

No.

Put on the lights?

I have to put on the lights.

Malin presses the switch by the bathroom door and the hall
lights up. Jackets and coats hanging in a neat row under the
hat-rack.

Listens.

Nothing but silence.

She goes quickly from room to room, then back to the hall.

All clear, she thinks.

She looks round the hall, pulls out the drawers of the chest.
Gloves, a hat, some papers.

A wage-slip.

Fifty-seven thousand kronor.

The computer fantasy. But what does a bit of money mean?

Malin goes into the kitchen. Rifles through drawers, checks the walls, empty apart from a cuckoo-clock.

The clock says almost one. Don't be startled if the clock chimes. Which it will do in a few minutes. The living room. Drawers full of more papers: bank statements, saved adverts, nothing that could be regarded as out of the ordinary.

Then it hits Malin: there are no wardrobes, no cupboards anywhere. Not in the hall, where they usually are in a flat like this.

Malin goes back out into the hall.

Only the painted-over signs of where they had once stood.

. . . she locked him in . . .

Malin goes into the bedroom. Flicks the switch but the room stays dark. There is a table-lamp on a desk by the window. The room faces the rear courtyard, and the light from a lamp outside casts a weak grey glow over the walls.

She turns on the table-lamp.

A dim cone of light on to a desktop covered with knife marks.

She turns round.

The sound of a car stopping in front of the building. A car door closing. She feels with her hand for her holster. The pistol, she usually hates it, but now she loves it. The front door of the building closing out in the stairwell. Malin creeps into the hall, listening to the sound of footsteps on the stairs.

Then a key in a door on the floor below.

A door being closed carefully.

Malin breathes out.

Goes back to the bedroom and there she sees it, the wardrobe. It is at the foot of the bed. She switches on the wall-mounted lamp above the bed to get more light, and realises it has been set up to shine directly at the wardrobe.

A padlock on the handle.

Something locked in.

An animal?

With a practised hand Malin applies the skeleton key to the lock. It has a tricky mechanism and after three minutes of trying she feels herself breaking into a sweat.

But eventually the lock lets out a click and slips open. She carefully pulls the door towards her and looks inside.

I see you, Malin. Is it the truth you see? Does what you're looking at make you feel safe or scared? Will you sleep better at night?

Look at him, look at me, at Rebecka, or Lotta, as she will always be to me. We are lonely.

Can your truth cure our loneliness, Malin?

Malin looks at the inside of the wardrobe, covered with wallpaper whose pattern represents a stylised tree full of green apples. On the bottom, beside a packet of plain biscuits, are various books about Æsir beliefs and psychoanalysis, a Bible, and a copy of the Koran. A black notebook.

Malin leafs through the book.

Diary entries.

Neat handwriting, letters so small that it's hard to read.

About work at Collins.

Visits to Viveka Crafoord.

Further on in the book it's as if something inside the writer has capsized, as if another hand is holding the pen. The writing becomes shaky, there are no dates any more, and the style is fragmented.

. . . in February it is midwinter . . .

. . . now I know, I know who has to be sacrificed . . .

And in various different places: *Let me in.*

At the back of the book is a detailed map. Blåsvädret, a field with a tree marked on it, close to the site where Ball-Bengt was found, and then a site in the forest, close to where the Murvalls' cabin must be.

He sat here talking to us.

With this book behind him, with everything inside him.

The whole world, at its very worst, was right here in front of us, and it managed to maintain its mask, it managed to cling to reality as we know it.

Malin can hear all his voices roaring. Out of the wardrobe,

into the room, and on, into herself. A chill passes through her, a chill far worse than anything below zero outside the window.

Fault-lines.

Within and without.

The fantasy world.

The real world.

They meet. And right up to the end his consciousness knows what is required. Plays the game. I'll escape: the last remnant for his mind to cling to before awareness and instinct become one.

Another map.

Another tree.

That's where Rebecka was going to be hanged, isn't it?

Don't lose heart, Malin. It isn't over yet.

I see Rebecka in her bed. She's sleeping. The operation to transplant skin to her cheeks and stomach went well; maybe she won't be as beautiful as she was before, but she's long since abandoned vanity anyway. She isn't in pain. Her son is sleeping on a bunk beside her bed, and new blood is pumping through her veins.

Karl isn't doing so well.

I know. I ought to be angry with him, because of what he did to me. But he's lying there in his cold earthen cellar, wrapped in blankets in front of a stove where the fire is fading and I can't see anything but that he is the loneliest person on the planet. He doesn't even have himself, and I always had that, even when I was at my most despairing and cut off Dad's ear.

So I can't be angry with such loneliness, because that would mean being angry with humanity, and that, if it isn't impossible, is no consolation whatever. Fundamentally, we're all basically good, we mean well, don't we?

The wind is getting cold again.

Malin.

You have to go on.

I won't get any peace until that wind has dropped.

★

Malin puts the book back.

She curses herself for leaving her fingerprints on it, but it doesn't really matter now.

Who shall I call?

Zeke?

Sven Sjöman?

Malin pulls out her mobile, calls a number. It takes four rings before anyone answers.

Karin Johannison's voice, full of sleep.

'Yes, this is Karin.'

'Malin here. Sorry to disturb you.'

'No problem, Malin. I'm a light sleeper anyway.'

'Can you come out to a flat at 34 Tanneforsvägen? Top floor.'

'Now?'

'Yes.'

'I'll be there in fifteen minutes.'

Malin examines Karl Murvall's clothes.

Finds several strands of hair.

She puts them in a freezer-bag she finds in the kitchen.

She hears another car pull up in front of the building. A door closing.

She whispers down into the stairwell, 'Karin, up here.'

'I'm coming.'

Malin shows Karin round the flat.

Back in the hall Karin says, 'We'll have to examine the wardrobe, then the rest of the flat.'

'That's not why I wanted to get you here first. It's because of these. I want DNA tests on them.'

Malin holds up the bag containing the strands of hair.

'Right away. And compare the results with the profile of Maria Murvall's attacker.'

'Are they Karl Murvall's?'

'Yes.'

'If I head off to the lab now, the results will be ready first thing tomorrow.'

'Thanks, Karin. As quick as that?'

'It's easy with perfect samples like this. We're not completely useless, you know. Why is it so important?'

'I don't know, Karin. But somehow it's definitely important.'

'What about all this?' Karin gestures at the rest of the flat.

'You've got colleagues, haven't you?' Malin says. 'Even if they're not as sharp as you?'

As Karin pulls away from the pavement Malin calls Sven Sjöman. Passes it on. Sets in motion things that need to be set in motion.

75

The bedroom of the flat is lit up by the arc lights brought in by the forensics team.

Sven Sjöman and Zeke look tired as they search the wardrobe. Earlier, over the phone, Sjöman had asked her why she had gone to the flat and how she had got in. 'Just a feeling. And the door was open,' she had said, and Sven had left it at that.

Zeke pulls on a pair of plastic gloves and reaches for the notebook again, leafs through it, reads, then puts it down once more.

Malin showed Sven and Zeke the book with its writing and maps as soon as they arrived, explained and drew connections, told them what she'd done, that Karin had already been there, gave them an outline of what must have happened, of the events leading up to this point. She noticed them getting even more tired from what she told them, that the fact that they had only just woken up was getting in the way of her words, and that they weren't really absorbing what she was saying, even if Sven was nodding as if to agree that this must be the truth.

'Bloody hell,' Zeke says, turning to Malin. She's sitting on the chair by the desk, longing for a cup of coffee.

'Where do you think he is now?'

'I think he's in the forest. Somewhere out near the hunting cabin.'

'We didn't find him.'

'He could be anywhere.'

'He's wounded. We know that. Rebecka Stenlundh said she hit him.'

A wounded animal.

'We've put out a national alert,' Sven says. 'There's also the possibility that he's killed himself.'

'Are we going to send dog-teams into the forest?' Malin asks.

'We'll hold off until first thing in the morning. It's too dark now. But the dogs can't pick up scent in this cold, so maybe it isn't such a great idea. The dog-handlers will know,' Sven says. 'We've got all our cars looking for him. And the only thing that suggests he's in the forest are the marks on the maps in that notebook.'

'That's quite a lot,' Malin says.

'He wasn't in the cabin late yesterday afternoon. If he's injured he would have found his way somewhere at once where he can lie low. Which means that it's highly unlikely that he's in the cabin now.'

'But he could be nearby.'

'It will have to wait, Fors.'

'Malin,' Zeke says, 'I agree with Sven. It's five in the morning, and he wasn't in the cottage as recently as early yesterday evening.'

'Fors,' Sven says, 'go home and get some sleep. It would be best for everyone if you got some rest before tomorrow, and then we'll take a thorough look at where he might be then.'

'No, I—'

'Malin,' Sven says. 'You've already gone too far, you have to get some rest.'

'We've got to find him. I think . . .'

Malin lets the sentence die; they wouldn't understand the way she's thinking.

Instead she gets up and leaves the room.

On her way downstairs Malin bumps into Daniel Högfeldt.

'Is Karl Murvall suspected of murdering Bengt Andersson and attacking Rebecka Stenlundh?' As if nothing had happened.

Malin doesn't answer.

Pushes past him down the stairs.

She's tired and stressed, Daniel thinks, as he climbs the last steps up to the flat where two uniformed officers are on guard outside the front door.

Might be tricky getting in. But if you don't try . . .

Malin didn't seem bothered that I turned down *Expressen*.

But was I expecting her to be? We're nothing more than fuck-buddies, are we? Something for the body, not the soul.

But you looked beautiful just now, Malin, when you pushed past me. So fucking beautiful and tired and exhausted.

The last step.

Daniel smiles at the uniformed officers.

'Not a chance in hell, Högfeldt,' the taller one says with a smile.

Sometimes when Malin thinks that sleep will be elusive it comes to her in just a minute or two.

The bed is warm beneath her in her dream.

The bed is the soft floor of a white room with transparent walls that are swaying in a warm breeze.

Outside the walls she sees them all as naked shadows: Mum, Dad, Tove, Janne. Zeke is there, and Sven Sjöman and Johan Jakobsson, Karim Akbar and Karin Johannison and Börje Svärd and his wife Anna. The Murvall brothers, Rebecka and Maria, and a fat figure lumbering with a football in his hands. Markus pops up, and Biggan and Hasse and the security guard at Collins, and Gottfrid Karlsson, Weine Andersson and Sister Hermansson, and the Ljungsbro bullies, Margaretha Svensson, Göran Kalmvik and Niklas Nyrén and lots, lots more; they're all in the dream, like fuel for her memories, as navigation points for her consciousness. The people in the events of recent weeks are buoys anchored in an illuminated space that could be anything. And in the middle of that space beams Rakel Murvall, a black light radiating from her shadow.

The alarm clock on the bedside table rings.

A harsh, loud, digital noise.

The time is 7.35.

After an hour and a half, the time of dreams is over.

The *Correspondent* is lying on the hall floor.

They're behind on developments for once, but probably

only because of the inevitable delay caused by the printing process.

They've got everything on Rebecka Stenlundh, that she's the sister of the murdered Bengt Andersson, but nothing about Karl Murvall, or that they carried out a raid on his flat last night.

The paper must have gone to press by then. But they're bound to have it on the net. I can't be bothered to look right now, and what could they have that I don't already know?

Daniel Högfeldt has written several of the articles in the paper. As usual.

Was I too abrupt with him earlier? Maybe I ought to give him an honest chance to show who he is.

The water in the shower is warm against her skin, and Malin feels herself waking up. She gets dressed, stands by the draining-board to drink a cup of Nescafé made with water heated in the microwave.

Please, let us find Karl Murvall today, Malin thinks. Dead or alive.

Might he have killed himself?

Anything is possible now as far as he is concerned.

Might he commit another murder?

Did he rape Maria Murvall? Karin would soon have the results, some time today.

Malin sighs and looks out of the window at St Lars Church and the trees. The branches haven't given in to the cold, they're still sticking out defiantly in all directions. Just like the people at this latitude, Malin thinks, as she catches sight of the posters in the travel agent's windows. This place really isn't habitable, but we've managed to create a home for ourselves here nonetheless.

In the bedroom Malin pulls on her holster and pistol.

She opens the door to Tove's room.

Most beautiful in all the world.

Lets her sleep.

Karim Akbar is holding tight on to his son's hand, feeling the eight-year-old fingers through the glove.

They are walking along a gritted path towards the school. The blocks of flats in Lambohov, three and four storeys high, look like moon-bases, randomly scattered across a desolate plain.

Usually his wife walks their son to school, but today she said she had a headache, couldn't possibly get up.

The case is cracked. They just have to catch him. Then, surely, this will all be over?

Malin has delivered. Zeke, Johan and Börje. Sven: their rock. What would I do without them? My role is to encourage them, keep them happy, and how feeble it is compared to what they do. Compared to the way they deal with people.

Malin. In many ways she's the ideal detective. Instinctive, driven and, not least, a bit manic. Intelligent? Certainly. But in a good way. She finds short cuts, dares to take chances. But not rashly. Not often, at least.

'What are you going to do at school today?'

'I don't know. Normal stuff.'

And they walk on together in silence, Karim and his son. When they reach the low, white-brick school building Karim holds the door open for him and his son disappears inside, swallowed up by the dimly lit corridor.

The *Correspondent* is in the postbox by the road.

Rakel Murvall opens her front door and steps on to the porch, notes that the cold is damp today, the sort that gives her aches. But she is accustomed to that sort of physical pain, thinking, When I die I shall fall down dead on the spot. I'm not going to hang around in some hospital, rambling and unable to keep control of my own shit.

She walks carefully through the snow, worried about her hip-joints.

The postbox seems a long way off, but it's getting closer with every step.

The boys are still sleeping; soon they'll be awake, but she wants to read the paper now, not wait for them to bring it in to her, or read the latest news on the screen in the living room.

She opens the lid, and there it is, on top of some half-covered dead earwigs.

Back inside she pours a cup of fresh coffee and sits down at the kitchen table to read.

She reads the articles about the murder of Bengt Andersson and the attack over and over again.

Rebecka?

I understand what has happened.

I'm not that stupid.

Secrets. Shadows from the past. My lies, now they're seeping out of their leaking holes.

His father was a sailor.

As I always said to the boys.

Was everything a lie, Mother?

Questions that lead to other questions.

Was Cornerhouse-Kalle his father? Have you been lying to us all these years? What else don't we know? Why did you and Dad get us to torment him? To hate him? Our own brother?

Maybe even more.

How did Dad fall down the stairs? Did you push him, did you lie about what happened that day as well?

Truths need to be stifled. No doubts must be sown. It isn't too late. I can see a chance.

She, Rebecka, was found wandering the fields, naked, like Maria.

'Well done, Malin.'

Karim Akbar applauds her as she walks into Police Headquarters.

Malin smiles. Thinks, Well done? What do you mean, well done? This isn't over yet.

She sits down at her desk. Checks the *Correspondent*'s website.

They have a short piece about the raid at Karl Murvall's flat, and the fact that a national alert has gone out. They don't draw any conclusions, but mention the connections to the ongoing murder investigation, and the fact that his mother has complained about police harassment.

'Great work, Malin.'

Karim stops beside her. Malin looks up.

'Not quite according to the rulebook. But, between the two of us: it's results that count, and if we're ever going to get anywhere, we have to apply our own rules sometimes.'

'We have to find him,' Malin says.

'What do you want to do?'

'I want to harass Rakel Murvall.'

Karim stares at Malin, who looks back into the police chief's eyes with all the seriousness she can muster.

'Go,' he says. 'I'll take responsibility for any repercussions. But take Zeke with you.'

Malin looks across the office. Sven Sjöman hasn't come in yet. But Zeke is hovering restlessly over at his desk.

76

Silence in the car.

Zeke hasn't said he wants music, and Malin likes hearing the monotonous sound of the engine.

The city outside the car windows is the same as it was two weeks ago, just as greedy as ever: Skäggetorp full of rigid life, the retail boxes at Tornby just as blunt, the snow-covered Lake Roxen just as compact, and the houses on the slopes of Vreta Kloster just as inviting with their radiant sense of wellbeing.

Nothing has changed, Malin thinks. Not even the weather. But then it occurs to her that Tove has probably changed. Tove and Markus. A new note has emerged from Tove, less contrary and inward, more outward and open, confident. It suits you, Tove, Malin thinks, you're going to make a really great grown-up.

And maybe I should give Daniel Högfeldt the chance to prove that he's more than just a shag-machine.

There are lights on in the houses of Blåsvädret. The brothers' families are at home in their respective houses. Rakel Murvall's white wooden home looms at the end of the road, isolated at the point where the road stops.

Clouds of snow are drifting to and fro around the house, and behind the pale veils of winter there are still secrets hidden, Malin thinks. You'd do anything to protect your secrets, wouldn't you, Rakel?

Child benefit.

A child that you only kept for the money. A few meagre coins. But maybe not so meagre for you. Enough to live off, almost.

And why did you hate him so? What did Cornerhouse-Kalle do to you? Did he do something to you in the forest, just like someone did to Maria? To Rebecka? Did Cornerhouse-Kalle take you by force? Was that how you got pregnant? And so you hated the child when he arrived. And maybe you wanted to have him adopted? But then you had your brilliant idea and invented the story about the sailor and got child benefit. That must have been it. That he took you by force. And the child you had as a result had to pay.

Why else would you have hated your son so? The pattern runs through modern history. Malin has read about German women, raped towards the end of the war by Russian soldiers, who rejected their children. The same thing in Bosnia. And apparently also in Sweden.

Unless you loved Cornerhouse-Kalle and he treated you just like all the rest of his women? Like nothing? And that was enough to make you hate your son.

But I'm guessing the first explanation is the right one.

Unless you were tainted with evil, Rakel?

From the start.

Does such evil exist?

And money. The desire for money like a black sun over all life on this desolate, windy road.

The boy should have been allowed to have a different family, Rakel.

Then the anger and hate might have had an end; maybe your other boys could have been different. Maybe you too.

'What an awful fucking place,' Zeke says as they're standing on the drive beside the house. 'Can you see him standing here among the apple trees in the snow as a child? Freezing?'

Malin nods. 'If there is a hell . . .' she says.

Half a minute later they are knocking on the door of Rakel Murvall's house.

They can see her in the kitchen, see her disappear into the living room.

'She's not going to open the door,' Malin says.

Zeke knocks again.

'Just a moment,' they hear from inside the house.

The door opens and Rakel Murvall smiles at them.

'Ah, the detectives. To what do I owe this honour?'

'We have some questions, if you don't mind—'

Rakel Murvall interrupts Zeke. 'Come in, detectives. If you're worried about my complaint, forget it. Forgive an old woman's ill temper. Coffee?'

'No thank you,' Malin says.

Zeke shakes his head.

'But do sit down.' Rakel Murvall gestures towards the kitchen table.

They sit.

'Where's Karl?' Malin says.

Rakel Murvall ignores her question.

'He isn't in his flat, or at Collins. And he's been fired from his job,' Zeke says.

'Is he mixed up in any funny business, my son?'

Her son. She hasn't used that word of Karl before, Malin thinks.

'You've read the paper,' Malin says, putting her hand on the copy of the *Correspondent* on the table. 'You can put two and two together.'

The old woman smiles, but doesn't answer. Then she says, 'I've no idea where the lad might be.'

Malin looks out of the kitchen window. Sees a little boy standing naked in the snow and the cold, screaming with cheeks red with crying, sees him fall in the snow, waving his arms and legs, a frozen angel on the snow-draped ground.

Malin clenches her teeth.

Feels like telling Rakel Murvall that she deserves to burn in hell, that there are some things that can't be forgiven.

In the official sense, her crimes fell under the statute of limitations long ago, but in the human, social, sense? In those terms, some things are never forgiven.

Rape.

Paedophilia.

Child abuse.

Withholding love from children.

The punishment for such things is a lifetime of shame.

And love of children. That is the first sort of love.

'What really happened between you and Cornerhouse-Kalle, Rakel?'

Rakel turns to her, stares at Malin, and the pupils of the old woman's eyes grow large and black, as if they were trying to convey a thousand years of female experience and torment. Then Rakel blinks, closing her eyes for a few seconds before saying, 'That was so long ago. I can't even remember. I've had so many worries over the years with the boys.'

An opening, Malin thinks, for the next question.

'Haven't you ever worried,' she asks, 'that your boys might find out that Cornerhouse-Kalle was Karl's father?'

Rakel Murvall fills her own cup with coffee. 'The boys have that knowledge.'

'Have they? Have they really, Rakel? Being found out telling lies can ruin any relationship,' Malin goes on. 'And what power does the person who had to lie possess?'

'I don't understand what you're talking about,' Rakel Murvall says. 'You're talking a lot of nonsense.'

'Am I really, Rakel?' Malin says. 'Am I really?'

Rakel Murvall closes the front door behind them.

Sits down on the red-painted rib-backed chair in the hall, looks at the photograph on the wall, of herself surrounded by the boys in the garden when they were young, Blackie in the picture too, before the wheelchair.

Fucking little brat. You must have taken that picture.

If you disappear, disappear for good, she thinks, then maybe my secrets can remain my own.

If he disappears there will only be one or two rumours left, and I can lock those away in a dark wardrobe. He needs to go now, it's as simple as that. Be got rid of. Anyway, I'm so tired of him existing.

She picks up the receiver.

Calls Adam.

The little lad answers, his boy's voice high and innocent.

'Hello.'

'Hello, Tobias. This is Grandma. Is your daddy there?'

'Hello, Grandma.'

Then the line goes quiet, before an older, gruffer voice says, 'Mother?'

'You need to come over, Adam. And bring your brothers with you. I've got something important to tell you.'

'I'm coming, Mother. I'll tell the others.'

I used to cycle up here.

The forest was mine.

You would go hunting near me sometimes. I could hear your shots all year long, and even then I wished that you would come to me.

Mother, why were you so angry?

What had I done? What have I done?

Images and warmth. I am an angel under an apple tree of biscuit crumbs. The fire is warm again. It's nice here in my hole, but I'm lonely. But I'm not scared of loneliness. Because you can't be scared of what you are, can you?

I can sleep a bit longer here in my darkness. Then you'll come and get me, to let me in. And then I'll become someone else, won't I? When you let me in.

'What do we do now?'

Zeke is driving towards Vreta Kloster, the church like an ancient fortress on top of a hill maybe a kilometre away, the stables of Heda Riding Club on one side of the road, open fields on the other.

Malin wanted to knock on the brothers' doors, ask them if they knew whose son their brother Karl was, but Zeke told her to think about it.

'If they don't know, the old woman has a right to her secrets, Malin. We can't just blunder into her past and stir things up.'

And she knew that Zeke was right, in spite of the possible consequences of not telling them. If they stopped considering other people, no matter who they were, how could they ever demand consideration from anyone else?

In answer to Zeke's question: 'We wait for Sjöman's search teams. They're getting ready to go through the forest, but it's too cold for the dogs. They're taking a couple with them anyway, apparently.'

Then: 'Do you think we should get up there first?'

'No, Malin. We didn't find anything yesterday, so how would we be able to find anything today?'

'I don't know,' Malin replies. 'We could take a look at where the body was found, and the site of the other tree. Well, where it ought to be, anyway.'

'We've had a car looking since last night. We would have heard if they'd found anything.'

'Have you got any better suggestions?'

'None at all,' Zeke says, and does a U-turn. They head back the same way they've just come, past the houses in Blåsvädret, where they see the brothers heading together towards their mother's house.

'How long do you think it'll take Karin to have the results of the tests on Karl Murvall?' Malin asks. 'I want to know if he was the one who raped Maria Murvall.'

'Do you think he did?'

'No, but I want to know. I think she's deceiving us again. I just don't know how. But I know that she'd never have let us in if she didn't have something to gain from it herself. She's still directing this. And she'll grasp at any straw to protect what she thinks of as hers.'

Malin takes a deep breath.

'And to preserve her secrets.'

Adam, Elias and Jakob Murvall are sitting round the table in their mother's kitchen. Sipping cups of freshly brewed coffee, eating biscuits their mother has just warmed in the oven after getting them out of the freezer.

'How are the biscuits, boys?'

Rakel Murvall is standing by the stove, with the *Correspondent* in her hand.

Appreciative noises from the table, and they listen to what their mother goes on to tell them, what she didn't want to say until they had sat down and been given some coffee.

'Martinsson and Fors,' she says. 'They've just been here, asking after Karl. If it wasn't him who tortured and forced himself upon that girl in the paper, the one they found by the side of the road, why would they have come out here? What with the complaint of harassment I made and everything? Why would they risk it?'

She holds up the *Correspondent* to the boys.

Lets them read the headline, see the picture of the road.

'The police are looking for Karl. And it says in the paper that they found the girl with exactly the same injuries as Maria. And if you look on the computer you'll see that the police raided his flat last night.'

'So it was him who took Maria in the forest?' Adam Murvall spits out the words.

'Who else could it have been?' Rakel Murvall says. 'He's missing now. It must have been him, this was done the same way. Exactly the same way.'

'His own sister?'

'The bastard.'

'Monster. He's a monster. Just like he always was.'

'But why would he do that?' Doubt in Elias Murvall's voice.

'And why do we hate him so much? Have you ever wondered about that?' Rakel pauses, then continues in a lower voice: 'He was a monster right from the start, never forget that. And he hated her. Because she was one of us, and he wasn't. Because he's mad. You know yourselves how he used to hide away in the forest. And that hole of his is only five kilometres or so from where Maria was attacked, so it must have been him. It all fits.'

'Five kilometres is a long way in the forest, Mother,' Elias says. 'We may have had suspicions about him before now, but even so, Mother.'

'It all fits, Elias. He raped your own sister in the forest as if she were nothing. He destroyed her.'

'Mother's right, Elias,' Adam says calmly, then takes a sip of his coffee.

'It makes sense,' Jakob says. 'It all makes sense.'

'Now you'll do what's expected of you, boys. For your sister. Won't you, Elias? Boys?'

'But what if the police are wrong?'

'The cops are often wrong, Elias. But not this time, not this time. Stop arguing. What's wrong with you, are you on his side or something?'

Rakel Murvall waves the paper in the air.

'Are you on his side? Who else could it be? The whole thing fits. You have to give your sister some peace. Maybe she could come back if only she knew that the person who hurt her is gone.'

'They'll catch us, Mother, they're going to catch us,' Elias says. 'And there are limits to what can be done.'

'No there aren't, boy,' Rakel Murvall says. 'There's more sense in the henhouse than in that police station. And you know where he is. You'll see, if you just do as I say. Listen . . .'

The oak on the plain where Bengt Andersson was found hanging would have looked like any other isolated tree, were it not for the broken branches.

But the oak will always be associated with what happened in that coldest of Februaries. In the spring the farmer will cut down the tree, doesn't want to see any more flowers on the ground, any more curious visitors, any more meditating women. He will dig out all the roots he can find, not stopping until he knows for sure that no trace of the oak is left in the ground. But deep beneath the surface there will be a piece of root, and that root will grow and a new tree will spring up on the plain, a tree that will whisper the names of Ball-Bengt and Cornerhouse-Kalle and Rakel Murvall across the wide expanses of Östergötland.

Malin and Zeke are sitting in their car, staring at the tree.

The engine is running.

'He's not here,' Zeke says.

'He was here once,' Malin replies.

The Range Rover's interior smells of oil and engine grease, and its frame rattles as the vehicle passes through Ljungsbro at high speed, past the Vivo supermarket, the café and the Cloetta chocolate factory at the bottom of the hill, beside the bridge across the river.

Elias Murvall is sitting on his own in the back seat, twisting his hands, hears his voice say the words, even though he doesn't want to: 'What if she's wrong? If he didn't do it? Then we'll always regret this. What fucking right have we got to—'

Adam Murvall turns round in the passenger seat up front.

'He did it, the bastard. Raped Maria. It fits. We're going to do this. What is it you always say, Elias? You must never show you're weak? That's what you say, eh? You must never show you're weak. So don't now. Watch yourself.'

And the vehicle lurches, sliding towards the ditch just before the Olstorp curve.

'You're right,' Elias yells. 'I'm not weak.'

'Fuck it,' Jakob Murvall shouts. 'We're doing this, no more talk. Understood?'

Elias leans back, soaking up the assurance in Jakob's voice, in spite of his anger.

Elias breathes deeply, feeling the determination of the vehicle's motion, as if it had been on its way to this very destination long before it was even made.

Elias turns round.

Looks down into the baggage compartment.

It holds a stained wooden box, and in the box three grenades from a break-in at a weapons store, freshly unearthed from their hiding-place under an outhouse floor; a hiding-place the police missed during their raid the other week.

'Bloody lucky the cops didn't find the grenades,' Jakob

said when Mother explained her plan to them back in the house.

'You're right there, Jakob,' Mother said. 'Bloody lucky.'

Malin and Zeke are wandering the plain, searching for another isolated tree.

But the trees they find show no signs of struggle. They are just lonely, windswept, frost-damaged trees.

Zeke is at the wheel as they head towards Klockrike, along a scarcely ploughed road by the edge of an apparently endless field, when Malin's mobile rings.

Karin Johannison's number on the display.

'Malin here.'

'Negative, Fors,' Karin says. 'Karl Murvall didn't rape Maria Murvall.'

'No similarities at all?'

'He didn't do it, that much is certain.'

'Thanks, Karin.'

'Was it that important, Malin? Did you really think it was him?'

'I don't know what I thought. But I do now. Thanks again.' Malin ends the call.

'He didn't rape Maria Murvall,' she says to Zeke, who receives the information without taking his eyes from the road.

'So that case still isn't solved,' Zeke says, his voice gruff, a statement that sets Malin thinking.

The brothers walking towards Rakel's house just after she and Zeke had left.

Brothers who don't know that Karl didn't rape Maria.

Who listen to their mother. Obey her.

A mother with secrets to keep.

And only one way of keeping them.

Zeke stops the car at yet another tree.

Roots, Malin thinks. Blood that has to be eradicated. Actions that must be avenged. That's what we do.

And so he must be eradicated. Rakel doesn't know we got hold of Karl's DNA, that everything is going to come out.

Or else she knows deep down, but is suppressing the knowledge, grasping at one last imaginary straw.

If you force evil into a corner, it'll attack...

'I know why she let us in earlier,' Malin yells, just as Zeke is opening the driver's door. 'Get us to the cabin, as fast as you can.'

77

The houses of Vreta Kloster line the road.

A sense of wellbeing shelters behind the façades, close but still far away.

After this journey she doesn't want to come this way again for a thousand years.

They drive across the bridge down by Kungsbro and swing up towards Olstorp, past the Montessori school in Björkö where the blue- and pink-painted buildings, with their anthroposophically angular architecture, look just as browbeaten by the cold as every other building.

Hope they raise good people in there.

Janne had once talked of Tove going to a Montessori school but Malin refused, had heard that children who go to school in protected environments like that could rarely deal with the competition outside the security of the school walls.

Cutting out dolls.

Making their own books.

Learning that the world is full of love.

How much love is there up in the forest? How much dammed-up hate?

The car slides along the slippery road surface as Zeke hits the accelerator.

'Just drive, Zeke. It's urgent. I promise you, he's out there somewhere.'

Zeke doesn't ask, just concentrates on the car and the road, as they pass the turning to Olstorp and head on towards Lake Hultsjön.

They drive past the golf course, the flags still flying, and Malin imagines the flags as the brothers' bodies blowing in the wind, the breeze their mother's breath with the power to send them whichever way she pleases.

Jakob Murvall grips the wheel tighter, turns off on to the road leading to the summer cottages around Hultsjön, little white-painted shacks covered in cotton wool.

The green Range Rover swerves over the snow, ice crystals swirling out over the ditches, like the polished shards of a cluster bomb, but he manages to keep the vehicle on the road.

Elias hasn't said anything more.

And Adam is sitting silent, focused, in the passenger seat.

We're just doing what has to be done, Jakob thinks. Like we always do. Like we've always done. Like I did when I found Dad at the bottom of the stairs. I pulled myself together, even though I wanted to scream. I closed his eyelids, so Mother wouldn't have to see those frightening eyes.

We do what we have to. Because if we let someone rape our sister without doing anything about it, what sort of people would that make us? There'd be no end to the crap that followed. What we're doing now, it says stop, think again.

At the end of the track he stops the car.

'Out with you,' he yells, and the brothers jump out, and, if there was any doubt in Elias's body, it's gone now.

They're all dressed in green jackets and dark blue trousers.

'Come on,' Jakob shouts, and Adam opens the back door and takes out the stained box, putting it on the ground as he shuts the door.

'Ready,' he calls. Then he puts the box carefully under his arm and they clamber across the heaped-up snow and on into the forest.

Jakob in front.

Then Elias.

Adam at the back with the box.

Jakob sees the trees around him. The forest where he's been hunting so many times. He sees Mother at the table. Maria in bed the only time he could bear to visit her in Vadstena.

He thinks, Bastard. You bastard.

His brothers behind him.

They swear whenever their boots cut through the white crust, breaking up as it does under their rapid, heavy steps.

How can three grenades weigh so much, Adam thinks, yet still so little, when you consider the damage they can do?

He thinks of Maria in her room. How she always shies away when he visits, shrinking into a corner of the bed, and he has to whisper her name over and over again to get her to calm down. He doesn't even know if she recognises him. She's never said anything, but she allows him to be there, and after a while she's no longer scared, accepts the fact that he's in the room with her.

What then?

Then they sit there in the middle of her hurt.

Fuck it.

His boot crashes through the crust, sinks right down towards a root, and he has to pull hard to get it out again.

It was that bastard who did it.

To his own sister.

There's no other option. Away, he has to be done away with. No reason for doubt. Doubt isn't for us.

The box under his arm. He holds it tight. Doesn't know what might happen if he drops it.

He's short of breath. Sees his brothers ahead of him, feels the cold and remembers that time by the canal when the two of them took care of that Turkish fucker for him, when they showed that no bastard could get one over on us, we stick together; that means you too, Maria, and that's why we have to do this.

Kicking, kicking, kicking.

Much more than that.

We're grown-ups. And we have to behave like grown-ups.

Elias only ten metres or so ahead of him. Adam can still feel his body, the wind in his hair. He is still sitting behind him on a Puch Dakota moped, will always be sitting there.

★

There's the vehicle.

The Murvall brothers' Range Rover has been driven right into the bank of snow, and Zeke parks close behind, taking care to block it in.

They've called in, a helicopter is on its way. Malin to Sven Sjöman: 'Trust me on this, Sven.'

But it takes time to get a helicopter in the air in this sort of cold, so they have to rely on themselves, on their legs. The dog-patrols have just left the station.

They scramble over the bank of snow, following the Murvall brothers' tracks, head in among the trees, running, landing so hard on their feet that they break the crust of the snow, stumble, run again. Their hearts are pounding in their chests, their lungs are working overtime, overdosing on the cold white air, their bodies straining forward, forward, but not even adrenalin lasts for ever and soon they are stumbling more than running, as they listen to the forest, for the brothers, for signs of activity, of life, but neither of them can hear anything.

'Shit,' Zeke pants. 'How far in do you think they are?'

'A long way,' Malin says. 'We've got to go on.'

And Malin starts running into the forest, but the crust can't take her hard, heavy footsteps and she falls, gets up, rushes on.

Her vision narrows to a tunnel.

'He wasn't the one who raped your sister,' she wants to shout through the forest.

'Don't believe your mother. He didn't rape her, he's done some repulsive things, but not that. Let all this end now, it isn't too late, whatever you think, whatever she's beaten into you. He's still your brother. Do you hear? Do you hear? He's your own brother. And he didn't rape your sister, we know that for certain.'

The tunnel closes.

I've got to get there, Malin thinks.

Screams, 'He didn't rape your sister,' but she's so short of breath that she can barely hear her own voice.

★

Never show your weakness, never show your weakness, never. . .

Elias mutters the words to himself like a mantra, thinking of all the times he's showed his strength, how he smashed his fist into that teacher Brogren's face when he called him a filthy brat from Blåsvädret.

Sometimes he wonders why everything's turned out the way it has, why they're on the outside, and the only answer he can find is that it was like that from the start. There were all the people with jobs, with proper lives, decent houses, and it was never, ever us, and the world let us know that.

Adam behind him.

Elias stops, turns round. Thinks how well he's carrying the weight, his brother, and how his forehead glows pink in the winter light and the cold, how his skin seems healthier.

'Keep hold of the box, Adam.'

'I've got it,' he replies, his voice tight.

Jakob walks silently ahead of him.

His steps are determined, his shoulders are drooping in his jacket, angled to the ground.

'Fuck,' Adam swears. 'This snow's really dodgy.'

He's gone through yet again.

'Let's speed up,' he says. 'Get this over with.'

Elias says nothing.

There's nothing more to talk about. Just one thing to get done.

They walk past the cabin.

Pass it without stopping, carry on across the clearing into the forest, even darker, even thicker than on the other side, and there the crust of the snow is thicker, more stable, but still it gives way every now and then.

'He's hiding over there,' Elias says. 'I know he is.'

'I can smell smoke from the stove,' Adam says.

Adam's fingers holding the box are starting to cramp, shaking uncontrollably against the wood. He switches arms, flexes his fingers to get rid of the cramp.

'A fucking hole in the ground. He's no better than an animal,' Jakob whispers.

Then he says out loud, 'Now it's Maria's turn.'

He shouts the words into the forest, but the sound dies out against the tree trunks, the forest absorbing his voice.

Go on, Malin, go on. It isn't too late yet. The helicopter has left the airfield at Malmslätt, it's whirling its way towards you across the plain, the dogs in the patrols are scrabbling, barking, their numbed senses searching in vain.

Like you, Malin, I think enough is enough.

But even so.

I want Karl here beside me.

I want to drift beside him.

Take him away from here with me.

How is it possible to feel so tired?

Malin's body is full of lactic acid and, even though the brothers' tracks lead further into the forest, the two of them have to sit down and rest on the front steps of the cabin.

The whistling of the wind.

A whisper, above the noise of their bodies.

Their heads seem to be boiling, in spite of the cold. Breath rising like smoke from a dying fire out of Zeke's mouth.

'Fuck, fuck,' Zeke says, as he catches his breath. 'If only I was as fit as Martin.'

'We have to go on,' Malin pants.

They get up.

Chase off, deeper into the forest.

78

Are you coming?

Are you coming to let me in?

Don't hit me.

Is it you? Or the dead?

Whoever's out there, tell me you're coming in friendship. Tell me you're coming with love.

Promise me that.

Promise me that much.

Promise.

I hear you. You aren't here yet, but you'll be here soon. I lie on the floor, hearing your words out there as muffled cries.

'We'll let him in now,' you cry. 'Now he can be one of us. Now he can come in.'

It feels good.

I've done so much. There's none of that other blood left. Surely we can ignore the bit that's flowing through my veins?

You're closer now.

You're coming with her love.

You're coming to let me in.

The door to my hole isn't locked.

Elias Murvall sees the smoke rising from the little pipe above the bulge in the snow. Sees in his mind's eye how Karl is cowering in there, scared, pointless.

He must have done it.

Doubt is a weakness.

We're going to bite him, kick him, all that.

What Mother said must be right: that he was a monster

from the very start, that all three of us felt it, that he raped Maria.

Karl found this hideaway himself, when he was ten and cycled up to the forest and the cabin without telling anyone, then he had proudly showed it to them, as if they were likely to be impressed by some ruddy hole in the ground. Blackie used to lock him inside, leave him there for days with nothing but water when they were at the cabin. It made no difference what time of year. Karl protested to start with; they had to drag him there, the old man and the brothers, but then he seemed to get used to it and even made himself at home in there, turning it into his own little hovel. It was no fun shutting him in there if he was happy with it, and for a while they considered filling it in, but no one could be bothered to go to that much effort.

'Let the little bastard keep his grave, then,' their old man bellowed from his wheelchair, and no one protested. They knew he was still using the hole; they would sometimes see the tracks of his skis leading to the cabin. Sometimes there were no tracks, so they assumed he came from the other direction.

Elias and Jakob get closer.

The bastard. Get rid of him.

The green-painted box in Adam's hands is heavy and he follows their footsteps steadily through the white and black landscape.

'Do you hear that, Zeke?'

'What?'

'Aren't those voices up ahead?'

'I don't hear any voices.'

'But there's someone talking, I can hear it.'

'Don't be daft, Fors. On we go.'

What are you saying?

You're talking about opening the door, that much I can understand. Opening and letting in.

'You open, and I'll let it go.' This from Elias.

So it's true. I've succeeded. I've done it, something is finally being put right.

But what are you waiting for?

'First,' he says, 'you chuck one in, then the others, and last of all the box.'

Malin is racing, hearing voices now, but more like whispers whose meaning is impossible to determine from the sound waves moving through the trees.

Muttering.

Millennia of history and injustice summoned down into this moment.

Is the forest really opening up? Zeke isn't keeping up with her pace. He's hanging back, he's panting, she thinks he's about to fall. Then she pushes a bit harder, running between the trees, and the snow seems to disappear beneath her feet, proximity to the truth making her drift along.

Elias Murvall takes the first grenade out of the box. He sees Jakob standing by the door of the earth cellar, the smoke from the chimney like a veil behind him, the forest standing to attention, all the trunks goading him on: Do it, do it, do it.

Kill your own brother.

He destroyed your sister.

He isn't a human being.

But Elias hesitates.

'For fuck's sake, Elias,' Jakob yells. 'Let's do it. Chuck them in. Chuck them in! What the fuck are we waiting for?'

Elias, whispering, 'Yes, what the hell are we waiting for?'

'Chuck them in. Chuck them in.' Adam's voice.

And as Elias pulls the pin from the first grenade Jakob opens the metre-high wooden door to the hole.

You're opening up, I can see the light. I'm one of you now.

At last.

You're so kind.

First an apple, because you know I like them. It rolls towards me, green in the soft grey light.

I pick up the apple, it's cold and green, then two more apples roll across my earthen floor, together with a square box.

So kind.

I pick up another apple, it's cool and hard with the cold.

You're here now.

Then the door closes again and the light vanishes. Why?

You said you were going to let me in.

I wonder when the light will return? Where does all the crashing light come from?

Zeke has fallen somewhere behind her.

What can she see up ahead? Her field of vision is like a shaky hand-held camera, the image lurches back and forth and what is it she sees?

Three brothers?

What are they doing?

They're throwing themselves down in the snow.

And then a bang, and another and another, and a flash of fire shooting out from a bulge in the snow, and she throws herself to the ground, feels the cold force its way into each of her bones.

Weapons from a weapons store.

Hand grenades.

Fuck.

He's gone now, Elias Murvall thinks. He no longer exists. I didn't show any weakness.

Elias gets up on all fours, the noise from the explosion ringing in his ears, his whole head full of noise, and he sees Adam and Jakob getting up, and how the door of the hideaway has been blown off, and how the snow that covered its roof has become an impossibly white dust in the air.

Whatever must it look like inside?

Let a firecracker go off in a clenched fist...

Stick one up the arse of some fucking cat...

Bloodstained snow.

The stink of sweat, burned flesh. Of blood.

Who's that screaming? A woman?

He turns round.

Sees a woman holding a pistol approach from the edge of the forest.

Her? How the fuck did she get here so quickly?

Malin has got up, is walking, pistol drawn, towards the three men who are all clambering to their knees, getting up, putting their hands above their heads.

'You've killed your own brother,' she yells. 'You've killed your own brother. You think he raped your sister but he had nothing to do with it, you bastards,' she yells. 'You've killed your own brother.'

Then Jakob Murvall walks towards her.

He yells, 'We haven't killed anyone. We were coming to get him, we knew you were looking for him and when we got close to the hideaway it exploded.'

Jakob Murvall smiles.

'He didn't rape your sister,' Malin yells.

The smile vanishes from Jakob Murvall's lips; now he looks offended, misled, and Malin takes a swing with the pistol, allowing it to cleave the air as fast as it can before the barrel connects with his nose.

The blood pours from Jakob Murvall's nostrils as he staggers forward, colouring the snow dark red, and Malin sinks to her knees and screams up into the air, she screams again and again but no one hears her cries, slowly turning into a howl just as a helicopter glides in above the clearing and stifles the sound coming from her lungs. The despair and pain and the fragments of human lives that the drowned-out howl contains will echo through the forests around Hultsjön for ever.

Can you hear the rumble?

The unquiet muttering.

The rustling from the moss.

That's the dead whispering, the stories will say. The dead, and the dead who are yet living.

Epilogue

Mantorp, Wednesday, 2 March

'I'm not scared any more.'

'Me neither.'

There's no rancour. No despair, no injustice to forgive.

Here there is only a scent of apples and balls flying weightlessly through a space that never ends.

We are drifting side by side, me and Karl, the way brothers should. We don't see the earth any more, instead we see almost everything, and we're fine.

Rakel Murvall is sitting at the head of her kitchen table, her back to the stove, where a cabbage bake is almost done, spreading a sweet smell over the room.

Elias gets up first.

Then Jakob. And finally Adam.

'You lied, Mother. The articles in the paper. He was our . . .'

'You knew.'

'He was still our brother.'

'You lied . . . you made us kill our . . .'

One by one they leave the kitchen.

The front door closes.

Rakel Murvall pushes back her long white hair.

'Come back,' she whispers. 'Come back.'

How did it happen?

Malin is sure, as she hunts through the racks of clothes in H&M in the Mobilia shopping centre just outside Mantorp.

They threw the grenades into the hole, and their mother had tricked them into doing it.

But the brothers' stories match; it's impossible to prove that Karl Murvall himself didn't pull out the pins of grenades that he somehow acquired. The brothers will get a month in Skänninge in the summer for poaching and possession of illegal weapons, that's all.

Tove holds up a red flowery spring dress. Questioning, smiling.

Malin shakes her head.

The case of the murder of Bengt Andersson is regarded as solved, along with the kidnap and assault of Rebecka Stenlundh. The perpetrator in both cases was the victims' own half-brother, who blew himself into thousands upon thousands of pieces in a hole in the ground that was the closest he ever got to a home on this earth.

This is the official truth: 'He couldn't live with what he'd done.'

Jakob Murvall reported Malin for excessive use of force in connection with the event, but Zeke supported her version. 'Nothing like that happened. He must have been wounded in the explosion,' and that was the end of it.

One question remains: Who raped Maria Murvall?

Malin fingers a light blue pair of overalls.

Do all questions have to be answered?

Outside the cold has eased, even if the snow is still there. The white skin gets thinner every day, and beneath the ground the first snowdrops are preparing to break through the darkness. They are moving through the soil, soon ready to greet the sun.